The New Illuminati

The New
Illuminati

By

DAVID–MICHAEL
HARDING

The New Illuminati

Photograph of the author by
William Tillis and Harold Hutchinson © 2011

Cover by Kerwin Designs

DavidMichaelHarding.com

Printed in the United States of America
October 2016
First Edition

1 3 5 7 9 10 8 6 4 2

ISBN-10 0985728531
ISBN-13 987-0-9857285-3-3
Library of Congress Catalog Number: 2016954042

Novels by David-Michael Harding

How Angels Die

Cherokee Talisman

Losing St. Christopher

The New Illuminati

The New Illuminati – Return to Power

Short Story Collection

The Cats of Savone

Find free reading excerpts and preview upcoming
novels at the author's website -

DavidMichaelHarding.com

For Kathryn

Support & encouragement does not come without cost

"The penalty good men pay for indifference to public

affairs is to be ruled by evil men."

– Plato

1

The beer would warm in the glass before the cable news loop ran through its next cycle. No breaking stories to cut into the repeating drone. Just the too perky, too perfect, smiling then serious, practiced sincerity, happy pleasing torso of the anchor, cart wheeling from the rescued kitten to the dead soldiers through elder care and the DOW Jones. Regurgitation with titillation. Just enough to hold a viewer through the next money maker – an ad for a medication to control an illness unheard of a year before, but which now, "affects millions of people just like you."

The lukewarm beer listened to the numbing lecture alone as Clayton Rand had forgotten it and was anesthetized to the attention grabbing scam sandwiched between ever more desperate commercials. Even his beautiful massive curved plasma screen couldn't reel him in and turn him into a consumer. Overhead, a gentle hum from the ceiling fan provided subtle white noise and worked with the air conditioner to keep the stifling heat of a summer night in Florida outside the walls of Clayton's sprawling home.

He sat in the formal living room – a room away from the plasma – one leg dangling loosely from the arm of an overpriced, immeasurably soft brown leather chair, which offended the neglected ottoman that rested unused nearby. Clayton's propped up thigh was his desk and he covered it with a yellow pad and scratched notes with a cheap pen.

The advertising pen had a short life span, meant to be given away and read a few times in passing or boredom before changing hands or running out of ink. For now it worked with enough efficiency to capture the thoughts of its short term owner and those thoughts were coming in a flurry. Ninety minutes earlier the pad had been empty, the cheap pen still, and the beer cold.

A gratefully quiet evening in a busy life had been in pleasant predictable bloom. But it was shaken by twenty-three seconds of airtime, inadvertently captured from a local channel, as Clayton surfed while he waited on the soft white foam of his beer to fizzle itself into oblivion. Sealed indictments had been opened and implicated a local county commissioner in a bribery scandal. A land developer had donated forty-five thousand dollars to the commissioner's election campaign following his own failed attempt at pushing a housing development plan past the Regional Resource Impact Committee. Weeks later, with the freshly minted commissioner at the helm of the impact study appeal, the decision was reversed and chainsaws began immediately biting into cypress trees that had provided shade and relief for peoples as widespread as the Seminole Indians, Spanish conquistadors marching inland from sandy beaches, migrant workers, citrus growers, and tourists of six decades. Seven seconds of video showed the site with a voice-over describing the incalculable damage. Three hundred pristine acres stripped bare with only the beginnings of concrete pads and block walls held closely together by ribbons of still dark, uncured concrete curbs bordering bare dirt roads. A water truck drove through the frame spraying its load to keep down the dust. In the background, a mountain of two-hundred-year-old cypress, scrub pine, and oak, choked with brush, burned violently as it raced to consume the evidence. The fire triggered a reminder in Clayton of the flame of Wyatt's Torch and he knew – as an epiphany – that it was time for Atlas to shrug again.

The pen snatched ideas and the paper trapped them between faint blue lines. Almost immediately, entire sections were crossed out – deemed undoable, illegal, too illegal, or merely laughable. Others stuck. By the time the news loop broke into its new cycle with a new painted face, a straightforward plan had emerged from the yellow pad. Clayton re-read his work, made the last of his simple choices for the night, and put the pad aside.

"To those whom much is given, much is expected. Something like that," Clayton said stiffly as he stood and stretched an ache which had settled into his back compliments of the awkward dangling leg. "Yea, much is expected, you sonofabitch," he poignantly directed while the mumbling television went quiet as though it had committed the crime and had not simply been the messenger. "And tomorrow comes the accounting."

A nearly soundless click from the rocker light switch signaled the end of the long day. The yellow pad rested quietly as a placid darkness followed Clayton away from the soft chair and down the hall. As he moved closer to his bedroom and the king-sized bed that waited there, the dark overcame the trailing light with each successive click. Soon the yellow pad and its outline sat in pitch blackness while Clayton brushed his teeth by the glow of a single light on his nightstand. In a few moments, even that light faded beneath a touch to the lamp's base. In the blackness of well after midnight, Clayton breathed a tired breath and welcomed the relaxing feeling that followed. A few more deep sighs and he slipped away, never noticing that he had given himself over to the sandman with so little effort.

Sleep was a prescription he needed badly. On other nights he would have turned into the comfort of the bed over and over looking for a position that would free him from the waken world. Clayton understood it wasn't the bed's fault or even his body's, but rather it was his mind that was keeping the door to sleep closed. Thoughts and ideas raced through the days and reflected the needs, which were few, the wants, which were less, and the desires of his heart – a quest for justice in all things. This, and visible, viable production – all moving with an ebb and flow like a constant tide beneath the remarkable workaday life he had carved out of nothing.

On other nights, after the clock next to the bed flashed the dim recognition that hours had passed leaving him caught by sprinting thoughts, Clayton would get out of bed slowly, upset with himself for not controlling his restless mind and drift to the bathroom where he would force a piss if he could – one less reason to be woken up when he eventually did fall asleep. He'd pull open the small side drawer in the vanity and fumble through the litany of bottles for the Ambien, the muscle relaxers, and Xanax.

He would have already glanced at the enemy by the bed and checked the time. If the night had completely escaped him, he'd break the pills in half, otherwise he'd never be up on time. Three AM was his unofficial cut-off. Pre-three was a whole pill. Post-three was a half if it was a work night. If it was the weekend he might treat himself and take two at nine o'clock with a couple of beers with a gin chaser and enjoy an induced sleep that would seem good, but not satisfy as it should.

Desperation to silence the clamoring in his head pushed him to pause over the myriad of bottles and conjure up cocktails of halves and wholes – combinations by color and shape dependent on his temperament amid the self-diagnosis. It was not without risk. A body pummeled to unconsciousness as a semblance of sleep was a leaky vessel for a mind that had boundless energy and no seeming requisite for sleep. But neither his body nor his mind could keep up the pace so he'd limp along nightly until it would all collapse in a monthly ritual of a fourteen-hour deep sleep. Then the cycle would begin again.

It was an unending battle to occupy, stymie, stimulate, or deaden brain cells. This struggle is what drew him into the complex work of electronic security he had pioneered. The demands challenged his skills and overactive anatomy to create higher, more intricate forms, languages, codes, and conventions until his hands and his company created firewalls of such astounding complexity, government and corporate giants begged for his protection.

The burdens of the day – contracts and codes – were seldom troublesome. His thoughts skipped ahead and raced to the inevitable conclusion long before his hands perched over the keyboard. It was the manufactured encumbrances of tomorrow that teased and tormented him at night. But not tonight. Tonight, with his mind laced around the well-conceived outline on the yellow pad, an easy foundation had been laid for sleep to rest its head. A mind prepared for rest welcomed it and comfortably left the concerns of the day behind with the dousing of the lights. The pill bottles went undisturbed and the clock changed its faded blue digital lights unnoticeably and numbered the hours until dawn.

The following morning gave Clayton up for the day rested and renewed. There was a vigor that propelled him ahead as he settled into his home office. He would ferret his usual productions through the sieve of his company's mainframes and on into realizations of projects he'd left for himself. Contracts went from proposal to reality with minimal effort. While his hands plied his trade, his mind collected the thoughts from the yellow pad. It had traveled with him from the soft leather chair to the corner of his glass desk, upside down though it were.

His generation had eschewed paper for the electronic note, but surrounding his wizardry, there was a pleasure and fascination in things he saw as timeless. The nondescript notepad was such a thing. So simple. So beneficial. In this aged admiration was an explanation of his delight with black and white films and what he referenced as examples of modern classic writing – currently constrained to Steinbeck and Hemingway – accomplished in their time with pad, pencil, and loud hammering typewriters. Perhaps it was merely the tactile function. Or the clarity that followed the structure – the archetypal western movie's reliance on black hats and white hats that revealed intentions and agendas that were neither lost nor hidden, as well as the justice that was metered out before the closing credits. Clayton hid access for a living and there was none better. None. But in his life away from the keyboard and the whirling drives, he reached for the simple conscience of John Wayne, the Texas Rangers, or the denizens of *Cannery Row*.

So he pumped out the necessary work before him while his mind danced on ahead of its own accord. It tightened the formulation from the scratch work held between the faint blue lines of the pad into more and more of a patterned, concise roadmap. Before noon, the inconsequential concerns of the day were complete and Clayton turned the yellow pad face up, looked with an air of cautiousness around the room – for the first of many times – and began the accounting in earnest.

"Time for payback," he said to both the note pad and his keyboard. He adjusted his monitor slightly, though he was alone in his home, and absently and foolishly leaned to the side to see for certain if the monitor filter was in place. At the extent of his lean the screen went to black. Then he turned his fingers loose.

They were long, thin and fluid – a match to his frame. Just thirty-one, he was in good shape, but not athletic by the stretch of anyone's imagination. Back in the days when such things were done, he was toward the end of the group of boys to be picked for flag football, basketball, or baseball. He had a tight look about him with unruly brown hair framing a narrow, unspectacular face.

His hands skimmed the keyboard and immediately brought up the security folio and disabled the forensic software which he had himself devised and installed on every computer in his company. With clicks and sequences and codes he could very literally see every computer's activity in the company with ease and those outside the company, or outside the country, with only minimal effort. Clayton could review each site a computer visited; each email sent or received; each and every keystroke made – all captured in the computer and server's memories and coaxed out by forensic software he had developed. It had made him wealthy beyond measure. However, enough had become enough. The thrill and even the thought of more – more money, more of anything – had been relegated to a lesser standing. Now the scribbled notes on a yellow pad were paramount. With his standard production behind him, he moved on to his new, his real, his true purpose.

With the forensic protocol disabled, he performed a few tests. He typed "FL + lotto" in the search engine and hit enter. One hundred and six thousand plus sites came back in .37 seconds. He clicked the main Florida lotto site and was instantly there, looking at the results of last night's drawings. Six random numbers and you were a multi-millionaire. Five would have given you a quarter million in another game. Four, a thousand or so and on it went. But that meant nothing. What was important was that he was outside the initial blocking firewall of the company's restrictions.

He would test one more time. "Porn + Tampa strip club." Another click and the search was complete. He chose the third site for no particular reason and was rewarded with the presentation of a surgically enhanced blonde with breasts no bra would dare attempt to corral. All around flashed quasi-lights and signs promising 'Pure Pleasure,' 'Private Lap Dances and MUCH More!' There were phone numbers to call and other links to entice the viewer away from his money.

Clayton only smiled. The content of the site only interested him insomuch as it would have normally been prohibited by his own handiwork, but he had by-passed his own creation. No blocks came up. No warnings about corporate security alerts. No references to be passed on to internal security for review, action, and possible termination. As his screen continued flashing the digital equivalent of neon lights and beautiful wanting women, Clayton clicked his mouse and entered coding that put him further beyond the firewall.

Now he was operating beyond the reach of tracking software and off any memory path that might be retraced. With a few more flicks and clicks from his fingers, divergent reversing blocks were in place in the event that at a future time someone, not unlike himself, invented a way to retrieve the irretrievable. As he sat comfortable before a blank screen he entered a blur of coding. Should anyone begin to stumble toward him in this virtual world, they would find themselves looped into the Library of Congress reviewing the millions of pages of text in each of its volumes, automatically and without a way to stop or circumvent the process.

Clayton relaxed and breathed that same breath he breathed the night before as he went to sleep. He was that relaxed and that content with the promise of his next steps. He pulled the yellow pad closer and reviewed the list he had all but committed to memory. His hands rested in his lap, a short distance from the keyboard, but close enough to the portal that would begin something new that Clayton had mused over for more than a year. The errant commissioner had provided the final spark, but the powder keg had been slowly packed full by months and months of headlines and scrolling news bytes of misdeeds by those in power.

He brought his hands up to the black keys and flexed his fingers with sincere deliberation. This was serious business. The pause was not wrought of a true hesitation, but more a self-check of the digitized path and the possible shortcomings. The pitfalls were few by his estimation, and easily avoided by the sleight of hand he sent through his keyboard like so much magic.

"Well," he said to himself and his hands before him. "Let's delve into the black arts for a time and see what spells we can render on the good Mr. Commissioner and his developer buddy."

Clayton's fingers began to skate over the keyboard without effort. Like an ice skater of flesh and bone, his hands jumped in well-practiced leaps, seeming spins and twists, double axles and toe loops between 'Enter' and the space bar. Beneath his touch, the whole of the computer's repertoire was in full dance. In the computer's multi-towers, drives whirled and squealed as they kept up with the fluid commands. Information, encoded, encrypted, decoded and more, rocketed along the wired and wireless connections to retrieve, pull, and cajole bytes and digits into material and then push them to places Clayton wished them to be.

He started with the County's permitting department. His electronic scans slipped through the simple firewalls without effort. In seconds he was looking at a listing of permits pulled for construction. Clayton referenced his notes on the pad for names and performed a half dozen simple searches. Again, seconds were all that stood between his efforts and reward. The company's huge mainframes provided the power and he provided the precision.

In a moment, the shaded veils that had been erected in an attempt to cover the tracks of the commissioner and the developer – fictitious companies gilded by innocuous titles and apparent ties to reputable business and projects – had been replaced with people's names. Straight forward, easy to follow names. Names given by parents to sons years earlier. Names to make parents proud. Perhaps they had said, "My son, the new commissioner."

The calendar had flipped its pages and the bloom had lost its luster. Petals withered and fell, not drawn out by nature's course and gravity, but under the force of greed and want for money. The stalk was bare. Perhaps too bare for the district attorney to stumble upon enough evidence to convict. An indictment was already in hand, but Clayton sought to give the prosecution the smoking gun. "Beyond a reasonable doubt," he mused to himself.

More rattling keys, adjusting dates and more names, not too much. "Let's not make it that obvious," and a wry smile appeared. He backed up and replaced a few lines with the original smoke screen.

The first request of the yellow pad complete, Clayton moved away from the county pages to another cyber world – email. Again, practiced typing made firewalls disappear and mass market virus software ignorant to Clayton's entry. He was at the commissioner's personal email. Click, and Clayton sat a moment as his impromptu search looked for the developer under a dozen different guises in the sent, received, saved, and garbage histories. They began to trickle in. First just a few followed by only a few more. Most of these were tagged as unanswered. He sat and read them all. Each held a vague reference to "problems" and "delays," but nothing like he had hoped. It was time to dig a bit deeper.

The dancers began again on keys worn shiny by use. He was in the commissioner's text garbage pile – the bottom of the heap – far beyond the 'empty recycle bin' of a computer or the delete of a phone, into the bytes thought deleted and stated as such by the commissioner's own machines.

Clayton understood however, that each and every stroke of the keys, once typed or received, left an indelible trail. There was no way for a novice, or even someone with considerable skill, to completely erase the black board on which had been written a dirty word. Those simpler times were long behind the entire world. Another search among the forgotten debris and the true deluge began. Clayton scanned the dates and saw very readily the pile up as the Grand Jury convened and the indictment was handed down. Worded terror was visible as the men feverishly wrote back and forth, ending each email or text with the reminder to delete. They had followed their own advice, but never counted on Clayton seeing those old cypress trees burning.

Perhaps the police could and would find this, but perhaps not. Clickity click. Now they couldn't help but find it. Phase two was complete. Now for the money trail.

The stops and firewalls were more complex in some, almost non-existent in others. Through public records he found addresses for cross reference and the real estate holdings of each party. Another search via public domain revealed old divorce documents on file with the county and, much to Clayton's surprise, the commissioner's social security number buried inside. "This will be easier than I thought," he mused as he copied the holy grail of thieves. The developer wasn't much harder. Soon he had social security numbers, dates of birth, mothers' maiden names, and addresses going back for years.

Records had indicated which banks the men had used. "Creatures of habit," he said to the screen as he began to crack his way inside the listed institution. "Hmmm...," marked only a slight delay. Another avenue in, around, over, and through, and the maximum security walls began to crumble.

Searches and scans presented scrolling lists that sped by the screen at such speed they were indecipherable. It was taking longer than Clayton had expected and he was startled by the ringing of his cell phone.

While the scanning continued, he glanced at the calling number glowing below the name Raphael. He accepted without hesitation.

"Hey, Ralph." Clayton's voice betrayed that the caller was a friend – best friend – closer than most brothers. "What's up?"

"The market. That's why I'm calling. I'm in need of a celebration. It has been a very, very good day."

Raphael was at his own desk on the other side of Tampa. He was built thicker than Clayton, but only by enough to actually get picked for high school gym class sports. His longish sandy hair fit the beach better than the boardroom, but it lingered as a testament to an earlier era and also covered ears that he thought – real or imagined – stuck out more than they should. Minus the ear issue, braces had long ago fixed his teeth and a laser had corrected his vision and allowed him to toss his glasses. After it all, Raphael was left just shy of handsome.

He had more screens on his desk than Clayton as he monitored several exchanges simultaneously. While he was excellent at anticipating the temperature of individual stocks and the market in general, he could not come near his friend's technological know-how. Their skills weren't more than a source of occasional ribbing, but if Raphael's market predictions left his bank account more than comfortable, Clayton's company packed his accounts to bursting and beyond.

If there was another major distinction between the two it was that Raphael's desk faced the high rise windows. He watched every available sunset while Clayton allowed the sun to set over his shoulder. This difference surfaced often but provided the ying to a yang chemistry that kept the two men balanced and their friendship enduring. At the other end of their personality spectrum was a common interest reflected in nearly every conversation. The two watched old films together ad nauseam. Their shared wit promoted the borrowing of dialogue from memorized movies. The habit had become a mainstay for Clayton and a measuring stick he used on Raphael often.

Clayton looked at his watch. "It's only eleven. That topsy-turvy world of yours has a few hours to go. You sure you want to start crowing so early in the day? You could tank by the closing bell then you're crying on my shoulder all night like–"

"Not a chance."

"–like last time."

"You're full of shit," Raphael said laughing. "I've been on a roll. Cyclic ups and downs. That's all."

"Cyclic ups and downs?"

"Yes."

"That's what you're calling it these days?"

"Calling what?"

"Losing enough money to put some poor kid through college."

"We're done. Sorry I called. Just looking for a friend to celebrate with, not a lecture from the Pope. Gotta run. Have a good day."

"I think last week it was, 'market trends.'"

"Watch your step before you trip on your vow of peasantry."

"Vow of poverty."

"With you, it's peasantry."

"Is that even a word?"

"A rose is a rose. And as I recall, Saint Clayton, you've made a few bucks along the way following my 'cyclic ups and downs' and 'market trends.' Probably enough to, what did you say? 'Put some poor kid through college?' Like you need more money. You could buy and sell me in two minutes."

"Touché," Clayton said in submission. "I bow to your swift justice, sire."

There was a silence that stretched across the invisible airways.

"Touché and ouch!" Clayton continued, smiling as he broke the thin, warm ice. "For someone who's ready to celebrate at mid-day, you're carrying an awfully sharp sword."

"Life is cheap on the front lines of Wall Street, my friend. Life is cheap."

"You live in Tampa, Raphael."

"I reside in Tampa. I live and die on Wall Street."

"Why is it that I can always tell the amount of money you've made in a given day by the demeanor of your language? There must be a Freudian connection there somewhere I've yet to unravel."

"As you ponder my life," Raphael countered, "I was wondering if you, Dr. Freud, and the Pope would join me for a late lunch, slash early dinner, and extended happy hour? It's been that good of a morning and I'm done for the day."

"So, you're concerned that the afternoon's trading could cause the flower to wilt?"

There was another pause, but this one ended in mutual laughter. "Clay, you own the business and you've probably got your feet up watching Cary Grant and Ingrid Bergman. Are you going to meet me for lunch or not?"

Clayton thought of the non-related work beneath his fingers. "You know? Not just yet. I'm in the middle of something I can't step away from. How about dinner? My treat, Daddy War Bucks."

"Done. But forget the 'my treat.' This one's on Conoco Philips."

"Fair enough. We can leave a drum of oil as a tip."

"We'll discuss the tip over a Rob Roy. Where and when?"

"Yankee's?" Clayton answered as if it were a foregone conclusion.

"No surprise, but it'll serve the purpose. Time?"

"Four o'clock. Beat the traffic."

"And hit happy hour on the nose. I like your timing. Perfect. See you then."

"Hey! Raphael? You still there?"

"What's up? Still need a contribution to the orphan's fund?"

"No," Clayton said as he formulated his next words with a noticeable degree of caution. "This might sound like my strangest request to date, but I need a stock that's dying."

"A what?"

"If you had to pick a stock that's definitely moving in the wrong direction, which would it be?"

"You mean you're looking for something that's ready to bottom out and bounce?"

Clayton hesitated again. "No. More like an Enron type of bottom out."

"You looking for a write off?"

"Sort of. More like, call it a research type thing. What would be the last stock you yourself would buy, knowing what you know? Knowing, or at least surmising that this one's headed nowhere but south, and in a hurry."

Now it was Raphael's turn to leave a gap in space. "Have you read the papers? Check that. I forgot. You're a total cyber-geek. Let me re-phrase. Have you read the online papers?"

"What do you mean?"

"Xephclenor's been recalled."

"What's a Xephclenor?"

"A drug. And it's the only real seller Med-Pharm has left. All the rest have had their patents expire and are getting pumped out as generics by any company with a pharmacy license."

"And?"

"Damn, get your head out of your cyber ass, will you please? Med-Pharm was negotiating with GLK Pharmaceutical to sell out. Their stock jumped as soon as we got word on the buyout. We re-listed them from a caution to a very strong buy in less than an hour. Then yesterday, wham. The FDA sinks their flagship drug, Xephclenor, because it's killing people and Med-Pharm conveniently forgot to mention it. Xephclenor had billions in annual sales and seven years left on its patent, and, in truth, was the only thing GLK wanted. So that strong buy we ran up the flagpole got turned over in a heartbeat to an 'avoid.' Can you believe that – avoid?"

"That's bad I take it?" Clayton said as he scribbled 'Med-Pharm' on the yellow pad beneath his old notes.

"Bad? No one ever lists a stock as 'avoid.' Our thoughts are that by the end of the day they'll pull it off the Big Board entirely."

"That bad?" Clayton said, hiding a hint of glee in his voice.

"That bad and then some. Med-Pharm is a dead duck. Won't be worth the paper it's printed on as they say. If you need a loser to throw into your tax return, that's the one, but you better do it quick. Like I said, my bet is it's off the board by tomorrow."

"Good to know."

"You want me to run some numbers for you? Don't lose too much. Just a bone to throw the IRS and a small bone at that."

"Got it. Just a small bone."

"Anything else? Remember, I get paid by the transaction not the hour."

"Dinner's on me then. See you at four."

"Cool. Later."

The soft light from Clayton's cell phone hadn't timed out before he had tapped into the commissioner's bank accounts. He found several financial statements in the commissioner's name, his wife's, and his children's. The same was true of the developer. There was some simple math on the yellow pad and a pause, thinking about the wives and the children. Lines were drawn through the figures and new ones replaced them. These numbers were smaller, but still would cut deep. "Gotta leave something in the orphan's fund," he said quietly.

In moments he nearly simultaneously opened trading accounts for both the commissioner and the developer, then retreated back to the banking end. Account numbers were entered along with the proper passwords and with the click of his mouse, the commissioner and the developer were both the proud owners of thousands of shares of Med-Pharm stock. Even as Clayton confirmed the transactions and refreshed the page, the stock had fallen more. He smiled. "To those whom much is given."

There was one final misdirection magician's trick to be performed. The wireless pointed and clicked until a spammer's email account was tapped. Simple coding insured it would open automatically. The email was simple, "To those whom much is given, much is expected."

Clayton exited every site, backed his way out, left no traces, and restarted his computer. He sat back, leaning against the spring's tension in his chair as the computer stopped momentarily then began to whirl back to life. From the comfort of his semi-reclined position he reengaged the forensic software of his own creation. Secure, the computer opened itself.

"I don't know... I don't know... Let's take a look at the headlines and go from there, shall we?"

———————

2

As Clayton began to scan the e-papers, across town the hard copy headlines, plastered on paper that was scarcely dry, were being handed out by an old friend, Sam Ciampiano. It was a figurative hand out as Sam only touched the daily papers in bundles as he set them on the counter on front of him. He snipped the plastic bands with a razor sharp k-bar knife that was much more than needed to clip the simple strip. Passers-by scooped up the daily papers by ones, twos, threes, even fours and fives then shoved the money at Sam as if he was at fault for not taking it fast enough or making change fast enough or not seeing them waving their crumbled dirty dollar bills at him from the other end of the battered newsstand. Most buyers disappeared into the foot traffic minus a thank you and were out of earshot of Sam's half whispered obligatory, "You're welcome," if and when it came.

The process was almost automated for the regulars. For the tourists it was different, but for either group, the constant was Sam himself. He was as solid as the two by four that braced up the flap of the stand. Well over six feet tall and tipping the scales at two hundred and forty pounds he couldn't hide in the shadows of the glorified shed if he tried, and he did try. His arms were almost as thick as many men's thighs. His short haircut would have passed a basic training inspection on any Army base and his sharp features would have been comfortable on a movie screen. Any newspaper buyer waiting on a quip or a thank you would have ventured correctly that the personality behind the muscle aligned itself much closer to the Army than Hollywood.

Nearly half of the front wall of Sam's little haven was held up by the battered two by four that had been in service since Sam was a boy. Lifted up and out to form a neat weather break over the papers, the flap also shielded Sam and the patrons from the sun and rain. The twelve foot counter that held the majority of the dailies was covered with worn through linoleum – the same linoleum that was on the Ciampiano kitchen floor. There was no air conditioning. Two ancient box fans were slung from the ceiling by broken shoelaces of brown and dirty white. A Mr. Coffee machine, as old as the fans that looked down on it, sat stained and battered with a piece of black electrical tape over the burnt out switch that had stopped glowing red long before Sam's father had died.

This was not crunch time. That was early when the suburb people bolted into the city to their jobs. They parked their cars or streamed out of gray buses and made their way into the tall buildings, but not before stopping to grab a paper or two. For most, Sam's stand was a block or so out of the way, after all, this was Tampa, Florida – not New York – there wasn't a stand on every corner here. In fact, the Ciampiano newsstand was an oddity, but its uniqueness paid the bills and then some and had done so for longer than Sam could remember. Sam's father had sold newspapers, bolita numbers, and even Florida moonshine out of the shack seemingly forever. The bootleg business came to an end, but the numbers game went on as part of the Trafficante crime family's many interests. While bolita numbers were Sam Sr.'s day-to-day gravy, he occasionally left, all but unannounced, on long drives to New York, New Orleans, or Chicago. Sam had grown up with these absences and never thought to ask about them. He adored, idolized, and trusted his father. He could never bring himself to question him. As a teenager and later, the trips grew less frequent, but the hesitant shadow cast over them by his father's demeanor encouraged Sam to not press for the why and who at the other end of the trip. It was enough that his father came home, usually with enough extra money for a new set of sneakers for his boy.

So now, taking his turn in at least one side of the family business, Sam opened the newsstand seven days a week. And the regulars laid down their money and walked away over a faint, "Thanks Sam," not looking for any change.

After the crush and before the noonday crowd looking for information on a story shared at the water cooler that morning, business was slower. Depending on the weather there would be a steady run of downtown delivery people grabbing a magazine and the tourists moving between the historic cigar making section of Tampa, the sports complexes, beaches, and the museums. Sometimes they'd stop to buy a paper merely because there were no newspaper stands in their hometowns. It was the uniqueness of the sight, coupled with nostalgia for a few, which caused them to treat the newsstand as it were one of Florida's attractions. Some of these transient customers, all men, often tried to flip a quarter in the air and expected Sam to snatch it, like in a black and white movie they had once seen. Sam's dad had always grabbed the quarter then followed with something snappy to entertain, but not Sam. Not any longer. He often let the quarter fall and even pretended to not be able to find it – easy to do when he didn't even look – thus changing a dollar paper into a dollar and a quarter sale. It was his way of getting back at them all – the tourists who flaunted their money and even the wealthy businessmen who didn't need or want change. Sam stopped thinking they were being nice, leaving him a tip, years ago when he last ran the stand with his father and he had never been much of an entertainer.

Somewhere in those years the stand had become work and not a place to go to be at the center of the world. Twenty-five years earlier it was a mini-Disney that whisked Sam and his young friends, Clayton Rand and his older brother Carl, and Raphael Bordaine, into the heart of downtown Tampa. There they raced and played all day until Sam's father signaled the day was over by dropping the wooden front flap with a resounding crack that called to the boys for blocks around. With that clap, any game instantly ended and the quartet raced for the newsstand with Sam always slapping the side of the building first.

A few years later Sam, Clay, Carl, and Ralph – a nickname Raphael had rebelled against from the onset which only reinforced it – worked the stand in earnest. Mr. Ciampiano began taking longer and longer breaks while delivering a wine stained drawstring leather pouch containing slips of paper, fistfuls of change, and crumpled dollar bills from the bolita game to a back table at The Columbia Restaurant. Conveniently, the restaurant was only a few blocks away and at a mid-point between the newsstand and the Ciampiano stilt-built shotgun style house. When Mr. Ciampiano was engaged in a lively debate across the linoleum counter of the stand – the newspapers at rapt attention beneath his flailing hands listening to a language not captured in any of their papers – Sam would run the bag to the restaurant's back table.

The men there would smile and tousle his hair, give him lemonade and ice cream, but Sam could see they were hard inside and out – like his father. They were a tough, respectful lot who remembered his name, but usually called him, *Po' Martello* – Little Hammer – which pleased him to no end as he heard them refer to his father as, *Il Martello*, The Hammer. The guardians of the back table also waived him past the long waiting line of the lunch crowds like he was special though his sneakers might have ten knots in the broken laces and most of the soles had long been left on the sidewalks and streets of Tampa.

Sam was about ten when someone grabbed him by the neck and jerked him off his feet as he went to the head of the line with the pouch.

"No budging, kid," the man barked through a sneer as he looked at his eventual lunch date, an admin assistant he was trying to bed.

The bag seemed to hang in the air for a moment in the place Sam's skinny frame had been. When the bag hit the floor, countless quarters spilled and escaped in as many directions. The racket begged attention and drew it from the maître d' who snapped his fingers toward the back table.

Two guys who wouldn't have fit through the wide front door of the restaurant side-by-side came up front. They stopped at the maître d and he whispered to them while several lunch guests knelt to help retrieve the errant change.

Sam was on his hands and knees picking up rowdy quarters when he saw the shiniest black shoe he had ever seen step on a quarter in front of his face. He looked up from the floor.

"Go open the front door, *Po' Martello*," was all the maître d' said.

Sam was up and at the door. He held it open as the crowd instinctively separated nearby and left a wide gap like flighty antelope might do when drinking in the company of a crocodile.

Both big men walked on Sam's scattered money and crossed the foyer to the woefully overmatched diner who had grabbed Sam.

"You need to get out," one of the crocodiles growled.

"Look. I don't want any trouble–"

"Now."

"I'm just here for lunch. The kid ran into me and–"

It was a blur, but when focus returned, the antelope was literally upside down, his feet straight in the air, and he was being carried through the door. Sam saw the man pitched like a bowling ball across the sidewalk. He was scraped and battered when he reached the gutter and moved, but stayed down trying to regain a sense of himself and what had just happened.

One of the bowlers walked close to him and squatted down. "Don't come back here no more. Be happy it was us and not the kid's old man. You'd wake up at the bottom of Tampa Bay. Get the fuck outa here."

Sam was still holding the door open when the big men stepped back in the restaurant. To a person, everyone in the lunch line was now busily bending down picking up scattered coins from the bag.

"Get your stuff, kiddo," one of the crocodiles said in his best rendition of a soft voice.

Sam grabbed the bag and walked down the line. People dropped in what they'd found. He thought about a scene from the old movies his father liked where Jesse James walked down the aisle of a train he was robbing and the passengers dropped their valuables in the nice-guy-robber's bag.

When his bag was burdened down again, Sam took it to the back. One of the men at the table took it with a thank you and vanished deeper into the restaurant.

"Sammy, listen to me," the head of the table, known to Sam only as Don T, said with some force. "You got to have your head on a swivel. All the time. See? You don't sleep on nobody. *Capisci?*"

"Yes, sir."

"Head on a swivel, *Po' Martello*. Or it could end up on a platter. *Capisci?*"

"Yes, sir."

"*Bene.* You like vanilla ice cream, Sammy? It's my favorite. You want some?"

Sam was a grown man again. He was back behind the counter of the newsstand, but allowed a small smile at the curious and pleasant memories of those days at the stand, The Columbia, his father, and running through the special little neighborhood called Ybor City.

"You got the *Enquirer?*" a voice asked over a loud yellow shirt plastered with seashells and flamingos.

"*Philadelphia* or *National*," Sam asked absently.

"Philly. I don't read that other shit. I wanna see what's happening on the home—"

"Beneath the *Times*, before the *Washington Post*," Sam interrupted as he pointed down the stacks of newspapers, each well depleted by this time of day.

The loud shirt walked down the front of the stand and began to rifle through the stack. "I don't see it."

"Sold out."

"Damn it. What else you got that's close?"

"The *Times*. Right in your hand."

The shirt pulled the thick paper up the counter. "Can't get away from New York even on vacation," the man said as he pulled the business and entertainment sections and a fist full of ads out of the paper in front of Sam and dumped them on the counter.

"No gutting of the fish, Philly," Sam said with no emotion.

"Just throw it in your recycle bin."

"We don't recycle here. Dollar fifty buys the whole fish – guts, head and tail."

The man laughed. "Everything's gotta be related to the ocean with youse people down here. 'Don't gut the fish.' That's funny."

Sam took the two dollars and instinctively had two quarters out and slapped them on the pile of 'guts' on the counter.

"C'mon, buddy. I don't wanna haul all that shit around," the shirt from Philly said.

Sam pointed to the trash bin chained to the streetlight at the curb in front of the stand.

"I got it. I got it. Youse people oughta recycle these papers. We do."

"We don't."

"You should. Makes for a lota trash. Recycling keeps the city cleaner, you know?"

"Then why are you coming down here if Philly's so nice?"

"I said cleaner, not warmer," the yellow shirt laughed again as he dumped half his paper in the trash.

Sam didn't bother with a hundred come backs. He just let the loud shirt wander up the street. That was one of the best things about the newsstand. The design was such that it looked straight out onto the sidewalk and beyond to the street. It didn't allow much peripheral vision with its sideboards hanging down from the big braced up door flap. The sideboards were like blinders on a racehorse, to protect the papers against the weather and protect Sam from the world. On some days he lifted one end or both, but not often. He rather liked the darkness and security the blinders gave. As it was, when traffic or customers or annoying tourists in loud shirts passed just a short distance, they vanished from view and vanished also from a memory well practiced in erasing the insignificant or the painful.

From Sam's limited scope, his immediate world was simple and had few rules, each of his own making. The greatest offense in the realm of the newsstand was unfolding a paper without buying. Thumbing the stacks was alright. Even pulling a paper from beneath other cities' rags was fine, as he had long ago recognized the conscious or otherwise need of tourists to scan the headlines from home. But to open a paper without buying it was a sin. No one, no matter how carefully, could put the paper back together with the exacting standard of the original press. Then they would stuff it in most anywhere, Sam thought, as a way to hide their sin. You couldn't hide sin. No matter what you tried.

"If you want to read, go to the library," he remembered his father saying. Or, "That paper's for sale, mister, not for rent." Mr. Ciampiano's thick arms ensured little argument.

Then Sam would echo the same words and embarrass the dollar out of the pocket that had been its nest. He'd tuck away George Washington in his new home and the reluctant customer would move away and be forgotten. But the wisdom of his father was never far and there were other words fresh from his father's lips that jumped to the front of his mind with little prompting. Like the calls down the narrow central hallway of their small house at 4 AM.

"Let's go! Let's go! Early bird and all that jazz! The drop offs will beat us there!"

"The trucks have never beaten us to the stand," young Sam would say sleepily as he tied his cheap, dirty sneakers.

"Why do you suppose that is?" his father would reply to no answer from Sam. "Because we're up and at 'em! That's why. We don't get there before the trucks, half the papers would be stolen."

"Nobody would touch that stand, Dad."

"How's that?"

"Nobody would touch the stand or take any papers."

"Why not?"

"The guys at The Columbia are your friends."

"So?"

"They scare people."

"They do?"

"Yep."

"You scared of them, Sam?"

"Nope."

"How come? You a tough guy?" his father said as he grabbed Sam as though to wrestle.

Sam wasn't awake yet and it was too early. He went limp as his father eased from clench to hug. "No, I ain't tough, but they don't bother me. They like me. They give me ice cream sometimes."

The hug tightened. "Yea, they like you," the Hammer said. "But I love you."

Sam only patted his dad's thick arm.

"C'mon, boy," the old man said as he squirted Sam up the hall. "Let's get to work."

As the father and son went down the single corridor that split their small house, out onto the porch, and down the steps to the street, they kept talking.

"Dad? Will I have big arms like you when I grow up?"

"Bigger."

"Bigger than yours?"

"Yes. I feed you too good."

"When will they be as big as yours?"

"Tomorrow."

"Really?" Sam said as he looked at his lanky arm as it stuck out from his t-shirt.

"It'll seem like it. Time goes too fast, Sam. You'll see. Don't wish it away."

"I'd like to have big arms now."

"Might be a good idea in case somebody has snatched the early drops. You might have to wade into them to get our papers back."

"I would too."

"I know it. That's a good boy. And the sonofabitch probably took the quarters any early *paisanos* left for us. Our money and our papers, Sam. What are we going to do about that?"

"The sonsabitches...," Sam said as he grit his teeth and walked faster.

"He probably took the whole stack and is peddling them papers right now from under his arm around town just like it was 1920 all over again. Hey..." Mr. Ciampiano's wheels were turning. "Not a bad notion. A paper boy. Town crier. And I know just the boy for the job."

"PAPER! Get your paper!" Sam cried out up and down the street. His beat was the block and saved people the steps of walking the rest of the way to the newsstand if their timing was good enough to catch Sam at their particular junction of his route. His father was hot on the idea for a short while, and then brought Sam back into the newsstand to help out through the crush. Clayton, Carl, and Raphael were hired to be Ciampiano Criers and even made it into the papers they sold as a novelty story, but the boys were unreliable at 5 AM and Sam was needed in the stand. Very soon the Ciampiano Criers were a thing of the past, as newsboys had been elsewhere for fifty years. A yellowed newspaper clipping of Mr. Ciampiano with Sam, Clayton, Carl, and Raphael in old style newsboy caps with bundles of papers under their arms was still in a dusty frame on the back wall of the newsstand. In the picture, Mr. Ciampiano's hands rested heavily on Sam's shoulders. There had been other pictures taken by the *Tribune* photographer of the boys with their newspaper satchels, but those pictures, like the boys in them, had disappeared. This one had lasted. Sam looked at it once in a while and let a smile slip out as he admired himself for not giving in to his father's idea of wearing knickers.

A few years after the short-lived days as a newsboy had passed, Sam filled out a thin card that had fallen from the *Sports Illustrated* magazine he'd been leafing through in the quiet library at his high school. The card carried with it the promise that he'd become an 'Army of One.' It was appealing with its picture of a gritty camouflaged faced warrior and its brief lecture on the advantages of enlisting – saving for college while saving the country.

It almost seemed comical to him, 'Save the world and get up to $15,000 toward tuition.'

"Doesn't seem like much of a reward for saving the whole goddamn planet," he remembered saying out loud to whispered hisses for library protocol as he filled out the simple card. "But, it's more than Spiderman makes," he laughed as he put the card in his shirt pocket beneath a faded light jean jacket he nearly always wore. Others saw the faded jean jacket with the worn out elbows and blanched creases as a symbol that stood for Sam as much as his name. Sam just saw it as a layer of protection against the rest of the world – sort of like Spiderman's suit. It also covered the fact that he only had three nice shirts in his closet. The jacket hid his simple rotation.

As he left the library that day he remembered being pulled out of line. He was seventeen now, his father's thick arms were filling in, but he always thought back to that day in the Columbia. It seemed to Sam he was always being pulled out of line for something.

"What'd you slip in your pocket, Ciampiano?" the head librarian was drilling. "Let's have it," the snap in his voice matched the snap of his fingers. "Our magazines are for everyone's use. Something make you think you're special? Well, you're not. Let's have it."

Sam moved slowly, "like 'lasses in wintertime," he'd heard in an old cowboy movie when the bad guy had the drop on the hero and wanted him to hand over his guns. Like the hero, Sam already knew the outcome, so his moves were deliberate and full of suspense for the movie goers in the library who watched him and the librarian face off on the carpeted floor that became for Sam a dark and dusty outpost in 1870.

The recruiting card came bit by bit into the view of all those who had gathered for the gunfight. The librarian was beaten – shot down dead by Sam's slow draw. But even dead, he tried to recover.

"That it?" he rudely questioned as he took the card then snatched open Sam's protective jacket.

Sam jerked away. "You don't tug on Superman's cape," he said with a grin, mimicking a line he'd heard in a song his father played on the oldies station in the newsstand.

"Easy, Ciampiano," the librarian said as he looked at the card. "Thinking of going in the military, are you? Probably the best thing for you. Teach you some discipline."

"What time did you get up today?" Sam asked abruptly.

"Excuse me?" the librarian said as he attempted to hand the card back to Sam.

"What time did you get out of bed this morning? It's not a tough question."

Caught off guard the inquisitor answered. "6:30. Promptly. Every school day to meet the buses."

"Four AM. No alarm clock. Seven days a week. Don't tell me I need discipline." Sam took the card, tore it in half, in half again, then tossed it in the librarian's face.

The librarian was at odds with himself, but recovered enough. "Pick that up, young man."

"You wanted it. You pick it up," Sam said as he headed for the door.

The next morning Sam was called to the office yet again and given in-school suspension. Nothing to do but sit at a desk in a miniature cubicle and think of ways to annoy the monitor at best, damage the system at worst. The thoughts made him think of how an inmate must feel when faced with simple confinement and nothing to do but watch the calendar flip by. For Sam it was only the clock, not a calendar, and his sentence was just three days, seven hours at a time, but he lingered over the thoughts of the oppressed and imprisoned and of what the pressure of time coupled with the prowess of the mind would have men contemplate.

Lack of stimulation forced him to whisper first then pass surreptitious notes to the cellmate in the adjoining cubicle. Sam learned his neighbor was Clayton from the newsboy days who had, by Sam's crude standards, become a geek. Still, there was the history between them though it was nearly washed away by the years and the divergent paths they had taken. Clayton didn't have a job now that he'd outgrown the newsstand and Sam was still tied to it and also the dishes in the sinks of The Columbia.

While at the restaurant he was once asked to drive to Miami to make a pickup of something unknown. After asking his father to use their old car, the need for the trip evaporated along with any future job offers from the back table. Sam only brought it up to the table one time as he delivered espresso when a senior in high school.

"If you ever need anything," he said shyly to the head of the table. "I can do it."

Don T, tall with thinning hair, simple classic features, a pockmarked face, and a mind for business ignored the expresso. "You need money, *Po' Martello?*"

"Everybody needs money," Sam grinned.

The entire table reached for their pockets. Tens and twenties flew from worn billfolds, tri-folds, and diamond crusted silver money clips, onto the table as if ante money was collecting to start a card game. Someone piled the money neatly and put it in front of Sam who looked at it, then to the head of the table.

"There you go, kiddo," Don T said proudly. "Problem solved."

"Thanks," Sam said without reaching. "But I can't take that. I mean, if you have any work, I can do it."

"I know you can, kid, but your old man says you're gonna be a General."

Sam smiled, a little embarrassed. "I don't know—"

"No, that's a good thing. This is the greatest country ever in the world. I'll sleep better knowing you're looking out for it – making things right. Keeping us all safe. Can you do that for me, Sammy?"

"I can do that."

"*Bene.* But until you're a General, you gotta concentrate on knocking the hell outa people on the football field." Don T stood up. "Make a muscle," he said.

"Aww—"

"Go on. Show the guys. Make a muscle."

Sam flexed his bicep and it stretched his white t-shirt. The man patted Sam's thick chest.

"Look at that! We got Jack LaLanne here. He's like hitting a wall."

"Built like the Hammer."

"Joe Weider."

"What are you guys, antiques? Arnold-fucking-Schwarzenegger."

"Superman."

"It's all good, *Martelletto*," Don T said as the boisterous table mirrored the boss's move back into his chair and settled down. "You kick ass on the football field and be a General." The Don folded the pile of money and stuffed it in Sam's pocket. "I'll let you know if something comes up."

Nothing ever did "come up." Yet all those men, and countless others, were at Mr. Ciampiano's funeral years later paying their final respects while the FBI took pictures from across the street. Each of them – hard men inside and out – gave Sam a hug that day. Lasagna dishes piled up at the house he had shared with his dad from birth until the freezer was packed and the refrigerator full. Taped to the casserole dishes were names to return them to. Also taped beneath the trays were envelopes full of cash. Sam never knew a single particular, but understood well enough.

While Sam worked and played football, Clayton and Raphael embraced the gaming and computer age. Carl, older by a year, left school behind for a paycheck on the Tampa docks. School had never agreed with Carl anyway. The genetics that provided gifts to one son led some to suggest had come at the expense of the other. Carl struggled with reading, math, and anything analytical, but if a solid back and kind heart were in the job description, he was your man.

The shared circumstances of the suspension room fostered a renewed friendship between Sam and Clayton that would normally have endured only the duration of the incarceration. However, and for reasons that escaped them both, they maintained a quiet friendship. Throughout the remainder of their senior year they talked at length when they ran across one another and ventured into unknown shared interests in the political structure of the day, college, and the military. They understood that neither would be fully embraced by the other's circle of friends, but they were content with the clandestine notion that they had a contact on the other side of the tracks. By the time their tassels were symbolically moved and later tossed into the air – a ritual Sam chose to ignore – there was a mutual sigh that before long, their admiration and respect for one another's stances on life would no longer be constrained by the caste system of high school.

Shortly after the suspensions ended, Sam filled out another card, slipped from another *Sports Illustrated* at the newsstand and dropped it in a street corner mailbox, no stamp required. Within a month of graduation, he was in boot camp writing letters to his father, but also to Clayton.

———————

3

Across the base Sam called home for several years was a miniature law office – JAG – the Judge Advocate General. It was somewhat disorganized, understaffed, and manned by inexperienced spanking new law school graduates. They were fresh from a specialized basic training with little in common with the rigors Sam and similar recruits had endured. The novice attorneys came here to hone their skills, pay their dues, and absorb the useless rhetoric the military shoved down their waiting throats in exchange for a respite from the tuition loans of law school. A few might be enticed to stay on and serve their country in uniform, but the vast majority were there to reap the benefit of a reduced law school bill and would bolt for the gate to chase the dream of high dollar, high power jobs the day their obligation expired. The JAG assignment provided lots of experience – the cases were endless – but the rules of military justice were well removed from what they would encounter in the civil environment. The young esquires knew this, perhaps their eventual employers knew it as well, but it didn't curb the tide. They came, served their time then moved on to jobs where the strict rigors of military protocol didn't apply. Many would flourish, but a good number would suffer the inevitable damage evoked by the lack of those same rigors and, nourished by greed and a form of lawlessness the profession seemed to foster, fall far from the stringent format of their earlier military training.

During the early years of his enlistment he had been trained as the advertised 'Army of One' and had demonstrated such a penchant and proficiency that he was permitted or invited, depending on the context, to apply for entry into the elite Army Rangers.

Sam excelled as a Ranger. It was the combination of discipline, ability and his unwavering diligence – his head always on that swivel – that set him apart within a group already set apart from mainstream soldiers. In sight of his fulfillment and release, Sam's talents brought him again to be invited to try out for still another choice group within the Rangers themselves and as before, he survived the initiation.

The selection process was little more than torture. Sam and the lucky few offered a shot at this best of the best troupe, were starved, left without water, and deprived of sleep until strong men wept like children. Those that broke down were whisked silently away.

In the end Sam made it, as he knew he would before the process ever began. He was still a member of the Army, and still a Ranger, but he was also a member of a very select team to which conventional Army practices no longer applied. Sam was in Delta Force.

They operated beyond the usual rules of engagement and ignored the regulations of the dated Geneva Convention with impunity. They were, to Sam, men in which his father's simple rules of life – hard work, discipline, strength – bubbled at the surface. And while many left families that blended in at parent teacher conferences and in little league bleachers, when they boarded planes at midnight on the far edges of the tarmac, they were all highly skilled assassins.

Delta Force traveled around the world as though covered by an invisibility cloak – flying in and out of countries, leaving misinterpreted destruction in their wake. Internal factions would blame each other and the bias of his own country's national news would fan the flames of strife with an overt bend toward the perceived good guys. All the while it had been Sam and his free ranging band.

Like men everywhere in all manner of work, Sam liked some guys better than others, though he wouldn't leave the least of them behind. But this was more out of a need to protect the operation, not something as trite sounding as bringing home a dead comrade in arms. They all knew why. Their uniforms – even the all black ones with no patches or labels - and their American faces gave away too much intel. Sometimes their uniforms were those of the enemy, but they couldn't change the set of their American eyes and chins. Everyone, dead or alive, came out.

Several times, Sam wore the disheveled rags of a goat herder and once he was stuffed into a suit and tie. Papers in his pockets would match the garments. The larger contingencies – teams, squads, and platoons – operated under similar guises with similar impunity, but the invisibility came with a price. Few things were as they seemed. Aircraft down, reportedly the result of a training accident or mechanical malfunction, could be members of the elite team killed in a place a thousand miles from the listed crash site. Code words and scanned bar codes opened every door and quieted every question, but left anonymous soldiers dead of quiet causes when they had sacrificed themselves in the most violent hidden trenches of a war that had no boundary.

The soldiers talked little among themselves for an inbred fear that any question from a comrade was part of a test by the upper echelon to gauge a man for weakness or vulnerability. This was all true. Sam himself had been asked to question another soldier once, in absent fashion, regarding his next deployment. When the soldier smiled back and said nothing, Sam smiled too, relieved to be out from under the weight of whether the man might be prone to talking.

Months turned to years and operations came and went. Sam still wrote to Clayton occasionally and his father if he was away from Tampa and his barracks on MacDill Air Force base too long. He was reasonably certain his letters were screened, but wouldn't have written or talked of work, where he had been, or where he was going even if he was assured otherwise. He was just a sergeant, he'd write, doing what he was told. Sometimes he was told to go overseas for six days or six months and he went, trips that filled his father with pride. Other times he would be at MacDill serving his country. Wherever the Army needed a simple sergeant, he would go, but each time he said it, it was a lie. Sam had long stopped being a simple sergeant. Tension of the missions kept him sharp, but concern for his father as the elder Ciampiano aged, was concerning and distracting – a dangerous combination for a man like Sam.

For Mr. Ciampiano, who knew much of guises and secrets, it wasn't long after Sam's induction in Special Operations Command that the Hammer pieced together his son's military life. He never asked, but his heart swelled to near bursting. Then one day, it did, and Samiste Ciampiano Sr. died.

"How you holding up, *Po' Martello?*" Don T asked at the graveside service with an unaccustomed softness in his voice.

Sam was pinched into a new black suit. Black sunglasses designed for shooting protected his eyes from anyone looking for a tear. *"Bene."*

A strong hug followed.

"You a General yet?" eased out through a tender smile.

"Just a sergeant."

"Just a sergeant..." The Don motioned to the casket, engulfed in flowers. "He told it a little different."

"I imagine he did."

"He never wanted our life for you, Sammy."

"I know."

"I've got some boys who were helping your father at the newsstand covering it." The Don was rubbing Sam's thick muscled shoulders. "All the businesses. Everything's taken care of."

"*Grazie.* Carl Rand has been helping Dad a lot. He's going to take it over for me. He's a good man. I'll probably close it up. It's way past time. It was Dad's thing, you know?"

"I do. Take your time. You'll get the Hammer's *vig* though. Let us know what you want to do and when."

"*Grazie.*"

"You stay in touch, right? You ever need something, you come to us."

"I will," Sam said as he put his hand over his heart. "*Grazie di cuore.*"

The Don and his handlers drifted away, each shaking Sam's hand, hugging him, and offering condolences in turn. Clayton, Carl, and Raphael took their place.

"Hey, Sam," they echoed softly.

Sam just nodded.

"I'm awfully sorry, Sam," Clayton half whispered. "We all thought the world of your dad."

Again, there was just a subtle nod and the three newsboys stepped away from the fourth and others slipped in. When the polite mourners had gone, Sam ran his hand over the gray granite marker and went back to the small house and the counters full of lasagna.

––––––––––––

4

Not long removed from the funeral, Sam flew into Andrews Air Force Base from points in the middle east and was immediately drenched in the oppressive heat and humidity of Washington, DC in August. The weather dwarfed anything Sam would have felt in Tampa. There was no coastal breeze from the Gulf. The air was heavy and stifling. He was still carrying grief in his heart and jetlag was carrying over from his last mission. Both conditions were clouding his mind and, combined with reactive training, aligned with unseen stars and led to an encounter that would impact the rest of Sam's life as well as many others. If a breeze existed at all, it happened to blow him out of line once more and into a corrosive drill sergeant's path. The sergeant, accustomed to having recruits jump beneath his words, bumped into Sam as the men met roughly at the door to the commissary – Sam going in, the other soldier coming out. The drill instructor reacted poorly and paid a price for it. In a fraction of a second, beads of sweat flew ahead of the man's face to the sidewalk and evaporated in a flash. The splatter of blood that fell with the sweat dried as quickly, but left a story and a trail though it wasn't needed. The stunned sergeant's screams and the honest and near honest statements of the two men after the fact were evidence enough – buoyed by the mangled condition of the sergeant's right arm.

The soon to be helpless man started to say, "Make way, mother–," just as Sam's own words were forming.

"Sorry, I didn't–"

But all the words were interrupted when the drill instructor's right hand touched Sam's chest in the birth of a shove that never matured. With the beginnings of the push, Sam snatched the man's wrist with his left hand. His right hand drove up under the sergeant's right armpit. In a well-practiced move that was as fluid and quick as water spilling, Sam spun to his left and ducked beneath the man's outstretched arm slightly until he was in the seemingly unenviable position of having his back to the aggressor. The sergeant's arm was now held over Sam's shoulder, braced against it by the weight of his own body versus the upturned and unyielding joint of his right elbow.

Then Sam stood up. He pulled the arm toward the ground with his left as his right pushed up on the sergeant's armpit. The sergeant's feet said goodbye to the ground as he was effortlessly leveraged head over heels and thrown with the force of both speed and strength to the concrete sidewalk within the shadow of the commissary door. It was an immaculately executed throw that had been all blur from start to finish, but the final passing frame of the blur held the real damage.

In that last nano-space of a second that the throw took, Sam, still holding the sergeant's twisted wrist, drove his own right forearm into the backside of the sergeant's already hyper-extended elbow and snapped the man's arm as easily as a twig. A vicious twist within the follow through brought splintered ivory white bone through the sergeant's skin like a pencil poking through paper toward Sam's face. Only then did the ingrained reaction stop. Start to finish had been a literal flash of lightning split in half.

Shocked and stunned from the coarse bully he had been, the sergeant laid helplessly with eyes widened by burning pain and fear. Sam's movement never broke stride as he slipped without notice from bone breaker to mender. As he began first aid and rolled the sergeant gently to his back, others from both in and outside the commissary gathered. The sergeant could now see his own blood and the tip of broken bone beneath Sam's hand as first aid was administered and pressure put on the bleeding compound fracture. The sergeant responded with a primal scream and tried to push away from Sam's continuing efforts when he took notice of his hand seemingly on his body backward and his arm nearly twisted off.

"Lay still," Sam said as he forcibly pushed the sergeant's chest to the ground.

"You... You crazy bastard... Get off me!"

"That's not a good idea. That splinter must have nicked your brachial artery."

While others made frantic calls to the military police and the base's medical unit, Sam continued working, fashioning a tourniquet from his belt and ID wallet which he neatly placed beneath the belt against the upper inner arm above the damage he'd inflicted. As Sam tightened the belt, the bleeding eased.

Two MPs appeared over Sam's shoulder. They watched for a moment as his bloodied hands worked the tourniquet. Sam didn't look up, but spoke to the police calmly. "Bring your first aid box."

"No need. Medical is pulling up. What happened to this guy?

"I broke his arm," Sam said.

The MPs looked at one another then were jerked away by the sergeant's scream.

"That sonofabitch attacked me!"

"That's not quite right, sergeant," Sam said.

"Looks to me like he's your best friend," one of the MPs said as he pointed to Sam's medical handiwork.

"Bullshit! Arrest him!"

Sam moved the splintered arm slightly beneath his hand and purposely ended the sergeant's need to talk as he nearly fainted from pain. Meanwhile, the MPs stepped aside and Sam gave way as paramedics took over.

The first medic to snap on latex gloves knelt down beside the sergeant, who was lost in a stage of fainting, screaming, and moaning, and examined the arm. He glanced at Sam then back to the sergeant. "Sgt. Dermitt?" the medic said as he pulled the man's shirt tight enough to read the name sewn on the front. "Sergeant? Can you hear me? We're going to transport you to the med center. Stay with me."

Another medic appeared with a massive red plastic case, opened it and immediately retrieved an inflatable cast which he began to adjust on the sergeant's bloody arm. The first medic stepped away from the moaning and walked a few feet to Sam and the police who were talking to him quietly.

"I have never seen a break that bad. Compound spiral. His arm is almost ripped off. Right through the muscle and skin. And he's not a little guy," he whispered. "What happened?"

"We've got it," one of the MPs said stoically. "Would you come with me, Sgt. Ciampiano?"

As one MP led Sam to the open jeep, the medic watched the other move through the crowd, jotting down names and what they'd seen. He saw some in the crowd point at the jeep and shake their heads. Others looked back and forth from the broken sergeant to the jeep and covered their mouths. And still others seemed to be mimicking a judo throw as they tried to demonstrate what they'd seen.

The MP in the jeep clamored out and jogged over to the prostate sergeant. He pointed at Sam's wallet still tucked beneath the makeshift tourniquet. "Can you get that out of there for me? And do you have something to clean up my guy with?"

The medics replaced the wallet with a roll of gauze and gave the MP some disposable towelettes just before they placed the sergeant on a stretcher. As they wheeled him to the open doors of an ambulance, the sergeant pointed at Sam and the jeep with his only good hand. "I want him arrested! I'm pressing charges! You're headed to the brig, soldier!" Then he rested back on the gurney, his strength and bravado drained.

Sam sat quietly as both MPs returned to the jeep – one holding Sam's ID and the other looking inquisitively at what his partner held.

In a minute the trio was driving to the base police station, Sam riding in the front. The MP behind him leaned forward and handed Sam the damp throwaway towels. As Sam wiped the blood off his hands. The MP asked respectfully, "Ranger, huh?" followed by a simple question. "SOCOM?"

Sam looked at him intensely, hesitated, and then said clearly, "Blackbird."

The MP leaned back slowly without a word and the driver gripped the wheel a little tighter as Sam tried to get all the blood off his hands.

At the station, Sam was asked to wait in a small holding room with a glass door and windows for walls on two sides. The two MPs who brought him in disappeared down the hall while Sam sat at a small table with his hands spread in front of him and waited. He realized he had insanely overreacted and was going to pay for it. What he didn't know was how much.

Between thoughts, an attractive Naval JAG officer with shorter than shoulder length brown hair burst into the room carrying a single page of paper she was snatching from a crisp manila folder. She might have been twenty-five, Sam guessed, and right from law school and induction in her crisp white uniform.

Sam snapped to his feet in deference to the lieutenant boards on her shoulders.

"You Ciampiano?" she asked abruptly, before the door was closed behind her.

"Yes, ma'am."

"Sit down, Sergeant," she said as she scanned the single page while she pulled a chair up to the empty table in the center of the room. Sam could see it was the MP report. At the top above his name was the single word 'Blackbird' and a question mark.

"Sgt. Ciampiano, my name is Lt. Auburn and it's been my fortunate luck to be the next available attorney to pick up incoming reports. I've drawn you," she said slowly as she read the report. "Or you've drawn me, depending on how you want to look at it. But either way, no perspective looks good. It says here you had an argument with a Sgt. Dermitt and that you summarily proceeded to try to tear his arm off. True or not true?"

"Partly–"

"True or not true, Sergeant?"

"Not true, Lieutenant."

"Okay. Not true. See, that wasn't hard, now was it? I ask the questions, you tell me the answers."

"Yes, ma'am."

"What was the argument about? The one you had with the victim...,
Sgt. Dermitt?"

"There was no argument, ma'am."

"So, for no reason, you attacked this man and broke his arm. Is that
what you're telling me? Not much for me to go on in order to mount your
defense."

"There was no argument and I didn't attack him. The sergeant put his
hand on me and I overreacted. I'm very sorry. I'd like you to enter a plea
of guilty for me."

A moment passed. The Lieutenant finally looked up from the single
paper at Sam. They stared at each other for almost a minute before she
spoke as she closed the folder on the one page report.

"Sam? May I call you Sam?"

"Yes, ma'am."

"Let's try again. Sam, my name is Karen Auburn," and she stuck her
hand out.

Sam's hand still carried dried blood in the creases and around his
fingernails. He looked at it then at Lt. Auburn. She thrust her hand at him
a bit further.

They shook hands, but the lieutenant kept his and took it to the table
between them. "Look, Sam. I'd like to help you, but I need a little more
than a full confession and an apology. That guy got mangled if I can believe
this," she said quietly as she glanced at the folder. "I need to know what
happened. Or maybe I need to know why. Instead of what, how about we
start with that? Why?"

Keeping to his code, Sam was silent. He looked through the officer
until a gentle yet firm clasp of his hand brought him to look to the hands
on the table. Sam allowed his eyes to drift slowly over her hands and away,
but with a constant intent about them that said they wouldn't stop until
they met hers.

He noticed her manicured nails – white ends painted so neatly it was
as if done by a precision machine – the tips looking as sharp as razors. Her
hands were youthful, porcelain, even fragile. The wrists were stick thin and
her forearms tight, muscled, and tanned. The white short sleeves of her
uniform were bright and starched, crisp as new money. At her throat he
saw the same muscled tan skin and from habit detected a pulse where her
carotid would be. The face was prettier than he had noticed earlier and
nearly void of makeup. A little on the high cheekbones, but that was it.
Her eyes needed no help. They were brown, dark as a forest, not black, but
a deep dark brown that looked elegant and regal. Sam recognized a natural

beauty he had never noticed in a woman before and he felt a change creep over him that he hadn't expected and had no defense against.

"I... I've had training...," he heard himself say unbelievably. "I reacted to a threat that wasn't there. He was... he was... the aggressor. I'm use to reacting in a certain way."

"What way is that, Sam?"

"Protect the mission. Protect yourself. Head on a swivel. I overreacted, as I said. I'm sorry," and he began to pull his hand away.

Karen reached for it again and grasped it just a little tighter. "What is your assignment, Sam?"

He baulked noticeably.

"It's alright, Sam. I'm your attorney. You can tell me anything."

"No I can't."

"Sure you can. What do you do?"

He looked for an easy way out of the conversation, but it was difficult to escape Karen's sincerity.

"I follow orders."

"You and everybody else," Karen smiled. "Where are you assigned?"

"SOCOM. MacDill."

"Special Operations Command?"

"Yes, ma'am."

Karen knew the structure. United States Special Operations Command, USSOCOM, covered the globe from MacDill Air Force Base in Tampa, Florida.

"That's pretty intense stuff. Anything troubling you, Sam?"

The hesitation was so slight it would have been missed by anyone watching the conversation, but from within, it was unmistakable. While Karen weighed the signs of posttraumatic stress for a defense, Sam was thinking of his father's death.

"That's okay, Sam. I imagine you've had defensive training."

"Yes. Some."

"Alright. We've got a start. I think there's something here. That's a defense. We–"

"No, Lieutenant. It's no defense. It's improper discipline. Improper action. Unacceptable," and he roughly pulled away, leaving her hands clutching at an empty space.

There was a long gap in the conversation. She was sizing him up and in the process saw something beyond the usual jar-head, macho, drunken assaults she was accustomed to representing. Beneath the thick arms and the rough exterior was another man. Somehow she caught a glimpse of the newspaper boy she had never known, now conditioned to be something else. A man who embodied the Army of One so well, he found it difficult to turn off. She saw a man who needed help.

The door flew open with such a shock that it shook the room. "Lieutenant, what's going on here?" The speaker was a full bird colonel in faded battle garb with sleeves rolled up just above his elbows.

Sam jumped from the table and stood at attention with a frozen salute. His thoughts instantly clear again.

Karen recovered quickly and said sternly. "I'm interviewing my client, Colonel."

"Not any more. You're dismissed."

"With all due respect, sir, this is client counselor privileged information. I respectfully request you allow me to continue."

"Out, Lieutenant. Now."

"Sir, my client has rights. He has—"

The colonel now ignored Karen entirely and returned Sam's salute. "Ciampiano. You come with me."

"Sir," Karen complained. "Are you assuming Sam's... Sgt. Ciampiano's defense?"

"That won't be necessary. All charges against the Sergeant are waived. He has been remanded to my custody."

Karen was stunned, but quick and defensive. "Colonel, if all charges have been dropped, why is he in anyone's custody?"

Now the colonel moved close to Karen. He spoke softly, but with great confidence. "Lt. Auburn. You will soon be debriefed. You should never have seen this," he said as he slipped the single page report from the table and crumpled it into a tight ball in front of her. "I understand that you took the next case that came in, but Sgt. Ciampiano will be coming with me and there is no case."

Karen thought for only a moment. "There's a drill sergeant in the medical ward with an arm nearly ripped off—"

"Lucky to be alive, I'd say. Ciampiano? Let's go."

"Yes, sir," Sam said as he moved in crisp military fashion toward the door.

Karen followed them out into the hall. "Colonel, I'm entitled to an explanation."

The colonel spun on his heels, his patience with the novice officer expired. "You, Lieutenant, are entitled to nothing, but I will tell you this. If you had been awake in your interviewing classes, you would have known that 'Blackbird' means something besides a fucking crow!"

Karen stopped in her tracks unable to catch her breath for a retort. She knew what 'Blackbird' was and the exemption it meant for ghost soldiers like Sam. The colonel stomped out the two sets of doors with Sam close behind, but between the two doors, Sam glanced over his shoulder at Karen. It was only a flash, but she saw something in his eyes that she had begun to see and hear across the table. It was a hint to a very private search and once witnessed, Karen was quite certain she could not ignore, regardless of a simple debriefing for her and the MPs that basically said, "Forget everything you may know or think you know."

For Sam's part, he had tipped his hand with the entire affair. His officers were beguiled and leery of a soldier who demonstrated poor command of himself and Sam agreed. He thought of his father and the closeness he pined for and mentioned his death as an explanation, not an excuse, for his lapse.

Soldiers and Rangers who were themselves limited to only pieces of the puzzle that was Sam's life, quickly began to connect dots. You couldn't say 'Blackbird' without inviting a crowd though the intent was just the opposite. 'Blackbird,' a simple word meant to open closed doors and protect men when their weapons could not, had been his undoing. Sam was asked to resign. He knew too much and his apparent lack of control could threaten himself, others, and operations. He signed the papers without question. All he said was, "I'm sorry." Within a week of the chance encounter at the commissary door, Sam was out of the Rangers, out of his 'Army of One,' and back at his father's house where he slipped into his old room and a dead man's life, burdened by secrets and buried in loss.

So Sam worked the newsstand where he had started. He wrestled himself out of bed to the ghostly echoes of his father's voice at ungodly hours and set the papers out by himself and missed his dad. When he dropped the large wooden flap at the end of the day, Sam put his hands in his pockets and wandered home where he sat among his father's things, his own old football trophies, and his increasing sadness. His father was dead. His military family was gone. He was alone.

In the beginning he just went through the motions. Later, after the shock of it eased, he fashioned a resume for job interviews as best he could, but it lacked any substance. He had a high school diploma and eight years undistinguished military service, which showed him as a simple infantry sergeant, with not a single skill transferable to life in this lighted part of the real world. There wasn't a big call in the classifieds for assassins though he did allow a slight smile as he considered a new definition of the term 'head hunter' and his potential jobs. Despite the brief smile, Sam came to realize that for all his specialized training and years of service, he had no skills to list on a resume that could land him a civilian job.

There was The Columbia, but he knew his father did not want that life for him so he stayed away. He thought about applying with the Tampa Police Department – maybe they could use a sniper who took his warm-up shots at four hundred yards – but after the commissary incident he began to second guess himself and his ability to gauge threats. Someone would get hurt bad, far worse than a shattered arm, so he never applied. Nearly ten years of discipline and extreme military training had left him with the skill set to be a greeter at Wal-Mart and even that would probably get some shoplifter's neck snapped. So he rolled out of bed seven days a week and sold the papers he still thought of as his father's.

5

On another Tampa street, three floors above the traffic, not quite high enough to block out the noise of the city, Jack Aaron, the county's District Attorney, was figuratively scratching his head along with others in an anteroom to his office. Jack's hair was gray throughout and messy as though it had been combed neatly at the start of the day then lost its will to stay in place as the day's troubles tugged at it. He had walked into his office, as he did each morning, as crisply coiffed as a candidate, but he morphed quickly into a coatless, loose tie, disheveled prosecutor. Though he was a candidate with the cycle of elections, he did not campaign – much to the chagrin of the political machine. Years ago he had been the epitome of elect-ability – handsome with a hint of gray at the temples that oozed maturity and reason. Now, the dark hair was gone and he carried a few extra pounds. His face was no longer as handsome having given in to the ravages of gravity and too much Florida sun. In exchange for the years, Jack had accepted an acuity for solving crime that rivaled any detective sworn in by the City of Tampa, the State of Florida, or a CSI television show. His considerable talents outpaced his current job title and transported him to the days prior to taking the Florida Bar Exam when he had been a criminal investigator for the State Troopers and the Florida Department of Law Enforcement. It had been so long ago, the FDLE hadn't even been pulled into existence from a half dozen other State agencies. With the passing of the Bar, Jack retired from the Troopers and took a post with the District Attorney's Office as a prosecutor. It suited him, but he never stopped carrying a small revolver tucked neatly in the back of his waistband. A District Attorney was a cop and according to Jack Aaron, cops carried guns.

Through the intervening years Jack had forsaken the altar and a family for interminable hours at his desk and on the streets building cases. Convictions as much as attrition positioned him as Chief Assistant and insured an eventual run for the office he had yet to leave. Though direct and coarse at times, he was never humorless. And there were no backward glances at the bottom line of political ramification. His reputation, effort, and results easily marginalized any political threat and at sixty-three years young, with over twenty eight years in the District Attorney's office, he felt he was just hitting his stride as Tampa's top cop.

Less than a week ago the indictments on his desk against a county commissioner had been opened. A week was a lifetime in the world of headline news, but what had unfolded in the last few days was a headline in and of itself, all but dwarfing the initial story.

"This a joke?" Jack asked as he tossed the papers in his hand to the conference table with such a flick of his wrist that they spun down like falling leaves in a brisk wind.

"It's no joke. Not that we can find anyway," Marcus Pete said as he unconsciously shrugged his shoulders.

"Petey. Listen to me closely," Jack said in a tone that was too accusing. "You are my primary investigator—"

"I know what I am, Jack."

"I expect you to bring absolutes to bear on this case. Not some kind of... of dreamy eyed speculation. No one does this. These people aren't stupid."

Marcus Pete, called Petey by no one other than Jack, looked away. It wasn't disrespect. It was his part of the cat and mouse he'd come to expect with his boss. Jack would rave – Marcus would provide the ballast. He was twenty-five years younger than Jack; northern black to Jack's southern white; Ivy League educated to Jack's hard scrabble rural red dirt roads. Eventually they would settle on the merits of a case, a topic, a movie, or even a cartoon and move along and away – still the most successful prosecution team in the State of Florida and still the best of odd fellow friends.

"Appears they are," Helfer Oakes said, uncharacteristically outspoken in the presence of the County's ranking prosecutor.

"Horseshit," was Jack's response. "I walk into court with this," he bullied as he flicked his hand again toward the papers Helfer was collecting. "I'll be laughed out on my ass."

Helfer focused on the papers.

"Not every crook is as clever as Batman's adversaries," Marcus followed.

"Batman... Jesus, and you're my top investigator?"

Jack looked with eyes that pretended to plead at Helfer, barely twenty-four, painfully thin, small, and vastly over qualified, but under courageous, for a job managing technology forensics in a busy District Attorney's Office.

"My top investigator gives me comic book stories," Jack begged. "Holy shit...," he continued as he reached for the papers Helfer had collected into a neat stack. Oakes dutifully handed them over and Jack began looking through them once more as he paced through the silence.

Marcus watched him for only a moment then let his eyes and mind drift to the wide sheets of immoveable glass that made up the windows behind his boss. He studied the glass and realized for the first time that they were bluish. It was hard to see without a comparison, but they were indeed tinted blue. It was an odd thing, he thought to himself. Blue windows. He'd have to remember to look at them from the outside and see if they looked blue from there.

Until the windows, he hadn't found things to be much different here in the South than they were up North. The weather was the lone exception. The people, regrettably, were not. They committed crimes with equal enthusiasm in the heat and the cold. Someone had told him when he moved from a smaller District Attorney's staff in upstate New York to Tampa's busy office that "heat breeds disease," in reference to the increase in crime he'd face, but it wasn't true. It seemed that people were people – unaffected by climate – and were the same everywhere. It was a realization that he knew before he moved, but its confirmation was still disappointing. Marcus hoped that paradise by the warm sunny blue waves of the Gulf of Mexico would be just that. It wasn't.

"Petey?" It was Jack. "Try to stay with me here. Has all this been validated?" he said, referring to the oft-tossed papers, for now still in his hands.

"I'll defer to Helfer on that. He's the computer whiz."

"But have you gone over these with him?"

"I have."

"What do you think?"

Marcus hesitated only long enough to look at the table and offer another involuntary shrug. "Hard to believe, I know. But there it is. I say we go with it. It is what it is."

"If it looks like a pig and acts like a pig and, in this case, smells like a pig, then it's a pig," Jack mumbled.

"It's a pig," Marcus echoed.

"You know why I can't believe it at least, right?"

"Hard for me too."

"Then you won't mind checking everything again. Give me everything. Exact. Right down to the time of each transaction – amounts, dates, everything."

"That's what you have now," Helfer spoke up again and pointed to the papers. "It's all–"

Jack shot the young man a harsh look and cut him off with the filtering of the papers spinning down to the desk again. "Check everything again, Petey. It's too good to be true." He left the door open as he walked out.

Helfer sat back and looked out one of the bluish windows. Marcus reflected the younger man's expression, but leaned forward and began sliding the papers back together.

"Take it easy, Oakes. You take everything to heart in this business and you'll give yourself a stroke."

"But it's all been done. It's right there for him," the young man's hands turned up in frustration.

"Yep," and the collection of the papers continued.

"So?"

"So, what?" Marcus finished and stood up slowly.

"So why doesn't he just go with it?"

"Spooked. Me too, for that matter. Like he said, too easy. He doesn't want to jeopardize a good case with what appears to an electronic confession. It's like he said. It's too good to be true. You know the adage – if it's too good to be true, it probably is."

"I liked the pig analogy better. And what you're holding right there is a pig. A big one."

"Ready for slaughter, is it?"

"Ready for slaughter," Helfer confidently sent back.

"But we don't sign the checks," Marcus countered. "Jack wants a second look, he gets a second look. Who knows, we might find something else."

The pair had the sorely tossed papers safely in gentler hands as they surveyed the room to make sure none had skirted to the floor. When Marcus came up from beneath the table he was face to face with the window.

"Hey, Helfer? Does that window look sort of blue to you?"

There was no thought necessary. "Of course. They're the best."

"Best what? Window?"

"In a way. They're the best at keeping heat out. Huge hit down here. You probably didn't have much of an issue with heat in New York."

"Blue, huh?"

"It has to do with a reflection principal, the refractive rays, and the color spectrum. Heat out. Cool in."

"They work?" Marcus said as he slowly walked to the glass and timidly felt it as if he were touching any glass for the first time.

"Best they make, so I'm told. You want me to pull an analysis on it? Temperature transference, energy consumption, cost comparisons? What are you looking for?"

"Nothing. Mostly I'm interested in whether the windows in my office are blue. Just curiosity."

Marcus tapped the papers again on the table until the edges were neat and trim then slid the pile across the table to Helfer. "Nice work on this, Mr. Oakes. Nice work."

"Even if Jack wants it done again?"

"He's just nervous. I'll hold his hand through your papers tomorrow and by five o'clock, he'll be ready to give you a kiss."

"I'd settle for a raise, but I still don't get why he doesn't believe the data."

"Old fashioned. Let me take you to lunch. I'll introduce you to a friend of mine. He can help explain. Mr. Rob Roy."

"Who's that?"

"Jack introduced me to him."

"Is he a County or State guy?" Helfer asked.

"No, not officially. He provides... support. He just provides support I'd say."

"Unpaid?"

"Oh, no. It'll cost and in fact the first round is on you. Follow along. We'll review this case and all its oddities and see if it looks quite so odd by five o'clock. My guess is that we'll be feeling ready to charge the jury by then."

The pair cleared the doors to the street and hit the bright sun head on. Helfer's sunglasses were already on.

"I haven't gotten use to carrying those things," Marcus motioned. "I never had much need of them before I came here. We used to say we had three months of winter and nine of bad sledding. I'll never go back."

"That miserable?"

"It was for me. No one ever mentioned to my senior class that you could actually move away and make a life somewhere else." He paused, though not with great purpose. "You remember anything from your high school or college commencement addresses?"

"Not a word."

"Who gave them?"

"No idea."

"Can you stand one last question before I introduce you to my friend?"

"Sure."

"Just to help me satisfy Jack, why would that commissioner and his developer friend leave such an easy trail, I mean, with the permits and all those waivers?"

"I could guess my commencement speakers easier."

"I lied. One more question. Instead of transferring their money to their wives or kids or one of those James Bond type Swiss bank accounts, or even stuffing it under their mattresses, they blow thousands of dollars on the most worthless stock in the world? Why?"

"Guilty conscience is the best I've got. They must have known we would freeze their assets."

"Why not move it out of the country?"

"It's not as easy as you think. It takes time to set up an offshore account."

"An act of contrition? Why not donate it to a church or charity?"

"Too slow. I mean, anybody can buy stock with a click of a mouse."

"Can't you donate it to St. Anne of the Redeemer or the Red Cross as easy?"

Helfer answered with a question of his own. "Well, I'd have to say no. And here's why. You want me to buy some stock for you?"

"Maybe. Have you got a good tip?"

"No, but within the context of our conversation, if you wanted me to buy a stock for you, I'd know exactly where to go and how to do it. If you wanted me to donate money to some church, I'd have to do some leg work. Same for you, right?"

Marcus shook his head. "Right you are. Poor commentary on our world that we know how to buy stock easier than we know how to donate money to the church on the corner."

"If it was a simple twenty bucks on your credit card, that's something pretty easy, but tens of thousands? Makes it tougher. The stock was the easiest way."

"But why a stock that was already tanked and just waiting to hit bottom?"

"Beats me."

"Me too. Let's ask Rob Roy," Marcus laughed a little as they passed Sam's newsstand. The *Tampa Tribune's* headline reached out behind the men as they passed.

'COMMISS CUTS FINANCIAL THROAT AS NOOSE TIGHTENS.'

Sam sat in the soft shadow of the stand and read the story beneath the headline and wondered to himself what Marcus and Helfer wondered aloud.

At the same time, Clayton's phone was ringing. It was Raphael.

"Hey, Ralph. What's up?"

"I dunno. You tell me. I think, or maybe I don't want to know."

"What'd you do, drink your lunch?"

"No."

"Start makin' sense, lad," Clayton said, almost giddy, in his fake Irish. "Or off with ya."

"Holy shit. I'm right. You are way too happy. I knew it. I knew it! As soon as I saw the paper, I said, 'That crazy sonofa–'"

"Hey," Clayton said, all the levity gone from his voice. "I gotta go."

"I'm stopping by later. What time are you letting yourself off work?"

"Late."

"What time is that?"

"Past your bedtime."

"Not tonight it's not. No school tomorrow. I'll be over around eight. I want to talk to you, man."

"About what?"

"I thought you had to go?"

"I do, but I'd like to be prepared for your visit."

"Read the papers. I'll see you at eight."

Raphael hung up and Clayton set the phone aside on his desk. Beneath the phone was the same headline that had by then forced a sellout at Sam's newsstand.

The rest of the day passed as any other for Clayton, but he found himself glancing at the headline far too often and wondering ahead to the upcoming meeting with Raphael. They had been friends since they were boys. Following college and graduate school they met again at a hiring seminar put on by the financial firm Raphael continued to work for. The company hired Clayton as well and the two worked together in the early years, though their specialties varied. Clayton eventually kick started his dream in a spare bedroom and rode his prodigious talent to the top of his field while Raphael stayed in the financial business and prospered alongside the market bulls and bears. The two stayed in close touch. They often shared drinks and dinner, cruised the clubs as a team, went to the beach with past and present girlfriends, toured the local off beat theaters, and watched old movies they had seen dozens of times. They often ventured into philosophical discussions on a wide range of topics. Injustices mostly. Corruption in political circles. Unjust wars. Poverty. What-ifs. And how far you would go to right a wrong.

Clayton knew already what Raphael would ask. "Did you do it?" he'd say, only half wanting to know the answer and Clayton would stand there; "Do what?" only half wanting to tell him.

Telling him would involve him, but he was too smart. He'd know in an instant. As soon as he saw him. That was alright. Clayton wanted to involve him, or better put, he wanted Raphael to want to be involved. And Clayton was sure he'd want to be. Especially when he told him who the next target would be.

A gentle motion alarm sounded that someone was nearing the front door – the only door – of Clayton's home. There was a quick knock on his door then someone tried the knob, but found the door locked. The doorbell was ignored, but the motion sensors lit up a twelve inch monitor alongside the door and showed the stoop and the opposite side of the heavy door.

Clayton glanced at the clock and saw it was too early for Raphael. He was always prompt. Like Clayton himself, working with numbers and programs of numbers, sheets upon sheets of data and code, had conspired to make them both addicted to numbers and hence, time. Perhaps they were struck with this affinity well before and this led them to their careers. The chicken or the egg. This is the type of thing they found themselves talking on and on about. What leads a person, or where a person leads, and why? Does the situation cause the action? Or is it the person? Would an honest man steal if the opportunity presented itself? What if everyone was stealing? If it, whatever it is, becomes the norm, then does it, if by mere weight of numbers if nothing else, become the unwritten law of the land? Sort of a common law wife ruling applied to thievery or any of a thousand scenarios they had crunched like a quality check of coding, looking for breaks, errors, trends, and output. The hands of the clock would whiz around when these discussions raged. Another unasked for, but accepted beer slipped in the dialogue unnoticed. And they would talk on and on about the chicken and the egg and the reason a man did as he did. This and much more and sometimes, much worse.

But the time wasn't right for his friend and the knock was not his. The knock and the hand behind it belonged to Clayton's brother. Carl Rand had rattled the solid knob as he usually did, trying to let himself in, but the door was always locked with vault-like pins that embraced the steel frame on all four sides. Clayton triggered the electronic mechanism and the pins retracted.

Carl opened the weighty but balanced door and walked straight in as soon as he heard the deadbolts slide back under his younger brother's hand. He brought a blast of humid summer in with him.

"What's the matter?" Carl said as he looked at the locks then to his brother as he passed. "You been chattin' up little boys on your computer again and got the cops after your ass?"

"Funny. How you doing, big brother?"

Carl moved to the living room and flopped down in a rather elegant dark maroon leather wing-backed chair and threw his head back. It was only there a fraction of a second before Carl lifted it and looked left and right for something then raised both hands, palms up, in surrender.

"What?" Clayton asked, frozen for a moment between the closing door and the chair by his brother's actions.

"Where's the remote?"

"Side pocket of the chair."

"Side pocket. Side pocket," Carl said as he looked left and right. "I didn't know chairs had pockets." Carl fumbled until he found the remote, but continued his searching, this time for the power button. "I can never remember which one turns the damn thing on. This thing's got too many buttons for me, Clay. I love the TV, but damn, kid. This thing looks like the cockpit of a airplane or something."

No matter what button he pushed the television didn't come on. He compensated by pushing the buttons a little harder and jerking the remote faster toward the screen as he pushed.

"Here. Hand it over before you screw it up. Look. This one turns on the audio. This activates—"

"Put it on ESPN, will you? I never remember anyway. Oh, wait. Put on that outdoor channel. Let's see if they're hunting or fishing. If they're fishing we'll go to ESPN, unless it's basketball."

"Here," Clayton said as he handed the remote back as the television came to life behind him. "This one takes you up the channels and this one goes down. You want a drink?"

"Why do you even ask?"

Two fizzes came from the granite and stainless kitchen and announced Clayton's return to the living room. He tapped Carl's shoulder with the frosted bottle to draw him away from the television.

"Sweet," said Carl as he took the beer then held it up to his little brother. "Cheers."

There was a soft clink of the glass and the two drank together as they had done since the bottles had been soda or chocolate milk twenty years earlier.

The beer and the company of blood was good. Carl had been born with a setback and had encountered others that conspired to take a toll. Somewhere along the way roles had gotten reversed. Back in the days of chocolate milk, Carl protected Clayton from bullies and gave him weak advice on everything from girls to what high school teachers to avoid. When Carl dropped out and opted for the paycheck of the docks, he'd give Clay a little money on payday for beer or to sponsor a date. It made Carl feel solid and responsible to slip his baby brother a few bucks. Then Clayton went to college. Carl sent pizza money from time to time, but fell off into the routine of a job and found great comfort in the predictable and simple expectation of labor and the biting but friendly banter of men at work. For reasons Clayton could surmise, but never confront, Carl did not go back to school, even for his GED. Somewhere in the middle of old heated discussions, and some not so long ago, Clayton came to understand that the carrot was firmly embedded on Carl's stick and it held him even when the carrot was often not big enough to pay all the bills. Rising interest rates and falling housing prices had caught up with the adjustable mortgage Clayton had advised against. At the time, Carl had glowed over the house he could never afford. Then his mortgage changed with the fluctuating market.

Today, in the company of the big TV and the cold beer, was like others when the carrot had again proved insufficient. Clayton knew it almost immediately when he heard the familiar knock on the door. Carl was a little short. "Just 'till payday." Clayton saved his brother the embarrassment and jumped ahead of him as soon as he could, knowing that "Just 'till payday," was largely symbolic. He knew Carl appreciated his generosity, but neither could hide the fact that Clayton was now the one who stopped the bullies.

"What's up?" Clayton asked as he looked absently at his television.

"Not much," Carl said with even less enthusiasm. "Same old, same old. How's things on your side of the tracks?"

"More of the same."

"What you got going tonight? Computer nerd stuff?"

"More or less. Raphael's coming over later."

"Shop talk?"

"Shop talk."

"Politics and all that shit."

"Maybe a little."

"Bunch of thieves. Every one of those political bastards," Carl said as a long hard pull on the bottle punctuated the proclamation.

"No argument there."

Carl looked at his beer bottle and picked at the label, talking to it as much as his brother. "Think this is okay?"

"Is what okay?"

"This," Carl said as he raised the bottle exactly as he had done to cheer.

"A beer? Hell yes."

"Dad had all that trouble, you know."

"You're not Dad."

"Don't I know it. Not even close."

"Don't be silly, Carl. Dad had a disease. He couldn't stop and it killed him."

"You never worry?"

"Never."

"I was wondering if it was, you know, generic, like inherited in your blood."

Clay smiled a little at his brother's word choice, but wouldn't correct him to 'genetic.' Brothers understood each other anyway. "Do you drink every day?"

"If I got it."

"Falling down?"

"No."

"Black outs?"

"No."

"Then relax. If it makes you feel better, I'll keep an eye on you. If you start to drink too much of my beer, I'll shut your ass off. That feel better?"

"Hell no," Carl laughed and Clayton with him.

They raised their bottles again. "To sobriety," Clayton said.

Carl smiled. "In other people."

"In other people."

"Hey, Clay," Carl started up, much more animated. "What'd did Dad used to call every bar in town? I think he stole it from an old John Wayne movie. John Wayne was a boxer in Ireland or something. I remember Dad going on about politics and saying it with a bullshit Mick accent. Whenever someone starts talking about Republicans and Democrats and all the rest of those liars, I think about it."

"Dad had lots of old lines from movies, but I think you mean *The Quiet Man* with Maureen O'Hara."

"Was that Irish?"

"Set in Ireland, yes."

"That's the one then. In the movie, them little Irish guys are yakking on about something political and they talk about a pub or a bar."

Clayton smiled broadly and threw the old Irish baroque into his voice. "I t'ink I'll be goin' down to the *Fist o' T'orns* and ta'k a little treason."

Carl clapped his hands together in a great smack. "Ha! *Fist of Thorns*. He called every bar the *Fist of Thorns*. Damn, that's a helluva movie."

"No, that is a 'film,' a 'motion picture.' A classic. Show respect. What they make today are 'movies.'"

"Right. Right. Helluva film. How's that?"

"Better. And you pegged Dad on *Fist o' Thorns*." Clayton laughed at the memory. "That was so Mom wouldn't know which bar to go to trying to find him."

"Yep. That's right. Our old man was a good guy, Clay."

"He was."

"To Dad." And they raised their bottles.

"And the many *Fist o' Thorns*."

There was the slightest break in the dialogue. "Hey, Clay, I was wondering—"

Clayton set his beer aside in a rush. "One sec." He stood up and walked into the adjoining room. Clayton opened the center drawer of his dark mahogany desk before Carl could finish. Instead, Carl stood up as well and followed his brother, but much slower and at a comfortable distance. He didn't want to intervene nor did he want to see what was happening.

The check was being torn from a large leather ledger. Clayton walked to his brother, folded the check in half and in half again so it felt like a smaller handout than it was, and put it in Carl's hand before it could move up from his side.

"Thanks, Clay. I'll hook up with you next week or so."

"Sure thing. C'mon," Clayton said as he walked back into the television room, distancing himself and Carl from the monthly ritual as quickly as possible. "My beer's getting warm. The other night I got doing some writing and forgot all about a brew I'd left in here. I went to bed and it was waiting for me the next morning."

"I've done that before – fall asleep next to half of one. I down 'em as soon as I wake up next morning."

"Warm?"

"Piss warm. Flat. I don't give a shit. I ain't throwing no beer out."

The brothers had returned to their places. Clayton held out his bottle in salute. "Good man." And the bottles clinked again.

They drank and watched as Carl surfed through the cooking shows, handyman shows, and animal shows. He stopped at an entertainment news program that followed the evening national broadcast news. The reporter was discussing a music mogul's arrest for DUI.

Clayton pointed at the widescreen with his bottle. "These shows follow our supposedly hard national news, but I can't tell when one ends and the other begins."

"Music's louder on this one," Carl quipped.

"And the anchor's show their legs," Clayton added.

The brothers laughed. Carl was leaning forward. "And their racks. Never see Katie Couric toss hers around like that bitch right there, do you? Not that she's got a pair like that."

"No she doesn't, but I just as soon she didn't if she'd stop lobbing softballs at us. The other night I had one of the networks on and they spent two and a half minutes telling us about some damn cat that got caught and eventually rescued after the fire department and the police sent in video cameras and rescue squads. Meanwhile, in the time it took to tell that dumb ass story, ten more people got butchered in Darfur and another soldier got blown up in Iraq. I don't understand the reasoning. Who picks the stories that air, anyway? Stupid bastards. Insulting."

Carl took a moment to formulate a response, taken aback by his brother's frustration. "Stop watching it if it pisses you off. I don't watch none of it. But I'll watch this show now and again to get the dirt on somebody, you know, behind the scenes shit."

This time it was Clayton's turn to hesitate a minute. "Alright. So, you watch this show and get the skinny on some movie star. How does that help anybody, including yourself?"

Carl leaned toward his little brother. "It's not supposed to help anybody, dumb ass. That's the point."

"What point?"

Carl hesitated yet again. "For someone who everybody says, got all the brains in the family, you're dumber than a post. You know that? The point, Mr. Harvard-assed graduate," Carl said as only a sibling could. "The point is that it's en-ter-tain-ment. That's why they call it that. It don't have no point. It's something to watch to be entertained. Something to make you forget, for a half hour anyways, that you gotta get up at four-thirty in the morning five days a week. Got it?"

"Escapism."

"Whatever."

They both looked back at the television as if it somehow held the answer. They watched for a moment as the screen flashed pictures of a gently wrecked SUV on the side of a road and the music entrepreneur's mug shot.

"See that asshole?" Carl said as it was his turn to point with his bottle. He didn't wait for an answer. "That sonofabitch has been arrested at least three, maybe four times for driving drunk. Always makes the news. Never goes to jail. Never. If I get stopped driving home right now, after this one beer? I'd do thirty days and lose my license. Not that sumbitch."

"Why is that?" Clayton asked, not even looking at his brother.

"Money, dumb ass. I swear, you have got to get out of here more. You're locked up in here like its Fort Knox. What are you scared of? 'Fraid somebody will steal your kick-ass TV?" Carl finished the last vestiges of his beer and climbed out of his chair. "You oughta have a recliner for when I come over."

"I'll get right on it."

"Mines got a handy-ass lever on the side. Comfortable as hell. Puts me to sleep every night."

"I'll see what I can do."

"I'm outa here, Clay. Thanks for the brewskie," Carl said as he wandered slowly into the kitchen where he slid open a cabinet and dropped his empty bottle in the waiting trash.

"No problem."

Clayton met his brother at the door. "Call me. Maybe we can go out to dinner."

"That'd work," Carl said as he reached for his brother and they hugged. "Love ya, even if you're not as smart as people say."

"Thanks. Love you too. See ya."

The door didn't close. Instead, Clayton stepped onto the threshold and watched Carl get into his truck and drive away, offering up a honk of the horn and a hearty wave as he did.

"Good guy," Clayton said to himself as he stepped back into the air conditioning. Other thoughts followed. He knew his brother very well. They had been the only children of one of the hardest working men either had ever known. He knew the strengths and the faults. He knew Carl's opinion of the world, though sometimes he baited his older brother just to hear it again. Carl was a touchstone for him – the pulse of the common man. And the common man was pissed.

Clayton finished his own beer and immediately pulled two short, thick glasses from a dark cherry cabinet with a glass front panel. He referred to them as hard drinking glasses, something Carl never enjoyed, but he knew Raphael did, so he would set the table – drink wise – and have a stiff Tom Collins ready for his friend when he arrived. The gin was pulled from the freezer and poured without measuring. Clayton gave up on jiggers long ago when it was just for himself and Ralph. Three quarters full over ice would be about three shots. Then enough mix for the soft gray color. Any more and it'd be too sweet. That was their standard fare. He could count off the shots if he wanted to be more accurate or pour four bottles at once, two necks clenched between the fingers of each hand, if he wanted to show off behind the bar at a party, but what was coming was no party. He was sure of that, but as with Carl, Clayton knew his friend and was moving ahead with a reasonable degree of certainty that Raphael would be falling in right behind.

He stirred the drinks too quickly and the ice pushed small amounts of mix and gin over the rims. When he set the thin spoon aside, it too carried away a few drops and deposited them on the black granite. Clayton smiled in his mind as he thought of his brother while he wiped up his mess. Carl would be wringing the sponge out over his mouth, but then again, Carl didn't like gin. Maybe he'd let this much alcohol escape him just this once.

On cue, the sensor whispered from the door and the monitor came to life followed by the ringing of the doorbell. Clayton didn't hesitate, even though he hadn't completely laid out the plan that would lay his deed bare before his friend. He carried the drink with him to the door and opened it to find Raphael leaning against the jam.

Neither said a word. Raphael looked at the glass Clayton held up to him and then moved his gaze up to his friend's eyes. Continuing without a word, he took the glass and tested its mix.

"Mmmmm," he grimaced. "You must have a lot on your mind to have to ply me with jet fuel."

"I figured you can handle it."

"This," he said as he gestured with the glass. "Or what you're going to tell me?"

"Both." Clayton stepped out of the doorway and moved to the kitchen to retrieve his own high octane cocktail.

Raphael came inside and for the first time in his life, insured the door of his friend's house locked behind him.

6

Eight hundred miles away, Karen was going to be working late. There were many nights like this – never enough hours to do all that needed doing. Cases came in as a constant flow of falling water, but unlike a natural stream this current of criminal cases and the associated paperwork was unaffected by climate or season. There was never a drought, only runoff from more melting snow and sheets of rain like the proverbial cats and dogs. Those sheets coming at her were paper and gained weight as they settled into her hands and mind day after day until the pressure forced her shoulders to literally bend beneath the load. Her body whispered to her in a voice that was increasingly growing louder. It told her she was due for a break. A vacation. Time in the sun with gentle rolling waves of warm salt water that would miraculously cure her, lift the load, and wash the tension out of her neck. The thought had been gaining a foothold for some time and the last several days had cemented the deal. Tonight, between prepping briefs for court, she would walk out to the empty front desk, where everyone else had gone home hours ago, and find the simple vacation request form that would free her for a while. Before the form was complete, Karen knew where she would travel and why. Instantly she felt the burden lessen and three weeks later she felt the airliner's wheels shudder as they touched down on the runway of Tampa International.

It had been months since she'd been debriefed regarding Sgt. Sam Ciampiano. At the onset she continued to protest, if only to gain a better understanding of that glimpse of a heart she saw in the man who could snap another's arm with so much ease. Her defense as to how and why she had even spoken to Sam was simple and straight forward. The responding MP's report had been inadvertently put in the hanging incoming case file. Karen had merely picked up the front folder and began her investigation and initial interview.

No one mentioned the word 'Blackbird' at the debrief and the single page report had vanished. The debriefing colonel had said, "Things like that aren't put in writing, put in email, or even put in the shredder. They never happen. They don't exist." When the smoke cleared, Karen had nothing to show for it except that short but impacting meeting with Sam. However, the colonel had told her explicitly, "Not a word. Not even a thought. No follow-up and, God help you, no paperwork. Do we have an understanding?" Karen had looked him straight in the eye and said yes.

Thirty minutes later she was trying to find out all she could about Sam. The computer record held nothing to suggest an association with special operations, black ops and, as would follow, playing the ace, Blackbird, but she didn't expect there to be. The colonel had seen to that. Even what did come up was unremarkable except in its uniformity with a hundred and fifty thousand other members of the armed services. Date of enlistment. Basic training. Assignment to a nondescript infantry unit stateside. No overseas deployment. With all the bases in Europe and the Far East, forget about the many seen and unseen wars, Sam had stayed on American soil. He hadn't even gone to the Middle East when nearly every cook, mechanic, and truck driver had served at least one tour, most two or three. Sgt. Sam Ciampiano had led the quietest, most uneventful term of enlistment as any soldier Karen had ever seen. He had signed on, got basic training, and then apparently cleaned his rifle at a lost barracks in Kansas for the last six years. Then somehow he pulled a Wizard of Oz trick from Kansas to the commissary door and met the drill sergeant. From an enlistment that was all but invisible, to Andrews Air Force Base just outside of the Nation's Capital – all in a few non-descript pages. And then there was Blackbird.

Karen looked at the nearly blank computer screen and tapped her fingers on her desk. "What were you doing in Kansas, Sgt. Sam Ciampiano? Protecting an empty missile silo? And if this says you're there, how is it you're here?"

Intrigued, Karen searched – first one way then another. Now backward. Now forward. But there was no more information on Sam than there had been after the first attempt. An hour or so later she was compelled to temporarily shelve the process and attend to the real files in the incoming hanging folder, but Sam never ventured far from her mind.

A couple of days later, she had another thought and started searching the subset of Army Rangers and on to other special forces. These groups would be predisposed to code words like Blackbird. Still no Sam, even though she was certain she had seen something in the initial one page report from the investigating MPs about the Rangers. Ready to give up and return to the tangible work on her desk again, she brought Sam's original computer file up.

Date of enlistment. Basic training. Assignment to post.

"What the...?" she scarcely heard herself say.

Date of Discharge.

Sgt. Sam Ciampiano was no longer a soldier. He had received an honorable discharge. His commitment complete, Sgt. Ciampiano was now Civilian Ciampiano. Sam wasn't in Kansas any longer.

Karen electronically scrambled back to his enlistment and opened rudimentary forms. At the bottom, above the waiver saying the United States Government would not be held accountable for any misfortune that might befall the incoming soldier, was a small set of boxes to list next of kin. In the box was Sam Ciampiano Sr. of 2998 E. 8th Avenue, Tampa, Florida.

Karen wrote down the address, then looked up with a bit of wonder and surprise at what she'd done. She closed the computer file on the innocuous and bland soldier then tore the address from her yellow legal pad, folded it neatly and put it in her pocket.

Now, in a Tampa hotel room near the airport, Karen unfolded the yellow scrap of paper and read the address for the hundredth time. She pushed aside the room service menu and the plastic coated card that showed a patron how to operate the television and order movies, then laid the solitary paper on the corner of the desk. Two hands worked in unison and caressed the piece flat. Her eyes read the address in increasingly smaller script as she backed away from it and literally wrung her hands, rubbed her face, and ran her fingers roughly through her dark hair as she anxiously wondered – for the same number of times she'd read the address – if she should follow through with what she was about to do.

Karen went to bed that night not certain what her answer to herself would be – at least that's what her mind said to her – but she slept as soundly as a child. It seems that beneath the cacophony stimulated by the address, her subconscious had long ago made a decision. In the morning, Karen dressed and headed out, yellow scrap in hand, to find the Sergeant who had crossed her path for a few minutes, but in doing so, had captivated her mind and strangely, possibly her heart with a hundred words and a woeful glance.

The GPS in the rental car had been perfect. In an instant it seemed, she was standing at the address on the now crumpled and sweaty piece of yellow paper in her hand. The house was small, just a single story, but neat. A wide covered porch adorned the entire front of the modest home and was itself home to a pair of plain wooden rocking chairs, the white paint of which had been crushed by years of shielded weather and was faded and peeling. It struck Karen as peculiar that there was no railing, just the open deck of the porch, but as soon as the feeling appeared strange, the recognition of how open and inviting the house was overwhelmed it. There was no barrier to the street or any neighbors and guests that might happen by. The nearby houses were in the same low slung, unique style, each with a similar covered porch. The colors varied widely from the sedate – soft taupe, muted greens and white – to rather garish reds, bright blues, and even orange. Almost every one of the exceedingly bright colored houses had an equally bright corresponding color as trim. The front door of many were framed by bright mosaics of tile in primary colors and intricate patterns. Twenty-nine ninety-eight was plain white. Beneath the porch, facing the street and Karen, was what appeared to be more of the unique tile, hidden beneath several layers of the same aged white paint to match the rocking chairs.

She hurriedly marched across the cracked concrete sidewalk and up the steps before her courage escaped or reason caught up. Now that the act was done, the nervousness peaked. She had given herself over to coming some time ago, but that often onerous discourse had consumed her to such a degree that what she was going to say had not been planned out. Karen suddenly realized that her presence would not mean to Sam what she hoped the sight of him would mean to her. Undoubtedly he would think he was under investigation or, worse yet, think he was being recalled to duty – being sent back to Kansas or wherever he was really from – only to be told, by her, that there would be no reenlistment. Merely the sight of her might be a bad memory and she knew he was certainly capable of violence. In a broken heartbeat she came to see this trip was not a good idea.

"You gonna knock on that door, or jus' stare at it?"

Karen jumped at the voice then recovered only slightly, her head swiveling as she looked around.

"Hey. Missy. Over here." The voice was coming from the house next door. More specifically, it was coming from a frail old man sitting on a rusty glider. Now he was waving a boney hand at her to help Karen locate him. "Over here. The place next door. Oh, come on. I ain't a ghost just yet."

Now Karen saw him and took a few quiet, tip-toe steps toward him and away from the door.

"I'm sorry to have troubled you. I guess Sam's not home. I'll try later."

"How do you know he ain't home? You ain't knocked yet."

She'd been caught. She looked back at the door as if it might vouch for her, but even that glance left her exposed.

"Nope. You didn't knock," the old man said again.

She caved. "You're right, of course. I realize I've come at the wrong time. I was supposed to be here later. Later than it is. Later. Later this afternoon."

"Who you lookin' for?"

"Sam," she said hesitantly, realizing she was still standing on the porch and that the door could open at any moment, hastened by the old man's interrogation.

"Senior or junior?"

Karen headed back near the door and retreated down the steps.

"Umm... Junior, but it doesn't matter. I'll come back."

"Figured it to be Junior. You about a hundred years too late to see Senior. You a friend a Sam's?"

Karen was on the sidewalk now and didn't want to yell, but answered. "Yes."

And the reply shot back like a gun. "Hell you are! If you was a friend a Sam's, you'd know damn well he weren't here this time a day. That boy's working. Been gone out the house five hours by now. He can't sell no papers on that porch at half past nine. Any damn fool knows that. And any friend of his knows it for damn sure!"

"Papers?" Karen asked, her confidence restored by the fact that Sam was acknowledged not to be home.

"See there!" the old man shouted as he started to come up from his seat. "Right there. Anybody with a lick a sense knows that no Ciampiano is home this time a morning because they's at the onlyest paper stand here abouts. Workin.' Workin' hard."

Now Karen was headed for her rental in earnest. She'd gleaned what she needed, if she decided to continue on, from the neighbor's tirade. "Thank you. Sorry to have troubled you. Have a pleasant day!"

The car door slammed and the engine quickly came to life as the old man continued with less enthusiasm and even less acknowledgement from Karen. She did look at him sincerely and offer a pleasant wave as she pulled off, hedging a bet, not certain if she might run into him on another day.

The non-descript white rental car, with Karen at its helm tenderly prowled the streets for a newsstand and passed anonymously beneath the Tampa City Office Building. Three floors above it, Jack Aaron was yelling down the hall from his office door.

"Petey! Petey! Where the hell's Pete?" he scolded a passing young intern, who scarcely knew her own name on this first day, let alone the whereabouts of the city's senior investigator. Before she had time to divulge her ignorance, Marcus's face emerged from a conference room into the busy hall.

"Jack. Right here. Two minutes."

"Make it one."

Both men simultaneously ducked back through their portals like rabbits down holes leaving the intern alone in the hall. Still dazed, she looked from one doorway to the other as if she had just witnessed a magician's trick. Before she could pull herself from the allure, Marcus reappeared and walked briskly by her as though she had intended to be standing mystified outside Jack's office.

"Has it been a minute yet?" Marcus asked with a smile.

She returned the smile and relaxed.

"When he says one minute," he continued, motioning to Jack's door, "He means now. It'll all make sense in a couple of weeks. Keep moving, but take it slow."

Marcus rapped his knuckles, backhanded, on the door then opened it without waiting for an answer. He was already closing it as Jack, not bothering to answer the knock, launched into his diatribe without looking up from behind and nearly beneath stacks of papers, manila folders, and this morning's newspapers.

"What in the Sam Hill is going on in this town, Petey? I'm... I'm befuddled by it. Befuddled. Befuddled's a word, right?"

"Befuddled is indeed a word."

"Then that's what I am. I am befuddled."

"Over what?"

"You read the papers?"

"Not this morning. Somebody kill somebody I haven't heard about yet?"

"I wish it was that simple. Here. Take a gander at page one."

Jack spun the paper thru the air to the edge of his desk like a dying maple seed that dreamed of being a helicopter. He snatched up another and began rifling its pages as Marcus picked up the first. Page one, columns one thru three, shouted the headline – 'MED-PHARM SCANDAL SNAFU?'

Without waiting for Marcus to read further, Jack, true to form, launched again. "You know Med-Pharm, right? Has offices not a stone's throw from where I'm sitting."

Marcus was reading and didn't answer, knowing as he did that his response was neither needed nor expected.

"It seems the company's tanked," Jack continued, himself not looking up from another flurry of rifling newspaper. "They stepped on their dick with some drug. Bastards knew it could give you a heart attack and kept right on pumping the crap out. Nobody gives a shit anymore. Cock suckers. You heard about it, right? Was all over the news last week. Could have been a few weeks maybe. Time goes so fast. I so bad would have liked to put the screws to those big shot corporate boys."

Marcus spoke absently and continued reading the article in his hands. "Still could."

"Why bother? I mean, we'll go through the motions, that is, if we have jurisdiction. But, I mean, really, if half of this is true, these greedy sonsabitches will have shot themselves in the head before we get to trial."

Marcus stopped reading and dropped both hands down in front of him, still holding the paper. "Is this correct?"

"Damned if I know. I've already made a few calls to the *Tribune*. I've got the editor rounding up the writer. I'm waiting on a call back."

"How would the papers have all this and we don't know about it?"

"I dunno. SEC and FTC shit isn't our party. Fed crime. The rest of your class probably studied on it in law school while you were nursing a hangover or banging a co-ed. My guess is the Security & Exchange Commission had to have wind of it. They're quoted in there somewhere. They were probably... It's in one of these articles. I saw it a minute ago," Jack said stiffly as he flipped the thin paper from hand to hand. "They were about ready to crawl up the CEO's ass and grab him by the nuts and then poof! This comes out this morning."

Marcus pulled the paper back up and sat in an armless chair in front of Jack's desk. He crossed his legs and began to read again. Jack read as well, stopping only long enough to call the local FBI office and leave a message for an agent he had often worked with. Jack and Marcus were remarkably quiet as they read.

The articles reiterated the drug recall that gutted the pharmacy giant, but went on to detail how the top executives and all the board members had mysteriously re-purchased millions of worthless shares of their own company's stock after a recent history of massive selloffs. Their combined losses were measured in billions.

After several minutes, Jack lay the papers aside and turned slowly in his chair until he was looking out the window. He rubbed his eyes as if it was the end of a long day, but it was only eight forty in the morning.

"Something funky is going on in this town, Petey."

Marcus lowered the paper. "Did you say, 'funky?' Tell me you didn't say 'funky.'"

"I did, and what of it, Mr. Harvard-ass-graduate? You couldn't get a real job so I felt sorry for your dumb ass and took you in. I've been paying for it ever since. Harvard. Horseshit. They'll let anybody in that shithole."

"Sure. Anybody with a sixteen hundred SAT. And for the record, I'm certain 'funky' was not in the vocab section."

"Don't half our politicians come outa that shitbox? What's that tell you?"

"Another day, boss. Back to Med-Pharm. Granted it's odd, that is, 'funky,' but it's not our game anyway. Apart from being interesting, I don't see any reason to come unglued."

Jack turned around. "Am I unglued? Tell me you didn't say 'unglued,'" he said facetiously.

"I did and you are. You are also an elected official. That makes you a politician. You better go easy on your Harvard kindred spirits."

"Horseshit."

"It's federal, Jack. You said so yourself. If the CEO of Med-Pharm does some insider trading, then gets cold feet, or gets wind that the FTC is watching, or... or finds God and wants to repent and give back all his ill-gotten goods, that's between him and the FTC, oh, and God, if indeed that's what happened." Marcus stood up, walked to the door and opened it. He stood holding the edge of the door for a moment. "We've got enough on our plate without trying to horn in on a case that's not ours. Interesting case to be sure, but not ours nonetheless. Call me later. I'll let you take me to lunch so I can watch you beg my forgiveness for the Harvard comments."

Marcus had gone into the hall then returned rather triumphantly to stick his head around the door casing and point to the disheveled papers that now littered Jack's desk. "Nice articles though. Thanks for the law lesson." Then he smiled broadly and retreated again.

Jack yelled at the empty doorway from his desk. "What stock did your corrupt commissioner and his developer crony buy?"

There was a thick pause in sound and motion. Jack eased back in his chair and rested his elbows on its arms. He clasped his hands in front of his face and slowly tapped his lips with his outstretched fore fingers. The tapping could have been the ticking of a clock. In only slightly more time than it took Jack to lean back, Marcus began to slink into the picture frame that was the doorway. He allowed himself to be captured there for the obligatory moment it took to form words in his mouth. But before they were spoken, Marcus knew the answer and, more profoundly, recognized the stall tactic he was employing while he began to piece together a puzzle his boss had already completed.

"Med-Pharm."

"Med-Pharm, Petey. Close the door."

Jack was right, of course. The articles splayed on his desk recounted the facts concerning the CEO of Med-Pharm, but the writer had not thought of or considered the correlation of Med-Pharm and the influence peddling crime that was in Jack's jurisdiction.

"Got your attention now?" Jack asked as he leaned forward on the newspapers.

"Maybe. What are you thinking?"

"Not sure," Jack announced as he leaned back again. "Just strikes me as…, as funky, that our commissioner blows his bribe and then some on a stock that is already dropping like a rock and his partner in crime pulls the same dumb stunt. Then Mr. Bigshot CEO of that very same company and fifteen or twenty members of his high command, who are under investigation for selling a ba-zillion shares just before it comes out that their dope is killing people, turns around, for no reason whatsoever, buys all the shares back, and then some, totally bankrupting themselves."

Now it was Jack's turn to play the stall technique. He wasn't certain where he and his conspiracy were going. Time and a fresh perspective should help. So he just threw the facts as he knew them on Marcus and waited for their digestion and the thoughts of his extremely capable second.

"The FTC and Med-Pharm is not our case," Marcus began slowly as he eased back into the armless chair.

"Agreed," Jack muttered through his tapping fingers as he leaned back further in his chair.

Marcus continued laboriously. "Both bought the same stock when, A – they're both in trouble, and B – the stock is bleeding to death before their very eyes. Quite a coincidence."

"Could be more than that."

"How so?"

"Don't know. That's why we're having this conversation," Jack motioned with a hand temporarily freed from the tapping. "Keep peeling the onion."

"Is there a relationship between the two?"

"Are you talking the two events or the two primaries?"

"Either, I suppose. If the men have had dealings with one another it may fall in our lap somehow. Is that what you're after? You want to prosecute the CEO? Never happen."

"You're probably right. But I think I want to prosecute someone else. Maybe." The word hung heavy by itself.

"Who?"

"Whoever made those assholes buy that worthless stock."

"Blackmail?"

"Has to be. I can't think of anything else. A partner, another bad guy, hell, could be someone in their family, their priest, I don't know, but somebody with enough of a stick over these characters that they coerced them into cutting their own throats."

Marcus laughed a stifled laugh and flashed a Cheshire cat grin at his boss. "Are you sure you want to prosecute this person? Based on your theory, they might be working for us."

Jack flashed the identical grin. "That's my maybe. Could be right. Call it the cop in me. I'm the inquisitive type. Be nice to know, wouldn't it? Let's flip over a few rocks and see if anything scurries out, know what I mean?"

"I do."

"I've already reached out to my guy in the local office for the feds. You know him. Denti?"

"Yes. Very capable. Professional."

"Capable? He's forgotten more about being a cop than I know, but don't tell him I said that. He once said I was coarse. Me? Coarse."

"No, he said you were an asshole."

"You heard that, huh?"

Marcus stood up, much slower this time and retraced his steps to the door. "Are you certain you want to review this with a federal agency? They might assume the case under a federal conspiracy umbrella."

"It's a thought. Good thought. You're right. That's why I don't fire you. I'll keep a few cards close to the vest. Where you want to start?"

Marcus shoved his hands into his pockets and spun slowly on his heel in the doorway. "I was thinking maybe I'd reach out to a guy I met over at Raymond-James Financial. Try and find out what I can about Med-Pharm."

"Sounds like a start."

"You?"

"Well, I think the County's District Attorney is going to pay a visit to our old commissioner buddy. Maybe spending some time in the crowbar hotel has refreshed his memory a bit. That's if he ain't hung himself with his bedsheet yet."

"You need to have a discussion with his council first, don't you think?"

"No shit, Sherlock. I give the law lessons around here, remember?"

"And it was a good one."

"I've known his attorney for forty years." Jack pounced up from his desk. "He'll see me."

"Sure, he'll see you, but will he talk to you?"

"I'll let you know," Jack said as he eased by Marcus through his own doorway. "Mind the store for a while, will you, Petey? I'll be at the jail. Let's swap stories at the end of the day."

"Got it, boss."

Jack was already down the hall when he stopped and took a couple of steps back toward Marcus, who was himself walking slowly, thinking, down the hall to his own office.

"Hey, Petey? Next time you take a class. You know, one of those in-service things on legal shit or whatever. You know, your job?"

"Yes?"

"Sit in the front row."

"You're an ass."

Jack was laughing as he whirled around and half danced up the hall. "Oh yeah, I'm an ass. Agent Denti calls me coarse, but you go straight to ass. Helluva a world we're living in, Harvard. Helluva world."

Marcus smiled to himself then smiled even broader at the picture of an old cliché Jack was as he disappeared around the corner. But age did nothing to diminish the appropriateness. Jack was Jack. He could be rough – he could be an ass – but in a very amenable fashion. Marcus had worked for Jack almost ten years and each agreed that they spent more time in one another's company than with their families, if they had any. Neither did, so the bond was even stronger, even if it was merely by default. There were noncompulsory limits that somehow erected themselves as if by their own accord – such as the shortfall of social events and the like. Apart from the frequent six o'clock work sessions, the discourse of which occurred over and around several frosted glasses of beer and a wide variety of sandwiches, the two men never did anything together that required thought or planning or sandals, shorts, and sand. As a matter of practice, Marcus had once considered that he had never seen Jack, not once in ten years, without a tie on. He'd seen it loosened daily and askew plenty, sometimes just prior to entering a courtroom, but Jack had never been without it. Curiously, Marcus had come to depend on the tie. Jack and the tie meant Marcus was at work – a place he was comfortable and in control. A place where he would be productive and contribute to the better good of his adoptive city and put the small town north behind him.

His own hyperbole was Marcus's reality and he wore it inwardly as a badge of valor. He would allow the doors Harvard had opened to hang like empty children's swings in summer breezes while he chose to labor in semi-anonymity at a mid-sized District Attorney's office in the Deep South. His aspirations were minimal and nearly blotted out entirely by the brilliant light that radiated from his desire to serve and speak for those who could not.

Some couldn't speak for themselves because they were dead, but the vast percentage were lesser victims of either a sole crime or of a system, a culture, and a nation he thought was losing its way and had left them without a voice of their own. So he stayed on with the DA's office and relished the work as well as the frosty glasses of camaraderie that came with a sandwich and a side of Jack with tie.

Once Marcus had retreated to the comfort of his office he sat quietly looking out the bank of windows that dominated the moderate high-rises of Tampa's skyline. There were several much taller buildings overshadowing him, most of which had names of major banks emblazoned in corporate colors across the facades of their pinnacles. But those buildings, like his, had architects that had understood the allure of the bay and the gulf beyond and had incorporated huge amounts of glass in their designs. The trade off, of course, was the heat that the glass, in conjunction with the ancient workings of the sun, produced in a measure that was nearly inconceivable. The amount of energy the buildings consumed in order to make them tolerable in summer was therefore enormous. Massive coolant systems hummed and whirled without ceasing on their rooftops and still struggled against the combined effects of the glass and the sun. The upside for Marcus and thousands of others who recognized it was that they could work without the harsh glare of fluorescent bulbs that subliminally beat down on their northern counterparts.

In the gentle ambient light, supplemented by the backlight of his computer, Marcus now flipped through his e-directory until he came across the name he was scrolling for. It was a name he'd forgotten, but it was attached to a name he remembered, Raymond-James Financial. That was a name impossible to forget, at least in this city. The name Raymond-James was plastered in glowing letters as big as the banks' logos which radiated down from the high rises in the clouds. Except it drew a million viewers each week of the season to the big and beautiful football stadium that was home to the Tampa Bay Buccaneers.

Massively successful, starting in the Reagan inspired 80's, Raymond-James had exploded in the financial market and its shotgun approach covered everything from small portfolio monitoring to international investments on the scale of small countries. Its own net worth rivaled its largest clients and manifested itself in the high tech stadium. It was a game – both on the field and in the boardroom – but it was a game everybody involved with was winning. The fortunes of the team would vacillate, like Raymond-James itself, but today they were both all in and both ahead on wins versus losses.

Right now Marcus was interested in contacting one of the players of the bigger game. They had met briefly at a financial seminar a few years before – one of those things where your financial future is diagnosed free of charge. "When do you want to retire?" and, "What lifestyle do you want after you retire?" were the questions he remembered.

The electronic cards flipped by until he came to Ray J Financial. Beneath it was an office number, a cell number, and a name. Marcus would be polite and go with the office first. If this were a violent crime, he'd be knocking at the office door. A homicide – he's rattling up the cell and kicking in the door in the middle of the night. But this was strictly white-collar stuff and to be sure, he wasn't convinced a crime had been committed in his jurisdiction at all so he'd let Mr. Raphael Bordaine continue through his day and interrupt him with only a few questions. From there, Marcus would follow his instinct and see where it led.

———————————

7

Though the mid-morning sun was bright and seemed to be reflecting from every available surface straight into her eyes, Karen felt like she was in a shadow. There was anonymity on the bright city streets that cloaked her as surely as any dark corner. She sat in her car, bathed by the hushed breeze and the clicking cycle of the car's motor in response to the demand of the air conditioner. She watched the newsstand living its quiet ebb and flow not realizing it was under surveillance. As she had repeated again and again, Karen re-accessed her position and thoughts. As quickly as the notion of a direct frontal assault came, it was supplanted by another that feigned a thinly veiled ruse or pure happenstance. Neither extreme was the right fit. Too tight. Too loose. Each was subject to the shortcoming of not being able to go back. Even as one hand turned the ignition off and pulled the keys, while the other popped open the door, the plan, if there was one, hadn't taken a solid form. "This was no military engagement," she reasoned, and suffered a weak smile. "Sometimes you just go." These last thoughts cleared her mind as the slamming of the door jolted her to the reality of where she was and what she was about to do.

True to its world famous reputation, the Florida sun was brilliant and warm. It was almost directly overhead and Karen caught herself noticing how little her own shadow followed her on the sidewalk. Her sunglasses swung from one hand, a gyrating prop to dispel nervous energy. The coastal breeze that spilled over the open water of Tampa Bay so easily, was baffled by the city's buildings and, here on the street, had been relegated to an every now and again wisp that left the city streets hot to the touch. The foot traffic was light at this hour, but the street was busy. Taxis took corners without turn signals and white rental cars, small and impeccably clean, stood out like sore thumbs and crept slowly, impeding the flow as their confused occupants looked awkwardly at street signs for hope. She could tell the difference between locals and tourists merely by their gait, whether walking or driving. The tourists ambled, purposely or otherwise, sometimes lost or nearly so, while the locals rushed along in practiced strides and turns that led to well-worn destinations. As if that weren't enough of an indicator, one could always resort to color and costume. The distinction between walkers and drivers this time was polar. The rental cars were barren of color while the sidewalk bound tourists were all ablaze in the brightest and loudest summer filled colors the catering clothing stores could muster. The tourists were pictured against the city's year round dwellers who drove big bright Corvettes, red Mercedes, and Escalades whose paint was so shiny they glowed regardless of their color, while the permanent residents on the sidewalk dressed in subdued business attire. It was an interesting convergence, Karen thought, and a wonderful distraction, but the mini-dissertation in her mind fell away as she noticed the newsstand coming closer.

The large flap of the gapping front door was propped up, acting as an unwritten sign that yawned, "Open for business." Looking into the deep shadows of the newsstand was like looking over the rail of a boat down into the depths of dark, still water. The closer you got, the more hints you saw of things in the deep. There were shapes with no movement, and void of color. But as the water grew clearer, or the denizens of the deep came nearer, shapes crystallized and moved in the shadows. As Karen drew up on the stand, a rather hulking shape slowly took form and eventually demonstrated signs of life. It was Sam of course and he was half perched on a tall barstool styled chair with a low backrest. One foot rested on the metal ring well beneath the seat – designed for such things – while the other hung limply to the ground where its heel served as a pivot point for the lazy swaying of Sam's foot. The stool itself seemed to flow and fit Sam as if it were an extension of his clothes. It was covered in worn black Naugahyde. Dirty yellowed stuffing peeked out from the seams that were covered with gray duct tape – itself nearly worn through. The steel frame was rusty from the encompassing salt air except for where Sam rested his feet. The chair was, Karen would soon discover, much like Sam himself. Parts were worn, ragged and poorly patched. Other pieces showed sparkles of polish from constant use, but these were few and each was beginning to rust with every five AM salty opening of the stand.

Karen saw Sam clearly now for only the second time in her life. His face was turned down, along with his spirit, toward what appeared to be a leather backed hard covered book which he held in one hand. Along the book's spine, Karen caught the glimmer of a golden page marker dangling as loosely as Sam's foot. Karen caught herself thinking that it wasn't the *Law Review*, but it was better than *Mercenary Monthly*. The sudden check on reading material brought her up short and she put on the sunglasses she'd been carrying as an impromptu disguise or a wall of protection against what she'd come here to do.

"Did she really intend to go through with this?" she thought in a flurry as she absently and nervously flipped and touched every paper laid out on the counter. It was nonsense. She'd met the man one time and then under less than memorable circumstances.

"You'll have ink on your fingers," Sam said abruptly without looking up from his book.

Caught, and caught unaware, Karen could only manage a startled, "How's that?"

Sam still didn't look up from the reading. "From flipping through all that newspaper. Your fingers will have ink on them."

Karen immediately addressed the issue as if it were the most immediate thing on her mind. She looked at the fingers on her outstretched hand and saw that Sam had been right. Then she felt and looked for a tissue. Not finding one she began to ask. "Do you have a–"

"End of the counter. Inside around the corner on the wall. Just take one," Sam said with a degree of annoyance in his voice that betrayed that he'd said this same thing a thousand times.

Karen moved to the end of the counter as directed then reached, stopped to look, then leaned again and carefully, very carefully, tore one sheet of paper towel from the cheap plastic holder. As she drifted back toward Sam wiping her barely dirty fingers, she thanked him. "Hey. Thanks for the advice and the towel."

"Forget it. I'm made of money. It's my lot in life to give stuff away." Sam had not torn himself from the book.

"I just took one. Like you said."

"Very kind."

There was a pause and Karen, content with the state of her fingers knew the conversation and the meeting could hinge on that pause and take a harsh turn. "I'll pay you for the towel, if you'd like."

"Skip it." And the pause lingered.

Karen could walk away now, knowing Sam was an inconsolable defeated man, curt and uncaring in defense of what the world had done to him and he to himself. There was a lean in her body, figuratively and otherwise. She agreed with her body and took a hesitant half step away.

"No paper?"

Karen turned only a little, as resigned to go home as she had been to fly down, when the spark that had ignited her interest and caused her to buy that plane ticket, flickered to life. In a millisecond of time, a single beat of her heart, she saw the battered man in the battered chair and immediately understood that what had filled the well of callousness and disregard for humanity was what had drawn her to this sidewalk at this very moment.

She had been there. She had been an eye witness to the destruction of a soldier and the disembodiment of a man. Karen knew his secret.

She pulled her sunglasses off in a rush of movement that from the corner of Sam's eye told him an un-aimed diatribe was headed his way for his apparent insolence. He didn't care. He'd been subjected to this before. The lecture wouldn't phase him, but ring just enough in his ears, sting just enough on his skin, to remind him that he was still alive. Still, he read on – his eyes moving slowly over words in a story he had read enough times to not be put off course by the trivial ranting of yet another vengeful tourist who felt offended by his lack of attention.

"Like I give a shit," he said to himself as he waited for the sting.

"Sam? Sam Ciampiano?"

His name brought his eyes from the book for the first time, but the next words brought them into sharp focus and snapped the muscles in his back tight.

"Sergeant Sam Ciampiano? Is that you?"

The muscles were nearing spasm as he lowered the book and searched the face in front of him. Karen's sunglasses were gone, but, though pleasing, the dark hair was longer, the crisp white Naval JAG uniform gone. Above all, the décor, situation, and circumstances so different, Sam could not put a name to the pretty face that he recognized ever so slightly. Karen saw the searching in Sam's eyes and felt a twinge of disappointment that bordered a pain she hadn't anticipated.

"Hi. Karen Auburn. Andrews Air Force Base. I was your attorney of record for a short while. How'd you ever make out with that?"

Before the words cleared her mouth, she wanted them back. Sam's reaction showed her she was right.

"Nothing. It was no big deal," and he retreated back behind his book.

Karen wanted to kick herself, maybe slap herself to boot. "Eight hundred miles to say that, of all things," her mind whispered. Then it countered. "Try it again, stupid."

"Hey... Ummm..., Sergeant, I was–"

"I'm not a sergeant," and like before, Sam's eyes stayed in the book, but now Karen recognized he was holding it substantially tighter.

"I apologize, Sam. Mr. Ciampiano. Could I–"

"How is it you remember my name?" Sam suddenly exploded and snapped the book shut with one large vise-like hand.

"I don't... I..."

"Forget it, Lieutenant. Whatever you want, you're not going to find it here. If you remember, I didn't have much to say to you then and I've got even less to say to you now." Sam leaned forward menacingly on the counter. His eyes flashed a fierceness he knew had never really gone. "So why don't you and whoever brought you down here, turn around and get... the... fuck... out."

"It's not like that," she struggled.

Sam stood up and grabbed the two-by-four that held up the flap of the stand. Karen might have thought he'd crack her with it if she'd had time to think at all. But Sam pushed the weight of the roof up and relieved the two-by-four of its duties then let the side of the stand crash down. Karen jumped back to avoid being slapped by the falling door as she heard Sam yell one last time from inside.

"Leave me alone!"

She stood there encased by stunned silence. If the situation had shown a star's twinkle of promise, she might have chuckled to herself, "That did not go very well," and found the joke inside the emasculated attempt. But there was no twinkle of a star's hope. It was apparent that Sam Ciampiano had drawn the curtains of his world tight around him. The reminder of anything from the days of service to his country and shallow dismissal did nothing but layup concrete blocks to replace the drawn shades.

The last few minutes had gone as badly as Karen had thought possible when she considered the worst case scenarios. Rejection had been on the table from the start. She saw it laying there, surrounded by other possibilities. It was briefly mulled over then set aside while she concentrated on the more promising outcomes. "Thanks for caring so much to look me up." "You've gone to so much trouble, let me buy you dinner." Or, hope against hope, "Funny. I've thought of you as well." But instead, the wooden flap of the newsstand bounced to stillness in front of her.

As she took her first steps in shunned retreat, Karen instantly thought about the things she had hoped to hear. Beyond her hopes, were more simple things she had never completely answered. Why did she think of this guy? What really made her get on that plane? He was handsome and interesting, but others carried those qualities. Why was she at a beat up newsstand on a city street, eight hundred miles from home, trying to woo a discharged mercenary who shattered people's arms with equal amounts of ease and disregard? There were a few more steps back toward the rental. Instinctively, Karen scratched a tickle on her cheek and realized it was a drying tear.

It all came down to those few seconds back at the interview room when Karen looked across the table at a seasoned, dedicated veteran of many things, and caught a glimpse of a young man, perhaps even a boy, who was in pain and needed help. That was what drove her into his past and what brought her to the newsstand. She could deal with that part as her steps quickened and became more deliberate. However, the watery eyes were something she hadn't counted on. They came from somewhere else – a pain or emptiness of her own. Perhaps there was a commonality behind all of this, she thought as she blinked away tears and wiped the evidence of her own ills from her face.

She had thought it all through and decided to come meet Sergeant Sam Ciampiano, a brief memory from her past that was as vacant as his own. And she'd done just that – meet him. He rejected her out of hand. It was over before it began. She had come. She tried – fulfilling a mission that was part fantasy wrapped in a strange cloak of sincere concern. Karen had done what she could – tried what she'd dared – and the results were what they were. It had been on the table from the onset. So there it was.

Karen reached for her keys and pushed the remote door lock. Ahead of her she heard the car respond and saw the lights flash. Perhaps she'd honk the horn as she drove by the stand and say a prayer for the man inside. As she opened the door she thought he needed it, but in truth, she didn't know how badly.

"Hey. Hey! Hold on!"

Karen looked over the open doorframe down the street toward the stand and saw Sam shouting and running across the four-lane street with abandon. Tires squealed and horns blew as the big man dodged vehicles like a running back clearing the line of scrimmage. His face, even from a distance, matched the intensity in his voice. Rather than wait on someone who saw her as a vivid reminder of a vicious turn in his life, Karen dove into the car, slammed the door and hit the electronic lock button. All four knobs retreated into their doors with a comforting thud. Then she hurriedly fumbled with the large plastic tag on the rental's key ring until she got the key into the ignition. Unlike the movies, her moves were efficient. There was no dropping or cursing for dramatic effect. Sam running at her was ample drama all its own. The car started easily.

Outside, Sam was running fast and bearing down. Karen slipped the car in drive and hit the gas, but as she turned into the street Sam appeared in front of her and slammed his hands down on the hood of the moving car.

Karen locked up the brakes as the others had done when Sam had darted into the road. The car lurched, helped by the strong arms pressing down on the flimsy sheet metal of its hood.

"Stop!" he yelled. "Stop!"

This was getting ugly real quick. Karen put the car in reverse and turned over her shoulder, but the parking spot was tight. Her attention was drawn back to the hood of the car by fierce pounding and also by the fact that she had nowhere else to go. She was effectively trapped, unless she wanted to run over the angry man slapping the palms of his hands on the hood of the rental. Karen quickly checked the locks on the doors as she began rummaging through her purse for her pepper spray, which as far as the airport security had been concerned, was a lipstick canister – one of few perks in working for the Federal Justice Department. But there were no thoughts of perks or anything else at the moment. She had a hood ornament on her rental that was very big and highly upset with her presence. All she wanted to do was get out of there.

Karen had the pepper spray in her hand and laid on the horn. She couldn't hear what Sam was saying any longer, but he lifted his hands from the car and took a half-step back. Karen still couldn't get by him, but she at least had him in retreat. Sam was holding up his hands and waving them at her, shouting something, so she eased off the horn.

"I'm sorry!" he was shouting. "One minute! Wait one minute."

"Okay," Karen thought. "Now what's this?"

Sam stepped forward again, slower now and with tremendous balance. He eased gracefully, like a dancer, Karen thought, off to the side of the car and up to her door. She had the locked door and the window between them and the pepper spray clutched tightly. Sam motioned for her to roll down the window. She shook her head no and in doing so dislodged a couple more tears from the wells of her eyes. In her blurred vision she held up the pepper spray for Sam to see.

She saw the reaction in Sam's face behind the fingers he held up a scant inch apart. "Just a little. I've got to ask you something. And maybe you have to ask me something too."

Karen hesitated and argued with her eyes. He beckoned, then begged, for the inch of unencumbered space, the crack of the window. From somewhere in the recesses of her mind, or perhaps in the corner of her heart, she recalled that it was as much the space between the bars that kept the tiger caged as the bars themselves. Only then did she reach for the button, being careful to push the window and not the door locks. The window slipped, too far, and Karen ran it back up until it was down only a half an inch. The pepper spray was aimed at the small gap.

"What do you want?" she said speaking to the crack.

"I'm sorry I yelled back there," Sam said as he threw a glance toward the stand. "I was a little surprised to see someone from Washington."

He waited politely for a response that didn't come so he pushed forward with what had caused him to bolt up the street.

"Anyway... What I was wondering was..."

Karen felt the tears drying and her heart racing for new reasons.

"Did the colonel send you?"

Karen shook her head no, slowly and with little thought.

"Who then? Wait! I don't need to know. Tell them, whoever it was, that I'm ready. I've stayed in shape and I'm ready. Did they say where they want me to report? Just tell me where to report."

The heart in Karen that had been racing from anticipation to fear, nearly stopped. Though crushed, it continued to beat in its mindless way, unaffected by the disregard or callousness or miscommunication that had brought her to this point on a hot blacktop street, speaking through a tiny gap in a rented car's window.

Unconsciously or otherwise, Karen's head fell away from the crack in the window and took the pepper spray with it. She closed her eyes and lowered her face until her chin nearly rested on her chest. Fresh tears began to form. It had gone more wrong than she had ever thought possible. She had first been a painful reminder, then it had grown in the space of a minute into what was now a wrenching wound that was about to bleed this damaged man dry. Karen was nothing more than salt being rubbed into it and she'd never be anything more. She was going down.

What's the worst that could happen? He'd body slam her like a rag doll into the concrete sidewalk? Right now that would be absolutely painless compared to how she felt inside. She had it coming, for fostering this crazy dream and pulling Sam down with her. She'd take the broken arm or broken face and never press charges. She opened her eyes and, without fumbling this time, pushed the button and unlocked the doors.

Karen forced her door open with such suddenness that it clipped Sam's shin as he stepped back. She didn't take time to apologize – a scrapped shin was nothing compared to what she'd already done to him or what he was about to do to her. In a fraction of a second she had cleared the door and eased it shut behind her – purposely shutting off all avenues of escape. She'd take whatever Sam had for her and then limp back to Washington to heal her injuries, knowing already that her heart would be the last to return to normal.

"Sgt. Ciampiano," she began. "Sam. No one sent me. I'm not here for any... any work related... I'm not here to offer you your job back. Your career back. Your goddamn life back. I don't have anything like that. I came here..." Karen saw her words were penetrating their target and she baulked. "I came here... To see you."

Sam's forehead wrinkled and his face took on the look of a child who had just seen a dime store Santa remove his beard and light up a cigarette. His lips parted as if to form a word, but nothing came out. Unknowingly, he took a slight step back. Karen saw the recoil from her and knew again all was lost. Her arms were still attached, but there was time for that.

After a few more rented and local cars sped by, Sam choked out a single word. "Why?"

Karen heard it, understood the single syllable's definition, but couldn't match so clearly an answer. Was he asking, "Why would you come to see me?" or, "Why did you come to Tampa?" or the most painful why of all, "Why did you do this to me?"

She was suddenly cold though it was ninety degrees. She felt as though she had somehow slipped out onto the ice of a frozen Potomac. Now, in the middle of the river, she didn't know which way was the safety of the shore and beneath her feet she felt the ice crack. She couldn't stand there not answering – not moving off the ice – and she couldn't run. Her toes crept out as though leaving her body and felt for a safe foothold on the frozen ground in her mind while words, nearly as few and simple as his, began to edge out of her mouth.

"I was... I was here by chance," she lied, then as quick tried to take it back. "No. I knew, that is," she said slowly. "I found out you lived here. I was due for a vacation," and she forced a smile, but it was soon lost in her mangled words. "I thought I'd check on... Look you up and see – say hi."

Sam's puzzled look began to erode. Beneath it was the sharp edge of anger sired by disbelief and disappointment. "What for?" Sam said with a little force.

"Okay," Karen said as she looked away for a moment. "We've gone from one word to two. Things are moving in the right direction."

"What do you want?" Sam asked the same thing as if he hadn't heard the remark.

"Nothing. Absolutely nothing. I swear."

"Then what are you doing here?"

"I heard this was a nice place," Karen said as she gestured to the city that held them in its hands.

Now the step reversed and Sam closed in. "Bullshit! You blood suckers are all alike. Looking for a debriefing that'll make your career? Want to know where all the skeletons are buried?" Sam reached up in a blurred move no one could have seen and stopped his hand a fraction of an inch from her throat. Karen brought her own hands up and clutched his hand in a defense that wasn't needed and would have done nothing had it been. "You people are unbelievable," Sam muttered as he tore his hand from hers and stepped away toward the newsstand.

Karen should have been counting her lucky stars that the high cheekbones in her face weren't cracked, but she dropped her own hands and went after him. "Hey. Hey! Who the hell do you think you are?"

Sam stopped and spun around. "What?"

"You can't curse me out like that and walk away – like some spoiled kid who didn't get their way."

"I thought you came here to give me back my life! Yeah, you said that, didn't you, smart ass? I don't have a goddamn life and you don't have one to give me."

The whole thing scared her. Not the hulk in front of her, veins popping in his neck, but the loss of a life, of a dream. What had made her think she could make it right?

"I'm sorry!" she screamed in self-defense and at herself at the same time. And she was sorry – for raking this up in him again and sorry for herself in a pitiful way that she had been a part of it. "I'm sorry," the voice cooled. "I'm sorry."

Sam just stood watching as Karen began to cry for the third time today and the third time in the last eight years. If this had been planned by some dirt digging bureaucrat, he couldn't have found a better actress. Or if not, then what was making this officer fold up in front of him?

"Hey. Hey, Lieutenant?"

Karen looked up and Sam saw the black streaks of what had been neatly applied mascara running from her eyes.

"You... Your face," Sam said as he slowly slid his fingers down his own cheeks. "Must be makeup."

"Oh, doesn't matter." Karen wiped at the streaks with the palms of her hand making it worse.

"Didn't help."

Karen wiped her face with the backs of her hands. "I need a tissue."

"There's towels in the stand."

"I know. But I don't want to use any more of them up."

"C'mon, Lieutenant. You get one more. On the house." Sam turned back toward the stand then looked over his shoulder and waited until Karen fell in alongside. He didn't say another word, not then, not in the entire walk back or for several more minutes at the newsstand. Neither did Karen. But both of them were thinking, "What is it with this person? What makes them do what they do? And why are they here? More importantly, what do I do now?"

Raphael was thinking the same thing as he stood outside Clayton's house, ignoring the brass encircled lighted doorbell knowing the sensors would have already announced him. He began knocking, becoming pounding, on the door. He was still pounding as the door opened and was so entrenched he actually knocked twice more as the door was opened.

He stormed inside and immediately launched into thoughts he had been harboring since Marcus Pete had called his office.

"Jesus, Clay!" His face was flush and he was nearly screaming. Then he checked himself long enough to glance back out the still open door Clayton was holding, take it from him, and close it. "The goddamn District Attorney's Office? What happens next? The FBI? It's over."

"Relax."

"Done. *Fini*. Before we get in any more trouble."

"What trouble?" Clayton said as he walked away from his pacing friend and pulled two short tumblers from behind the etched glass faced cabinet.

"What trouble? Are you joking? The DA's office, Clay. There's not much worse trouble than that."

The clink of the glass bottle to the rim of the glasses provided the bookends to Clayton's sentence. "Follow me a minute. That's not trouble, Ralph. That is some of the best news we could receive. It puts us smack in the driver's seat." He ended by holding the tumbler out to his friend who could only stare incredulously.

Clayton had to move to Raphael and actually eased the glass in his hand as he continued. "Deep breath, my friend. Deep breath. There's not a soul in this world who knows what really went on with those sorry assholes. Hell, they don't know what happened themselves and who would they tell if they did? How about this? 'Oh, Mr. DA? Mr. SEC? By the way, all that money I stole? Someone bought worthless stock with it and I'd like to press charges.' Yep, that'd go over real big."

Clayton took a good drink. Raphael managed just a sip as Clayton continued. "This guy that called you. The flunky from the DA's office—"

"Senior Chief Investigator."

"Even better. A guy like that is going to have the skinny on the caper."

"Christ, Clay, you talk like it's a cartoon. We could end up in prison."

"How?"

"How? We broke the law, Ricochet Rabbit."

"Where?"

"Tapping into other people's accounts, for starters."

"Prove it."

Raphael hesitated a second. "You know I don't know all that cyber bullshit."

"That's right, you don't. And guess what? No one else does either."

"I'm sure the FBI has got a couple of fellas running around with pen protectors and taped up glasses who know their way around a computer."

"True enough, but remember – I build the forensic software they're using. I build it," Clayton echoed his own words for effect and took another drink as he walked deeper into the comfort of his home.

"Clay, I know you're clever–"

"Please, it's a little more than clever."

"Right. Right. You're a goddamn genius, but you're not the only genius. Now, are you following me?"

Clayton didn't miss a beat. "Ralph, check this out. No one is on top of this stuff like me. Granted, there are other people who can work this stuff, but not like me. Not right now."

"Pride goeth before the fall," Raphael said before he took his first full drink from the glass.

"I know. I know. But not here. Not now. This is the time. Today, I am the one. Tomorrow someone may come along who knows it better or more or differently, but not today. Not today. Today I write the programs that protect nearly every one of the Fortune 500 and the feds. They come to me. My company is creating this stuff – re-creating, updating – every day. Even the military comes to us. Hell, they're the ones who put the bank vault door on my house." It was Clayton's turn to breathe. "Now's the time, Ralph. We hold all the cards. And that DA friend of yours is just another asset."

Clayton lowered himself onto the arm of one of the leather covered chairs. He worked his drink and watched the ice swim in the glass while his efforts slipped into his friend's mind as their own version of an intoxicating elixir. Raphael walked across the wide room and sat in the chair farthest possible from Clayton's perch.

"The DA's Office, Clay," he said weakly.

"I know," Clayton answered in a softer voice. "But he didn't ask one single question about you, did he?"

"No."

"Or even why someone would do this to themselves."

"Of course not. Who knows what another person thinks."

"Exactly. And not even a hint as to how someone other than those two dumb asses and a barrel of greedy execs could have done this."

Raphael didn't answer.

"Nothing like that, right, Ralph?"

"Right."

"So, he's asking questions about the stock and ups and downs and margins and options. Typical market questions from a guy who by pure chance happened to still have your card."

"And who happens to be the Senior Chief Investigator for the County in which I just committed a crime."

Clayton stood up slowly from the arm of the chair and went back behind the island of the kitchen where the gin bottle had remained. He freshened his drink then silently held the bottle out to Raphael who shook his head no. Clayton stirred the drink with his finger then put his finger in his mouth before dabbing it on a towel.

"For the record, or off the record, whatever makes you feel better," Clayton said as he wandered from the kitchen back into the living room toward his friend. "You didn't commit a crime. Not a felony, a misdemeanor, nothing." He sat on the arm of the chair Raphael had dropped into. "You didn't do a single thing. Didn't break any laws." Both men sipped their drinks. "I did... and I'm not done."

The sentence was followed by an extended silence. Clayton continued to sip his gin and lose himself in the glass. Raphael however, waited until he was ready then took a long purpose ridden drink that burnt over and over with each gulp. He stood up in the strength he'd found in the pain. "Not me, Clay. Not me. I've done all I'm going to do."

"Figured that was coming."

"I was thinking about it already, but that investigator guy scared the shit out of me."

"You don't have to be, you know. It was nothing."

"It was something to me, Clay."

"I get it. But would you hear me out on one thing?"

"Go."

Clayton took a breath and waded into what he knew would be his last effort. "It was just coincidence. Nothing more. They have nothing on you or me. I'll access the DA's files tomorrow and—"

"Let's not do that."

"Okay. I won't, but know that there's absolutely nothing to connect us to this. Nothing. No need to be concerned. Not in the slightest." Clayton took a drink. "Trust me on this, I know."

"How?"

"I just do."

"You already ran through their files, didn't you?"

Clayton looked into his glass for an answer, a reprieve, or to give Raphael another moment to tell him if he truly wanted to know. It was a short wait. Raphael shot across the room in a resigned stomp, plowed to the far side, and back to the center.

"Jesus Christ, Clay. You already did it."

"Do you want me to say it or leave it alone?"

"I don't want to know anything." Raphael spun and sat the glass on the counter on his way to the door. Clayton didn't try to convince his friend any longer. He scarcely looked up as the door opened. "Don't call me, Clay."

"I'm sorry, bud."

"No need for that. I'm out. Fair enough?"

"Fair enough."

"See you." Raphael was nearly out the door, pulling it closed behind him when he stopped and looked back in and across what seemed an immeasurable distance to his friend. "Hey, take it easy, will you?"

"Don't you mean, be careful?"

"I do, but I was afraid it sounded too much like one of our movie lines."

"Yes, it does."

"Any chance you might walk away from this with me? If it's like you said, no one knows. Good time to cash out while you're ahead."

"Can't do it, Sallie."

"Robert Duvall. To Abe Vigoda in *Godfather Two*."

Clayton smiled. "*Godfather*, the original. You buy next round," he said as he held up his glass."

Raphael nodded. "I buy."

8

The door closed and Clayton slipped off the arm of the chair down deep into the seat. He sighed then emptied his glass. The ice cubes were rattled and nursed to melting, then chewed and crunched when they responded too slowly. In time there was nothing left to entertain him in the glass so he pulled himself from the chair and meandered to the kitchen. He picked up Raphael's glass and finished what remained from Raphael's melting ice then put both glasses in the sink.

Disheartened and discouraged by his unwitting partner's defection, Clayton retreated to electronic friends that always remained. He clicked on the television and let the news drone as he powered up his laptop and scanned clips from the world news summaries. From his chair he plumbed the digital depths looking for a new focus. There was a piece on theft and misappropriation of money by civilian contractors in Iraq. He read intently for a name. Finding none, he moved on, but reminded himself to follow up.

The national news had more specifics, but most of it was fluff about another Hollywood celeb headed off to rehab or a sports star finding Jesus on the way to his sentencing. "Pure crap," Clayton muttered as he flipped through the e-pages. Then another headline, seven minutes old it said, was on the screen as he refreshed the home page of the site.

His eyes darted back and forth in the computer's window to the world. The headline shouted, 'Congressional Sexual Misconduct,' in an attempt to separate itself from the drowning unspoken din of other stories.

"Here we go again," Clayton muttered, hardly impressed, shocked, or surprised, until a single word perked up his virtual ears and literally widened his eyes. Florida.

"Sonofabitch..." It wasn't Clayton's home district, but a member of Congress had been called out in an open letter to the Orlando Sentinel for propositioning male congressional pages and having illicit sex with more than a few over the course of several years. The national news wires had picked it up after the hard papers hit the morning newsstands. It was the twenty-first century electronic world. Clayton blew through the brief article which promised more details as they became available then leaned back in his chair.

"You sonofabitch." The slump into the chair was the calm before the storm. In a flash Clayton was doing what he did best.

"Well, Mr. Congressman-kiddie-cock-sucker. Let's see what you've got under your dirty little fingernails. Let's you and me show the world."

As ever, his fingers bounced around the keyboard like a kindergarten class on a summer trampoline. The keys were silent beneath his touch, but they issued direction like the sounding of a gong. Clayton paused only occasionally to watch a program unfold and surrender before his eyes or to reason several steps ahead of the firewalls in order to circumvent them without leaving an electronic fingerprint or an identifying shoeprint in the virtual landscape beneath his touch. And as he had done several times in recent weeks, he was soon reviewing the hard drive of a computer other than his own without the owner's knowledge at the moment, or in all likelihood, ever.

"I know it's in here, you piece of shit. Local boy makes good then steps on his dick. Come on. Give it up."

Clayton ran some elementary searches and as predictable as sunrise, files opened. His mammoth drives opened the pictures in nano-seconds and a portfolio of naked children, some bound, gagged, and blindfolded, others in sex positions and acts, began cascading onto the screen as fast as an ancient cinemascope. Clayton pulled his hands away from the keyboard as though they'd touched an electric wire. He leaned back to avoid the disgust on his monitor. In a flash he'd seen enough of what he'd come for and reached to stop the revolting parade of pictures. But before he could, the pictures stopped themselves.

An open file along the bottom of the pirated screen flashed then disappeared. Clayton leaned in and unconsciously wiped the sweat off his upper lip, brought on by the gin and the chase. He watched the screen. The eleven year old boy tied with pantyhose vanished. Then the little girl. Then the next and the next until the photos were retreating as fast as they'd appeared. Caught off-guard, Clayton took another moment to realize what was happening and another long moment to stop it.

"No you don't, asshole." And the fingers raced like sin before Judgment Day. His hands became a juggernaut of disjointed thoroughbreds bolting from the starting gate and leaning hard into the first pole. Change. Rename. Open. Secure. Timed. Save. Shift. Disclose. Divert. The commands went on and out and across airways and hard lines for an explosion of forty seconds. Then Clayton relaxed. The pictures continued to slip off the screen until they were all gone.

He plied the keyboard again, slower now, crossed his arms and watched. An email account opened without his influence and a mass deletion project began, just as had been done with the photographs.

Clayton smiled and wiped the sweat from his face with both hands. "They're still there, shit for brains. You almost dumped the lot, but not today. They'd have found the trail anyway, unless you chuck your tower in the river, but that would look pretty obvious, wouldn't it? Your wife might even raise an eyebrow at that little move, you cock sucker. Hopefully they're smart enough to find them eventually, but it'll be more fun my way."

Half way across the state in a dimly lit personal office in his home, lined with the prerequisite law books and surrounded by plainly framed pictures of him shaking hands with Presidents and Heads of State, a pressured, harried, and very anxious United States congressman sat back from his computer. He had discarded his red power tie hours earlier and his thin hair was gone astray – sweat making it stick to the side of his face as the comb-over collapsed under the weight of scrutiny. His throat felt tight, his breathing short and quick. There was a pain in his chest as he fumbled across the keyboard, hunting and pecking with his stubby index fingers.

"Alright. Think clearly. Plan for the expected as well as the unexpected. Files are cleared. Check. Probably some kind of retrieval program in that damn hard drive though. Take your time. Lots of time."

In the soft glow of a single lamp, the congressman had already copied all his tax forms and pertinent personal documents to a worn thumb drive. Deleting the photos was the last stroke of his plan before he slipped out of his chair and onto his knees. He tugged at the computer tower until it was out from beneath the elegant dark cherry desk. He craned his neck around the back and looked instantly lost as he absorbed the snake pit of wires protruding from the back.

"I can do this," he muttered. He stood back up and leaned over the keyboard, clicked the start menu of the old operating system, and chose 'shut down.' In a few seconds the machine complied.

Clayton's screen went black as well, but his towers continued their efforts. He smiled. "Calling it a night, Congressman? Going to go to bed and dream of eight year olds? Tomorrow the press will be camped outside your house and you'll take up hours on CNN. You plan on dodging every bullet, don't you? But there'll be a few surprises."

It was a few minutes until Clayton shut down his own computer. He'd retraced his unseen steps from earlier. Then he glanced at his watch. "Probably hauling your fat ass under your desk about now. I can see you fumbling with your hard drive – nervous as hell. That would work, in a way, but not tonight you sonofabitch. Not this time. Sleep tight, you piece of shit."

Clayton had seen the future across the miles. Indeed, the congressman was on his side laying on the floor and had removed the side panel from his computer tower. "I'm too old for this shit," he groaned as he stared, overcome and helpless. Through trial and error he eventually impressed himself with being able to locate and remove the hard drive. He tested its heft in his hand then smiled as Clayton had done moments before. "It'll be my word against yours," he thought. "You little bastards. I'll ruin them. I'll make their lives so unbearable and discredit them so badly, they'll be flipping burgers forever." Then he paused in his aggrandizing self-speech as he hauled himself out from under the desk and shoved the tower back in place. "Gotta say it," he said to his ego. "I will miss that Jeff. Perfect ass and was a great source for new talent. Could have made something of himself. But not now you ungrateful prick."

The congressman struggled to his feet and set the hard drive on his desk. He bent and picked up his expensive soft leather attaché case. A wave of dizziness washed over him. "I need a sandwich," he said as he made room for the hard drive in the case, dropped it in roughly, then zipped the case closed and laid it on the center of the desk as gently as if it had held a bomb, which indeed it did. The lone light clicked into darkness and the congressman left his home office behind and wandered to his kitchen. The refrigerator light trickled up the hall like the last rays of a vanishing moon and crept into the office, on the desk, and across the attaché case.

The following morning cast another gray light across Florida announcing the earliest hints of sunrise. The routine of the day was underway well before the sun broke over the Atlantic coast horizon. Sam was at his station. The papers had been arranged, no neater, no messier than any other day, and he sipped his first coffee from a dark blue ceramic cup that showed white where the broken off handle would have been. The headlines on his counter barked out the report that had driven Clayton the night before. But while the static words on the newspapers relayed what little they knew, the live news coverage was competing for prime real estate outside the congressman's house.

Since the wee hours, trucks with satellite dishes pointed skyward had converged on the idyllic upscale neighborhood. With dawn only a distant certainty, they had begun spewing reporters and cameramen out their sides and long lines of cable out their asses in order to catch the five second walk of shame of the alleged pedophile law maker as he wrangled to his car, dodging reporters and questions with equal enthusiasm. State troopers crept their cruisers up the street and over the cables, easing the throng aside in answer to complaints from well-heeled neighbors and the congressman's wife. They waited in their cars at the end of the driveway despite pleas from inside the home for an escort to the car and beyond, but no crime had been committed – not by the journalists anyway. As long as the reporters stayed off the property, their bleating and baying would pass for lawful assembly. So the mass jockeyed on the sidewalk and at the end of the driveway with microphones held at the ready like soldiers with their rifles, ready to attack.

In Tampa, Jack was watching the circus unfold above the crawling CNN ticker. He stood in his stocking feet in his living room as he tied his tie between bites of peanut butter covered toast and sips of fresh coffee. "Sick bastard," was all he said between mouthfuls.

He walked back to the kitchen for a warmer when the reporter's perfunctory account of the congressman's legislative voting record was interrupted by a bustle of rough elbows as the alleged perpetrator suddenly emerged from his front door. Cloaked in the semidarkness of pre-dawn, some thought he was attempting to beat the late arriving news crews and catch the others off guard, but the reaction was predictably quick and powerful.

Jack was drawn back to the television by a cacophony of questions aimed at the member of the United States House of Representatives. What happened next was as predictable as the horde's convergence. The congressman, soft leather attaché case in hand, stopped by the door of his car and held up his hand in an attempt to halt the strafing. It worked well enough for him to give a crafted speech meant to appear spontaneous.

"I understand why you are here. And I fully understand and appreciate the public's right to know. But the absolute truth is that in this case, there simply is no story to tell, to report, or to be uncovered. I have done nothing, absolutely nothing, in regards to the allegations leveled against me."

Harassing questions signaled an all-out bombardment. So many that even had he wanted, the congressman could not have responded. In the verbal melee that continued, a few reporters suddenly fell away from their colleagues and as one, pressed a finger into their tiny earphones in order to hear better. Each mirrored the others as their faces contorted with disbelief at the news in their ears, then moved into a confident nodding of the head. Three went to their satellite trucks – one running – and disappeared behind the pictures of a giant number eight, a number ten, and a thirteen painted over their respective doorways. It was only a few moments and station number eight emerged the winner, a fistful of paper waving in her hand as her trophy. Ten was a close second and thirteen just behind and all three were racing back to the fracas in the congressman's driveway.

Number Eight very physically crushed into and through the throng until she was face to face with the target of her attention. Separated by the legal trespassing boundary of the driveway, she balanced on the narrow crack in the sidewalk and waved her papers in the air at the congressman and her colleagues. "Congressman! Did you write these? Did you write these emails?"

He smiled politely. "I have no idea. I don't even know what you're holding," he laughed.

"Sir, would you glance at these and tell me if you wrote them?"

"I don't believe that will be either necessary or appropriate. In this age, we are all aware that almost any person can fabricate anything with basic software. Regardless of what a person may contrive, or conspire to type out, the fact is that I have done nothing inappropriate and certainly nothing illegal." The punctuation was the congressman beginning to step into his car.

"But, sir, these were sent by you, just this morning, to my station. Why would you do that?"

"Again, most anyone can send anything anywhere. Rest assured, I did not send you an email this morning." He smiled. "It's an invitation to come camp out in my front lawn I suppose," he laughed. The laugh was genuine and a few uninformed reporters couldn't resist joining in.

"No, sir," Station Thirteen shouted. "I received similar emails and far from being an invitation to your home, these are countless emails, perhaps hundreds, detailing your many, many sexual encounters with children."

"That's absurd."

"And among the emails are pictures – hundreds it seems, of children in highly suggestive sexual positions."

The congressman was losing his patience. His practiced confidence was next to erode. "Once again, anyone can manipulate most anything these–"

"But, sir, these came directly from you. From your account. Care to comment?"

The congressman smiled again, in a rehearsed play of his lips and teeth that had disarmed many constituents over the years and had allowed him to continue in a conversation that he was able to control. This time however, unseen hands plied their trade and pulled the wires behind the smile and he had been rendered powerless, but it was something he had yet to learn. So, drawn as much by curiosity as an impulse to refute the allegations once and for all, he abandoned the comfort of the intended escape route of the open car door and walked with a weak confidence across what had been his cushion of safety, his own driveway, and approached the dividing line of the light gray concrete sidewalk where Number Eight was perched with her papers.

Prefaced again by a weak smile, the congressman held out his hand and quipped, "You guys need to check your sources a bit, don't you think? I've said it before and I'll say it again – anything can be sent from anywhere by anybody. But I'll glance through your papers if it will pacify you on the subject, then we can move on to the real story here – namely that the allocations are utterly false and it is the accusers in this case will be prosecuted."

With that pronouncement, he grasped the small stack of papers from Number Eight then stepped back to read them in the comparative quiet and safety of the car's shadow. As he scanned each document, his countenance and his mood darkened. The still photographers caught the mood much better than television. He was a man under siege and it was readily apparent.

Waves of emotions came and went on his face like time elapsed photos of an eroding beach. First, the slim to skinny confidence shook and crumbled under the weight of the initial reading of his name above what he planned to do with Jeff when next they met. Astonishment followed rapidly as he hurriedly leafed through the emails, completely astonished at what he saw – original emails, complete with his IP address and more, sent to more young boys and girls than he'd remembered. Then came the photos – grainy colored and the odd black and white.

The congressman's face was ashen and his hands trembled, despite his feeble attempt at recovery.

"This is... is absolutely obscene..."

He didn't notice the whirl of the cameras and the flashes of light, which caught each mood as well as his rush to rid himself of the trail which led directly back to his hands. In those hands was a picture of a grown man's hip on a child. The camel fell under the weighted straw of another picture of him and a teenager, both naked. In a flurry of confused motions he began to retreat inside the car, then stopped long enough to scurry to the end of the driveway and literally throw the papers back at the reporter.

"Trash!" he yelled, meaning the reporter as much as her files. He spun and headed for the quiet of the car. Those who hadn't received the email trail, scampered and tore at the flittering papers to have their own piece of the day's second biggest story. The biggest story was falling on the ground twenty feet from the papers. The congressman was collapsing under the weight of his sin.

Pain gripped his chest like a fist, in a chokehold, in a vise. Sweat burst onto his face and the morning light, still struggling to gain a foothold on the horizon, faded to near nothingness in his eyes. He fell toward the car, dropped the treasure of his briefcase, slid down the car, and sat awkwardly upright against its dirty tire. The troopers who had been watching sprang like lions from cages. One spoke loudly and forcibly into the microphone on his shoulder and ordered an ambulance before he even reached the congressman. When the troopers came to him, the reporters had long forgotten the boundaries of the driveway and had crowded around. One tugged at the barely conscious man's tie as if to loosen it as another knelt beside him and asked inane questions as he and his kind normally did. The inquiries echoed as absurd, under the circumstances, even to the sharks themselves.

While some continued to bark questions, others elbowed their cameramen into better positions, grasping that their verbal assaults were nothing to the video of the man dying by the dirty tire. Reporters further back – unable to jockey through to the front – couldn't see death's pallor creep up the man's face. They shouted over their competitors' backs. "Ask him if he wants to confess!"

The troopers broke through the throng before the prize winning question could be put to the dying man with the face and hands left smudged with dirt from the wheel. They kicked the precious briefcase aside without words, and while the digital film continued to virtually roll and the digital shutters silently snapped, the troopers pulled the congressman the rest of the way to the ground. His eyes were useless as his heart choked to a stop. "My briefcase..," he slurred before conceding to death completely.

A reporter picked up the case and looked sheepishly at those around him. The troopers had begun resuscitation and never saw the newsman unzip the case and feel inside followed by glancing eyes. He began to pull the hard drive to the light, recognized it immediately and pushed it back in, leaned forward and placed the opened briefcase between the congressman's lifeless legs.

Marcus Pete's cell phone rang. He glanced at his watch then returned to his kitchen where he snatched the phone off the counter. The ID said, 'Jack.'

"Good morning, boss."

"Got the TV on?"

"No. I was just on my way to the office. What's—"

"Turn on your set. Go to CNN."

"What is it?" Marcus asked, anxious, as a hundred scenarios shot across the screen of his mind.

"Turn the damn thing on, will you?"

"I am!" he snapped, dumping his shoulder strapped briefcase into a chair and snatching up the remote in a single move. "What am I watching?"

"CNN."

"I know that much, Jack, and who calls a television a 'set' anymore? How old are you?"

"You're an ass. Got it on?"

"What's happened?"

"There's a guy having a heart attack right on the news."

"Okay...," Marcus slowed as the news came up. "You almost gave me one. What's the big deal? I feel bad for the guy, but—"

"Don't feel bad for this sorry sonofabitch. He's the kiddie porn king of Florida."

Marcus settled into a chair and was more interested in the phone conversation than the television screen and hadn't noticed the ticker spelling out the details of what was happening. "Which one of our old customers is he?"

"Nobody! Out of our jurisdiction anyway, I imagine. His district is over north of Orlando."

"District? What district?"

"His Congressional District. That sorry sonofabitch on the ground by the car is a United States Congressman and he just had a heart attack when the press showed him emails from some kid he was plowing in the ass. Believe that?"

Now Marcus sat up. Jack continued rambling in his ear, but Marcus had tuned him out. He scanned the ticker and listened to the broadcast over Jack's voice until a phrase from his boss wrenched him away from the television and back to the phone. "What did you just say?"

Jack moaned. "Are you listening to anything I'm saying?"

"Of course, but I've got the TV in one ear and you in the other—"

"And damn little in between. I'll see you at the office."

"Wait! What did you just say?"

"I said – since all of a sudden you're interested – they're saying he did it to himself."

"What do you mean, did it to himself?"

"Yea..., now you're thinking. That's my boy."

"Did what, Jack?"

"Cut his own throat. He sent the emails and pictures of naked kids from his own computer to the press. Can you believe that?"

"No."

"Me neither. Remind you of anything?"

"A couple of cases come to mind..."

"Damn right they do! I'll see you at the office. And wear your work clothes!"

Jack hung up. Marcus held the phone absently by his head and watched the replays of the congressman dying narrated not by the zealous reporters, but by Jack's words in his head. "He did it to himself."

———————————

9

The early morning meltdown in Orlando had been ripe for the networks and their million dollar satellite trucks, but it was death on the day's newspaper sales. Sam's dad never saw the internet and the cable news networks coming, no one did, and the apparent fact that news print might be unceremoniously shoved aside. But hey, Sam reasoned, it was one day out of three hundred and sixty five. Besides, now he could do his own reading – as if the customers were that big of an interruption anyway as he ignored the vast majority.

As it was, people were waking up to the story of the day being splashed across a million screens as the insultingly soft morning news broke away from their vanilla layouts and spent their entire broadcasts devoted to showing clip after clip of the congressman's stumbling fall and painful death. No one was passing out crying towels, to be sure, as news programs pasted together their snippets of the congressman in better days delivering speeches and kissing babies. That baby scene caught lots of air time, but few save FOX News openly addressed the irony as they leaned in from the right on the corpse.

The story continued to unfold and unravel around the feet of the reporters who were in it at the end. And Sam's buffet of newspapers had not one word on the whole fiasco. From a going to press and insuring delivery standpoint, the story broke at the absolute worst time of the day for morning newsprint. But it was what it was, so Sam leaned back, wedged the heel of a boot into its place along the bottom rail of the old counter stool and picked up his book, content to let the papers sit as he read away the morning. He leafed through the Turow paperback Karen had given him until he came across the bent corner where he had stopped.

Predictably, few people stopped that morning, so the interruptions were slight. What interruptions came were mental jumps, pictures, and recent memories from Sam himself as the holding of the book translated into thoughts of Karen and that first day in Tampa that had begun so crudely and ended, not in the clothes-tearing, near naked throes of passions, as it would have in a movie, but instead in subdued late lunches and fumbling conversations that spilled in and around Karen's vacation.

Sam didn't officially ask her out and she didn't impose. They had a few late lunches that grew more relaxed, following the daily close of the newsstand and took in a baseball game at Tropicana Field in St. Petersburg where the Tampa Bay Rays played. The Tampa namesake playing home games in St. Petersburg sparked a lively debate which proved the most animated conversation from Sam during Karen's entire stay. There had also been a couple of dinners, none of which would have resembled a solidified date. There had been no buildup, no nervous laying out of clothes and pickup, and no obligatory movie. With no dark theater, there was no shared popcorn with its intentionally inadvertent touch that ended with a hand hold as fingers sparked in the dark. This while hoping against hope to impress the other that somehow the gentle manipulation of the hand in the flashing glow of the theater would somehow make known their equally gentle skill as a lover. There was none of that.

Rather, each encounter was unassuming and strangely relaxed – as if their brusque beginning had sapped most of the awkwardness or poured a foundation that was between, "This can only get better," and, "This can't get worse." When the conversation lagged – which was often as they tried to figure out why they were here, what it meant, and where it was going – Karen enjoyed the water and the sunshine while Sam saw it with eyes refreshed by Karen's enthusiasm. Each day, each small and casual event, became a stone laid in a foundation and this suited them both very nicely.

A commonality was exposed in dribs and drabs during a drive across the city when Karen's joke about Sam's neighbor eventually led to a question about the Ciampianos.

"He's like your own private neighborhood watch program."

"That's Mr. Abreu. He's one of the last of the old Cuban families in Tampa. He was born rolling cigars. Good people."

"He's pretty protective. He thinks a lot of you."

"Him and my dad were tight."

"Mr. Abreu. Did I pronounce that right?"

"Yep."

"He mentioned your father had passed away–"

"Just before we met in Washington," Sam said as he steered the rental toward the beach.

"And your mother?" Karen asked innocently.

"I don't know."

"You don't know?"

"I mean, I know she's not here – not here as in Tampa. She's not dead. At least I don't think so."

"Really?"

"She beat it right after I hit the ground."

It would have been disturbing for most people to learn of a new friend growing up without a mother, but the impact was different for Karen. "At least you had your father."

"Yep." It was a long minute before Sam picked up his cards and followed suit, never expecting the direction the obligatory background first-date-styled conversation would go. "How about your family? Your parents still living?"

"No. I never knew either of them."

It was Sam's turn. "Really?"

"My father died in the first Persian Gulf War when I was little. My mom died before I can remember. A cancer I think, but I never could learn much."

"Wow... I'm sorry about that."

"It's okay. I mean, there's nothing to be sorry about. It wasn't your fault–"

"I meant–"

She stumbled a little. "Now I'm sorry. I didn't mean it like that. People always say they're sorry, and it's the only thing they can say." She reached across the seat of the rental car and touched Sam's arm as he drove. "Normally I just tell people they've both passed away and leave it at that. Growing up without parents begs too many questions, even from strangers – especially from strangers." She took her hand away and was rewarded with a fresh ease in the conversation.

"I used to get that about my mother," Sam said. "It doesn't happen so much when you get older."

"Yea, it gets less frequent," she echoed. "In case you want to know but are too polite to ask, I grew up in foster care for the most part."

"I won't ask."

"It's fine. You're easy to talk to. I mean, easy because I don't have to wait my turn very often."

They both waited on the pause then laughed a little.

"Yea, I guess I'm kinda quiet."

Karen patted his arm again, but much more roughly and playfully. "Nonsense! You're just right!"

The exchange had been easy and disarming.

"You never met your mom? All this time?"

"Never did."

"Did your father talk about her?"

"Never."

"And you didn't ask?"

"Not that I can remember. I guess I must have somewhere. Dad kept a picture in his top drawer of her holding me in the hospital when I was born. I remember sneaking a look at it once in a while. I think he said she went north to college and never came back. I don't know. After a while you stop asking."

"I know that feeling. I was that way, except I couldn't find anyone to ask. I'm glad you had your father."

"He was a special guy."

"And he had a special son."

Sam didn't acknowledge the compliment, but it echoed inside him and felt good.

Shockingly, to a world grown expectant of the timely progression of things such as this, they did not hold hands as Sam took her to the state run beaches, bypassed by many locals more than tourists, because of the slight admission fee of a few dollars. "Why pay when there are free beaches all along the coast," they'd complain. But the price of solitude was a Godsend to Sam and Karen. They often had beaches to themselves as they walked endlessly on the soft sand as the waves and tide snatched at their ankles. She fought a desire to take his arm and won. He thought of sitting closer on the sand, but was held at bay by seeing lieutenant's bars and a white Naval officer's uniform in his mind's eye.

The conversations stayed more than a little one sided – enough to make a girl think her companion was not remotely interested in her. Except that Karen had that briefest of histories with her new friend and understood from that day on the Air Force base, and her run up the Tampa street, what Sam's demeanor and nature was, though she continued to search for the why. His absent mother was suspect of the lion's share.

After the vacation ended and she was walked into the airport – Sam effortlessly pulling her big bag to the check-in – she did chance the snap of a kiss on his cheek over a sincere thank you for the time and the tours, but it had all the appearances of being harmless. Still, the woman in her wanted to plant the seed of a touch, of closeness, of possibilities. Though he had enjoyed her company and conversation, Sam could barely hug her in return.

Afterward there had been a few phone calls, all from Karen. The first was to advise she had safely returned to the Nation's Capital. Another came several days later to thank Sam again for the great time which was followed a couple of weeks later by a short call to deride Sam for the beleaguered performance of his Tampa Bay baseball team versus her Washington

Nationals. Sam laughed and defended the un-defendable, but hung up feeling a spirited warmness inside and caught a smile lingering on his face for some time thereafter. The smile at the thought of a woman, any woman, was something he could not remember.

From the relentlessly vigilant corner of his eye, Sam saw the man come to the stand and begin the time honored tradition of touching, thumbing, and looking at the newspapers. However, Sam took note that the man was exceedingly careful to not disrupt the pages and circumspectly, with near reverence, place them back with a profound exactness to the places where they had originally rested. This was a nice alternative and he even smiled, albeit inwardly, but then smiled broadly on the outside as he considered Karen and deemed that she had made him soft and uncharacteristically cordial. The smile and recent memory brought Sam from his book and he realized what was behind the careful placing of the papers. The customer was Carl Rand, Clayton's older brother. It had been a while since they'd seen each other. They had talked on the phone, but most conversations were quick ones as Carl had taken over much of the newsstand before Sam's discharge ended his days of painting himself black, tan, and green and crawling on his belly through a desert mountain pass in search of prey.

Sam lowered the book entirely, stood up and extended his hand. "Hey, Carl. How's it going?"

"Good, Sam. How about yourself?"

"Alright."

"Minding the store?"

"Yea, minding the store."

"Ever need somebody to cover, just give me a holler."

"Thanks, Carl. I know. I've been able to keep the flap up pretty well."

"Done with the Marine stuff?"

"Army. I had enough."

"Don't fault you there. I don't think I could take all that marching and shit."

"Lots of marching," Sam said with a smile. "Still on the docks?"

"Still on the docks. Pays the rent, pretty much."

"How's your brother?"

"Mean as ever."

"Shit. He's too good a guy. He can't spell mean."

"I know it," Carl said as he rapped the back of his hand across the headlines of the *Tampa Tribune*. "Surprised they don't have that dead congressman on page one."

"Missed it. One of those things."

"Nobody reads the paper anymore."

"I hope a few keep reading. I've got to eat."

"Damn CNN is trying to starve you out, Sam."

"Taking food right out of my mouth, my friend. Right out of my mouth." Sam sat down, but kept his book in his lap.

Carl looked across the headlines and recounted what he'd heard of the missing story. "They said that asshole keeled over right in his driveway. Had a heart attack right on the news. Grabbed his chest and flopped around like one of those snook your old man use to catch off the mangroves. I guess he'd been tapping a bunch of little kids or some such bullshit."

"Doesn't sound like much of a loss. He might have got off easy."

"Ain't that the truth. Hey, Sam. You know, I must of heard twenty people say that same thing at the diner this morning. Everybody was saying, 'Oh, they should of cut off his pecker,' or 'Put his nuts in a vise.' 'Ram a pipe up his ass.' All kinds of stuff, you know, for messing around with kids."

"Sounds about right."

"Help me out here, Sam, because this is where things get screwy. Seems everybody always wants to pound these guys, but nothing ever happens to them. Nothing! A bunch of times there's been headlines right here – right on this counter – where some politician gets caught and everybody throws up their hands. 'Kill the bastard!' But what happens? Nothing. A year later he's running for office again."

"What are you recommending, Carl? The guy's dead."

"Sure. This one's dead, but there's others. Lots of 'em. There'll be a new headline in a week. Bunch of assholes and thieves." Carl paused to allow his own thoughts to catch up. It had nothing to do with dramatic effect, but along with his next words, the impact on Sam was pronounced. "To those who much is given, much is expected."

"What?"

"'To those who much is given, much is expected.' Your dad told me that. I never really understood it, but it sounded smart. I memorized it. Impresses women. Your old man said it whenever something happened like with this congressman. I think I get it now. I'm getting older. Smarter. You get smarter when you get older."

On the outside little changed though Sam's eyes fell away from Carl as though following his words to the counter, the papers, and the ground below. Inside however, there had been a tiny muffled snap. Rattling around in Sam's head among the things he knew to do and the things he wished for, held tightly together by bookends of upbringing, training, and bearing, steeled a resolve to regain or contribute or something – some way to find meaning, direction, and purpose. His father's words wafted through him like a sour scent in his nose, the taste of a nickel in his mouth, and a low rumble like an elephant's inaudible roar in his head.

"To those who much is given, much is expected." It was no longer Carl, but Sam Sr. speaking to his son as clear as Carl at the counter.

Carl looked away from the missing headlines and over to Sam who was lost in thought and still listening to his father's voice.

"Hey, Sam? Sam." Carl snapped his fingers in front of his old friend as though trying to wake someone from a trance, but the snap was weak, more brushing skin than brisk crack. It was enough just the same, and Sam was pulled away from his father's echo, a position he was not yet ready to relinquish.

"What!" he yelled as he leaped up as though rudely woken from a sweet sleepy dream, as he nearly was.

"Whoa there, big fella," Carl said as he jumped back from Sam and the counter. "Just easing you back to earth. Looked like you were really out there somewhere. Sorry, man."

Sam looked at Carl then surreptitiously around the stand for a glimpse of the dead man who had carried his father's voice. There was nothing to see. Sam regained his traction and looked back across the newspapers. "Hey, Carl. Don't apologize. I'm the one who's sorry. I didn't mean to break on you like that."

Carl eased cautiously back to the counter. "You can scare somebody like that, man. Thirty inch neck and all that Marine Corps shit. I mean, what the hell?"

It was another moment before Carl was back to normal. Sam would not be normal again. A glimpse of where he was peeked out from the newsstand at Carl and frightened him more than Sam's sudden outburst just a minute before.

"Hey, Carl?" Sam said slowly and far too softly for his voice, his bulk, and for Carl. "Have you ever heard of a way to measure the dark?"

"Huh?"

"A way to measure darkness. You know, lights come in watts – sixty watts, seventy-five watts, a hundred."

"You need a three-way bulb?"

"No. Measure–"

"You said a sixty, seventy-five, and a hundred. That's a three-way."

"Listen a second," Sam said as he leaned closer to Carl and hunched over his hands as they tried to form a design or words or a motion that would convey the disjointed thought that was spilling from his mind. "Light can be measured. By watts... or by candlepower–"

"Oh, I got ya. I got one of those fancy ass spotlights. Says it's a million candlepower, or something like that. Maybe two million. Bright as hell, but it doesn't hold a charge for shit."

"That's it. Now, Carl, light is measured in number of candlepower. How do you measure darkness? If you can measure light, like your spotlight – how many candlepower – it seems to me you should be able to measure dark. What do you think?"

Carl thought seriously. "There's dark... then, like, there's dark as night. And I guess the darkest dark would be pitch black. You know, can't see your hand in front of your face dark. How's that?"

Sam seemed almost not to hear and was adrift. "I've been thinking. If you're in a room that is dark and you have a container of some sort that's closed up tight, but there's a candle in that container. You can't see it or the light it's giving off. So the room is dark. Then you open the container. All of a sudden the room isn't dark anymore. One single little candle pushes back a whole room of darkness. Got it?"

"Sure, Sam. I got that."

"Now, check this out, Carl. You're in that same room, except it's light, maybe just from one candle. Just enough to call it lit. Not bright dazzling light, but still light. And you've got that same container, but this time there's no candle in it and it's sealed up. What's in the container?"

Carl was lost. "Damned if I know."

Sam was almost impatient. "Dark, Carl. It's dark in there."

"Well, duh. No shit. It's dark in there 'cause it's all sealed up."

"Right. So what's in the container?"

"Nothing."

"No, Carl, there's dark in there. And if you open the container the light goes in and kicks the dark's ass. No more dark."

"Wait Sam. The first container, or whatever, had a candle in it. The second thing had nothing in it. It was empty. Yeah, so it's dark in there?"

"Right, just for argument's sake, let's say it's full of dark."

"Full of dark?"

"Full of dark."

"Full of dark."

Mental gears were slipping on both sides of the counter.

"Don't you get it? One candle can dispel an entire room of darkness, but darkness can't do a thing to light. And where there's darkness, I think all that it would take to end it is one candle. One person with one candle."

Carl was quiet again. He looked around. "Sam, we've been friends a long time and I've never heard you say anything like that."

"I've had time to do a lot of thinking lately," Sam said. "About what I should be doing now. I haven't really figured it out, but you reminded me of something."

Carl was as hesitant as before. "Oh, yeah? But I don't know what the hell you just said."

"That's alright, Carl. Thanks. You're a good friend."

"Damn right I am. But you know what? Clayton is the one you should tell your idea about sizing up dark and three-way bulbs. He's a smart sonofabitch. Damn, he knows a lot of shit. He's got a huge ass TV with a remote bigger than your book. He can turn a computer inside out on itself before it even knows the goddamn switch is on. He's smart as shit."

"Yea, maybe. I haven't seen him in a long time."

"Doesn't matter. Call him. He thinks a lot of you and your dad. Remember all of us running the streets peddling papers?"

"Long time ago."

"Yep, but friends is friends, Sam. I know I'm not as sharp as Clay, but I do know that much. Friends is friends. Remember that. I do."

"I will, Carl. I'll remember."

"Good."

"I've got some work to do on my light/dark thing–"

"That's right. But I'm telling you, Clayton is still cool with you."

Sam leaned back. The protective air that normally encompassed him and flowed out across the counter came over him again and covered his shoulders like a long overcoat. It had felt good to hear his words out loud, but having been given life, it was time to close down again.

Carl sensed the change right away. "Hey, I better run along. Good to see you, Sam. If you need somebody to cover the stand, let me know. If I ain't scheduled at the docks, I'd take a few hours. Couple extra bucks never hurt, you know?"

"Absolutely."

"Thanks, Sam. See ya around."

"Definitely."

Carl was about a half block away when he heard Sam calling him. He turned and saw the lumbering ex-Ranger loping up the sidewalk toward him and instantly admired the ripples in his arms and beneath his shirt.

"Hey, Carl. You know, I'm going to be taking a short trip, a little vacation in a week or so. Could you cover that quick?"

"You got the same number at the house? What's your cell? Carl asked as he pulled out his phone to record Sam's number.

"Same number at the house. Dad's."

"No cell?"

"No."

You don't have a cell phone?"

"I'm getting one."

"Clay can't go to the bathroom without his. He's a geek. About a week?"

"More or less."

"More or less... You don't know when you're going?"

"I've got an idea, but it's open ended. It's contingent on a few other things."

"No problem. Still cash? I don't need to be on no books, do I?"

"All cash."

"Cool. Thanks, man. And I'll tell Clay to get in touch about the dark thing."

"Thanks, Carl. I'll call you."

They drifted away in different directions – Carl to the docks beyond downtown and Sam back to the newsstand and a plan that was hatching rapidly. Sam was a candle of one he told himself. A candle of one could defeat an entire room of darkness. He would become a candle of one as soon as the next headline appeared. The transition had already begun. The thick veins in Sam's neck were bulging and his eyes narrowed. He'd taken on another assignment. He didn't know a parallel course already existed nearby.

———————

10

Neither Jack nor Petey knew where to start. What they did know was that they were hot onto something or someone and they didn't have a single clue to steer them in any particular direction. Instead, they were taking the sum of consequences and attempting to put together a five thousand piece puzzle with no edge pieces or corners. Any ideas they had may have been coincidence. But when Petey mentioned this fact – one of only a few facts they had and it of little value in the fledgling investigation – the notion was quickly waved off by Jack. He had a feeling growing inside his gut.

"Naw, Petey. There's something here. I can feel it. Too many coincidences add up to fact in these old bones. Things like criminals leaving themselves broke. The CEO's crowd 'changes its mind' and buys worthless stock and loses everything in a day after it took them years to steal it. And now this senator..."

"Congressman."

"Whatever the hell he is– was. This sorry sonofabitch flips himself in to the press then is so gassed up by it, he has a heart attack. Really, Petey? Answer one question for me. Just one. What the hell?"

There was a pause that left a smile on Marcus's face. "That was a question?"

"Well, yeah. 'What the hell?' That's a fair question."

"You have reached an all-time low in your assault on the English language."

"You're an ass, Petey. I swear to Christ. This is serious and it's going somewhere."

"Sorry, boss. I agree it's serious, but I'm not certain there's a connection between all this."

"Doesn't it strike you, Mr. Harvard, that criminals, thieves, and philandering baby raping politicos, are not prone to acts of charity or stupidity and stepping on their dicks when no one's chasing them?"

"There have been some peculiar turns around here of late, but Jack, come on, who are we dealing with? Like you said – criminals. No one ever said you had to be smart to qualify."

"Horseshit. You don't believe it as soon as you say it. Cut the crap and tell me what you make of all this."

Another pause, but this time no smile. Marcus sank into his usual chair in Jack's cluttered but comfortable office and looked beyond his boss to the bright skyline near the bay. He could see the big bridges rising toward the sky then vanishing as they dropped down beyond the midpoint – high enough to allow ships and sailors to pass beneath. He had nearly formed his thoughts with words when he was distracted by Jack poking him with a verbal sharp stick.

"C'mon, Petey! What do you think? Help me out here."

"Alright!" Marcus was loud and he was never loud. Jack had forced a burr under his saddle and backed him into a corner whose walls were made up of the 'peculiar turns,' as he himself had just described them. "Alright," softer now. "I'll pacify you," he said as he glanced up at Jack who had been glaring from behind his desk. Marcus returned to the bridges, the sunlight, and the glistening water of the bay. "For argument's sake. Let's presume there to be a connection, and note I said 'presume' not assume. There's a difference, though its subtlety is no doubt lost on you."

"I know the difference, wise ass. Make your case, prosecutor."

There was another short lull as Marcus bit his upper lip and pierced the window of the office with his eyes though they were no longer seeing the sun bouncing on the bay. Instead they were running down a list of scenarios that had been formulating in his mind since Jack's phone call. "No one does the things we have witnessed without cause."

"True. That's true," Jack said as though trying to prime a slow churning pump.

"From a purely investigative point of view, who has motive? Who benefits from all these instantly righteous criminals? Certainly not them."

"Not them," Jack echoed as though coaxing a kitten from a tree.

"Not them," Marcus continued. "The only person I can come up with who has motive in all these cases is... is us."

It was Jack's turn to linger, but only long enough for his brow to furrow deeper than it always was and his mouth to curl up as though he'd just taken a bite out of bad stew.

"Us? Us what? Us, as in us are the bad guys?"

Marcus couldn't stifle the laugh, but he hid it in his answer. "No, not you and me, but someone like us. If anything, it's a cop, or a prosecutor, maybe a judge — someone who knows the law, has seen it denigrated and decided enough is enough."

"A rogue cop, huh?"

"It's a maybe, Jack. Who else knows what we know, has access to what we see, and can get to these guys? It has to be a person in authority who has access to the info, then can present himself, sort of like a quid-pro-quo plea deal and say, 'Do this and you skate on the superior charge,' or 'Do that and maybe a charge goes away, evidence disappears.' Something like that."

"Okay," Jack said slowly, thinking as he relaxed, stood, and walked around his desk. "That works. That works. Cop gets fed up — can't blame them for that. Knows about our casework, might even be in on the pop and decides to take matters into his own hands. Probably lost a few big cases on technicalities and says, 'Not this one.' Chop-blocks the sonofabitch and takes their knees out. Know what I mean, Petey?"

"You had me up until the chop-block something or other."

"Football, Petey. Football. Watch the game instead of the cheerleaders sometime. You want to take a guy down? Maybe for the rest of his career? You block him real low, at the knees. Snaps 'em. ACLs and MCLs can't take it. Snap a ligament like cheap string. The guy's out for the rest of the season."

"Good to know. Now how are you going to ferret out our phantom cop?"

Jack was smiling as he returned to his desk. He sat down, got comfortable then leaned way back and heavily dropped his feet on the desk, scooting papers, some tearing, under his leather heels. "Might not."

"Might not what?" Marcus questioned as he leaned forward, caught his own anxious move, and settled back too late.

"Might not try to catch him. He's doing a helluva public service, if you ask me."

"No one is asking you, Jack, and you'll need a better quip than that for the reporters or they'll turn on you so fast you won't get elected dog catcher."

"Relax, Petey. Jesus, you're wound up tight. This is a stressful job, you know? Young fella like you gets all wound around a simple case, doesn't do his heart and mind any good at all."

"And?"

"Okay. Okay. Let's put our heads together and decide how we want to handle this thing. You're right. It might be nothing. Then again, might be something. Let's flip over a few rocks and see what comes scurrying out. Why not start out with the case files on the local shitbirds we got here.

See if they've got any common enemies or if any personnel's names shows up in all the cases. Let's check the State level too."

"And you?"

"I'm going over town and have a chat with my boy at the Federal Office. They'll have the lowdown on the senator."

"Congressman."

"Whatever–," Jack began, but Marcus helped him finish.

"–the hell he is."

"Ha! Now you're starting to think like an elected law enforcement official."

"Or at least talk like one."

"Just a touch of the common man, my friend. The common man. That's how he talks."

"Maybe the common man on the docks, but I don't think he votes too often."

"I'm on my fourth term. Somebody's voting right."

"Or somebody's fooling them all."

"By God, but you're sassy. Why the hell I don't fire you escapes me."

"True love."

"I think it's pity."

Marcus enjoyed a last glance at the distant bay, slapped his thighs and stood up. "Well, I'd love to sit here and point out all the reasons why you keep me around – like making you look good, saving your job, buying your drinks – but I've got to go chase down a wild goose for my boss."

Marcus had said it with a soft smile – a carryover from the rest of the bantering – but a weak pale came over Jack and now it was his turn to look to the water.

"Hey, partner. Give it to me straight up. Is this a wild goose chase? Tell me. I get so damn worked up about this job I suppose I could go off half-cocked now and again. Probably that's the real reason I keep you on – you pull the reins in on me – the voice of reason."

Marcus didn't jerk the reins at all. If the bit was in Jack's teeth, it'd stay there. Jack had proved himself right more times than anyone could remember. It wasn't the language – from a florist to a butcher – that kept Jack in office. It was dogged skill and a mind that saw the pieces of the puzzle before most others had the lid off the box. So Marcus shoved his hands deep into his pockets and hunched his shoulders.

"I don't know, Jack. I truly don't. Certainly bears a look. Let's flip a few of those rocks of yours and see what we find."

Jack was refreshed and instantly buoyant. "Just see what we see. If there's nothing, we'll move on and fry some other fish, but by God it sure sounds interesting. Imagine that – one of our own out there as a vigilante."

"Has all the markings."

"You bet it does. Hey, get at those files, will you? Why you hanging around here? You're cramping my style. I got to get over town. If somebody's name comes up in more than one file, give me a shout." He was walking fast out his own door. "See you for supper." Before Marcus could finish shaking his head, Jack was back in the doorway. "And bring some money this time. I'm going broke pouring liquor down your throat. Where we going?"

"Quinn's at five-thirty."

"Quinn's at five-thirty. Don't be late."

Marcus' hands were still buried in his pockets when he drifted up the hall to his own office. He slipped into his own chair and stirred the computer to life. The hard drive whined and whirled as the screensaver of the Hillsborough County Seal vanished. He tabbed, typed, and entered his way through the log-in process and verified manual and internal passwords before he was at the case files for the last quarter. A search and the case files began to electronically pour out. Scrolling, clicking, pointing, and more clicking, highlights, searches, screens, and filters. It took several hours, but when the files were being returned to their e-cabinets there were only two common names from the cases on Marcus's simple yellow pad and even those had no connection to the dead congressman. The names were his and Jack Aaron. It seemed the wild goose had just had its head cut off.

"C'mon, Jack, you know better than to ask me that." The speaker was Calburn Denti, Special Agent in charge of the Tampa area office of the Federal Bureau of Investigation. Cal was as seasoned a cop as Jack, but carried it better. He was an articulate and dapper Sherlock Holmes to Jack's crumpled Lt. Colombo. Like Jack, he was on the backside of a long productive career, but also like Jack, there remained a lot of fight in him yet and calculating savvy to spare. He was thinner over the length of him than his surprise guest, especially through the face, which would have appeared gaunt on a less streamlined frame. His light tan suit was much more fashionable than Jack's dated clothes and the crease of his pants razor sharp. The shirt was FBI white. The cuffs were heavily starched and held in place by black and gold cufflinks which bore the Bureau's seal. Over all the finery, Cal's hair was totally gray like Jack's, but shorter and sharply styled. He claimed his gray hair was a memorial to the job. Past years had witnessed numerous attempts to color, dye, highlight, disguise and masquerade, but they had given way to simple acceptance and a balance that suited him as neatly as the crisp white collar.

"Don't ask again. I mean it this time."

"I won't. Christ, you're touchy," Jack whined as he paced around Cal's oversized office and absently flipped open a manila folder resting at the corner of the desk.

"And you're not supposed to be reviewing those files either," Cal answered, trying to be serious, but unable to hide the farce of it all as he reached over and closed the folder.

"Okay. Okay. I won't ask nothing. I won't touch nothing," Jack said holding up his hands as though it was true. "Just tell me what is it about this pedophile old bastard that's got your ass in a pucker?"

"How about the United States Congress for starters. Hell, Jack, it's not even in my region and they're pulling us into it. Orlando's swamped because of it. They're not doing anything else. I've got TSA cases at the airport, a sting going down at the docks, illegal Mexicans, Cubans crossing the Straits on rafts, the Vice-President comes to town in three weeks, plus the usual smugglers, horse and dog dopers, and all the crap you send me."

"Nobody gives a shit about the Vice-President. And since when do I send you crap? Hell, you made senior grade off my cases."

"Your cases... One of your whims in the middle of the night hardly constitutes a case."

"You sound like Petey. But listen a second. Lots of those have turned out to be what I said, right?"

"A couple–"

"There you go. That's what's got me thinking there's something here that don't add up. These sonsabitches don't pack it in on their own. You know it too, Cal. C'mon. What's the deal with the stiff in the driveway sending all the evidence to the TV station?"

Cal sat back hard in his chair, as though exasperated, which he was not. He held his hands out, palms up, in a feigned state of resignation. "Did I just say something or was that somebody else?"

"C'mon, Cal."

"Why I let you in my office remains a constant source of wonder for me."

"Bemusing, isn't it?"

"Now I know that's not your word. You stole that from Marcus. I'm certain of it."

"Cal... The senator?"

"Congressman."

There was a delay that silently asked if Jack was truly pursuing an official investigation or merely satisfying an old cop's curiosity. The tenet of the dialogue changed as Jack fielded the unasked question and expounded on the reasoning he had flippantly mentioned when he first walked into the Regional FBI complex.

"I've got a feeling, Cal. I won't deny it's thin, but there's some solid facts behind it. Understood, the connection is damn loose, but it's there – even if there's no other reason than the cock-eyed way all these things are playing out."

"Keep going."

"These local shitbirds. There is no way they were all of a sudden going to wake up and smell the coffee. Hell, we hadn't even got the coffee on the stove yet. I mean, Cal, we hadn't had a single hearing. They didn't, we didn't, even know what the charges would be by the time we got to trial." Jack walked a little, back and forth in front of the desk, and let his eyes wander around the room. He searched the floor for the elusive reasons he needed.

"It's quite a jump from a county commissioner to a congressman, Jack. You see that, correct?"

"I do. I do. But here's the similarity. Both guys were politicos, know what I mean? I know, I know, there's a helluva gap between them, but that's their business – politics."

"Okay. One point."

"There's more."

"I hope so."

"Every one of them had been indicted, but that's all. No actual charges, you know what I mean? Hell we can indict a ham sandwich if we want – the formal charges for trial were a long way off."

"Point two, but a weak one. Damn weak."

"No argument. But stick with me a minute. No one is hot on these guys, Cal. That's where I'm going. It's not like we're beating down the front door so they have to jump out the window. You know how these things play out and so does everybody else. White collar crap. Lots of play in the papers. Then when all's said and done, a fine and probation. Happens in ninety-nine percent of these things. Some sonofabitch steals a million dollars and he gets community service and probation. Same schmuck steals twenty bucks from a convenience store and he gets ten years. You know the routine."

"There are generally a number of mitigating circumstances, Jack, and you know that routine."

"True enough."

"What else do you have? Tell me you have more than this."

"What I have is a group of assholes who are fighting to give away the proceeds of years of theft without an incentive to do so. They gain nothing by it. They're still headed to trial. Still going to get convicted. Might even get more time because of all the notoriety around them and the money trail they left for us. If they'd laid low, things would have taken their course, they'd have pled to lesser charges, paid their fines, and had it reported on page fourteen somewhere. Instead, they give away all their money and force themselves into the headlines. It's too much. It's just too much."

Cal was thinking and in those thoughts were seeds of consideration. "How's the dead congressman fit into all this? He's not even near Tampa – had nothing to do with anything in your jurisdiction."

Jack smiled for the first time in several minutes. "Right you are, Mr. FBI guy. But even you know something wasn't right in that driveway. Admit it, Cal. No sonofabitch does what he did. Nobody sends incriminating evidence to the press. Not even the biggest nut cases we've ever had. Not when they're still breathing free man's air."

Cal pushed back from his desk and stood. He turned his back to his friend and stared out over Tampa Bay. Jack waited and wondered. He wiped the beads of sweat from his upper lip, wanted to speak again, but didn't because he had nothing else to say. In another moment he silently drifted to a distant chair, sat quietly, and leaned back as a slouch weighed him down. Across the room, Cal stretched his shoulders in small circles and slowly twisted his head and neck to relieve a slight ache.

Following a sigh Jack couldn't have heard, Cal turned back to the room and took up a position in his chair behind his desk. He leaned forward, adjusted his cufflinks, folded his hands in front of him and looked Jack straight in the eyes. As though drawn up from his slouch by the invitation of the stare, Jack sat up slowly until he was the picture of perfect posture.

"The congressman's dirty pictures were sent to the press," Cal began slowly. "That part you've gotten right. But we don't think he sent them."

Jack bolted to the edge of the chair and left behind any decorum. "I knew it!"

"Relax," Cal continued. "The timing is really a puzzle. We know when the emails came into the news stations, but the congressman was already in the driveway chatting up the press."

"His old lady!" Jack jumped. "She finds out she's married to a pedophile and sends the shit to the press to bury the bastard. Not realizing she really would bury him."

"No good."

"Why?"

"The congressman's computer didn't have a hard drive in it when we searched his house. We found it in his briefcase. In the driveway. He had it with him when he died."

"So..., she has her own."

"We checked. The pictures weren't on hers. Understandably."

"No shit?"

"No shit. Our guys have been tearing into it and everything on his system at home, at his office, everywhere. Nothing. Oh, we found all the pictures and all the bullshit emails he had sent and received since he created an account, but we wouldn't have it without that hard drive in his briefcase. It was with the body – adjacent to... you know the law. Having it, gave us probable cause for our warrants. If the press hadn't gotten those emails and pictures, we'd have been a long time scaring up a warrant. Even with all that, we have no idea what happened before that hard drive got pulled out of that tower. We can't find a single thing."

Jack's naiveté showed and he didn't try to hide it. "What does that mean, 'you can't find a thing?'"

Though Cal was following at only a measurable distance in his own understanding, he did carry the results of a briefing which had been completed moments before Jack arrived. "There's no point in saying I know for a fact when I truly don't. Hell, Jack, I'm like you. If I can get to my email, I'm having a good day. The guys who use to wear the pocket protectors and have taped up thick black glasses are now running the world–"

"And driving BMWs."

"And driving BMWs. They tell me that a couple of things could have happened. One is that the congressman sent all that crap himself, but it took a few minutes to load or download or whatever it has to do to get through the router or cable or however it gets from point A to point B, because of all the pictures." Cal was exacerbated by his short comings in the field. He got up and stomped across the room. His hands flew up and down grasping for straws and coming up empty. "I don't know what they're talking about. But regardless, the congressman had a ton of porn on his computer and it would have taken a while to send it out. Somehow, that's scenario number one – a major delay from when he sent it, pulled his hard drive, and went to the driveway."

"And two?"

Cal baulked. "I'm going to sound just like you. And that's the only reason I'm telling you this. Only someone who reasons the way you do would be able to make sense out of this."

"If you're thinking like me, chances are you might become a good cop yet."

"You want to compare old cases, don't you? Look for more like these?"

"No," Jack played off his exact want. "But I'd like a peek at your paycheck later."

"Money's not a very good indicator of professional prowess."

"I said 'a good cop,' not a rich one, but we'll go over paystubs when the check comes after lunch."

Cal came up short and diverted his attention from the thin line he'd been following to the day minder on his desk. "Do we have a lunch scheduled?" he asked seriously as he opened his calendar.

"Not really, but next time."

"Let me know," Cal said as he slammed his calendar closed. "So I can plan to be busy."

"Sure thing. How about right now you finish filling me in on option two?"

"Obviously this stays here, Jack. Even the geeks in IT haven't got all the answers – they talk mostly about possibilities." Cal paused again, still trying to get his arms around the briefing. "Apparently, they tell me, if someone knew how... I guess they could get into your computer and do... do whatever."

"With no hard drive in it?"

"If everything is on the cloud."

"The clouds? What the hell are you talking about?"

"Servers. Data storage. A snapshot of everything you do on your computer. Maybe–"

"Maybe?"

"I don't know, Jack, and neither do our tech guys. But they did tell me one thing that they were absolutely certain about."

"Wow. A certainty. Haven't seen one of them since I walked in here."

"That's exactly what I told them, but they said that in no uncertain terms, if we start working this option two–"

"I don't think there should be an 'if' in the same sentence as 'a certainty,' but I'm not an English major."

"I agree, but this is what I've got. You want it or you want me to follow Bureau protocol and shut up?"

Jack's answer was on his face and in his eyes.

"I thought so. Anyway, here's what they tell me. If... If we go with that second option and start trying to scratch out a lead or two, it will start or end with one clever sonofabitch. Our guys are top shelf, Jack. We've got the sharpest computer people in the country working for us. They can tell me in two minutes what website you were on five years ago at twenty-three minutes after four in the afternoon on July eighteenth. They can go backward. They can go to a website and tell me if Jack Aaron was ever there and when and for how long. Then they'll tell me what you wrote about it in an email or some note you jotted down or a tweet or posted on Facebook. They can tell me every keystroke you ever made on your computer since you took the thing out of the box. But they can't see what happened with the congressman's naughty pictures."

Cal took a breath and Jack joined him. They recognized that this new front on crime had taken them far away from the element they knew. Each was tentative. Each was afraid of the unknown and of losing control. They were already in trouble and they hadn't even begun.

"Any chance they'll still find something?"

"I suppose," Cal offered in resignation as he lowered himself back into his chair, signaling Jack to resume his slouch. "They're still at it, but if it's not there, I guess it's just not there. I don't know. But that's what we've got. Not much, Jack. Hope I didn't burst your bubble."

Jack stood up. Not fast, as though shot from a gun or energized beyond what the chair could hold, but sharply enough to tell Cal that he'd somehow struck a chord.

"You did just the opposite, my friend. I love you Bureau types. Sharp as tacks. That's the part Petey and me weren't seeing. Some wizard vigilante is running around trying to clean up the world."

"Sounds like."

"So, Cal, do we catch this guy or let him run awhile?"

"Come again?"

"Do you really want to loose the hounds of hell on a guy who's doing the things we'd like to be able to do?"

"Jack. Tell me this is one of your sad attempts at satire."

"To tell the God's honest truth, Cal, I don't really know what satire is. I'll run it by Petey. We're going for drinks at Quinn's around five or so. Come out with us."

"How about the congressman? And those hunches of yours? And tell me again that it's your job to catch bad guys, not look the other way."

Jack walked to the door and opened it. He was leaning heavily on the knob. "Maybe this guy ain't so bad, Cal. Maybe he ain't so bad."

"It's a crime to hack into someone's computer."

"I understand that, but hell, you know what I mean. And you know I don't mean anything by it."

"This is interesting. I'll grant you that. We've got somebody with that kind of smarts devoting himself to being a caped crusader, so to speak."

"Like Batman, you mean?" Jack suggested.

"Like Batman, but not quite."

"How, not quite?"

"As I remember my comics, Batman used to punch a guy in the mouth from time to time. Our guy doesn't do that."

"At least not yet."

"I'd rather he did. He'd be easier to find if he exists at all."

"He's out there," Jack said plainly.

"Maybe. Probably. But if he slugged somebody we'd have a body to chase down. Contact makes for an easy chase, you know that. This guy, like I said, if he exists, and I'm not certain he does or where and how, he doesn't get within ten feet, ten miles – maybe a hundred or a thousand miles. A person like that might be overseas for crying out loud. It's going to be tricky."

"You're with me though, right, Cal? You're seeing the connection?"

"Not entirely, but I do see where your hunch originates."

Jack was satisfied. "Let me know what your geek squad squeezes out of those discs and drives and whatnot, will you?"

"Will do. What are you planning to do with all your new found knowledge?"

"Cop stuff. Knock on doors. Flip over a few rocks. Pound the pavement."

"You do remember that you're the District Attorney, not a detective?"

"Sure. Sure. I like to keep my cop license current – play with the lights and siren in my car."

Calburn smiled. "I'm afraid that won't get you far with this one. This one's going to be cracked by one of those boys with the pocket protectors."

"Maybe. But I got a few more hunches I'm already working into a lather."

"You sharing?"

"Let me put a little flesh on their bones first."

"I showed you my cards. You should put yours down, don't you think?" Cal wasn't pushing hard and smiled again.

"Ha! Probably scare the shit out of you. I'll just say, our boy ain't done yet. He's really, really good at this. You said so yourself. Somebody that good at something isn't going to stop just because the congressman's toes curled up."

"Your rock flipping, that might scare him a bit. He could go underground. He's picked up a body now, albeit indirectly. He might hold up in the Bat Cave for a while and decide if scaring people to death – literally – was what he signed up for."

"The Bat Cave. I like that. He's holding up in the Bat Cave. I'll tell Petey that one. He'll get it right off."

"Tell him I said hello and ask him when's he going to apply to the Bureau. We'd take him in a heartbeat."

"I know. You tell him every time you see him."

"What's stopping him? Great benefits, retirement, gets to work with me. No downside I can see."

"I think it's the working with you part."

"Hardly."

"Nothing personal, Cal, but if Petey was working with you, he wouldn't be working with me. You're a smart guy. Figure it out. And call me if you come up with anything on your dead congressman."

That was Jack's goodbye. Cal took it in stride and settled back to his desk. He tugged at his cuffs out of habit then hit the speaker button on his phone. When the dial tone clicked in he punched a speed dial number, heard a single ring then a male voice pick up.

"Forensics. Agent Meyer."

"It's Cal Denti in Tampa. Anything new on the congressman?"

"Sorry, Agent Denti. It's as clean as a whistle. If he did it himself, he should have retired from politics and gone into programming."

"And if he didn't?"

There was a pause that lingered. "Then we're chasing a ghost."

11

Blue and white sneakers with silver accents flashed by in alternating strides beneath Clayton as he ran up the wide sidewalk that paralleled Bayshore Boulevard. To the right, he was separated from the waters of Tampa Bay by ancient concrete columns that squatted low and carried a wide elegant mantle for a hat. Between the rush and hum of passing cars, Clayton heard the water kissing the seawall as gentle wakes from boats long since passed commingled with the changing tide. To the left, across the manicured divided thoroughfare, rested a wide row of houses so prim and proper they looked as if they'd just fallen from the pages of *Architectural Digest*. Each stately mansion rose, ruled, then gave ground to the next while the progression gained in splendor as the numbers on the houses signaled they and Clayton were nearing the city. In another mile the towering buildings of downtown began to block out the early morning rays of sun. The shadows were long and low and in a matter of strides encompassed Bayshore, Clayton, and everything around them. The brim of Clayton's hat did its job against the low slung sun and made the transition to shade easy. Apart from an occasional dodge to avoid another runner, walker, skater or biker, the morning's run had been uneventful. It was another beautiful, warm, brightly lit, sparkling day.

The rhythm of the run kept an easy metronome's pace for Clayton's thoughts. They flirted with the recent death of the congressman, but abandoned him quickly. They did not reach back to any of the others, instead finding contentment beneath the process of accomplishments tallied thus far. Following his capture by the morning shadows, Clayton began to review an unwritten list of persons and events which seemed acceptable candidates for his unique intervention. There was a local police officer who had been picked up for DUI, but he was hardly worth retaining. One promising character in this one sided play was a principal who redefined 'high' school by buying dope in his office and getting stoned while his charges strolled the halls just beyond the door. "He's worthy of a good ass whipping," Clayton smiled.

The smile was wiped away by a tight look that shielded a question which had begun to plague him the last several days. The concern was whether or not he – in corporate speak – could take his initiative national. The notion had been sparked by one of those infamous twenty-two seconds long, fifteen minutes of fame splashes that passed for the nightly news. The Mayor of San Francisco had hit the trifecta of politics as usual – corruption, campaign money, and concubines. He'd been caught with his pants down – literally. The good mayor was reportedly having simultaneous affairs with two different employees while claiming strict allegiance to his marriage vows. Clayton felt a sincere heartfelt impulse for the beleaguered wife, but moreover, wondered how a man was attending to the affairs of a large, vibrant, metropolitan city while servicing two mistresses and managing a wife and family. "Affairs and affairs," he thought and the smile returned.

The scandal had surfaced after a house of cards surrounding a campaign financing fiasco fell and exposed bribery, corruption, and collusion in its wake. The infidelity was the least criminally culpable, but was lingering in Clayton's mind and served as the flash point for his disdain.

Several gray blocks of concrete passed as Clayton toyed with the idea of the philandering, thieving mayor. "How many meetings did he miss while he was pile driving a secretary against a file cabinet? How many line items in the budget did he overlook while his mind and/or his hands were on some woman's ass? Did he charge the hotel room to the city?" Expense account. Entertainment. "The price of holding the office," he'd tell his wife. "Late nights come with being the mayor, honey," he'd decry then slip off for a piece of ass while she put the kids to bed. He'd grab a quick blow job in the back seat of the mayor's limo while his police officer driver adjusted the rearview mirror away, turned up the radio, and took a few extra unreported days off. After the mobile tryst, his Hon. Mr. Mayor would emerge, pants zipped, none the worse for wear, at the First Presbyterian Church for a photo op, ribbon cutting, or a fund raiser. And all the while, the city was relying on itself as the mayor cashed his payroll checks and lauded himself for juggling three women, billing the city for his trouble, and taking no-bid contract kickbacks in envelopes stuffed with cash.

"If a man will lie to and cheat on his own wife – a woman he vowed to love always – and neglect his children, what will he do to a mere job he also took with a vow?" The answer was obvious to Clayton. This wasn't about morality or the sanctity of marriage, but that did serve as a marvelous point of contrast. Clayton's problem with the Mayor was the abandoning of the personal and political oaths for private gain. "To those whom much is given..," but now he had to figure out a way to get the Mayor's goat. He could transfer all the money to the wife. Not a bad start. Shuffle some funds under the control of the Mayor's office and tip off the press. That'd rile him up. It would insure the California investigators had all the evidence they needed. Go after the financiers, the bribing businessmen, even the cheating women. Turn up the heat on all of them.

Several more sidewalk slabs passed under the prancing sneakers as Clayton picked up his pace to match his darkening mood. The smiles were totally gone now. What he really wanted to do was bitch slap him. The pace increased as he considered going beyond the man's checkbook. What a thrill it'd be to snap him up by the scruff of his neck and give him a good shake like Clayton and Carl's old dog used to do to woodchucks who were too slow or too distant from their burrows. He'd take them by the back of their neck and crack them the length of their bodies as smoothly as a whip then drop them, crouch, and stare at the corpse, hoping it would run or at least twitch. Clayton was running hard, panting, much like the dog he was remembering.

But it wouldn't happen. The pace tailed off. The Mayor was twenty-five hundred miles away. The stride broke and Clayton stumbled awkwardly to a winded walk. He wasn't going to California and if he did, he knew full well that he wasn't the snapping-up-by-the-scruff-of-the-neck kind of guy.

The walk slowed further then drew up and Clayton turned toward the glistening bay and leaned heavily on the old concrete mantle. Like so many others, he stared at the thousand twinkling sparks of reflecting light for answers. The water whispered as it struck the seawall beneath him. It had nothing profound for Clayton to hear, yet the gentle rhythm of the water's soft caress was relaxing and shunned away the anger, violence, and disappointment from Clayton's mind. In the quieted reasoning reflection, he uncovered the solution he'd been chasing. There would be no baseball bat to the head. There would only be, for now, a simple throwback to a decade earlier – before email gained a foothold. Clayton would write the mayor a letter – something more than the anonymous email warning he'd used before. There on the concrete banister, he began to doodle with his finger – signing a name, or perhaps a slogan that would represent the new cause and the demand for ethics, honesty, integrity, and right mindedness. His finger traced out stars and circles, even a crucifix on the stone, but the invisible figures didn't linger on the rock face or with him. They weren't right for the purpose, but he did begin to fashion the words of the letter itself.

Clayton stared again into the twinkling waves.

"To the Honorable Mayor of the City of San Francisco." Already Clayton recognized the flaw. He would have to send the mayor's letter to his personal mailbox or he'd never see it. Even sending it to the mayor's home, there would be a chance someone else might divert it from the guilty party's hand. A new idea hatched on the fly amid the gentle waves under Clayton's gaze. He remembered what prompted the recently dead congressman's descent – an open letter.

"Sure, there'd be challenges," he reasoned to himself as the plan grew legs. "But a click here and there and it'd be in the electronic typeface of the *San Francisco Chronicle.* 'Mr. Mayor: You can't be doing your job and doing a secretary at the same time.' Something along that line."

Contented so easily and quickly, Clayton pushed off the old concrete like a ship edging away from a pier. He began to turn away from the bay slowly, as though reluctant to leave the place that had been so fertile for his new plan. All that remained was to compose the letter and crack the newspaper's firewalls. Neither would take much effort. Clayton rapped his knuckles gently on the concrete railing with his fist as if pointing out an empty plate after a wondrous meal. "That was good," he mused. "That was good." And he began to jog away.

A half hour later Clayton was stepping out of a hot shower. The towel roughly dried his hair then his fingers combed it smooth enough. He tossed the towel over the glass door of the shower to dry before he moved with purpose to his bedroom. A quick rummage through a tall dresser produced a non-descript well-worn t-shirt and a pair of faded sweat pants with a frayed hem on one leg. He pulled on the comfortable clothes quickly, nearly losing his balance as his foot caught in the ragged fray of the sweats. He was dressing as though he was late for work. To him, he was late and the simple clothes were standing in the way of what he wanted to be doing which was penning the letter he had concocted by the bay. He pulled a pair of short topped socks from the dresser and flopped onto a loveseat at the foot of his bed to complete his outfit for the day. Once the socks were close to being in place, he left the room quickly and slapped the light switch as he passed, leaving the room as it had been. In a matter of a few seconds he was in his favorite perch at the computer.

The power up took a few moments as always, while the soft blue lights twinkled a welcome, the drives whirled. The wide monitor sprang to life and waited to confirm Clayton's directions. His desktop icons popped up in unison signaling all systems go. He could cruise the internet for the news, sports scores, or music. Maybe open a spread sheet from the office and set in motion a vast number of computations that would run without human intervention through the entire day and reveal stacks of data with no effort on Clayton's part. But that wasn't even close to the intent in his mind. He was going to compose his letter from the scenes he had glimpsed at the concrete railing.

The letter, his public message to the mayor, would be simple in its format and design, but grave in its message. It occurred to him that there could be collateral effects – that was the hope. Others who shared a similar line of work as the big city mayor whose pants couldn't stay up, might make a note of their own false lives. While they might be appropriate recipients of such a message or such a warning, this wasn't their time. Clayton would ply this use of the media as an experiment. He'd analyze the resulting data as he would any other program, measure the outcome then decide on his next tact.

So the words began their soulful journey through his mind down his arms and out the tips of his fingers.

> *Mr. Mayor: We see you. We see what you've done and what you are. We watch you neglect the business of our city while you satisfy yourself with women who are not your wife and fund your sin with the taxpayers' money, misappropriated campaign contributions, and bribes. Your pathetic confession is dust in the wind. You are sorry to be sure, but you are not sorry for what you did. You are sorry you were caught.*
>
> *Admit this. Admit this and pay the city back 100% of your pay from the last twenty-four months. Donate the bribery funds to local charities. Consider these punitive and compensatory damages due the city and for misconduct as an elected official. If not, retribution will be sudden.*
>
> *If a man will lie and cheat the woman he professes to love above all else (a quote from your teary confession), what will he do to us, mere citizens, a million in number who you do not even know? What will you do to us to satisfy yourself?*
>
> *Pay the city back what you have stolen by not tending to the needs of the mayor's office. Beg your wife's forgiveness. Resign. Fade away and leave the business of our city to someone who can reason beyond base impulses.*
>
> *You cannot draw a line between the public man and the private when the public man abuses his privileges.*
>
> *Remember, Mr. Mayor, to those whom much is given, much is expected. We see you and will be both swift and severe. Time is short. Do the right thing. And do it quickly.*

Clayton relaxed and his hands fell away from the keyboard. He pulled his shoulders back and stretched as he took a deep breath that was nearly involuntary. He didn't re-read what he could see on the screen, rather, he played and re-played, as though forwarded in time, the reaction of the Mayor as he read the words Clayton had penned just for him. A hand crept up slowly and triggered the mouse. The screen scrolled quickly by and Clayton now read his words in earnest as the wayward mayor and a million others would in the font of the *San Francisco Chronicle*.

The plan had evolved into something tight. But Clayton still toyed with a slogan or perhaps a symbol that would punctuate the open letter, encapsulate his efforts, or provide a rallying cry for like-minded citizenry. As on the concrete railing hours before, he began to doodle, but this time he used pen and paper. He managed squares with circles in and half out – zigzagged lines across some unknown backdrop – but nothing clicked, nothing stood out. Then a triangle lingered empty on the page. A small circle went inside then crept first to the sides then to the top in the last rendition. There was a pause in his hand, a noticeable shiver in his spine.

Clayton stared for a moment at his latest handiwork then pushed away from the desk and returned quickly in his stocking feet to his bedroom. From the nightstand he retrieved the sterling money clip set there an hour before. The clip slipped off beneath his hand and he rifled through the currency which was wrapped over his driver's license and a single credit card. He set the plastic aside and continued leafing through the money for what he was after – a simple one dollar bill. There was none. He scanned the twenties and the sole ten and even the front and back of the couple of hundreds he kept for his father's sake. "Always good to have some walkin' 'round money. Just in case," he'd said many times. Today one needed hard currency less and less and 'walkin' 'round money' was as easily plastic as green.

Clayton, like so many others, had all but given up on straight currency long ago. He had reverted to plastic cards with their speed and simplicity, but generally there were a few bits of folding money in the clip for parking and bottles of water from machines and the testament to his father. There was cash, but not what he was after. The C notes were worthless at the moment. Clayton looked over the bills again. There was something there, he reasoned, that his simple sketch had brought to mind, but he needed desperately to hold it and see it for himself. He needed a One.

His search was becoming a bit too frantic. He brought himself up short of throwing things out of his dresser drawers like a character in a Three Stooges film. Quite literally he flopped on his bed and thought. Like many other people, he had squirreled away a few dollars here and there –

tucked in books and the back of drawers in case an event should catch him unaware and distanced from an ATM. He had to think differently for a moment. Money was seldom on his mind. He lived by that single card. Personal hand-written checks were a thing of the past except for Carl. Cash seemed almost a forgotten relic. It was another long moment, spent in contemplation of where he had tucked a few dollars for Girl Scout cookies and the like. He didn't have the proverbial cookie jar to raid and cold cash in the freezer was something left for corrupt congressmen – something that instantly sparked a mental note to revisit as the overall schematic of his agenda continued to unfold in the coming days, weeks, and months.

Clayton fingered again the twenties and hundreds in his hands – flipping them over and over – searching until he tossed them aside as if they were worthless scraps. He stood, hands on hips and turned to survey the room. The nightstands, the dressers, the couch – without rummaging he knew they held nothing. Dejected, he walked out, leaving the money clip on the dresser and the cash strewn across the bed.

He meandered rather aimlessly down the long hall past the empty spare bedrooms glancing in each as though they held an answer. In the spacious foyer his eye caught a marble topped table and his steps quickened. The small antique table with its gleaming white top with grayish steaks held just three items. There was a small lamp that a timer told to turn on and off at given hours. And there was the hand turned wooden bowl, brought home from one business trip of many to a country in South America he'd long forgotten. The bowl caught his keys each time Clayton came in the door and guarded them until he was ready to leave again. The third item gave the appearance of some foreign and exotic blue ceramic vase, but in fact had been purchased stateside, not many miles distant. It was a simple piece of clay pottery – the shape of a quart-sized pitcher replete with handle and spout. The color faded from steel blue at the rim to earthy brown at the base which matched the wood of the table and led to its purchase. Although the piece began life in Clayton's home as an ornament of sorts, its place on the table advanced it to a position of functionality on its first day of service. Immediately it began to collect the change that occasionally weighed Clayton's pockets as he entered his home. Along with the coinage, Clayton remembered he often dropped in dollar bills that proved excessive in the limit of his money clip.

Clayton went to the pitcher and picked it up to see inside. The weight surprised him, but he wasn't disappointed. His fingers scarcely scratched the top of the silver and brown coins before revealing the paper he was searching for. It was a single dollar bill wedged between the tightly packed coins. Clayton caressed the bill to gently flatten it out then turned it over, away from George Washington's familiar face. On the reverse, Clayton saw what his simple sketches had brought to mind. He took the dollar back to his computer and laid it down flat alongside his simple drawings. There was the match and the perfect symbol he was after.

On the back of the bill, to the left was a pyramid, Clayton's triangle. At the top was a radiating eye and he found himself riding a speeding luge down a slick ice track through his memory's own search engine for the correlating thoughts he knew were there but couldn't quite grasp.

It was the eye. That was what he wanted. The eye would be the signature to his open letter to the Mayor. But at the same time there was a definition, a reason for the eye on the pyramid that still escaped him. Finding his own internal search engine uncooperative, Clayton returned to his keyboard and tried another version, the electronic one, that he mastered with as much deft as his own mind.

Dollar. Eye. Enter. The results, over one hundred and eighteen million, came back in point one four seconds. They ranged from Dollar stores selling eye glasses to sites with an 'eye toward the silver dollar of yesteryear.' But all it took was a quick scan and Clayton had the piece that had been eluding him. It was a single word. Illuminati.

His hands slipped away from the ebony keyboard gently and with a quiet reverence reserved for safecrackers of old and ministers who believed their hands truly held the Word of God when they leafed through their worn Bibles. There would be no need for additional searches via electronic engines. Any search now would be reserved for his internal memory. Somewhere in the past, intrigued and inspired by the casual glance of a Masonic ring, Clayton had immersed himself in a course of study that led in a hundred directions and none at all. When his unofficial personal dissertation had run its course, all he had to show for the hours of research and reading were stacks of material that ranged from clubs to cults – the benign Loyal Order of the Moose to Nazism. He never discovered the Holy Grail, in either a literal or figurative sense, which would lead from a local group of men bent on deeds of good and promise, to the horrors behind the Holy Crusades, and perhaps back again. Instead, he had only succeeded in expanding his intellectual horizon, never a wasted effort in his eyes, and added new volumes to a personal library which reflected the eclectic taste of its caretaker.

Somewhere along the path, the traveler had stubbed his toe on the Illuminati. Clayton could not say then or now if the intent of the men behind the formation of the group, if it existed at all, was order for the sake of all, or a not so subtle guise for domination. But he did recall and continue to marvel at what might have been, or might still be, if the intent was global benefit for humankind. Now, tonight, in the dim light of a computer's monitor that triggered in Clayton's mind the soft light of candles from hundreds of years prior, he recalled, perhaps selectively, the goals he bemused the founding fathers of the Illuminati milled over as they constructed an unwritten charter.

Integrity would have been paramount, as would honesty in the hearts, minds, and souls of the men who discovered themselves in stations of power by virtue of birth, right, or appointment. Clayton smiled as he considered chastity – perhaps an honorable trait in the days of the founding – but not today, not in today's Illuminati. Rather, he considered that he would, and the original Illuminati would agree, prefer that a man be well rounded, to put it in terms palatable to them, and would thence carry a more complete palette of colors from which to paint. That rolled off his tongue well. But as with so many of his thoughts, it was a preceding one, 'today's Illuminati,' which remained on the computer screen of his mind long after the smile wrought by his mind's meanderings of chastity faded.

What would the Illuminati of old think of Clayton's consideration of their all-seeing eye as a symbol for his technologically driven designs on the wayward of the twenty-first century? Would they understand his thoughts of underlying integrity in a congressman with perverted sexual exploits on his mind and in his heart and connect the dots to a leader of men and maker of decisions who, by Clayton's standards, was fit for neither? Would they endorse the draining of bribery money and ill-gotten gains as punishment for abuse of office and the misplaced faith of the electing body? His hands still rested in his lap and he wondered. Perhaps he was well wide of the mark on all fronts. Moreover, was the Illuminati – as some of his revisited research indicated – more part of the problem than the solution?

A lone finger crept back to the keyboard and exited the results of his earlier search. Once again that hand slipped back to his lap while he stared at the wallpaper of his computer screen – a stunning baby blue forty foot sailboat anchored in crystal clear water yards off a pure white sandy beach. Clayton would leave the history of the Illuminati to scholars and cult theorists, past and present. He'd plagiarize their seal, or purported seal – whatever it was and whatever it represented. Clayton's Illuminati of today was to be the all-seeing eye and his hope was to spread the message throughout the halls of power from coast to coast. And he'd start with his letter to the corrupted Mayor of San Francisco.

12

Two days later saw a run on the *San Francisco Chronicle* at the newsstand. Sam watched the flurry of papers being snatched open while the new owners never bothered to count their change. He had heard an early report of the open letter to the Mayor of the City by the Bay as it headlined the news breaking in the wee hours. There were still several copies of the *Chronicle* on the counter at that hour and Sam had opened one, something he very rarely did.

His eyes scanned the letter with a soft smile beneath them. He couldn't fathom how something like this could happen. Surely there were security checks in place to guard against such things. But whatever the reason, whatever the means, even if it was a ploy induced by the mayor himself and or his entourage, it sold papers and made for interesting copy. And if it were real, sponsored by a group of concerned citizens, or a political rival, this could play out for days and days, selling lots of papers in the process. Sam smiled again, at the content of the letter and thought of his recent dissertation to a struggling Carl about light, dark, and a single candle. Strangely, it seemed to fit. He found himself drawn to the unique symbol that served as the punctuation to the piece. Clayton had utilized the seal of the eye and the pyramid and beneath it, typed the letters 'TNI.' It was all part of his design of course, a teaser to when he would make the complete name known to the world and, like a book series or story line, raise the stakes and increase the anticipation. Though Sam couldn't know all of this part of the scheme, he wondered like thousands of others across the country, who TNI was and what their next step would be. Certainly there would be a next step. No group or person placed a full-page ad in a major city newspaper for the sole purpose of antagonizing one man. There'd be more, Sam thought, and each would sell papers.

Another thought welled up in Sam that was as far removed from the sale of a few extra papers as anything could be. His fingers ran over the all seeing-eye and the initials after reading the letter one more time. The last lines seemed bolded on the page though they weren't.

Remember, Mr. Mayor, to those whom much is given, much is expected. We see you and will be both swift and severe. Time is short. Do the right thing. And do it quickly.

T N I

Carl had just quoted that line a few days before. Sam had heard his father's voice saying it in his head. Now it was at the heart of a national story. There was something else.

"Swift and severe." That line captured him. Sam intrinsically knew what the writer or writers meant and there was a part, a rather large, heavy part, which longed to be a player in the culmination of that line's promise, especially the word severe. Severe was Sam's forte. Swift wasn't a half-step behind, but severe – that was Sam when he was in his element of days gone by. It was an element he missed, longed for, would dare to regain if the circumstances were right.

After reading the full page open letter to the mayor, his hands put away the paper from thousands of miles away neatly and with great care. He'd hold it as a favor for an old customer, though in truth, he had no idea who that might be. Perhaps a familiar face interested in the scandal.

If TNI was as smart as Sam thought they were, there'd be no tipping of the hand to outsiders, willing though they may be. He couldn't have known how far off he was from the very truth as it now stood across the counter from him.

"Hey, Sam. How goes it?" Clayton said nonchalantly.

The pair hadn't seen one another since Mr. Ciampiano's funeral. They had been close and were still comfortable, but had fallen away as most people did when the tug of life took them deeper in other directions. There were plenty of shared memories, though they were all dated, as Sam's life became shadows and Clayton went on to jobs with easier hours and more pay. Each had been kept slightly abreast of the affairs of the other through Carl's disjointed explanations. Kindled by the allure of the antiquated newsstand, in-school suspension, and the memories for both of early hours and the driving force of Sam Sr., the pair shook hands across the counter and the years.

"Pretty well, Clay. It's been a while. How've you been?"

"No complaints," Clayton remarked as he slipped away from Sam's firm grip. "You?"

"Alright," Sam said with a noticeable shrug of indifference.

"Just alright? I thought you'd be a General by now, or on the Joint Chiefs. Carl mentioned more than once that you were running some top secret operation for the Pentagon."

"Not today," Sam said through a begrudging smile as he looked down. "You know Carl – always talking trash."

"That's true, but there's generally a grain of truth or often more, behind what he's spouting off about. So I figured, if not a General then a Colonel or however ranking goes."

"Carl's always been Carl."

"Yeah, Carl's Carl. I didn't expect to see you here. Are you home on leave? I thought you'd be chasing down some Taliban terrorist or jumping out of a plane into the Afghan mountainside. Under the cover of night," Clayton added for effect as he quickly shuffled his hands in front of himself, as though performing some devious sleight of hand.

Sam looked away, embarrassed that he wasn't doing just that. Clayton picked up the cue and tried to offer his old friend a way out of the uneasiness. "Or maybe you've got the whole thing solved. 'Mission Accomplished' and all that. Are you taking a break?"

Sam was reluctant, but felt a peculiar sense of ease with the face from his past. "I guess you could say that. No more GI Joe."

It was an expanse of an opening – more than he'd allowed anyone apart from Karen. Clayton saw it all immediately. "Did you get in a scrape, Sam?"

"Sounds like how my Dad would have put it."

"I learned a lot from your father, Sam. He was a helluva worker and damn proud of you, I know that much. Whenever I'd swing by here, even years after I'd stopped working for him, he'd always whisper to me where he thought you were, based on your letters. He said they were coded. Any truth to that?" Clayton hesitated just a moment. "If you can tell me."

Sam smiled for the first time. "He was pretty good at figuring things out. Maybe we should just leave it at that."

"How long are you home?"

Sam leaned forward and rested his thick forearms on the papers and the worn counter beneath. "No more deployments for me, Clay. I'd like to be able to tell you I'd seen enough, done enough, but I'd be lying to you. And we both know Dad didn't care much for liars."

"You're through? No more military? You mustered out, or whatever they call it? Discharged, I guess. Are you done? Really?"

"Really."

"No shit? I thought you were a lifer."

"Me too," Sam said as his head dropped unconsciously toward the papers beneath his arms. "I'm done. I took an honorable discharge, but that's about all there is to it."

There was a true pause from Clayton and it was rooted in absolute respect. Another patron stepped along the length of the newsstand and casually interrupted the silence by asking for a copy of the *San Francisco Chronicle*.

"Out," was all Sam could muster.

The would-be sale drifted back down the length of the counter, mumbling something that didn't matter even to him, let alone anyone at the stand. Clayton was too focused on his old friend despite the casual reference to the newspaper he himself was there to pick up. Sam didn't notice the mumbling and if he had, he wouldn't have taken offense. That was something he had left behind at the commissary door with the sergeant and his snapped arm.

"Hate to see you lose out on a sale," Clayton pushed a forced smile.

"Happens," Sam answered, brought back from the casual indifference that had layered itself over his hurt. "Been a run on the *S.F. Chron*," he continued.

"Why's that?" Clayton answered in a completely believable tone.

"They ran a full page open letter to the mayor. It seems he's been banging secretaries two at a time and not doing his job. Or at least somebody thinks so."

"That doesn't sound like much of a story to me."

"It wasn't just that. Whoever bought the ad said they're going to bust a cap in his ass if he doesn't straighten up."

"I can't believe they'd print that."

"Didn't say it exactly like that. Here," Sam said as he reached beneath the counter and pulled up the copy he'd set aside. "Take a look."

Clayton took out his money clip and put a five on the counter. "I thought you were out?"

"Saved one just for you," Sam said through a smile as he made change and set it beside the paper.

For his part, Clayton couldn't stop the flush of embarrassment as though he'd been found out. He quickly pocketed his change and rubbed his eyes as though it were early morning and tried to brush the shock off his face, but it was too late and Sam too sharp.

The flashing moment of hesitation and involuntary withdrawal drew an instant response from Sam – half unintentional.

"Have you seen it already?" he said as a deeper question than the words themselves.

Clayton was still strangely caught in the headlights of a nonexistent car that was only turning by him and not attempting to run him down. At least not yet. His reaction was too slow for either him or Sam and he felt the first slips of his feet on this path that had begun as notes on a yellow pad in the safety, quiet, and comfort of his living room.

"No," Clayton said as nonchalant as possible. "I heard about it though."

"You didn't mention that."

Clayton saw his feet shuffle beneath him and they became a mouse's feet, wiggling as his neck was caught in a trap. On his side of the counter Sam was more confused than Clayton was actually trapped, but his training flooded in on him regardless of his intent and he was suddenly inquisitive bordering accusatory. The transition had been so quick from lost friends to the hunter and hunted that both were startled. Sam, an accustomed hunter longing to hunt once more, was quicker than Clayton, who had never been either.

Sam dropped the *Chronicle* abruptly between them and locked on Clayton's eyes. "Go ahead. See how it looks in print."

There was never a more open ended sentence uttered in the history of the spoken word. Still, Sam didn't know how close he was to springing the trap, but what he did recognize was the look and actions of a man who had something to hide.

Clayton didn't say a word which said volumes. He picked the paper up too slowly and Sam's mind raced ahead. Clayton handled it too delicately and sweat was coming to his forehead on a day that was cool by Florida standards. The beads of sweat flashed in Sam's mind as though they were on the faces of countless foreign fighters who were being questioned by himself and others before their answers, right or wrong, left them dead.

Clayton began to slowly leaf through the pages, picking up speed when he realized he was handling the cheap paper too gingerly. "What page. Do you know?" he said quickly.

"No. About two-thirds through. Left hand side. Full page. Lots of white space and no border. Stands out like a sore thumb. You can't miss it." All the while Sam's eyes were riveted on his childhood co-worker.

Clayton located the piece he had penned and covertly scanned it, strangely enough, for errors. There were none. The end of the article was punctuated by the Illuminati eye and the pyramid so familiar on the dollar bill. Now the symbol rested above the letters TNI - cryptic to every other reader in the world except him. The feeling was one of immense power, but he lifted his eyes to a stare from Sam that read as though Sam was pulling the curtain back and revealing the true power behind the Wizard of Oz.

They stared at one another across the counter and the paper Clayton was lowering. "Some piece," was all he said.

"Yeah," Sam echoed slowly, still grasping in the dark himself. "Some piece. What do you suppose that symbol means?" he said as he plopped his hand down abruptly on the article, taking the paper the rest of the way to the counter and nearly out of Clayton's hands, one scarred finger pointing to the eye.

Once again Clayton, for all his quiet prowess at the keyboard, was captured in a net of uncertainty regarding spoken words. "I... I suppose it could be anything. I mean, who knows what people are thinking these days. You know? Like, whoever would write something like that could be making up all kinds of things, you know?"

Sam was cautious now, but his senses seriously piqued. As before, he wasn't certain, yet, as to why, but he recognized a radical change in his friend. For no other reason than to see what would happen next, he tossed out an ace.

"Hell, Clay. I thought you'd recognize it right away. It's on the dollar." Sam pulled a small wad of currency from his pocket, mostly singles – wrinkled bills from the morning's sales. He spread one out on the newspaper and lined up the dollar's pyramid above the *Chronicle's* version. Then he just watched and waited.

Clayton wanted to run. He was far out of his element while Sam was deep in his comfort zone. Sam had once thrived on the intimate proximity of the kill whereas Clayton was strictly a long distance manipulator of numbers.

They both stared; Clayton at the two pyramids, dumbstruck; Sam at Clayton, interpreting every blink of his eyes and twitch of his cheek. Clayton's hand began to slowly wave back and forth between the two symbols. "Yea. I can see that. The guy must have been thinking about the money the mayor stole, I suppose."

"Did he steal any money?" Sam shot back.

Clayton was on the verge of squirming and Sam was on the cusp of outright accusation and it had come this far in a matter of minutes born when a mind accustomed to stealth ran into a careless look. "Maybe the money he wants the mayor to pay back then," Clayton countered.

"Maybe," said Sam slowly as he pulled away the dollar and shoved it back into his pocket. "Who said it was a he?"

"Okay, Sam, playing the devil's advocate here," Clayton snipped, getting agitated. "A she."

"I sooner think a 'they' wrote it."

Now Clayton relaxed a little, thinking that Sam had lost the scent. "Okay. They. But why a 'they?'"

Sam pointed again to Clayton's symbol printed in the paper. "That sign. It's been around a long time. You're telling me you don't recognize it and don't know what it means?"

Clayton tried to laugh. "I can make it and spend it, but I don't analyze it."

"It's not the money, Clay, and I'm having a hard time thinking you don't know who that symbol represents."

"I use plastic for everything," Clayton offered through another weak smile.

"That sign," Sam said as he tapped his finger for effect and continued to read Clayton. "That's the sign of the Illuminati."

The word was a scalpel that silently slashed Clayton's juggler vein and drained the blood from his face, the last trickle leaving as ice. Sam couldn't believe his own eyes. Purely by accident and happenstance, he was thinking he may have stumbled upon the man who had penned the scathing accusation. He knew Clayton. Had known him for years. He was brilliant and not prone to embarrassment or feigned ignorance. Another player – a real one. Another candle in Sam's mission to dispel darkness had walked right up to his counter. Clayton was a part of the tech brains of TNI.

"I know you've heard of the Illuminati, Clay. You read too much, study, and do all that forensic computer stuff. You have to have heard of them."

Obviously cornered, even if by nothing more indictable than an old friend, Clayton attempted again to wiggle free. "I guess so," he said casually as he gestured toward the symbol on the paper. "I mean, maybe I've run across them somewhere, but I imagine everybody has."

"I don't think so, Clay. People handle money all day and never notice it or give it a second thought. I think you would have to be looking for them and what they stood for in order to use their sign in a thing like that," he said as he pointed again to the printing.

"How is it you know so much about it?" Clayton said, going on the offensive.

"Work. Same as you," Sam said, stating again a fact that was obvious to him if not admitted to by Clayton. "Back when I was active," and the words uncharacteristically cracked. "We had to decipher and learn a lot about insurgent communication. Their codes. Somewhere early on I remember this old Major with service bars on his arm up to here," and he pointed to his elbow. "He came in one day and started us off with a history lesson on codes and symbols. One of the things I always remembered was him passing around a dollar bill and telling us about the Illuminati."

"Interesting."

"Isn't it?"

For at least the third time in as many minutes, Sam left the words to hang and just read Clayton's face. He was coming to a conclusion that would have never occurred to him had Clayton not walked up to the stand. As the conclusion gelled, Clayton turned on his heels, casual, but shaken.

"Hey, good to see you again, Sam. I've got to get back to work. Take care of yourself."

He didn't make it far before Sam put one hand on the counter and vaulted silently over it as easy as another man would have taken a single step. Without looking back he snatched up the *Chronicle* newspaper, still open to Clayton's letter and was at Clayton's back.

"Clay?" he said just above a whisper.

Confused and distracted, Clayton turned quickly as though Sam had spoken to him from within the stand. He gasped and physically lurched backward when confronted by Sam, now only inches from his face.

"Forgot your paper," Sam said in the same soft voice as he tapped the *Chronicle* against Clayton's chest. Clayton reached up, riveted by Sam's face. There was the slightest smile beneath Sam's piercing eyes that was sincere and seemed to whisper all was well. Shaken nonetheless, Clayton felt an odd relief as he took the newspaper he had intended to buy from the start.

"You know, Clay. You haven't stopped by here in years. Yet today, you stop and don't seem to want a thing, but end up leaving with the hottest newspaper in the country. Know what I think we should do?"

Sam didn't expect or wait for an answer. "I think you should swing by tomorrow and we can talk about the fallout of that article. There's going to be some, don't you think? See you, Clay. Take care."

This time it was Sam's turn to walk away, but he disappeared around the corner of the stand and came in the door instead of leaping over the counter. Clayton saw him for a moment as a shadow in the back of the stand and watched as he appeared to vanish in a deeper, darker recess. Clayton squinted to see better, then raised a weak hand and waved good-bye to nothing. Cloaked by the newsstand, Sam merely nodded his head in unseen reply before Clayton turned away for the second time. Sam settled back on his worn stool and began piecing together what had just happened and his own revitalized philosophy. What would happen if he were right on both accounts and when the two things met, where would it lead?

———————————

13

The uppermost echelon of the *San Francisco Chronicle* were collected in a rich, darkly paneled conference room circled around an immense oval table huddling with their lawyers, consultants, and members of the board. It was short of six am and the sun had yet to finish waking. There was gnashing of teeth and pointing of fingers as the blame game throttled down the track. Voices were rising and falling, replaced by fresh, louder ones that espoused their innocence while secretly searching for scapegoats and sacrificial lambs in their own department should they be pressed. The mayor's office had called the *Chronicle* in a frenzy less than a half hour after the first bundles of newspapers landed on sidewalks across the city.

"We could print a retraction."

"Oh, yeah, that'd work. Brilliant."

"The cat's so far out of the bag–"

"You'll never get it back in."

"Mayor's office is so pissed a suit is inevitable and it wouldn't surprise me if he attacks us with some sort of injunction."

"What do you mean?"

"An injunction. Make us stop printing."

"That'll never happen. Ever hear of the 1st Amendment? Freedom of the press and all that crap?"

"Ever hear of libel and slander?"

"If he tries to close us down, it would create more noise. I bet the entire thing gets passed off as a joke. It's not like he's going to admit to anything."

"True. He won't, but the City Council has called already and is requesting an investigation."

"That was quick."

"It was a well written piece."

There was a trickle of laughter through the room.

"Damn it. The legal wrangling will cost us a fortune."

A nondescript younger man on the fringe of the group spoke up, softly at first, but cleared his throat and tried again. "Sir, we would lose money if he could hold our presses for a day–"

"Is that possible?"

A well-heeled attorney answered. "He'll threaten, but unlikely he'll find a sympathetic judge."

"Doesn't he appoint them?"

"He is the mayor."

"But sir," the young man continued. "We could make up for it. Make it up today even."

"What are you talking about?"

"Our points of service have been calling. They're out of copy and they want us to deliver more papers. Everyone is sold out."

"How many units are we talking about?"

"Maybe... another hundred thousand."

"A hundred thousand additional papers?"

"I believe so, sir. Plus the internet site has had more hits this morning than in its history and it's still very early. I'm afraid our server will crash once everyone hears about the article."

"Don't we gauge ad rates by number of hits?"

"We do."

For the first time since the group had convened, it was quiet.

Finally the publisher asked his editor for thoughts. His answer was succinct.

"Publish a second run."

A hum went through the assembly.

"Can we do that?"

"We can."

Another quiet pause, but not as long.

"Run it. Make the run. Nothing extra on the ad itself. We'll save that for tomorrow. We got people on it?"

"We do."

"We know anything?"

"Not really. Not yet."

"Well, get something! Tomorrow will be bigger than today and we've got to cash in before the news services steal our thunder."

"What about the mayor, sir?"

"To hell with the mayor. When his term is up – probably sooner than later – we'll still be here. So roll the presses again. Same copy, just more of them. And get on the distribution pronto. I want these papers all over the country as fast as possible. And somebody get me some data on the website hits. Go go go!"

The room began to empty itself of the people who would actually start another run of the day's paper. Left behind were the lawyers and consultants. Even the board members, roused from their beds, trickled out the door in silence – apparently content with the decision – though they hadn't truly been asked.

Someone asked the publisher, "What do you think happened?"

The gap was long and the officer breathed deeply and often. "It could be a couple of things. One is that the ad went through our copy department and no one read the damn thing. Second, it could be a plant, someone here who either has it in for the Mayor or us or both."

"We'll find them."

"Not if it's door number three."

"Door number three, sir?"

The publisher seemed taken aback. "Door number three. Haven't you ever seen, 'Let's Make a Deal?' Helluva game show. That's the third option. One, it just got through. Two, it was an inside thing. And three – behind door number three – that's the scary one. The third option is we got hacked."

"Hacked, sir?"

"Yes, hacked. Hacked! Somebody tapped into our servers. They got to our copy department and slid that load of shit right into our paper while we were home sound asleep."

"Could that be true? I mean, could that even happen?"

"Hell yes! I suppose so, anyway. They're catching guys every day hacking into big banks and credit card companies. I heard someone even hacked the Pentagon, for crying out loud. We're not immune."

"But we have security."

"Apparently not strong enough."

"Get somebody shopping for the best. We can't risk this happening again."

"If it's true – that we got hacked – I guess we should be glad he didn't put it on the front page."

"No, this character's too sharp to do that. He buried it under enough pages so it wouldn't get caught by our internal reviews. Bastard. Smart though. I'll give him that."

"So what now?"

The publisher leaned back and smiled. "We sell a shitload of papers." He basked in his own sentiment before continuing. "I want to see every piece of copy on this for the next week. We will wave the 1st Amendment like it's never been waved before. You know, like I said, freedom of the press and all that jazz. The mayor will be crying foul, crying the blues, and helping us sell papers. I don't care if this is total nonsense or not. There's going to be a feeding frenzy over this and we're the ones with the bait. Whoever it was that did this, inside or out, he might have done us a favor. The *Chron* will be on every news wire, national and syndicated news program, and probably all the tabloid rags before it's over. Still, if it came from outside, I want that crack found and plugged. Next time, the little cocksucker might want to print something that would really get us in hot water like, 'Fuck the President,' or some such nonsense. Yeah, back track on this until we find an answer – pronto."

———————

14

The traffic on I-95 was heavy. Cars and trucks dodged rocketing tractor-trailers and plodding motor homes along soft gray concrete ribbons that rose and fell with the molded terrain. Far ahead, through the countless windshields, heat waves caused the road and sky to melt and waiver until the miles themselves melted away beneath the spinning wheels and the illusion vanished. More accurately, it moved down the road, always out of reach.

Karen was one of those chasing the mirage. The interstate led her southbound with a thousand others away from the cooling grip of autumn toward the still summer-like days of Florida.

This was her third trip south – the first driving. A few months ago Sam had invited her down for what turned into a long weekend. Carl had covered the stand and Karen stayed at Sam's place. The first night they had shopped and cooked dinner together. Somewhere between the dated appliances they found themselves crowded together by the confines of the tiny kitchen. Mutual taste testing brought their lips together for the first time. Though Sam was consumed by a single purpose, Karen managed to turn the stove off before they fumbled with and out of their khaki shorts. The few days morphed into a love fest that would have made a Kama Sutra artist blush. They went out to dinner at The Columbia once, but even it was sandwiched between the torrid sex common to new lovers.

The sand came beneath their feet briefly one afternoon, but it too was a witness to grab ass games in the surf and their soft rolling beneath a blanket brought expressly for that purpose. In a blur, they were locked in an embrace at the airport. This time the parting was slower and punctuated by long kisses. Karen boarded the plane already in the clouds. Sam drove home content, but wrestling the ebb of a tide that had never before swept across him.

Then came the chance meetings with Carl and Clayton Rand. The new feelings that tingled and teased at Sam's mind and heart were being overcome by a desire to return to the roots of his spirit. Karen heard it in their phone calls. Sam's philosophical dissertations scarcely resembled the man she'd first met or later fanned desire with. The voice had brought her to I-95 South and now to the northern Georgia border.

She lowered her windows and felt the warm air rush into the car and toss her hair. She fought with her dark locks, longer now than when she first met Sam, and tucked them in for a time behind her ears until the stiff breeze won again. She was reminded of her love making with Sam and how her hair was left tangled on her face. All that was lacking was the sweat and the soft touch of his strong fingertips as they caressed her body, frail in his embrace.

The short coast of Georgia passed quickly and she soon passed a mammoth weather-worn sign that welcomed her to the Sunshine State. Karen passed the smiling orange face, pressed the gas, and thought of gaining an extra moment in the arms of a man with a murky past and an uncertain future. Over the months their conversations had ventured near the events in his history, but she had known rather instinctively how far she could take him with her gentle probing. For his part, Sam was fine with sharing his interpretation of intimacy with someone who knew enough of his past to not ask much. It made things easier for him when he considered that Karen's glimpses of his past had staged her to know about as much of his future direction as he did. They seemed a perfect match in that regard to this point, but last night, by telephone, Sam had recounted again his peculiar encounter with a friend from childhood – his name wasn't important, he'd said – and accented again his own thoughts of toiling against the darkness. Now Karen was racing south to rescue her Sam from the tone in his voice that suggested he might cross back over into a clandestine world, but this time, one that wasn't sanctioned, one that wouldn't protect him from the rigors of normal law.

So the miles trickled away beneath her until the interstate succumbed to the speed traps of the smaller two lane roads as she short-cutted across the state. Though he didn't know she was on the road to see him and twist his thick arm until he relinquished any wayward thought, Sam had mentioned the radar money–making machines so she slowed when the sudden signs commanded and made up her time where she could. Before long she was back on the interstate system and soon she would be in her lover's strong arms. And after the initial passion cooled, she'd broach the thoughts in her head and pry the intentions from his. Though Sam was loath to say anything overt and even less likely to write anything in a card or letter that had the potential to one day incriminate him, it seemed to Karen that her lover was struggling against, or possibly toward, something. Perhaps it would manifest itself as retaliation toward the very institution he had worshiped. Maybe he'd single out someone or something else to bear the brunt of his misplaced anger. If the pressure of a lost career was shattering him, Karen reasoned he might strike out with an act that in an earlier time and place would have been promoted and pardoned by his government. But those days were past. The fear was that Sam was on the verge of reverting to the sort of things where – legalities aside – he was most comfortable, and unfortunately it seemed to her, incredibly talented.

The countdown from the occasional city distance signs picked up in earnest as she pushed south, flying along on smooth roads never affected by the freezing and thawing that impacted the streets of Washington. The sun remained bright and the fenced pastures that lined the road for miles were green, lush and scattered with short horned cattle and thoroughbreds in training to shock and surprise their Kentucky cousins. The horses' dazzling bay coats glistened as though wet and the twinkles of brilliance captured Karen's eyes away from the road.

The sites helped pass the time and within a few hours the skyline of the City of Tampa grew up from the southern horizon. Soon she was driving on the locally famous 7th Avenue. It was late afternoon when Karen stopped in front of Sam's place. Predictably, Mr. Abreu was on his veranda working the metal rockers of his worn glider. Also predictably, despite several passing meetings, he was not in good outward humor.

"Back again I see."

"Back again, Mr. Abreu," she echoed with a smile.

"Glutton for punishment is what I'm seeing."

"Could be, but I doubt it," Karen said as she jogged around the front of the car and onto the sidewalk.

"Sam know you're coming?"

"Sure does," Karen said through that same soft smile. "I called him when I was about ten minutes outside the city."

"Cell phone, I imagine. Don't own one myself. I don't wanna to be tied with no cord like a fresh baby to its mama. A body oughta have time to hisself when we wants it."

"That's a good point."

"Funny," the old man answered as he pointed to the front of Sam's place. "Oughta be a pulled back curtain or the door opening on the place. Seems as though he'd be on the lookout, know what I mean?"

"Maybe he's got a surprise for me."

"Doubt it. Ciampianos ain't the type of folk who like givin' or gettin' surprises. Predictability. That's our way. Might be it's drawing to a close."

"What's drawing to a close?"

"You know how men are – 'specially military types. 'Any old port in a storm.'"

This brought Karen up short. "I am not a port and there is no storm."

"Whatever you say, Missy. But I don't see that door openin', do you?" The ancient rocking resumed.

Karen returned to the house, secretly wishing for the door to burst open, but it didn't. She had to knock, but did it softly, as though Mr. Abreu wouldn't hear or see and his thoughts gain any justification. And as far as the storm was concerned, Karen had heard the rumbling in the distance through the telephone and – setting aside the absent pulled back curtain – it had been those rumblings that had brought her here in the first place.

In a moment she was semi-rewarded when she heard the multiple locks inside the house being shifted and the door eked open.

"Hey, you're here!" Sam said warmly as he stepped forward to kiss her and hug her affectionately on the porch leaving the door open behind him. "What a cool surprise, but you should have given me more than ten minutes lead. I could have picked up some things. I missed you."

Karen hugged him – encased beneath his bulk – and cast a glance and a wry smile toward the glider next door.

For his part, Mr. Abreu pretended not to notice, and instead drifted dreamily and jealously to recollections of his own love, lost years before to the premature ravages of time. But the years between had been unable to dampen the loss. Next door, he saw the lovers embrace from the corner of his eye as a tear welled up and blurred their sight. He pulled a large red patterned handkerchief from a side pocket, dabbed at his eye and blew his nose. When he stuffed the hanky back in the place it had occupied daily for decades, he heard the sound of Sam's door closing. Behind that door, the welcoming kisses he had witnessed were losing their luster and cooling too quickly for bodies that ached.

"What's going on?" Karen asked for the third time between kisses that were dwindling.

"Nothing. You didn't have to drive all the way down here. I told you on the phone."

"Let me put this in a word you can understand – bullshit."

"What's that supposed to mean? That I'm not smart enough to know what you're saying?"

"Apparently not. If you did, you'd answer me."

"I did answer. I told you nothing was going on. You just don't want to hear me."

"I hear you fine. My problem comes in the believing what I hear part."

"That's right!" Sam was suddenly untethered. "That's exactly right. It's your problem. Not mine. Now, let it go."

"I will not let it go! I think you've got plans to do something you shouldn't."

"You think."

"Tell me I'm wrong."

"You're wrong. Happy?"

Karen stormed out of the room to the kitchen, snatched a semi-clean glass from the cupboard, rinsed it then went to the refrigerator for a cold glass of water. Sam meandered in like a boy who'd been scolded or found out. He leaned heavily against the doorframe and buried his big hands deep in the pockets of his long shorts.

"Why are you so upset?" he asked too casually.

"Because every time I come here I have to drink from glasses that have barely been rinsed. Let alone cleaned. Why can't you wash your goddamn glasses? Why? If nothing else, answer me that?"

Sam's brow wrinkled as he looked away. His wide shoulders shrugged. "I dunno," he said with half a smile. "Just the way I am I guess."

There was a moment's indecision then Karen slammed the glass down hard after a brief sip. The water jumped from the glass and scattered around the counter. "You're absolutely right, Sam. You are absolutely right. It is just the way you are. And I know the way you are. I know exactly the way you are. You're going to go off some night, paint your face some camouflage disguise and do something that is one hundred percent illegal. Somehow you're justifying it in your head right now that it's alright, but I'm telling you it's not. It's not right. It's not legal. Not anymore."

"You don't know what you're talking about."

"I don't know specifics, that's true, but I know there's something going on."

"How do you know?"

Karen left the glass in the small pool of water and walked across the kitchen to Sam who was still leaning against the doorframe. The closer she got, the more her movement brought him from the door casing. By the time she was face-to-face, Sam was standing his ground.

"I know because you slipped up. You let your guard down just long enough." Then she stunned him. "You're not the soldier you used to be. That Sam would have never let on to anything. No," Karen said as she pointed a hard finger squarely upward in his face. "You do something now and you're going to mess up, just like you did with me."

He shrugged and looked away from the accusing finger. "You don't know what–"

She grabbed his thick shoulders and tried to push him against the doorframe. He let her. "Yes I do. I heard it."

"What'd I say?" Sam countered, suspicious of his own thoughts.

"That working the stand was getting to you. Boring, you said. That was two months ago. Then – and here's the topper – you start to tell me about some long lost friend who shows up out of the blue to buy a paper he doesn't even take. And in it is some far-fetched scheme, 'weird' you called it – about some secret society or something equally as silly. Now when I call, you're too busy to talk. Doing what, I ask myself? And you? No reply. That's a long fall from that day I first came down here, like some teenager with stars in her eyes. To think, I was worried about you then. I'm twice, three times, as worried now."

"Why?"

"Because I love you. Back then I... I don't know what I was."

Sam didn't seem to hear Karen's profession.

"You don't have to be worried," he said.

"Why? You never were an open book and I'm okay with that. But now you don't give me straight answers. And the vagueness in what little you do say is the true sign there's something going on in that beautiful head of yours."

"Don't you think you might be wearing your JAG hat a little too tight?"

"Don't be glib. You're going to do something, are involved in something – might have already done something."

Sam had heard enough. He effortlessly walked out of her grasp. "I haven't done anything."

"Yet."

"Karen, you need to let sleeping dogs lie."

"What does that mean?"

"As politely as I can say it, it means to mind your own business."

"You are my business. We, are my business."

"Skip it," he said and walked away.

There was an incredulous gap. "Skip it?" she asked. "Did you tell me to skip it?"

"I did," Sam said as he used Karen's glass and refilled it from a cold pitcher of water in the refrigerator. "Let it go. Are you hungry?"

"Let what go?" Karen's voice began to shake along with her confidence and demeanor as she ignored his question.

"Whatever. Whatever's bugging you. Leave it alone." And he took a long drink.

"Leave what alone?" she continued with a voice that was waning.

Sam set the glass down too fast and too hard. The water popped up from the glass like uncorked champagne, landed on his hand then was flung off just as quickly as Sam spun toward Karen and pointed a sharp finger at her. "Whatever! Are you deaf? Let. It. Go."

Karen had flinched as much from the drops of water that struck her face as the threatening posture of her lover. She wiped the water off her cheeks and felt them mix with the smallest of newborn tears. "Or what? You're going to throw me around and break my arm? Would that make you happy?"

"Don't be stupid," and Sam relaxed his finger.

Karen braved a quick approach to the tiger's cage and rushed him. She snatched his thick upper arms and did her best to initiate a quick shake and plea once more. The attempt that was meant to bring Sam to his senses moved his arms back and forth like palms swaying in a casual summer breeze. But even that gentle motion was more than the movement inside. She talked, shouted, stomped, paced, and pleaded, but Sam was rock solid set. His decision was long cast in stone. In fact, Karen would never learn of it, but his ticket was already bought. Sam was headed to San Francisco.

When the storm Mr. Abreu predicted had passed, they managed a walk hand-in-hand down the street and around a few corners to The Columbia for dinner. Sam complimented Karen on her dress, but the conversation lagged well below the quiet time they'd come to know and expect. When they finished their coffee and prepared to walk home, a bottle of wine was pressed into Sam's hands instead of the check. It had already been taken care of.

The lovers went to bed together that night with Karen resuming her search for the truth. Finding no willing partner in honesty, she kissed Sam's cheek goodnight and rolled away from him. He didn't stop her and the passionate couple slept quietly.

During the night, Sam slipped from bed and paced the old house. He looked in his room often at Karen sleeping motionless. In time he wandered to his father's bedroom and leaned against the doorframe. He drifted in and walked around his father's bed in the dark. Everything was as it had always been. There was no need for light. Sam could see it all in his mind as if it were noon day.

The top drawer of an old waterfall style depression era dresser slid open and Sam took out the picture of his mother holding him as a newborn. He didn't look long in the poor light creeping in from the streetlights outside. It was more the touch against a talisman, but in putting it back he felt a book, known by his hand to be an old Bible.

Retrieved, Sam carried the book and the picture to his father's bed, sat, and flicked on an old nightstand light whose cord was ratty and frayed. In the tired light, Sam leafed through the thin pages and found the obituary of his father he'd saved. It was marking the Book of Luke. Specifically it was marking an underlined passage – chapter 12, verse 48, which he read to himself. *"Much will be required of the person entrusted with much, and still more will be demanded of the person entrusted with more."*

Sam sat quietly, flicked the light off, and continued to sit, holding the old book on his lap. Minutes slipped away in the silent darkness. In time he would return the Bible to his dad's dresser, but not before carefully placing the picture of his mother alongside the obituary in Luke's embrace.

Twelve hours later, Karen was driving north through Jacksonville on the same concrete ribbon that had carried her south just a day before. The trip had been in vain. Sam, whatever his intent, was lost to her. While she crossed the Georgia State line, a casually dressed, muscular man with a soldier's haircut settled into a first-class seat on a non-stop flight headed west from Tampa. He was returning home, the story would go if he needed it. His name, according to his identification and the airline's manifest, was Daniel Jacobs.

In a few minutes the 737 taxied to first position then accelerated to over a hundred-seventy miles an hour and lifted off into the crystal clear bright blue Florida sky. Its landing gear grumbled slightly as it settled in beneath the nose and wings of the aircraft. The reduction of drag and a command for power brought the nose up as the pilot began his gentle bank, mid-climb, to point the plane toward the Gulf of Mexico, Texas, and California beyond. Four thousand feet below and sinking quickly away from the airliner, Raphael was standing with his arms crossed, one hand massaging his upper arm, looking out his office window. He watched the jet climb and bank until he couldn't hear the distant rumble any longer. In less than a minute it was a vanishing dot in the faraway sky.

———————————

15

The aircraft carrying Sam, as Mr. Jacobs, had been replaced by another's ascent and disappearance and then still another while Raphael remained transfixed by the magic of flight as if it were the first time he'd witnessed it. By the time the third plane began climbing toward the sun, Raphael was in a steadfast daze, almost a stupor. While his body continued to stare at the unchanging sky, inside himself, in his mind, the landscape was as tumultuous as a volcano birthing a new archipelago of new land that appeared on no maps, no charts. The islands would be a hazard to the wayward sailor, but Raphael knew where they were and was trying to convince himself that he could navigate without fear. Behind these thoughts came a sense of power, a knowledge of the unknown that no one else could see or share. No one except Clayton.

The flights were left to their strictly plotted courses and Raphael turned away from their mesmerizing ascents to rather gently slip his cell phone from its resting place on the desk. He hit the speed dial list and number seven, lucky number seven it just occurred to him, and listened to the ringing.

"Hey," was all he could muster when Clayton's familiar voice answered.

Clayton was caught off guard, a rarity in his strictly governed world even though the caller ID had given him a momentary warning. "Hey, yourself. How are you?"

"Pretty good," came a response – soft, but not timid or afraid.

"You alright?"

"Yea. You?"

"Of course. Why wouldn't I be? Business is on fire. Markets are soaring. You must be riding the crest of this wave too."

"A little."

"Hey, that's what it's all about right? Chasing skirts and the dollar. Watching classic films. The standard stuff."

"Yea, the usual suspects–"

"Claude Rains. *Casablanca*," Clayton said automatically. "Too easy. How about something a little tougher?"

"I've got a couple of real tough ones. They might be too much for you."

"Let 'em rip. I'm up to the task."

"Not like this," Raphael stumbled. The fact that he'd tipped his cards was made clearer by the silent pause from the normally bantering Clayton. In a moment, he'd recovered.

"Got it. I got it. 'What we have here, is failure to communicate.' Under the current circumstances anyway."

"Right," Raphael breathed a sigh, grateful to be understood.

"Want to stop by?"

"How about you come over?"

"Of course. When?"

"Seven'ish?"

"Deal. See you then."

"Hey, Clay!" Raphael nearly yelled trying to catch his friend before he hung up.

"Yea? What's up?"

"Strother Martin. *Cool Hand Luke*."

"Another easy one."

"Maybe, but I didn't want you to think you'd gotten one past me," Raphael smiled.

"Never. I wouldn't do that to you."

"I guess we'll see."

There was another pause as Clayton saw a trap approaching and he was in a corner. "No need to worry. I mean it. I wouldn't do that to you. You're the only friend I have."

"See you at seven then." And Raphael hung up the phone.

Seven'ish provided ample time for Raphael to lean back in his stylish black mesh chair and gaze at the airplanes again. His workday had effectively ended with the hanging up of the phone. Several hours would pass with his mind working behind his eyes as they traced the planes, wondering what he would say. Wondering what he himself might do. Wondering if he were right. The afternoon drifted away like that until Raphael cleared his desk of what little work had peeked out and drifted home, no more certain of where his conversation would go than when the phone was first hung up.

The knock on Raphael's door coincided with hard turbulence twelve hundred miles away. Sam woke only enough to recognize it was nothing and dozed off again just as quickly. Raphael, however, was wide-awake when Clayton stepped inside. The foyer was elegant, capped by a coffered ceiling that concealed low-glowing lights. A marble topped table held a Remington sculpture to one side and to the other, a large mirror with beveled edges in a thick gilded frame that captured assurance as the men hugged and patted one another on the back.

"Been a while," Clayton said as he moved down the hall with his arm still on his host's shoulder.

"I've been busy. You know how it goes."

"I could work twenty-four seven and not get done if I were so inclined."

"But you're not. You never have been."

"Guilty as charged. Guilty as charged. Too many other things to occupy my time."

"Do they pay as well?" Raphael asked, already knowing the answer.

"Not a cent. But," he added somewhat sarcastically. "I'm only in it for the intrinsic rewards. What's a warm fuzzy feeling worth anyway?"

"Priceless, I suppose, if you're making a MasterCard commercial." Raphael couldn't help hesitating. "But you're not making a commercial, are you?"

"All this talk is drying me out. Got a cold one laying around somewhere?"

"Corona's where it always is. Grab one for me," Raphael said as he lowered himself into his favorite chair, a simple pale green Victorian wingback.

In the kitchen, Clayton opened the double black door refrigerator and pulled two cold beers from the door's rack. He sat one on the black speckled granite counter top and perched the other with its cap just catching the edge of the stone and raised his hand to smack the bottle and knock the cap off.

"And don't use the counter as a bottle opener!" Raphael shouted from the other room. "I mean it! You're going to chip that granite some day and I will kick your ass. There's a bottle opener on the fridge and you know it."

Clayton pulled the simple magnetic opener from the refrigerator door and popped the tops off both beers. He let the caps fall on the counter and roll around until they quieted themselves. "I used your precious opener."

"Macho man," Raphael mumbled.

"Girly man," Clayton echoed.

"Why don't you use your teeth, tough guy?"

Clayton walked back in the room and handed his friend the cold bottle as if nothing had been said, and to them, nothing had.

"Christ, that tastes good," Clayton said as he took a long pull as he stopped briefly in his move to a pale green couch.

"Damn good," Raphael echoed as he took a short swig and held the bottle in his hand, dangling from the arm of his chair.

"I've never figured out the lime part," Clayton said as a question. "You know – stuffing it in the neck."

"Flavor. Tradition."

"Must be a Mexican thing – dropping things in booze. Worms in tequila. Limes in beer."

Clayton leaned to set the bottle on the coffee table.

"Coaster...," Raphael reminded. "That's antique cherry and you know it. In spite of your pretended affection for leather, marble and glass, I happen to know you understand what true, elegant, antique furniture really is."

"And therein lies the answer, doesn't it? With modern furnishings, you can rid yourself of such painful encumbrances as coasters."

"A coaster scarcely qualifies as an encumbrance."

"A hindrance then."

"Hardly."

"One halfway decent wipe and a marble top's clean – no damage – and no nerve damage as a result of stressing out over it. In fact, my arrogant snob of a friend, you can even use the condensation to dampen the rag. It's conservation, the way I see it."

"You're an idiot," Raphael said as he took another drink.

Clayton smiled and took another drink along with his friend of so many years. The bottle, already half empty, was returned to its place on an absorbing stone coaster. "So, Ralph, how goes it? Been too long."

"Yes it has. I've had the boat out a few times, but besides that and the gym, I've been reading a lot – mostly newspapers. There's interesting stuff going on."

"Only you economic geeks would find anything interesting in what's going on in the headlines these days."

Raphael took a drink. "I'm not reading the headlines or the financials."

"No? What then? The funny papers?"

"No. The good ones only come on Sunday anyway."

"You're not becoming a sports fan, are you?"

"Hardly. I do catch the Giants when I can."

"San Francisco or New York?"

Raphael lowered his beer even further. "I didn't think you would sink so low in your regard of me. What season is it? I bleed Giant blue."

"Thought that'd jack you up," Clayton said as he finished off the cold Corona.

Raphael stared at his friend. "There is some interesting things coming out of Frisco though. According to what I've been reading."

As Clayton returned the empty to the coaster he asked the question he knew the answer to. "Oh yeah? Hmm... So, no financial reports, no cartoons. What are you finding so interesting in the papers these days?"

"The ads."

Clayton chuckled. "The ads? You're not reduced to jerking off to Victoria's Secret again are you?"

Even Raphael had to laugh, but it was short lived. "Guess again."

"No idea," Clayton said faintly.

"No idea," Raphael mimicked and took another sip. "Maybe you need another drink to loosen up your memory or get up your nerve, I don't know which."

"I don't think so. I'm cool. I don't know where this is going though. I'm lost."

"I hope not."

"What's that mean, 'I hope not?'"

"I hope you're not lost."

"You don't make any sense, Ralph."

Raphael leaned forward and held his beer in both hands. He leaned heavily toward Clayton. "I saw the ad, Clay. *San Francisco Chronicle?* The whole goddamn world saw it. And all the rest of it. I've been following your maneuvers in the papers. A corrupt councilman and his developer buddy cough up a truckload of money; an entire board goes belly up buying back their own worthless stock; a congressman drops dead when the press flashes his kiddie porn in his face; and now an ultimatum to a mayor caught rifling the coffers and banging his secretary? Holy shit, Clay. It's got your fingerprints all over it."

"Nice work, Mr. Holmes, except for one very important thing."

"What's that?"

"There are no fingerprints."

"Jesus Christ, Clay. What if they turn the congressman's heart attack into murder?"

"Never happen."

"You don't know that."

"Nobody gives a shit about that kiddie cock sucker. Forget him." Clayton popped off the couch holding out his empty bottle. "You ready for another?" he said as he danced around the mahogany table and almost skipped into the kitchen.

Raphael stood and followed him as if he were moving slow on a highway past a car wreck. He was still cradling his own half full beer. "C'mon, man. This is serious."

"What is?" Clayton smiled as he held out another beer to his friend.

"No thanks. I'm good." Raphael answered the unasked question.

Clayton closed the refrigerator door and snatched the bottle opener off it in one smooth motion. He snapped the cap off the bottle and aimed it toward the counter. It hit, but bounced and spun until it fell to the dark hard wood floor. Both men bent down to pick it up. Their conversation renewed as they crouched on the floor, with Raphael's hand, just by a mere touch on his arm, holding Clayton down.

"It was an out and out threat on the Mayor of San Francisco. Do you think no one is going to notice? You really think no one will care to look for you just because the guy cheated on his wife?"

"And took bribes."

"They'll call it 'lobbying.' It happens every day."

Clayton looked around, as if the confines of the kitchen floor, surrounded by the rich cherry cabinets, afforded some version of protection. His hand replaced his friend's and he patted Raphael's arm. "It's okay. It is." His gentle hand tightened on Raphael's arm. "I've never felt so alive in my life. All that bullshit I do all day – that you do all day – doesn't mean a goddamn thing. This matters, Ralph. It really matters. I'm tired of watching the news, the net, the papers telling us how bad all these people are and then nothing happens to them. They cover each other's asses so when they get busted they'll have a marker to call in." His grip had tightened. "I'm sick of it!"

"But you can't juggle people's accounts, tap their computers–"

"Why not? It's what I do. I mean, it's what I stop people from doing. I can do it with my eyes closed. I build the damn stuff. Nobody really knows how I put this stuff together. Even the military hard-ballers don't know everything I've built into their own systems."

"I understand that, but just because you can, doesn't mean you should. You know that. C'mon, before you get jammed up so bad you can't get out."

"Won't happen."

Raphael stood up abruptly, leaving Clayton on the floor. "Spoken exactly like every person who has ever committed a crime."

"I don't mean it like that," Clayton said as he stood up, tossed the wayward bottle cap on the counter, and walked away with his beer. He was moving in the general direction of the couch and the coaster, but he meandered as though he was unsure of where to light. "It's not that way at all."

"What do you mean?"

Clayton stopped near the couch and turned to face his friend. "Getting caught. I don't know of a way. While statistically I recognize that anything's possible – especially as we go to the next level – it's just the opposite of what you're thinking – the opposite of what anyone would think. See, I'm doing this exactly because I can. It's not an ego trip deal, but like a duty. I can do it so I have an obligation to."

Raphael was frozen in his kitchen. He looked hard at Clayton, who stared back, confident but with a plea in his eyes. Neither spoke for a long minute, allowing the words, spoken, now still, and those unsaid, to find a place in the other's mind. Raphael began to speak with the movement of his feet back to the living room. "You're saying you have an obligation, you believe, to break the law."

"No. I have an obligation to make wrong things right."

"Like Superman?"

"C'mon..."

"Sorry. An obligation to right wrongs..., like a vigilante sort of thing."

"That's closer than Superman, yes."

"Charles Bronson."

"Maybe."

"But without the shotguns and stabbing."

"Maybe," Clayton said again, but slower.

"Christ, is that the 'next level?' Guns?"

"Look, that's not the plan."

"Well, what is, 'The Plan?'"

"To set things right. Let these cocksuckers know someone's watching who isn't above bending the rules to expose them or bankrupt them, if that's what it takes to get them to start flying right."

"And you determine who is 'flying right?'"

"No. And that's the true glory of the entire thing. We do. We all do." Clayton paused and pointed at Raphael across the room. "Tell me you didn't want to kick that congressman in the nuts when you heard about him tapping page boys in the ass and his porn collection. He's a goddamn congressman, for Christ sake!"

"Of course, but that's why there's laws and the police – to investigate and enforce the law when it gets broken."

"That sounds great, but the truth of it is they can't do it – not to the people I'm talking about. They're insulated, protected by power and privilege."

"Above the law?"

"Exactly!"

"No they're not. I see these guys arrested and prosecuted every day."

"Right. Every day one of them gets caught. And these are our leaders in government and business? Best and brightest?"

"They're not all criminals."

"I never said that. If they operate within the law and work for the good of the nation and not themselves, they've got nothing to worry about from me."

"That's a razor's edge and you know it."

"They run our country and our businesses. There's a higher standard for them. There has to be. Too many people are counting on them to do the right thing."

"There's only one standard. Equality under the law."

"What a bunch of bullshit. I know you don't believe that."

"I want to. I try to."

"It doesn't work."

Raphael rammed a much needed pause into the conversation. He sighed and wished he had better footing under his argument. "And so?" he asked. "Why do I think there's an 'and so' coming?"

"Jesus, lighten up on me, will you?"

"A man is dead."

"A piece of shit child molester is dead and the world's a better place without him."

"I doubt his widow and children feel that way."

"Fuck him! Did you hear me? Fuck... him!"

Raphael held up his hands as a sign of resignation and to diffuse the obvious. He drifted himself a bit until he came to rest in his pale green wingback. Clayton mirrored him in a fashion and settled back on the couch with his fresh beer.

Raphael began the conversation again. "You know that Bronson analogy? The one you preferred over Superman?"

"Yes," Clayton answered between long drinks from his bottle.

"The movies were all called *Deathwish*. Remember that."

Silence passed as conversation as they both tried to lean in their minds to see around the corner that was the future.

"It wasn't his best stuff," Clayton said, giving up on the unknowns of tomorrow. "*Mr. Majestyk*. That was good stuff."

"Little guy triumphs over evil?"

"Yep. Now you're talking."

The pendulum of an antique schoolhouse clock ticked in near silence on the wall marking time. Raphael reached over to the table and picked up the remote. The fifty inch panel sprang silently to life. The station was CNN Headline News and the volume was low. A neon green bar advanced across the screen as he turned it up. Clayton glanced at him and weakly pointed at the screen with his bottle.

"Do you leave it like that all the time? How do you hear it?"

"I hardly watch it. I think I had a game on last Sunday or something. Wasn't that interested, I guess."

"Apparently."

They watched the rattling news together for about three minutes in silence and saw six or seven different stories play out in the short span. Clayton pointed with his beer again. "This is how it got started, you know. Bullshit news. Just like this."

"I don't want to–"

"You already know, Ralph."

"No. I don't. I really, truly, legally do not know a thing, and I want it to stay that way."

"But then I want to ask you something. I can ask, just not tell, right?"

Raphael looked back and said nothing.

"I'll take that as a yes. See," Clayton said as he wriggled to the edge of the couch and leaned closer, still holding his beer but now in both hands between his knees. "If I did tell you something, it'd be hearsay, right? Inadmissible."

"I think that's right. I can ask my new best friend – the DA Senior Investigator – if you want me to."

"Let's not do that just yet."

"We finally agree on something."

"But if you really, truly, legally don't want to know, and I can't tell you anything more, you tell me something instead. Just one little thing."

"Alright," Raphael answered a bit suspiciously.

Clayton faltered a moment then asked in a voice barely above a whisper. "Why did you ask me here?"

Raphael looked at his friend. His eyes didn't look away, but they drifted closed.

"I'm not sure." His eyes opened as though they hurt. "Ask you to stop maybe? Stop you. Save you."

"Save me?"

"From yourself."

They both suddenly laughed at the series of clichés.

"'Oh, little Alex," Clayton said hysterically, laughing too loud for the event. "I'm the only one in this sore and sick community who wants to save you from yourself!'"

"Very nice." Raphael began to clap slow and laboriously. "Very nice. *Clockwork Orange*. Excellent selection."

"Thank you. Thank you."

"If memory serves, that was the probation officer talking to the killer. That sound right to you?"

"Sure was."

"Apropos, don't you think? Could be foreshadowing."

"No, I don't think so. It was an interesting picture."

"Too violent for me."

"Wuss."

There was a break bookended by sips of beer before Raphael reached back to the point.

"I don't want to know anything, Clay. I really don't, but you're right. I already know something – I know that you can do all the things I've seen and read about. I know you can, that's all. And I don't want to talk about whys, certainly not hows. But just because you can, doesn't mean you should."

"There's where you're wrong, Ralphy boy. Like I said, it's exactly because I can, that I should. Don't you remember? 'To those who much is given, much is expected.' Old man Ciampiano use to say that. Remember?"

"Yes, I remember. And I never understood how he thought it applied to him. He didn't have anything. Sam was the poorest kid in school. He'd show up with the coolest sneakers once in a while, usually right after a big horserace. Funny how that worked."

They shared the grins common to hints at shared but hidden knowledge. The respite was welcomed, but brief.

"All true, but I remember Mr. C talking about his parents or grandparents in Sicily and how rough they had it. He considered himself blessed. I think he was – I know he was –involved in a lot of rough stuff and probably worse, but he held himself to a higher standard than most people because of the opportunities he had in the United States."

"You've gone around the bend in a big way. Did you hear what you just said? An itinerate gambler, a criminal who beat people up, probably killed people, held himself to a higher standard? That's how slippery a slope you're on."

"What he was or did is irrelevant. The higher standard is what's important and he believed it and lived it."

"No way."

Clayton regrouped. "You thought the world of Mr. Ciampiano, didn't you?"

"We all did."

"Yep. Nicest guy in the world. Treated us like little princes when really we were little shits."

"Because he liked us. My guess is that if he didn't like you, or there was money trading hands, he'd kick you so hard you'd be wearing your ass for a hat. Or worse."

"There's a lot of people who need an ass kicking."

"And we're back to who makes that call and defines who needs one and who doesn't and you think you can do that."

"Alright. Alright. But Mr. C was no monster."

"Not to us. Oh, because we were 'flying right?'"

"Kind of. We did our little bullshit jobs for him, never stole a nickel out of the cash box, treated customers well–"

"Right, but I don't think he ever meant it like this."

"Why? I think it's precisely what he meant." Clayton leaned back, straight as a ramrod and touched his chest with both hands, one barely holding onto his beer. "I know this stuff. I've been given this ability. I should use it to do good. Much has been given to me, so, much is expected of me. It might mean some risks and so forth, but I can't sit on my hands and let this nonsense happen when I know I can do something about it. That's what Mr. Ciampiano was talking about the whole time."

Raphael kicked backed in his chair and grabbed the matching ottoman with one of his feet around a single mahogany ball and claw foot. He pulled it closer roughly, tossed his legs up on it, and took a long drink of his beer. "Wow, Clay. You are so far gone."

"Hardly. I'm spot on."

"Isn't it amazing how two people can look at the same thing and see it so totally different?"

"What is that saying, 'Agree to disagree?' Something like that. You want to leave it there?"

"It's, *modus vivendi*. Yes, 'agree to disagree,' but not yet."

"Okay," Clayton said, his tone bracing for a fight. "Take your best shot." But he was up. "After I freshen my beer. You ready?"

"I'm good. Listen a second, you lush. Just step away from it for a minute. Look at it from a different perspective. Turn it around a few times and see what's on the bottom, the sides, on the backside."

Clayton seemed to physically do just that as he corralled yet another beer, came back, and settled deep into the soft couch. He looked up at the ceiling – a clear indication of being on the proverbial shrink's inclined couch.

"Well?" Raphael asked after a moment.

"I'm looking. I'm looking."

"What do you see?"

Clayton sighed, as though honestly making the effort. "I see dead people."

Raphael couldn't hold back the smile. "*Sixth Sense*, but cut it out."

"Right. Right. Okay," Clayton baulked. "I see dumb people. Check that. I see greedy people."

"Forget I said anything," Raphael said as he put his bottle to his lips. "Why bother?"

"I'm serious. I see greedy pieces of shit who think they can do whatever they want and get away with it. That's what I see from every angle."

Resuming the role of psychiatrist, Raphael continued. "Alright. But let's go back–"

"To when I wet the bed?" Clayton laughed as he spun himself around and stretched out on the couch with his head toward Raphael's chair, completing the replication of the shrink's office diorama.

"You're incorrigible. That's psychiatrist speak for, 'You're an asshole.'"

"Thank you, doctor. Please continue."

"What I was saying was, let's go back to what you said about Mr. Ciampiano. That whole thing about much is given, much is expected. Let's build a little clarity around that."

"Clarity? I already know it by heart and I know what it means and I know these bastards are not adhering to it and I am."

"And do you know it comes from the Bible?"

"No. I thought a philosopher. But that could still be true. Jesus was a helluva philosopher as I recall."

Raphael laughed to ease the placid tension. "Using 'Jesus' and 'helluva' in the same sentence... Doesn't that strike you as just a bit odd, maybe even sacrilegious?"

"Does, doesn't it? Sorry."

"Listen, Clay, I remember it as well as you. Mr. C had a hundred little anecdotes he used to spin on us kids – one for every situation in the world. In hindsight, I think he was trying to teach us all something besides how to work. I remember him saying that piece came from the Bible somewhere. We were either a bit too young, or too silly—"

"Or too tired. It was usually five AM."

"Maybe. Just too tired to understand what he was trying to tell us."

"And Sam had to be there at least an hour before us with his dad. That had to be tough on him."

"Nobody ever questioned how tough Sam was. At anything."

"That's the truth, isn't it?"

"No doubt. I wonder what he's up to."

They each paused to drink from their respective bottles and offer up their silent recollection and respect to their friend. For Raphael, he hadn't seen Sam since Mr. Ciampiano's funeral. He couldn't know that the last time Clayton had met with Sam was only a few days.

"Anyway," Raphael continued. "Mr. Ciampiano was a sharp man and we never realized it. What a guy like that was doing peddling papers I'll never know, but a lot of what he said stuck with me. It made a real impression on me. I even looked up that one about much is given, much expected, thing. Actually, I've looked up plenty of them. Most of them I couldn't find. I think he made them up himself, like a modern day Aristotle, but that one, it's from the Book of Luke. I don't remember the chapter, but it's different than most people say it. It's not as simple as you said it, or Mr. C for that matter. I think it goes more like – 'Much will be required of the person entrusted with much, and still more will be demanded of the person entrusted with more.' I'm sure that's it."

"That doesn't sound much different from what I said, Ralph. Where're you headed?"

"That maybe you fall into the second half. These pieces of shit that steal and screw around, they're in the first half. Sure, much is expected of them. But you, Clay, you are in the second half, even more is expected of you. Making sense?"

"Absolutely. That's what I've been saying all along." Clayton sat up – feeling that he'd finally convinced his makeshift psychiatrist. "They have a little and are messing up. I have more, so it's up to me to fix it. Sounds like I've got a new recruit," he said as he winked at his friend and smiled before finishing his third beer, mindful to return the cool bottle to the coaster.

"Not just yet," Raphael answered as he returned serve. "You're not quite hearing me. The second person referred to is indeed the more powerful of the two in the parable, but there is no clear intention of what either person's expectation is really bent toward. If they have been given a talent to be evil, should they manifest it? And how can we mere mortals tell the difference? If we take the Bible at its word, it says go with what you have. If you have lots of talents in an area, good or bad – no distinction made – go exercise it. 'Much is entrusted. Much is expected.' See how it gets touchy?"

Clayton slipped to the edge of the couch again. "Almost. Except for that word, 'entrusted.' I don't believe there is a way to translate 'entrusted' to mean anything else but for good or at least a positive. I think maybe it's you that needs to take in the big picture now. These politicos as an example – their jobs aren't inherently bad – they, over all others, have been elected, have been entrusted by the people to do good, look out for the electorate – be a shepherd to the flock, to build on your Biblical reference – but they've chosen to do otherwise. They rend their flock like wolves until someone like me comes along who is entrusted with even more power and I set them straight. I stop the wolves. I believe you're right, there is a Part One and a Part Two in that verse, and I'd like you to join us in Part Two."

"Us?" Raphael asked softly. "What 'us?' It's spreading?"

"Don't say 'spreading' like it's a disease. Say 'growing' like the something good it is."

"I don't think taking the law into your own hands can be seen as good."

"I know you see stopping thieves and molesters as good, don't you?"

"Yes I do, but you're not a cop or a judge."

"True. We've got lots of them and it hasn't helped. It's time for something different. It's time for those 'entrusted with even more' to step up. And I want you to reconsider coming in. I believe you want to reconsider too."

Raphael finally finished his beer and though his argument still had legs under it, he let it go. It slipped away down his own throat like the last swallow of warmed hops. He set his bottle on the floor and looked across at Clayton. "There's some truth in what you said. I know that. Maybe you're right. Maybe somewhere inside all of us is a latent vigilante. I'm not all in, but I do want to help you if it somehow keeps you from slipping into deep water."

"Save me from myself?"

"Yes, poor innocent little *Clockwork* Alex."

Clayton didn't lean forward as Raphael had expected to reveal his part in the next level of the plan. Instead, he leaned back into the wide comfort of the couch – content.

"Keep me from getting too deep?" Clayton said smiling. "I'm swimming over the Marianas Trench, but I'm telling you, I've got buoyancy to burn. Buoyancy to burn."

A twinge of regret for relinquishing too easily welled up in Raphael's throat, but it was washed away by another beer and the anticipation of what lay ahead.

Clayton brought his legs up and rested them the length of the couch being careful not to let his shoes touch the fabric. The newest member of The New Illuminati watched him and waited. After several minutes of blank space, Raphael tested the ice.

"What's the plan?"

"We just watch the news."

"We watch the news?" Raphael questioned him.

"Just watch the news."

"Looking for the next victim?"

"Never. Just the next idea. They make victims out of themselves."

"Just looking for ideas then."

"Just ideas."

"Nice clean way to think of it, Clay."

"It is, isn't it?"

Raphael didn't answer. He too just settled back in his chair, turned the volume up on the news channel and began listening for ideas. Almost everything was pure fluff. Occasionally a story, which seemed to have some merit, caused Raphael to look in Clayton's direction, but each time Clayton shook him off like a baseball pitcher shakes off a catcher's sign. There was no hot scandal or political outrage assailing the country tonight. Eventually the news got to the inner pages and the lesser stories. Fifteen seconds were devoted to what had been the raging storm of news from a week ago around the Mayor of San Francisco's dalliance with several administrative assistants which seemed to take precedence over his bribery. Corruption was not as titillating as sex. But tonight the anchorwoman only played it all off, trying to squeeze the last bit of news mileage – reduced to a half-step above gossip – out of what had once been the lead story.

"It looks like the full page add in the *San Francisco Chronicle* a week ago was nothing more than an expensive prank," she said through a near giggle. "The ad, estimated to cost a hundred thousand dollars, initially caused quite a stir over at the mayor's mansion, and though it is rumored that the First Lady of the City has not been seen coming or going from the grounds, it has been business as usual at the mayor's office and there has been no sign of repentance or a refund as the ad had demanded. I guess the writer should have spent the money on a donation to the city. But, what are you are going to do? It takes all kinds," she said with a smile before moving on with a slight change in inflection in her voice to match the spin in her chair to follow the change in cameras. "In other stories..."

"Dumb shit," Clayton fumed. "Turn it off, will you?"

"What's the matter?"

"Nothing. It's cool."

"You don't like being yesterday's news?"

"No, that's not it. It's an insult to hear her go on like it was a joke when it's not funny. None of it is. Everything we're doing is serious. Turn it off. Would you mind?" he said as his voice faded.

The wide screen television blinked and went black.

"Why did you want it off?"

"They're missing the point."

"What is the point, Clay?"

"The point is that what we are doing is making a real difference and it's just beginning. I mean, we may not be making a global, or even a national difference yet, but we're about to and it starts tonight."

"How do you know it's going to start tonight? What's going to happen?"

Clayton stood up in the quiet room and made his way toward the door. As he walked by Raphael, sitting in his chair, he patted his friend almost tenderly on the shoulder.

"That is the absolute beauty of this entire business. The way I see it – the way I have it planned and the way it's coming together – not everyone knows for certain everything that we're doing. That way, there's an extra layer of protection built in for the players. See it?"

"I see it," Raphael answered. "But I have to admit a sense of curiosity about what you've got in the works. This... this infamous 'next level' I heard you mention." As he finished, Raphael turned his head in a rather crooked pose as he arched his neck to see into the kitchen in order to follow Clayton who had continued moving through it, stopping at the fridge for a beer and popping the top before heading to the door. "I guess I'm wondering if this is it and, more importantly, where's it end?"

"You know what? I truly don't know," Clayton as the accumulation of alcohol reached him and the words drifted together.

"Come on," Raphael said as he eased back into a normal position in his chair, looking away from his friend.

"No, I truly don't."

"If you don't know, who does?"

"Those bastards. They know," Clayton said slurring as he pointed toward the quiet television.

"Wow. Still a lightweight. Three beers and you're half-cocked. You'd better stay here tonight."

"You sir, are an ass."

Raphael bowed his head slightly as though he'd received a compliment. "Thank you." He hesitated long enough for Clayton to have another long, hard swig then posed the same question from another angle. "Clay, you can't stop all the corruption. You can't stop–"

"Why? Where's it say that? What dusty book of yours?" he clamored as he wandered into the room running his hands lightly over leather bound volumes of works by the Masters, cradled neatly on rich dark walnut shelves with blazon natural trim that glowed in the pinpointed lighting. "In which one of these does it say that corruption and malfeasance, disrespect and moral turpitude, should go unpunished with such frequency that it becomes commonplace? So much so that it's ignored, even expected? Which book, Raphael? This one?" he said as he pulled an indiscriminate book off the shelves.

"No–"

"This one then?" and Clayton crudely shoved the first book half-way back into its place and snatched another which he held out to Raphael.

"Come on, Clay. Easy on the books."

Clayton set his beer in an empty space on the shelves and pulled another book. "This one then."

Raphael jumped from his chair. He grabbed at the book in Clayton's hand, but Clayton dropped it and reached for another. "Then this one."

Raphael roughly wrestled the book away from Clayton. "That's a Steinbeck 1st Edition, you idiot!"

As Clayton lunged for still another, Raphael quite deftly set Steinbeck's work on a shelf near a faded colored Roseville vase then tossed a foot effortlessly behind Clayton's knee and with a push that seemed nearly playful, sent his longtime friend tumbling backward across the floor. Clayton folded in half on the floor then recovered, but when he had rolled to his knees he stayed there. A smile broke across his face.

"Fuck!" he said through a grimace. "That hurt."

Raphael removed his friend's beer from the shelf. "Whatever you're going to do next, I hope you do it when you're sober."

"Not to worry, old friend," Clayton said as he sat on the floor. "It's done. Sorry about the books. Did I bruise anything?"

Raphael was looking over his collection for that very thing. "I don't think so, but don't do that again. I mean it. Don't even come close to them," he said as the Steinbeck was returned to its place of honor alongside other 1st Editions. "Don't touch them when you're drinking," Raphael said as he stepped over to his friend and stuck out his hand to help him up. "I mean it. Don't even read the binding as you walk by. Deal?"

Clayton took his hand. "Deal." When he was on his feet he dusted his pants off though there was nothing on them.

They wandered back to their places on the couch and chair. "You were a little slow," Clayton added. "I managed to knock down a couple before you dusted the floor with my ass."

"Actually, I was waiting for you to set your beer down. I didn't want it to get spilled," Raphael said as he lowered himself into the chair, almost as though it hurt to do so.

"Ohhh…," Clayton said thoughtfully. "So now I know Superman's kryptonite. As long as I keep a beer in my hand, I'm protected."

"Somewhat."

The pair sat in the quiet room and finished their beers in silence – Raphael's first, Clayton had lost count. When each bottle was empty, Clayton asked a question answerable in several ways. "What now, my friend?"

"I'm still here," Raphael answered plainly.

"You live here."

"I'm still on the fringe of what's happening so I can rescue you if you start sliding down that slope."

Clayton had been slouching, but sat up as though he'd renewed interest in something, which he had. "That's not what I was thinking. I was after more like, a pizza maybe, or catching a flick, but I'll take it."

"Good." Raphael waited just a second longer then asked. "So, do I have a job or an assignment, or do I learn the secret handshake or anything?"

"No handshake," Clayton chuckled. "And no jobs tonight. We'll watch the morning news and see what happens overnight out west."

"Out west? You said that like you're expecting something."

"I am."

"Can you tell me about it?"

"No. Remember – less is more. It's protection. Think of it like a condom."

Raphael paused. "How you can be so flippant escapes me. It truly does."

"Because I am relaxed. Up here," Clayton said in a whisper as he pointed to his head. "Your head gets tense. No room for tense in this business. You know what you need?"

"Another drink and a date?"

"Good thoughts on both accounts, but wrong. What you need is a dose of the Duke."

"Hmmm. That's not bad medicine. It has been awhile." Raphael was slow in responding, but eventually slipped from his chair and pressed the top of one of the corners of the coffee table right above a leg, next to Clayton's coaster. From within the leg a deep sleeve of DVDs began to emerge vertically until a stack a foot and a half tall stood above the table. "Let's see," he said as he ran a finger down the plastic cases. "Here we are. Perfect. Haven't seen this one in forever."

"*Hondo!*"

"Good guess."

"I know you so well. Fire up that bad boy."

"Sliding it in as we speak," Raphael said as he did just that.

The words were still slurring in Clayton's mouth, but he pointed at the DVD player with an objection. "I moved everything to digital. I don't have a DVD in the house, I think. When are you moving up to the twenty-first century, young man?"

"Two words. Liner notes. I like to read the cases."

"It's online."

"I'm tactile." Raphael rubbed his fingers across the DVD case. "I like the touch. Keep me up to date on technology, but I'll keep a firm foot in the past, thank you very much."

"Like your old books?"

"Yep. That you will never touch again."

Clayton raised his hands in surrender as Raphael tapped the case against his hand.

"Here's one. Who had a bit part, but went on to be huge on television?"

"Make me think, will you?" Clayton puffed as he settled back on the couch. "James Arness. Ah, Marshall Matt Dillon, hello? *Gunsmoke*. Is that all you've got?"

"Sorry. Too easy." Raphael let the DVD dangle from his hand as he pointed a crooked finger at Clayton and launched a weak John Wayne imitation. "Don't mess with that dog, kid. I told you twice."

"Classic. Classic," Clayton smiled. "Twenty bucks for the name of the dog."

Reflex made Raphael pull the case back and glance at it for help, but John Wayne's image, distant deep eyes, with a rifle over his shoulder and a scruffy dog at his side, offered no clue.

"No cheating," Clayton scolded.

"Give me a sec. I'm running through a couple scenes in my head," Raphael said as his eyes dropped closed and he did exactly that. "The Apache have got John Wayne prisoner..."

"Not a terrible rendition of the American Indian for a film of its time," Clayton chimed in, the alcohol and his body riding off on a tangent of slurred words. "Shows some depth of character, a sense of values through Victorio. Reverts to the more accepted stereotype often, but I've always said it was a glimpse of what would come later in *Geronimo, Last of the Mohicans, Dances With–*"

"Hey! I'm trying to focus here."

"Alright. Alright. But you're not going to get the dog. Give it up. I can't even remember it. I'm not sure the dog had a name."

"No, there was a lot of dialogue about that dog – important to the storyline – independent, not relying on others, minding your own business stuff. Kind of that less is more thing you said."

"Exactly! Which is why I said you needed a shot of John Wayne. And why, again, I knew you'd pick *Hondo* – no more perfect example."

"So this independence connection – that comes from John Wayne? Very patriotic. I suppose I get to be your sidekick – the dog."

The analogy would have made anyone in Clayton's position smile and he was no exception as he waved off the comment. "Get out. You're not the dog. A sidekick–"

"It's Sam."

The name stopped Clayton cold.

Raphael noticed and thought it was part of the game.

Clayton sobered up in one breath. He didn't remember letting that name slip. "Was he that drunk? What else – who else – had he mentioned?" he thought. Though he trusted Raphael immeasurably he valued the insulation that surrounded 'less is more.'

Raphael snapped his fingers. "Pay up."

"What? What about Sam?"

"That's it. Sam."

Clayton's shoulders sagged involuntarily. A draining look – part wonder, part resigned despair – came across his face. "How the... How did you ever put that together?"

"When you think it over. It comes to you."

"Think what over? Christ almighty!" Clayton bounced to the edge of the couch and his face reddened in embarrassment and fear.

"Whoa. Don't play if you can't pay. Show me Andy Jackson."

"What?"

"Jackson. The twenty? Sam. The dog?"

"He's not a dog, man. Ease up."

"Who's not a dog?"

Clayton baulked. "What are you talking about?"

"Me?" Raphael bristled in return. "What are you talking about?"

"Sam! How'd you know? When did you see him last?"

"Him? Who is 'him?' The dog? I haven't watched *Hondo* in over a year. What's wrong with you? You must be shit-faced." Raphael turned toward the DVD player and thumbed the remote. "John Wayne yells at the dog somewhere in the picture. Clear as day. 'Sam.' You'll see, dip shit. If the dog in this flick isn't named Sam I'll pay twenty-to-one."

Clayton stumbled in his mind and put the preceding minute's worth of conversation together in a new way. He leaned back on the couch and listened to the DVD's soft whirl in the fresh quiet. Raphael mumbled something barely audible as he padded back to his own chair.

Typical of the pair, by the time Raphael settled in and the venerated Warner Brothers logo rose on the screen, the feigned anger, if it had been even that, was gone. Raphael asked Clayton if he wanted another beer as the score began to play, but there was no answer. Clayton hadn't even heard him and would barely see the film, apart from five rewinds confirming Sam was the dog's name. Clayton was nearly three thousand miles away, lost in his wondering about another Sam – ex-Sergeant Sam Ciampiano.

16

The following morning saw the lights of a 737 shimmer in the heat waves of its exhaust as it powered up and lifted its nose toward the rising sun. The jet was headed east, bound for Atlanta and the carrier's central hub. From there, its contents would spill out across the southeast and north up the coast to homes, business appointments, and vacations. These were travelers from the west going east to see things fresh and new, passing in the sky, travelers headed west to do the same. One traveler, with broad shoulders and thick arms partially hidden beneath a long sleeve neutral colored polo shirt and under a sharp tan colored Greg Norman golf cap, relaxed in his first class seat, closed his eyes and dozed off, unencumbered by the wake he had left on the ground several hours before. Even now as the plane leveled off at cruising altitude, the San Francisco press corps was rushing to the home of the city's mayor. Raphael, Clayton, and most of the east coast were still asleep, but they would wake to news of The New Illuminati's first physical confrontation and the accompanying confirmation that the ad, its message, and The New Illuminati itself, were no prank.

Four days before, Sam had touched down at LAX. He had ridden away from the airport in a hailed cab then covered several miles through the city on foot until he reached a non-descript bus stand. From the bus he ferried himself north out of town where he disembarked, walked another several blocks, and caught another cab.

The cab took him and his single carry-on to an aging strip mall outside the city. Though hidden beneath a cap and behind cheap sunglasses, he was certain he had already been videotaped coming and going from the jet way and taking the first cab. That was acceptable risk. As he drew closer to the target and the means of getting there, he would guard his look more closely.

Settled in the back of the cab, Sam slipped a black rock hard carbon fiber strip from the frame of his small suitcase and eased it up his sleeve. One end was a uniquely fashioned hook. It was a perfect undetectable slim-jim and would slip down a car window to crack a door's simple lock in less than two seconds. From other pieces of the suitcase's wheels, handle and bracing, plus a section of Sam's money clip, he quickly fashioned a trigger operated lock pick mechanism. He worked the trigger a few times and the pick responded, poking and swiveling on demand. The clicking caught the attention of the cabbie, which in turn brought Sam to catch the cabbie adjusting his mirror so he could see the back seat better than before. On another day, Sam might have ripped the mirror from the windshield and even cracked the driver in the ear with it, but today warranted a quieter entry into the city. Sam gripped the lock pick between his knees and brought his hands up holding the remaining pieces of the money clip for the hack to see.

"Broke my money clip," Sam said nonchalantly.

Satisfied, the driver returned to the traffic and continued to weave his way toward the sprawl of the city's suburbs. Sam slipped the lock pick into his pants pocket, adjusted the slim-jim up his sleeve and waited out the ride. He watched with a patience that strained most other riders around him as the traffic stopped, raced, trickled, and stopped again along highways that were six lanes wide.

A curious thought at a time such as this crept into Sam's mind – "What is the phenomenon and physics that control traffic?" How is it that cars on an otherwise open road can be brought to a standstill merely by volume? There were no red lights to stop the cars and trucks, but stop they did and for inordinate lengths of time. The mind gymnastics were a simple way to pass the time and maintain awareness and acuity in this gap between planning and effort. It was a rudimentary game Sam played often and at odd times. Even those times between pulls of the trigger at six hundred meters, he thought about not only windage and elevation, but also the architecture of the buildings he saw through the lenses of his telescopic sight, how keystones settled in mantles, and the curvature of stone and glass. But never had he lost a fraction of focus. Rather, his concentration was keener and coiled tighter like a spring bound to bursting in a relaxed mind. When it was time, the stored energy exploded forth with such a practiced precision it was seamless in execution.

So Sam gave all the outward appearances of being at ease while debating the oddity that prevented stopped cars from starting as one, like a connected train, down the road again. Driver reaction and delay accounted for most of the offset in timing. Inattention and diminished skills made up for the rest, with a small percentage thrown in for the mechanics of the internal combustion engine. With no fanfare, the traffic problem was set aside by the clicking of the cab's turn signal and its easing through the lanes to the right and down an exit ramp.

At the end, the cabbie turned right without stopping and passed through a red light. In a few hundred yards he was pulling into a disjointed strip mall.

"This is the Gallery Towne. Which place you want?"

Aware of the bountiful security cameras in the lots and the entrances, Sam opted for the far end of the lot. He pointed to no place specifically. "At the end of the row. Need to stretch my legs after that flight."

"Long one?"

"St. Louis."

"Coach or first class?"

"Coach."

"Try first class. Lot more room. You're a big dude to be jammed into a coach seat for six hours."

"Coach is all the company will spring for."

"You could upgrade."

"Too much money."

"It's your legs."

Sam reached for his wallet while scanning the parking lot for pedestrians. He adjusted both the slim-jim and the lock pick before coming out with his cash. "How much?"

The cab's top light flashed to available and eased away. Sam took a few steps then knelt down between two cars and tied a black sneaker that didn't need it as his simple carry on backpack sat next to him. As he did, his fingers worked as though blind, like any second grader tasked with tying his shoes without looking. That wasn't difficult. What would have been a challenge for others was to look around and find a car ripe for the taking while the apparent troublesome shoestring provided the cover. For Sam, it was a simple step in a professional lifetime of misdirection, stealth, and clandestine maneuvers that had served both him and his country well. Now he was working for the same country, he reasoned, but in a way that he considered might save it from those who would eviscerate it from within.

Two cars away sat a non-descript dark red Ford Taurus, looking, except for the sculpted name pressed onto the trunk, like most of the Chevy, Chrysler, and Toyota products nearby. "What's happened to the industry?" Sam mused silently as he finished the ruse of the lace. "Detroit looks like Japan, and Japan looks just like Detroit and all built in Canada or Mexico." He shook his head at the wayward thoughts that kept him relaxed on his tight and diligent rampart to the world. "Dad would want me to boost something American," he smiled softly. "Always go American-made," he thought to himself in his father's dry voice.

It would be the Taurus. Sam eyed the parking lot, but being the far edge, there was no vehicle traffic at the moment and just a single shopper walking with purpose toward her car some distance away. With a confident step, Sam waded through the cars to the Taurus. By the time he came alongside, the slim-jim was already sliding down his sleeve. In less than the time it would have taken the owner to unlock the door with the key, the slim-jim effortlessly pierced the window's rubber seal, grabbed the locking rod and tugged slightly. The lock gave way without a struggle. Sam was in. The carbon fiber strip went back up his sleeve like a magician's trick. Sam opened the door, tossed his carry on across the front seat and slid behind the wheel.

A glance around the car and back through the parking lot revealed nothing to discourage the theft. The trigger lock-pick was out and inserted in the ignition in a flash of his hand. A quick series of sharp pulls and the ignition gave up the secrets of its keying. It turned, the engine came to life, Sam slipped the car into gear, and pulled away. A preliminary step in the San Francisco Project – obtaining transportation – had been accomplished in less than five seconds. There may or may not have been security cameras panning the lot, but Sam was counting on being as far away from the building as possible and had kept his head down and his hat pulled low. Minor things, but more than enough to cloud the money conscious mall execs and their cheap grainy video systems.

It was almost six hours before Sam and the lukewarm Ford were canvassing the Mayor's home. Earlier, he had briefly visited a multi-story parking garage on foot and switched plates with another nondescript Taurus. He had passed by one that was a good match, giving up on it for something closer in color. Another level or two and a couple quick flights of stairs in between and he found a maroon Ford. It was astounding and it was easy. The shoe tying game was played again while one hand, holding a dime, worked as an impromptu screwdriver while the other hand played with the laces. When the screws were ready, the shoe hand slipped the original license plate from beneath the back of Sam's shirt, switched it and returned the new stolen plate to the spot just vacated by its replacement. As with all the things he had done in the shadows of his life, it had been imperceptibly smooth and fast. On his return to the car taken from the strip mall, the stolen plate fixed to the original Taurus. Now, it would be harder to trace and less likely to stand out to a very diligent policeman and in the event something went array, the switched plate, still matching the car, would buy Sam the time required to move out of the flashing glare of a patrol car's lights to the shadows once again.

The mayor's home wasn't the White House or even a governor's mansion, but it was secluded and secure, both of which had been anticipated and held with little regard. It was nestled in a quiet older neighborhood behind a white wall and iron gate. Despite the recent headlines, the Mayor did not garner many layers of protection and what protection he did possess was largely ceremonial, given over to members of the local police department. The city's finest took the rotating assignments in stride with the exception of the mayor's driver, who was the only constant. Even this role was only laid out as such to avoid training new men and women to the mayor's schedule. For the Mayor of San Francisco, the choice to maintain a sole driver for every day, barring days off and the like, the need was even simpler – the single driver had taken an unspoken oath as payment of sorts – an easy routine, unburdened with the rigors of 'police work' in exchange for silence and forgetfulness. He would drive the mayor to and from his dalliances and unscrupulous conferences with greedy businessmen without question or notation and had performed with virtuosity until it all unraveled on the national news. The driver had been summarily replaced by a veteran of the police force. This unwilling successor was now being stalked.

Sam had already ambled through the city parking garage with his hat and glasses in place, taking the stairs from ramp to ramp until he came to the emblazoned glass doors that proclaimed too loudly for a parking garage, "City Hall." Nearby he had walked without apparent notice by a medium blue Ford Crown Victoria, the Police Interceptor specialized model, with an XLT package that supplanted the interior heavy wire prisoner screen and standard police computer system for a plush interior with leather seats. It was parked in a reserved spot designated, 'The Mayor,' making Sam's job incredibly easy. Now Sam waited up the street in his own borrowed Ford for the mayor's blue Ford to come home.

The season that brought snow and ice to the states further north slapped the San Francisco region with an occasional cool blast, but while the cold meant nothing to him, the early setting fall sun was a different matter. With his work, Sam could tolerate the inconsistencies of the weather as it had little bearing on any mission in recent memory. The night, which would envelop the streets he prowled, was a different matter. That black cloak had served him well more times than he could remember and he knew it would again. He glanced at his watch then looked fleetingly at the darkening skies around him and the streaks of retreating sunlight and knew the battle for the day was lost. Sam allowed a small smile. He was pleased that while the day's weather may make or break days at the beach, weddings, ballgames, and thousands of other plans, night and its cousin, darkness, were as dependable as the rising of the sun the next day. But in those intervening hours, Sam did his thing and waited for the morning sun to expose his handiwork. The next few days would be no different.

He was slumped down, with the seat back as far as possible to let him stretch his long muscular legs, but the back was up – to recline would indicate too long of a stay and raise an alarm with any of the regular traffic. But even with the seat arranged like it was, Sam couldn't stay long. He watched and waited until his internal clock began to whisper. Then he started up the car and slipped away from the curb, unnoticed.

Like a vulture forced off carrion by the side of the road, Sam moved to another perch not far from the first, where he could still see the path of the prize. After another flight to yet another limb of the tree that made up the branching side streets of the exclusive neighborhood, the sun began to set in earnest. The approaching twilight would, as ever, provide an extra layer of cover. He reached over his head and snapped the lens cover off the interior light. He popped the bulbs out and tossed them in the glove box.

Suddenly the quarry appeared. Just as quickly, the mayor's interceptor vanished up its occupant's tight side street. Sam slipped from the car and walked to the corner. Again he knelt and retied an apparent troublesome shoelace. From the corner of his eye Sam saw the iron gate begin to slide open long before the car approached and in seconds held its gapping mouth fully open for the car. The blue Ford passed through the gate without fanfare, but the gate didn't close behind the car, just as Sam had predicted to himself.

Sam checked his watch and spun its stopwatch function into action. He watched and waited. In one minute thirty-four seconds the driver and the Ford Interceptor emerged from behind the walls of the estate. The gate began closing as the car cleared the columns of the gate. Atop the pillars were security cameras – big bulky ones – designed to be visual deterrents as much as for anything they might capture and relay to the house. They oscillated slowly, each one covering its twin and the gate space, but not quite. Sam took note that as one paned away and the other covered the gate, there would be a blind spot – small to be sure – but a blind spot nonetheless tight alongside the column, right beneath the camera. Even with a wide-angle lens, the camera's position on top of the white concrete pillar – designed to be seen and deter by sight – left a gap. It would work to an intruder's advantage perfectly.

Sam returned to his car and pulled away. He found an upscale hotel a few miles away, rented a room with cash and a credit card with the name Lyles imprinted on it, flashed a matching ID, and went to bed. The next day was spent bouncing from the History Channel to Animal Planet and back via Discovery. That evening Sam repeated the same watchful tactic from the preceding day. Nothing changed except the numbers on the stopwatch and even they varied by only a few seconds. The following day was spent the same except when evening came, Sam's surveillance was much closer. He'd go behind the wall.

On schedule, the Ford appeared and drifted casually toward the mayor's home. Sam slipped from the shadows and, shielded from the lights of the car, jogged easily behind it, mirroring the Interceptor from the sidewalk in its run up the street. When the car turned into the gated driveway, Sam was nearly on it. As he came to the gate he adjusted the speed of his jog until the security camera's panning was just right. Then he ducked into the driveway with so fluid a motion that had someone been staring right at him, he would have seemed to simply disappear.

Sam came up from a slight crouch on the other side of the wall as the mayor's car accelerated slightly and moved toward the house, a short distance away. Shielded again by the car's headlight glare and guided by its bright red taillights, Sam jogged along the edge of the driveway.

This was a city manor. It lacked the luxury of acreage and a long curving driveway amid the visual grandeur of an expansive front lawn. Instead, the home was tucked in behind its wall and a veil of trees that would serve as perfect cover.

Ahead of him, the car slowed and eased into the wide cul-de-sac at the front door, splashing its low-beams across the house. It was a stately place, suitable for the chief executive of a large city. White, carrying dark green shutters with an entranceway framed by squared columns, the house sat deeply nestled on pristine, manicured grounds. Everything about the home looked perfect on the outside, but there was turmoil within. The First Lady of San Francisco had not been there since the story broke regarding her husband's infidelity. The only resident at the moment was a butler/bodyguard.

The brake lights came to life as the car rolled to a stop. Sam dropped down in a small flowerbed of begonias and soft pine needles that had collected near the trunk of their tree and watched. As he did, the car honked its horn very briefly and came to a halt just as the back door swung open.

A muffled voice weaved its way from the car and over to Sam. He couldn't make it out, but he understood the mayor very clearly.

"You too, Jay. See you in the morning."

The mayor punctuated his sentence by slamming the door. Almost immediately, the heavy green paneled door to the house opened and the butler stepped out, holding the door open.

"Good evening, Mr. Mayor."

"Frankie," was all the Mayor uttered as he slipped past the guard and into his house. It was neither a hello nor a goodnight. It was merely an acknowledgment of presence. Sam heard it and wondered if Frankie would return such a greeting with a strong desire to lay down his life for the person who tendered it. For his part, the bodyguard watched the taillights of the Interceptor for a moment, glanced around the driveway and the front of the house, then stepped inside and closed the door, leaving Sam alone with the pine needles, the trees, and the dark. Instantly Sam bounced to a low running crouch and said goodbye to the begonias.

The jaws of the gate were closing as the driver turned the Ford back into the street and hit the accelerator. The sound of the engine overstepped the rattling of the gate for another moment as the mechanical arms eased it together. Sam was in a race.

He was forced to abandon his dance with the security cameras in exchange for simply getting out. There was little doubt he could scale the gate and perhaps even the wall if pressed into it, but the point tonight, and on most of the sorties he had completed, was to draw little attention. Having a man grappling up and down an iron gate, even in semi-darkness, was not on the menu. So instead, Sam sprinted hard, turned sideways at the last moment, and ducked thru the raucous gate as it hammered closed behind him. The escape was complete with the gate itself lending a hand by veiling Sam's silhouette against its black iron. His eyes automatically darted up and down the street as his feet took up the relaxed jog of an unassuming evening exercise regime. The street was empty and quiet. The only spectators were the taillights of the Interceptor, winking good night as they rounded the corner at the end of the block.

The final reconnaissance of the mayor's home and routine were complete. Sam jogged off toward his Taurus, parked several blocks away, to spend his last night in San Francisco.

17

In Tampa, FBI Special Agent-in-Charge Cal Denti was on the phone. The other end of the line reached to Atlanta and the FBI's regional headquarters and his boss, Alyn Nuary. Holding the opposite receiver, Nuary, a stunning, but painfully arrogant political bitch if ever one took a breath of life, was scarcely listening. She was more than twenty years younger than Cal, carried only eighteen months' worth of field experience with her, had an MBA, but more crucial to her fast track resume within the Bureau, she had high placed friends, acquaintances, and lovers. Her face was cut from a fashion magazine replete with cheekbones teased exorbitantly high by perfect makeup beneath deceiving doe eyes that held cutting blue lenses over pupils that in truth were a greenish brown. All of this was kissed on either side by a hair stylist's bottled blonde handiwork. She was petite, save her augmented breasts, and was firm all over with an athlete's physic. Her curves could have ground a polished chrome dancing pole to dust and she had used them to maneuver the ladder of the Bureau in shockingly short order. Any arrests were ancillary and could be counted on one manicured hand.

Alyn Nuary was the kind of woman who was attractive to the eye by any man's standards, but lost nearly all vestiges of that appeal as soon as she opened her mouth. The teeth were straight and true and perfect Chiclet white with the aid of porcelain veneers, but the words, tone, and inflection were a perpetual stream of venom. If she had a true friend, they'd yet to meet. Still, Nuary managed to have more than her share of lovers, as there were no shortage of equally ruthless and powerful men who were more than willing to ignore or block out her attitude and personality for an extended romp in her bed.

Alyn lived – by accounts ranging from her own to those of her coworkers and superiors – simply to hunt down, overtake, and consume power. Her curves gave her opportunities that her quick mind snatched and stacked up in her unyielding process of ladder climbing and empire building. She wasn't done – never would be done – but having recently ascended to head the regional office in Atlanta, she had a new launching pad for her next career move.

Alyn had only one trait that passed muster with rank and file law enforcement. She was one of the best rifle shots in the Bureau. Her intelligence and ability to focus comingled with a brutal competitive sense that sent rounds down range through paper targets in tight groups you could cover with a quarter. Even detractors couldn't take her championship scores from her. To maintain her top form, Alyn went to long distance ranges every few weeks and practiced. Employing just a hint of her arrogance, she loaded her own ammo, not trusting even finely tuned match grade ammunition. Along with seating primers, uniquely shaped jacketed bullets, and meticulously measured and calculated grains of a high powered cocktail of gun powders, she added a dose of attitude.

The shooting was always spectacular. It was enhanced by the sight of Alyn laying on a padded blanket with her custom .223 Browning on a stubby bi-pod rest while wearing a skirt. Her thighs flashed. She did little to control the hem as she braced her legs in a shooter's stance. The focus was all down range.

The loading, tweaking of weights and mixtures, the practice, and the competitions were her hobby, but not her vice. That was reserved for power, impact, and influence. The package was surrounded, as anyone might gather with even a glance from a distance, by a very healthy fashion forward wardrobe.

The bulk of Alyn's days were not taken up with shoulder to the wheel work pursuing criminals and terrorists. Instead, she studied organizational charts of the Bureau, looking for weaknesses and retirees, supervisor's shortcomings, and mid-life men in crisis who could be manipulated to her benefit. Other women who were in the path of her intentions suffered through all manner of orchestrated wrangling. The life long process had been summed up by a past conquest in a heated conversation preceding his summary dismissal from her bed. When asked what she wanted in life, her answer had been brutally simple and encompassed her to the core.

"What is it Alyn? What do you want from me?" the used man said as he propped himself up on an elbow stabbed deeply through her pillow.

"Nothing. You're nothing to me now," she replied curtly as she stared at the ceiling.

"I was once. I was when you needed me. You're the most calculating person I've ever slept with."

"It's good to be number one."

"You know, you're only about two steps above a whore."

"Sticks and stones," she said as she glanced at her French nails.

"Yet tell me, what is it you're after? When will you be satisfied?"

"Never."

"Those manicured hands are awfully calloused."

"Know what?" she answered as she turned slightly to look at him dismissively. "I don't give a shit."

"That's been made clear on many occasions to many, many men. Oh yeah, you think I don't know your trashy past? The story is you were handing out blowjobs at the academy ten years ago in exchange for skipping the five AM runs."

"Is there a point to this rant?"

"Sure, but it's mostly curiosity. You never answered my question. What is it you're after? A little empire of your own?"

Alyn continued volleying and didn't miss a beat. "Not a little one," she said as she reached too hard through the sheet and grabbed her partner by the crotch. "Little will never do."

He grabbed her hand, also far too rough, and pulled it away. "Stop it, Alyn."

This time she hesitated a few seconds before slipping from the bed and standing naked beside it. Alyn stared down at her most recent lover. "What do I want?" she said through a sinister smile as she stretched, ran her hands slowly over her breasts and down to her thighs. "What do I want?" she repeated methodically as she placed one knee on the bed, reached out with her hands to his shoulders, and leaned close as if to give him a kiss, before stopping short.

He felt the allure building again as he stared at her curves, smelled the hot scent of sex and felt her wet fingers on his shoulder. "What do you want, Alyn?" he whispered.

Alyn pushed back forcibly and slapped his face with a resounding whack. He was stunned. His eyes were wide and a hand instinctively came to his face and touched his stinging cheek.

"More. I want more," is all she said as she spun toward the bathroom and the days and years that waited on her.

Calburn was clicking through a series of notes he had typed into a simple document on his computer as he talked. He was using his notes as reference points as he began piecing together a case worthy of investigation though there wasn't a thread on a suspect. Alyn was looking at her own computer screen while she continued to listen little. Her screen however, was cluttered with four windows of Saks Fifth Avenue's latest clothing line. She found herself enamored by the Rag and Bone tank top at two hundred ninety-five dollars. Alyn kept clicking while Cal continued pitching his thoughts.

"I've been over this mess four dozen times, Alyn, and it doesn't gain much traction on any try."

"So... Tell me again why are we talking?"

"It's an interesting set of circumstances. And each incident we're aware of adds to the sum of the whole."

"But the sum is zero, Cal. You said so yourself."

"Not quite zero."

"Not quite?"

"Yes. Not quite. And it's that small space occupied by 'not quite' that keeps me coming back to some vague connection."

"Let's walk through it again. But make it quick. Show me a solid connection, not a vague one." She said as she flipped ahead to find a matching belt.

"I don't believe I can. At least not yet, but there is—"

"It's there or it isn't, Agent Denti. Can't be both." A black woven Gucci sash with an onyx buckle caught her eye. "Neither we at HQ, nor you in the field, have the time to manufacture cases. In fact, I'm more than a little disappointed you've even inquired on this... this nothing."

"Jesus, Alyn. Do you even listen?"

Her hand eased off the clicking mouse. "Excuse me?"

"If one thing happens, I agree, it's a fluke. Two things, weird. Happenstance. Even three odd ducks in a row. Coincidence. A maybe. But we're up to four now and I don't think we're through."

"What four? What are you talking about?"

"Goddamn it, Nuary. Do you even read the reports I send up?"

"Watch your tone, Cal. I understand you've had an illustrious career. Don't piss it away by pulling any bullshit with me."

"That a threat?"

"No, it's not a threat. It's a promise. You mess with me and you'll be picking up brass casings at the firing range for recruits."

"This is such bullshit."

"What did you say?" There was an answer in the silence. "What.. did.. you.. say, Agent Denti?"

"I said, bullshit. You're not going to touch me and you know it. And I know I have to work with you. You're the boss, until you can work your way into something better. So here's what's going to happen. I'm going to keep sending my reports and you're going to keep ignoring them. But if and when this thing gels, you'd be a whole lot better off to be on the inside track instead of pressing your nose up against the glass from the outside. Your call."

Calburn hung up the phone. It was a few seconds before he came to grips with the fact that he'd just cursed out his superior and hung up on her. This could be ugly. He'd find out in less than ten seconds. The phone rang.

"Special Agent Denti," he said.

"You ever pull a stunt like that again, you goddamn dinosaur, and I'll make you happy to be policing the range for brass! Understood?"

He hesitated, bit his tongue and relented. "Understood. But I believe you're missing out on something here and I want you aware."

"I bet you do. You don't give a shit what I think."

"Maybe. But I have to run my investigations by you just the same so there it is."

"What's the four?" she snapped.

"It's all in the reports," Calburn said purposely giving her another go round.

"Humor me."

"There was a local county commissioner who was in bed with a big-time developer. They both mysteriously gave away every cent they made following indictment."

"Remorse?"

"White collar remorse? Doesn't even exist. Sounds like an oxymoron."

"Next."

"Pharmacy company. Makes millions peddling a drug it turns out they knew was harmful. Made a billion dollars. Dumped it in a series of worthless stock trades within days of the scandal breaking."

"Silly to say remorse, I assume?"

"It's laughable."

"Third."

"This one you had to have heard of. Pedophile congressman. The kiddie porn king who–"

"Alleged."

"Granted. Alleged. But he supposedly sends reams and reams of pictures of young boys and him in compromising positions."

"I did hear about this one. He sent them to the press."

"Right. The very morning the story broke. He's in his driveway denying everything and the pictures get sent right to the news channel trucks parked in his lawn. They flash the pictures in front of him and he has a heart attack. Dies right there and then."

"And?"

"And his hard drive is in his briefcase. He didn't send anything."

"Interesting. What's the connection?"

"I'm not certain yet. But then there's number four. The Mayor of San Francisco. You heard about the ad?"

"Yes. What of it? Seems like political bickering."

"We've been looking into the threat on a sitting mayor and we haven't been able to connect the dots."

"How so?"

"Forensics have been working with the *Chronicle's* security staff and haven't been able to discover how the ad was placed."

"Probably an insider. So there's no trace because there was no violation of company policy. Ever think of that?"

"Of course, but it's too heavy and leaves the *Chronicle* with huge liabilities."

"And huge sales. C'mon, Denti. This isn't what you're trying to make of it."

"I'm not trying to make anything of anything, Alyn. All I'm doing is arranging some recent events and looking at them from thirty thousand feet. And what I see makes the cop in me consider that these things could be connected."

"How?"

"Nothing definite, but the scent of each one has the same smell to it. 'Bad guy gets busted. Turns over the ill-gotten gain or gives up damning evidence.'"

"And your mayor? What's he given up?"

There was a slight pause, but only enough to find the right words, not search for a plausible explanation. "He's the interesting one and the real reason I'm calling."

"Continue," she said, but had returned to scrolling through screens of business outfits.

"The mayor's deal is different. The open letter is an invitation to do the right thing on his own – without being forced into it."

"Copycat?"

"Maybe, but I don't think so. It's too well done. Well-crafted and placed without a trace. That's the same type of thing our guy with the commissioner, the pharmaceutical company, and the congressman would do, just more so. Escalation. I don't think there are many people who could pull off all this cyber manipulation."

"Alright. So in this pipe dream of yours, we're after one real clever geek. Is that how you see it?"

"That's the final rub, Alyn. I don't think he's satisfied with just being a geek who's good with computers. The open letter was like throwing down the gauntlet. From what the west coast office tells me, the mayor has dismissed it out of hand. Obviously, he's not going to put up any money or offer to resign. I think our boy is ready to cross the line and do something stronger, bigger. The congressman dying was an accident. The next time it will be on purpose. He's not going to run that ad just to be ignored. You can bet on it."

There was another pause, this time from the Atlanta end of the line. "Denti? I want this to go away. I–"

"No. Alyn. It's not much, but there's traction coming under this."

"You didn't hear me. This is stupid."

"It's not. I'm telling you–"

"It's stupid enough to stop right here. We're not going to commit any of our resources to this scheme and I see no point in sending this on to Washington. If the west coast wants to use the mayor for bait, they can, but we're not getting involved in something this flimsy."

"Something's going to happen. I want to be on the record as saying as much."

"Duly noted. Now, is that all?" she said as the Rag and Bone Collection began its runway walk again across her screen.

Cal sighed in part to relax and also to bolster his resolve. "I'd like to take it to Washington. I don't give a shit if they laugh me out of the place. I'll take the weight."

"Don't even think about it. That's a direct order. Anything you do reflects on me and I go down for no one."

"Then let me go on my own."

"No chance."

"You're wrong, Alyn."

"Here's the deal – if the Mayor of San Francisco gets kidnapped and held for ransom or starts throwing money out of an airplane over the city, call me. Apart from that, we're done here. It's not our region. There's no connection. End it. Understood?"

"Alyn, this is not the way to–"

"Understood, Denti?"

There was a predictable pause. "You're making a mistake."

"Are you getting deaf in your old age? And don't think I've forgotten your little tantrum earlier. It will make an interesting entry in your annual review."

"Fine."

"Fine? Alright. That's another entry. Care to keep going?"

"No."

"Good. How's the weather down there?" she offered, wanting to change the subject to anything other than Calburn's fantasy. "They say nothing but sunshine."

"Yes. Sunny. Sunny here, but I hear it's raining twenty dollar bills over San Francisco."

"I doubt it, but call me if it does."

This time it was Nuary's turn to hang up and she did so minus a goodbye. Calburn hung up as well, but slower as he had already begun to search for a new tactic. In a mind trained to analyze quickly, he found one – he'd send the report on to Washington without her endorsement. It flashed of folly at first, but in an hour he had mulled over the whole thing again.

It started taking form in his mind, begging to be pushed into the fluorescent glare of some northern office light. After a long quiet night, Cal emerged from home the next morning with a fresh step. By the time he was at his neatly kept desk, the plan was finalized. The Atlanta report, minus Alyn Nuary's seal of approval, would go on to Washington. If it flew back in his face, he'd take it like a man. Alyn and he had disagreed on its validity. Fueled by Jack, Cal felt strongly and had crafted the report with all the details and clarity he could muster. The fallout from bypassing his boss would be strenuous and he'd own it all. He'd stuck his neck out before. It had paid off often, though occasionally left a mark.

Sun drenched cloudless Tampa skies, with the waters of the region twinkling at him from all sides, eased the tension. It was a good day to take a risk. Cal sent the package off to Washington and Big John LaRoy, a man he had worked with on several cases through the years. LaRoy was as hardline as they came, but also had the nose of a bloodhound when it came to tracking misdeeds. His forty-plus years with the Bureau had gotten him to the top spot for the Eastern United States. He reported only to the Director. The politics wore him down, but the job was a plum that gave him the liberty to get in the weeds of a case if he so desired and had the scent. Cal would bank on the latter trait and hope it outweighed the political hardline rules and regs. His package hit the small pile of top-secret communiqués bent on the next transport north to DC and he resigned himself to waiting. He couldn't know his wait would be less than twenty-four hours.

———————————

18

Sam spent his last day in San Francisco prepping for the night's foray into the dark and the gray side of the law. Regardless of what stance the authorities would take, Sam was comfortable as he set about his final preparation. The clothes, basic black from head to toe, were ready. He had a very light fanny pack in which he placed a light pair of black gloves, a partial roll of duct tape, a razor knife, a small can of black spray paint, a single sheet of neatly folded paper, and several thick nylon flexible handcuffs – the style used by police officers in riots or protest demonstrations. Apart from the small knife, the only other weapons he carried were his own hands. Ever so briefly, Karen danced across his mind and his hands paused over his limited gear as he watched her form come and go. In his mind, he lingered after her for a time until he came again to his mission. He looked away from his mind's eye and saw the flex cuffs in his hands. He put one together at the tip and snapped it hard in an unwarranted test of strength.

It was nearing dusk. Everything was ready that could be planned for. A much longer list – unfinished and unwritten – was full of the things that couldn't be planned for. He would rely on training, experience, and quick reaction to handle that list. He understood these things – the exciting ones, the dangerous ones – that lay inside the mayor's mansion. Once he was standing there, there was no step-by-step plan, only a thin outline to follow, cover, and commit to memory. Once inside that door much more primal traits would take over and whether things worked, or even made sense, would be solely dependent on the timing and the target's reactions. Success was determined more by outcome than by adherence to strategy. The tactics didn't even matter. It was all about results and completing the mission. Sometimes operations just worked. Other times things went bad. He never knew it until it happened. If Sam entered, did his duty as he understood it, and escaped clean, the plan – though never rehearsed, written out, examined and rubber stamped by senior staff that no longer existed – will have worked.

Sam smiled openly for the first time in days, maybe weeks. It was an unintentional smile that just appeared in the final hours before a mission as it had many, many times in countries far from his own. It demonstrated quiet calm and a relaxed peace that came over him. These were rare minutes he enjoyed immensely. He laid down, relaxed his eyes as though to sleep, and basked in the quieted rhythm of his breathing as the last preparation. His meager tools and the stolen Taurus were ready. It was time to wander back to the upscale suburb and introduce the mayor to The New Illuminati. Breath. Relax. Another minute. He checked his watch. Time to go.

True to the form laid down on the preceding evenings, the mayor's modified Crown Victoria appeared on cue. In the collecting darkness Sam watched its blinker signal the last turn onto the mayor's street. Winked at by the Ford's brake lights – as if a prearranged signal – Sam walked to the corner and watched the iron gate open up the street. When the car cleared the columns and cameras, Sam glanced at his watch. The second hand was at the two.

He drifted across the street. Twenty-one seconds passed. He retied the faux troublesome and resourceful black sneaker. Fifty-nine seconds. He stretched legs already loose and ready. One minute fourteen seconds. Sam took off running with an easy stride toward the gate. One minute thirty seconds and he could hear the Interceptor approaching from the hidden driveway. As he came to the gate he adjusted the speed of his jog, timing his arrival with the outstretched fingers of the headlights across the sidewalk.

One minute thirty-seven seconds and Sam ran headlong into the driver's side front fender of the Ford. It was a hard hit by design and made a crushing thud of a noise. He purposely bounced backward and away from the headlights into the shadow of the gate's column. Much like a football punter who feigns being hit by the onrushing defense and tumbles to the ground, Sam acted out his part, rolled and came to a slumping stop. The driver was out of the car before it stopped rocking.

"Jesus Christ! You alright?" he shouted as he clamored from the open door. In a fraction of a second he was at Sam's side. The driver knelt and gently touched the shoulder of the unmoving counterfeit jogger. "Hey, buddy?"

Sam moaned slightly and struggled in a feeble attempt to turn toward the driver who quickly adjusted himself on the edge of the sidewalk and tried to help. The prey had been lured into the trap. "I never saw you coming. You okay?" the driver said in halves of pleading confession and hope for absolution.

"I think so." Sam's eyes snapped open so quickly the driver was startled. "What do you think?" In the same flash, Sam snatched the man's throat so hard the driver's hand leaped unconsciously from Sam to his own neck and clutched Sam's fingers. Right behind the strike came Sam's other hand in a fist that plowed the driver's gapping jaw like a sledgehammer. Without a word the man was knocked out cold. Efficiently but with no outward urgency, Sam looked up the street from his place on the ground. There had been no witnesses.

Backed by pounds of muscle and rock hard strength, Sam slipped from the ground and, still holding the unconscious driver by the throat, dragged him inside the gate and behind a column. If there had been a witness, a lion carrying off an antelope would have come to mind.

Sam dropped the driver and pulled out his thin black gloves and slipped them on. He snatched three of the nylon flex cuffs from beneath his shirt at the small of his back. In seconds the man was trussed up, bound hand to foot, behind his back. Even after he woke up, he wasn't going anywhere. For good measure, Sam took the duct tape and wrapped a long piece around the driver's head and mouth several times. A second piece went over his eyes. Sam sealed the tape down hard and frisked the cop for his gun and cell phone. He pulled the magazine and threw the gun in one direction, the bullets in another. The man's body was a stool for Sam's hands as he stood up.

The car sat in the driveway, straddling the sidewalk, door open, engine running, waiting for him. In a very casual glance, Sam noticed that the fender he had launched himself into was none the worse for wear as he slid in behind the wheel and dropped the driver's cell phone on the seat. Continuing the nonchalant manner of the commonplace, Sam closed the door and slipped the car into reverse. He backed through the gate and eased onto the lawn. There was what looked to be garage door opener on the driver's visor. Sam touched the button and the gate sprang to life. While the gate closed, Sam turned the car for the house, retracing the track it had taken moments before. From hitting the fender to spinning the car in the entranceway and pointing it again toward the house took only forty-nine seconds. A quick phase one was behind him.

Again, the headlights flashed across the colonial columns of the house. Inside, Frankie saw the flicker of light dash across the dining room walls of the front room. He wasn't concerned and the mayor wasn't in a position to even see them, having already retreated to his den in the back of the house for an evening martini and some ongoing fallout damage control with his wife and their shared personal finances.

Frankie moved back toward the front door in response to the headlights, as conditioned as Pavlov's dogs. A tap on the car's horn prompted only a slight reaction. "One dumb shit or the other forgot a folder."

By the time Frankie retraced his steps to the dark green entranceway, Sam had raced from the car and was staged low outside the door, like a coiled spring. He had one hand over the peephole and his shoulder a foot from the door, cocked and ready for an explosion. As soon as he heard the lockset move – an instant before Frankie opened the door – Sam drove it open, into, and nearly through the hapless bodyguard.

Frankie's hand and arm collapsed under the surprise crush and the heavy door punched him the full length of his face. He reeled under the blow and saw only a rush of movement between the stars in his eyes. Sam had followed the rush of the door as though he were part of it. When the door slammed into the bodyguard, Sam slid off it and delivered a snapping uppercut that whipped Frankie's head back as though he was a human bobble head. He was out on his feet. Before he fell, Sam was behind him and tossed his left arm around the unconscious bodyguard's throat. Sam grabbed the crux of his right elbow with his left hand then flexed hard – so hard that his right hand came to the back of Frankie's head and pushed his throat deeper into Sam's perfect A-framed choke hold. Frankie went deeper into unconsciousness. The pair stood that way for a few seconds in complete silence except for the raspy attempts at breathing coming from the incapacitated bodyguard. In a moment Sam lowered Frankie to the floor, but he didn't release his hold until they were sitting in a crumbled mass just inside the still open door. Only then did Sam ease up the tension on Frankie's throat, get up, close and lock the door.

In seconds, Frankie was trussed up exactly like the Interceptor driver who currently rested under a tree in the shadow of the estate's wall. Sam slumped Frankie to the side, patted him down, and took his pistol and cell phone. Sam stood up as he scanned the hallway with his eyes and ears. There was no sign of the target.

On the balls of his feet with the fingertips of one hand skating along a wall as if to pick up vibrations, Sam moved to the far side of the foyer. Above him, a circular staircase ended with a banister edged balcony. He paused, out of sight from the balcony at the end of the foyer and listened for sound coming from upstairs or down. A wide living room opened behind him through an archway off the right side of the hall and was laid out across the front of the house. Mirrored on the left of the foyer was an elongated formal dining room. Straight ahead lay the beginnings of the kitchen.

The mansion was quiet, dark and empty. Had the mayor been in the front of the house, Sam reasoned the subdued commotion at the door would have alerted him and he'd have appeared by now. He'd be found easy enough. There was no place for him to hide and no reason. Not yet. The final steps of the stalk began in perfect silence.

Beyond the living room in the hall was another doorway, but this one held a wide, raised panel white door that matched the rest of the elaborate trim in the entranceway. There was no knob or latch, just a smartly polished brass plate to push the door open, reminding Sam of what he might see on a swinging serving door to a formal dining room.

Sam reached for a bank of rocker light switches nearby then caught himself staring at the two lights glowing in either end of the foyer – one an intricate chandelier in the foyer over Frankie, who was just beginning to show signs of stirring, and the other over Sam, a much more conservative nearly flush mounted etched crystal globe. There were three switches beneath Sam's hand. He hesitated, looked around and up to the balcony, tried to think as an electrician might, then slowly, to muffle any click, eased the far switch down. The hallway lights went out.

His eye pried through the small crack between the swinging door and the casing as he leaned in close. There was little to see in the dark room. He listened closely. Hearing nothing he pushed the door in only enough to slip into the room along the wall and away from the door. He crouched and eased the door closed again, sat, and listened as his eyes adjusted to the poor light. Some came in through a bank of windows set into a far wall, but the bulk glowed from beneath another door on the far side of the room, directly across from the swinging door. In the light that crept into the room, Sam could discern a smallish table, perhaps six-sided. He immediately thought of a gentleman's poker table. This he quickly reasoned was the gaming room. A faint smell of cigar smoke solidified the deduction, though Sam's focus had not ventured beyond the far door.

If the mayor was there, he'd be working a martini and a computer with equal concentration. It seemed the practical set of circumstances. The computer might pose an issue if he were actively engaged in a dialogue, but it would be far from insurmountable. If he were on the telephone it would be another matter. Either way, good or bad, Sam could not afford to wait long. Unlike other operations where he might have been surrounded by sleeping enemy combatants and sentries, here in this affluent suburb all he had to truly concern himself with was the fact that the gate was still open. A visitor who possessed a gate opener or a code, unknowingly becoming a victim, could arrive at any time. It would be a trifling to Sam, but it was not the way he wanted the first sortie by this new enforcement arm of the people to play out.

Concerned anew with time, Sam stood and crossed the room. As he passed the table he could make out the rack of poker chips to one side resting near a deck of cards. He repeated his earlier tactic at the swinging door with the door to the mayor's office. He listened with an ear and a hand on the door. This door held a standard latch with a long curved handle. Several possible scenarios shot through Sam's mind and he promptly pulled one from the stack. It was not unlike other players who had been in this room and had retrieved a card from the deck and put it into play.

Sam grabbed the handle crudely and moved it as if to open the door, but didn't release the latch. He hesitated as the catch caught its own mechanism. Then he merely rattled the handle back and forth loudly.

"It's not locked, Frankie."

Sam responded by rattling the handle harder, careful to not let it slip past the point of opening the door. Whatever the mayor was doing, Sam wanted to pull him from it.

"Open the goddamn door!" the mayor snapped as he gruffly pushed himself away from his computer screen and pounded toward his office door. "Open the damn thing, for—"

No sooner had his hand touched the latch than Sam was through the door and on him. In a blink the mayor was thrown to the floor by his throat. Before he could mutter a protest, Sam had slipped behind him, A-framed his neck, and put him to sleep. For the third time that evening Sam pulled nylon cuffs and the duct tape from his bag. The man was trussed up exactly like those who served him and once again, Sam stood up, slowly, confidently, and closed the door. As he waited for the mayor to wake up he looked over the most prominent politician in San Francisco.

There was nothing uncovered by the duct tape from which to judge or even distinguish the man's features. The brown slip on tasseled shoes were polished except for a single scuff up the inside of one – probably a result of what just happened to their owner. The pale pink shirt was lightly wrinkled from a day's worth of work and the matching tie was pulled away from the neck, probably loosened by the mayor on the ride from his office. The pants matched a suit jacket that was slung over the arm of a wing-backed light tan leather chair that faced the wide desk, but for now towered above the body on the floor. The desk itself was neat, had no blotter but did hold a short tumbler three quarters full of whiskey and water. The computer monitor glowed and was the only light in the room apart from a faintly glowing lamp on a small marble topped table across the room.

Above and to the sides of the lamp were rows of bookshelves, but it struck Sam immediately that the shelves were mostly holding framed pictures and nick-knacks and not the rows of matching law reviews he'd expected. The only window was heavily draped.

A snorting gasp brought Sam's attention back to the heap on the floor. The mayor was having difficulty regaining consciousness breathing only through his nose. The tape had his mouth sealed absolutely shut. There was nothing he was going to say that would change anything and Sam didn't want to hear the line of bullshit that would come sputtering out when the reason for Sam's intersection with his privileged life became apparent.

There were a few more deep breaths then a weak attempt to move, followed by a growing surge of a struggle that took the mayor no closer to being free than when he first tested his bindings.

"Hey!" Sam yelled as he stepped forward and put a foot on a thrashing thigh. "Don't try it."

The mayor mumbled and hummed beneath his tape.

"Shut up," Sam ordered. "There isn't a thing you can say or think of doing or giving up that's going to change a thing so shut up."

The mayor lay on his side, still, but breathing as heavy as possible through his nose over his duct taped mouth.

"Here it is, shithead. You fucked a lot of people over. They trusted you. They gave you their confidence along with their money and their vote. Now you have to pay for that." Sam walked around until he was at the mayor's back. He could tell the nylon cuffs were tight and cutting into the flesh at the wrists. He slipped two fingers into the loop that ran to the mayor's feet then gave his bundle a quick harsh jerk. The mayor grunted and flinched.

"You don't like it when it's you who's getting stepped on, do you? But if it's John Q. Public, it doesn't matter, does it? Just nameless people. Blank faces. Votes. Necessary evils. Campaigning and all those promises. But the rules have changed, Mr. Mayor," Sam said so slowly it was contemptuous. "The people have a new voice and it's not coming from inside the ballot box. It's right here. Right now. You were asked to do the right thing. You didn't. You thought, 'I'm above the law. It'll take ten years to work through the courts.' Not this time. Not anymore."

Sam paused and thought about his next words and his next move. His internal clock told him it was time to go, but he wanted to leave the right message before he punctuated his visit.

"I've got a message for you to deliver. Understand?" Sam nudged him with the toe of his boot. "Understand?"

The mayor nodded and offered a blind muffled affirmation. "Umm-hmm..."

"I want you to tell all your corporate and political friends, with their fat cigars in their paneled offices that someone's looking over their shoulder every second of every day. The next time one of them even starts thinking about fucking the public, we're gonna rip their head off and shit down their neck. Got it?"

The mayor nodded quickly from the floor and mumbled again. "Ummm hmm. Umm hmm."

"Good," Sam said quietly. "That's good. Make sure you deliver that message."

Without prompting, the mayor nodded again, hoping the threat was passing by. "Umm hmm. Umm hmm."

"That leaves us with some unfinished business, Mr. Mayor," Sam said as he took out his razor knife. "You were asked to pay back what you took and admit to your dirty deeds. You haven't done that." Sam leaned over and cut the nylon loop that held the mayor's legs together. Feeling the release, he stretched them out, just what Sam wanted.

"I'd ask you why..., but I don't give a shit."

Like a professional wrestler, but backed with a real expertise that bordered on a perverse zeal for pain and punishment, Sam put the knife between his teeth, picked up one of the mayor's feet, and twisted it tightly until the mayor spun on the floor face up. With a seasoned move, Sam dropped his full weight coupled with an explosive downward force on the mayor's knee until it caught deep in Sam's armpit. The weight and the blow caused the knee to give way. The ligaments and tendons stretched beyond their limits and snapped in rapid succession. The mayor went into convulsions with the pain. Before he could consciously understand what had just happened, it happened again to the other leg. Not content with the feel and sound of the crunch and tearing, Sam dropped on the second leg twice. It gave way so completely Sam was left holding the foot upright as though it was hinged backward.

Sam crudely dropped the useless leg. For a moment he just stood and watched his creation writhing on the floor. Then he came down beside it and cut the mayor's hands free. The agony forced the man to let them fall, but Sam snatched one, spun as he had with the feet, and drove his shoulder into the back of the locked elbow. Muscles tore and bones cracked with the sound of a limb snapping off a tree. In a blur, Sam repeated the motion on the remaining arm and felt the grinding as the hinged joint blew apart. There was no resistance. The mayor – sweating and crying – passed out, went limp, and his bladder and bowels emptied into his pants.

A torn up leg was pulled up behind the mayor's back and zip-tied to a worthless arm. Its mates were rendered like treatment until the binding was complete. The face beneath the duct tape was bright red. Sam knelt and used the knife to cut a slit in the tape across the mayor's mouth. He nicked the man's lip. Air was sucked in and expelled with tiny bubbles of blood. The broken man smelled of shit, piss, sweat, and grotesque fear.

The knife was returned to the small pack as Sam stepped to the desk. The mayor's cell phone was on the edge. Sam slipped it into the small black bag. When he pulled his hand from the bag he held the single sheet of paper and unfolded it. He laid it out flat and picked up the drink. He downed the whiskey in one gulp then placed the damp glass on the top left corner of the paper. The simple note held only the Illuminati triangle and eye and the chapter and verse, 'Luke 12:48' and was signed, 'The New Illuminati.'

Sam walked out of the office and away from the stench. He didn't look back as he crossed the gaming room and back into the dark hallway. He heard Frankie struggling against his straps and breathing hard through his nose between his taped over eyes and mouth, but Sam didn't stop. He opened the door and stepped out, locked the door, and pulled it closed behind him.

The car was still running. As he headed down the steps, Sam tossed Frankie's gun in the bushes. In a moment he was rolling up the driveway until the headlights caught the driver, who had rolled from the grass at the base of the wall into the path of the car. With no fanfare, Sam stopped the car, got out, and picked up the driver by the arm and unceremoniously dragged him to the side and dumped him in the grass.

"Don't move," Sam warned as he stepped on the driver's neck, pinning him down, before going back to the car and hitting the opener again. As he passed the gate he punched the button for the last time, the gate lurched into action, and began to close.

Sam stopped the car in the street and got out. He walked briskly to the wall he had monitored several times, well away from the panning cameras. The small can of black spray paint came out and he shook it a few times for good measure and listened to its unmistakable rattle. As carefully as he could, he sprayed a large black triangle on the white wall. Next came the rough painting in of the eye. To the side he sprayed big bold black letters, 'Luke 12:48.'

Sam returned to the Crown Victoria and the car eased away as it retraced its path down the street. The deed was done. All that remained was to trade cars – leaving the cell phones on the seat of the Crown Victoria, keys in the ignition, and windows down inviting the joy riders that would send the police scurrying all around the City looking for the car and tracing phone records while Sam was over Texas.

————————

19

Before the plane touched down in Tampa, the networks had their breaking news for the week. The tale was told in bits and pieces. "Assault on the Mayor of San Francisco." "Attempted Murder by the Bay." It went on and on with few facts as they truly happened, but more than enough of what Clayton had hoped for. The most titillating reports for him were the constant news clips showing the white wall and the Illuminati symbol. He smiled, he laughed, he jumped around the room like a kid on Christmas morning. Sam had delivered far more than he thought possible and it seemed perfect.

For his part, Sam went directly to the newsstand and arrived along with the early bundles of papers. He dealt with a vigorous trade. From their local police contacts and because of the published letter, The *San Francisco Chronicle* had the scoop and was sold out except for one copy beneath the counter. The other rags had the wire stories and would also sell out. The next few mornings' business would be brisk, but Sam waited on the one sale he knew would be coming. Clayton would be by before long.

Before he could, inner offices across the country were buzzing. On the west coast the paneled offices of the *Chronicle* held shouting matches over column space, placement and word counts. Semi-clandestine calls to police officers were rampant – all bent on an inside story and a detail not yet leaked. On the east coast, Tampa was buzzing less noticeably as Jack and Petey hashed over the latest turn in what Jack still deemed their case. He had a call with Calburn Denti that was vocal and excited on both ends of the phone, but the greatest quiet interest came from Washington and John LaRoy. He was on the phone to the Tampa FBI office just moments after Jack had hung up.

"Agent Denti."

"Hey, stranger. John LaRoy."

"Hi, John. How are you? It's been a while."

"A couple years anyway. Time goes so goddamn fast. I can't keep up. One minute I'm rocking my baby to sleep on one arm and the next she's thirty years old, probably making more money than me, and giving me a grandson in a couple of months."

"I'm sorry about the time thing – same here – but that last part is pretty special, John. Congratulations."

"Thanks, but I called to congratulate you."

"On?"

"On that San Francisco call. You had it pegged."

"Nuary didn't think so."

"Screw that bitch. You forgot more about being a cop than she'll ever know."

"I should say thanks, but it rings a little hollow when you're talking about my boss."

"Well, now you're talking to your boss's boss."

"She won't be happy."

"What else is new? That woman is happy in increments of twenty seconds – picking out a pair of shoes or showering the sweat of some conquest off her belly. Don't worry about her. I'll rein her in. Tell me the story."

"Well, the jest of it is in the reports."

"I know all that. But what's the skinny? Forget the reports. They laid it out pretty well, you're a good writer – nice and concise – but you left the gaps no one can see but guys like you and me. I want to know what you weren't writing down. Especially now that this group, who I was calling 'The Samaritans' after I read your report, has publicly planted their number one target in the emergency ward."

"Samaritans? As in nice guys?"

"Like I said, that was before they grabbed the mayor's legs and made a wish."

"What's his status?"

"I talked to the West Coast twenty minutes ago. It looks like a bunch of guys tried to twist the mayor into a pretzel and several pieces damn near broke off. I wouldn't say this to anyone but you, Cal, but the mayor isn't going to be tapping any secretaries no time soon. They said he might never walk. Could still die, I suppose. He's in some kind of shock from pain."

"I never heard of somebody dying from pain."

"Me neither. The report at least has deciphered TNI for us and it's not The Samaritans, that's for sure. There was a note – same pyramid and eye thing you've seen on the news from the wall, but the note was signed, The New Illuminati. Not sure it helps much yet, but we're running it down. We're also not releasing it yet. It'll come out soon enough. The locals were all over the place as well as the mayor's mob before we got on site."

"Illuminati, huh? I saw what looked like a Bible verse painted on the wall from the news. Has anybody looked it up or confirmed that's what it is?"

"It's something about people with more have more responsibility, or something like that. I'm not up on my Bible reading."

"Nor me, but I'm about to change that."

"Religious nuts?" LaRoy quipped.

"Long shot. This group is too calculating, clever–"

"Add vicious."

"I think the Crusaders were pretty good at vicious if I remember my history at all."

"Yep. Better make a note on that. The Crusades gave birth to the Illuminati or vice-versa. Might be something to check out."

Cal jotted the notes as directed. "What else from out west?"

"They tell me the good mayor's arms and legs were shattered. Just about on backward. Like I said, we're looking for some real hard cases."

"From what I saw of it on the news, there isn't a lot of tears being shed."

"You got that right. There's already been a poll in San Fran. The overwhelming majority say he had it coming – and that from the liberal armpit of the country. That's why I'm calling. We need to get in front of this. What's your gut saying?"

"I'm not certain, to tell the God's honest truth. I'm thinking it's right here. Could be anywhere, but there are some strong threads that lead to Tampa."

"Good old Tampa. Takes me back to the Trafficante days and Tampan."

"You can't be a cop in Tampa and not know the Trafficante name. His grandkids are still around, but what's 'Tampan?'"

"It was a hundred years ago. I was working out of the Miami office, but everything kept pointing to Tampa–"

"Like now."

"Funny how that works, ain't it? Regardless, no one remembers it, but Santo Trafficante was Don of a big part of the country. His family had settled in Tampa. He was tight with the Cubans, see? Hell, Santo Jr. was damn near the mayor of Havana until Castro showed up and gave him the bum's rush. Anyway, Trafficante invents.., yeah, literally invents, his own language. He combines Italian with Spanish. His crew was Sicilian, but he dealt heavy with the Cubans, so he comes up with 'Tampan,' a play on Tampa and Spanish, I suppose. He drove the cops nuts. No one could understand them!" John laughed and brought Calburn with him. "That was a smart old man. Took care of business, made money, didn't trouble the locals. Decent sort. Stayed outa the papers, not like the New York and Chicago wise guys, though him and Giancana were tight. Died in his bed. Hospital bed as I remember, bad ticker I think, but for a guy like that to die in any bed says something about him. God rest his soul."

"I think you're leaving out the part about him maybe having something to do with having President Kennedy whacked."

"That's true, but we never could come close to him on that. Too many players – our government was one of them. That was a god-awful tragedy. But I got to say, for smarts, if Trafficante pulled that off and never got touched, it says a lot about him. Forget it. That Tampan thing got me thinking back. Damn, I'm old! I ought to retire.

"Anyway, tell me more about this new racket, Cal. What have we got – some wide-eyed vigilante?"

"I'm leaning in that direction."

"What makes you lean? You're no kid either. I haven't got excited enough about a caper to cross my boss in thirty years. Why this one?"

Calburn leaned forward into the phone and his grip grew tighter. His voice became tighter as well. "John, this guy or this group, they're serious and they're in it for reasons that are way to the right of what we usually see. It's not for money or power or prestige. It's a revenge thing."

"We've seen revenge."

"Not like this. This is... This is revenge for the masses, not some road rage nonsense. These guys want to take revenge for the public. It's a dreadful cliché, but I think they're out to make a wrong, right."

"Vigilante style justice. Like I said."

"But with a twist. These guys are beyond smart. They're not smash and grab, string 'em up vigilantes. They're thinkers capable of knocking the living hell out of people who're somehow associated with the public trust."

"That's cliché number two in less than a minute."

"I know it, John, and it makes me cringe. I don't know how else to see it."

"You think they're limited to public servants?" Calburn had paused and John answered himself. "You're hoping so, right?"

"I'm pretty certain of it.

"How's your pharmacy execs fit in?"

"Public health – physical and financial."

"Curious."

"I believe they're looking to hold people accountable. Whether it's an oath or part of a scam of the public. They're looking for justice."

"Back to my Samaritans."

"Yes, but it's their definition of justice. They're not thieves, John. They don't steal anything and given what little we know, or think we know, they could be robbing people blind. They move the money. Lose it. Never steal. Give it away."

"Robin Hood?"

"Robin Hood."

"Until last night."

"Until last night...," Calburn echoed.

The pause was noticeable and prolonged. John broke it with a loud sigh. "So... what does last night do to your theory? We still looking for pacifist money movers – geeks with a conscience? Or have we moved over into geeks who double as sparring partners for the MMA?"

"How was the crime scene?" Cal asked. "Sanitary?"

"Crystal. Pro job, from what I've got so far. They scaled the wall like a commando squad, trussed up the driver and a bodyguard like two old ladies, then tipped their hand a bit by snapping the mayor's knees like twigs. Not just anybody can do that. You're after quite a combination here – guys who have skill sets about as far apart as they make them. Mercenary assassins with the restraint to tear a man to pieces but not kill him, and computer geeks who can walk through fire-walls like they don't exist, but don't steal. Helluva combo."

"Sounds a lot worse hearing you actually say it."

"You know me well enough. I call 'em as I see 'em. And this is how I see this one."

"Last night does shake up my original theory a bit. I need to circle around it a few times. Any chance I can get the reports out of San Francisco?"

"They're already on their way. I knew you'd be interested in going over them with a fine toothed comb." There was a short pause. "Okay," John summed up in tone alone. "Delegate your current caseload and get into this neck deep."

"That'll have to be approved by Nuary. I'll have to call her and–"

"Shit. She already knows you had this thing pegged and has been flooding my office and most of Washington with emails about the groundwork she'd been doing on the Illuminati. Most of her chatter looks like it was cut and pasted from the reports you sent me. I sent out a blanket reply saying I knew about it already. My guess is she'll be calling you in the next ten minutes."

Calburn laughed. "Good point. How do I prepare for a cat fight?"

"Kick 'em in the pussy!" LaRoy's voice dropped. "I can't believe I said that. People are so damn PC. You make a joke and you get fired."

"I thought it was sound advice – not that I heard you say anything."

"Let her run off a little steam. Then, after she's hung up on you a couple of times, I'll step in and squelch it best I can." Thinking out loud, John continued. "She does have some strong players in her pocket."

"Problem?" Cal said a bit too nervously.

"Could be – especially if you turn out to be all wet. But here's how we play it, for starters anyway. You and me go way back. We're just talking – no shop, catching up – me telling you about my new grandson. You make mention of a caper you got going. I ask to see it. You say Nuary's not happy with it and refuse. Finally I pull rank and you send it. Rest is history. If it pans out, you walk on water – turns to shit, we both look like asses. End of story."

"Are you certain you want to play it that way? It puts a lot of heat on you, John. You just said she's got juice."

"She does. I can't deny it." Another short gap. "You haven't slept with her, have you?"

"Not a chance."

"That'd make it real ugly. So here's the deal. Get to work on this thing. Let's get some direction – maybe pull a solid lead out of your hat. Let's see if you can't get some answers before people even start asking the questions. In the meantime, toss me under the bus when your boss calls. These guys may sound like heroes today, but before long, they'll go too far or make a mistake. Some innocent civilian will get his knees capped like the mayor or worse. Let's get close and see where this is headed."

The call ended in the next ten seconds amid assurances to keep one another informed of which way the case and the political wind was blowing. Then Calburn waited for the phone to ring and his boss, sharpshooting Alyn Nuary, to call to rip him a new ass, but it never came.

John LaRoy had been right about the impromptu poll. As the story spread out like a wildfire across the country, there was little sympathy for the mayor. Carl had correctly reflected the sentiment of the citizenry when he remarked that people complain about nefarious headline makers, but no one makes a move. Now he echoed the prevalent and nearly jubilant attitude that was reverberating through coffee shops and careening around proverbial water coolers from sea to sea. Finally someone had raised a hand in support of hundreds of thousands of thoughts and comments from a public that had simply had enough.

The knee jerk reaction was predictable. The former wannabe evening news anchors who'd stepped away from being correspondents and taken the short money to headline their own short lived television shows, chimed in with their standard boring bias. It took another couple of shows before they stammered their way into a story line. Each claimed to be truth tellers, but few agreed on anything related to Sam's handiwork and the inscription on the mayor's wall. They rambled, postured, and were wagged by their tails until most descended into dribbling buffoons posing as journalists. Their uninformed hypothesis of the foundations under the acronym 'TNI', the group's intent, and the ramifications for corrupt politicians and greedy businessman were only blind banter. But it sold papers, garnered viewers, raised both ratings and commercial rates for a thirty second spot, and sold more of the drugs that no one knew were needed.

When the frenetic flash of the days following the mayor's accounting had melted, the pundits were found to still be rambling behind video of the mansion's white wall and Clayton's all-seeing eye. They were making weakening attempts at a scoop they were unable to carry. It fell to long established columnists in dailies as far flung as the *Colorado Springs Gazette* and *The Washington Times*, to *Mother Jones* and *The New York Times*, to craft articles that spelled out three thousand word pieces from the three letters at the bottom of Clayton's letter published via the *San Francisco Chronicle's* hijacked press.

The Gazette led with the connection of the eye and the ancient clandestine Illuminati – going so far as to nearly replicate Clayton's initial endeavor by comparing Sam's spray painting scrawl to the National Seal from the one dollar bill. From there, others pounced and built until the evening television shows stumbled onto the new fodder. Then the gloves came off in earnest as journalism gave way to sensationalism. The euphoric and supportive public, vast portions content at the release the mayor's thrashing had provided, became inflamed, incensed, and emboldened by the titillating diatribes of the talking heads.

On the heels of a groundswell of anger and mistrust, viewers became less inclined to be led from commercial to commercial by the droning television shows and more inclined to look across internet and hard copy headlines for the next possible victim of TNI justice. Fifty million people had passed through being numb to salacious scandal and had come out angry and increasingly aware and frequently armed, either literally or with the more powerful weapon of inside information on malevolent deeds. Betting pools popped up. Soon the looking became local as denizens of towns, cities, counties, and states distilled their searches and bets to local offenders. And as Carl had been a mirror held up as the voice of the public, law enforcement officers across the country at every level took the alerting memos from their sergeants then waivered as Jack Aaron had done when they thought through the concept of justice – vigilante or otherwise.

There were voices of descent, but they were cautious and reserved – it was becoming exceedingly clear where the voting block was positioned. Liberals and conservatives of all degrees and stripes immediately saw the inherent danger. Even ardent supporters of the faction known as TNI – pieced together hesitantly at first as The New Illuminati – were forward thinking enough to feel the slipperiness of the slope beneath their feet. There was a quiet concern for the rule of law. This TNI, minus constraint, or victims of their own moral compass gone awry, were more dangerous than a single amoral, greedy politician. They could easily find themselves on an equally dangerous plane with corporate manipulators whose mantra mirrored Alyn Nuary's conceited concept of "more."

While these polarizing wrestling matches took place across the country and kitchen tables, the mayor battled for life. Shock nearly claimed him, but he lived. He would never fully recover physically and politically he was even more badly injured. There would be no sympathy wave to ride. He was finished. His only claim would be as the poster child for what could and would happen to others. Photos, leaked from his hospital bedside of casts and tubes and traction, reinforced the danger to the chagrin of the guilty and the chuckles of others. Most importantly to Clayton, Raphael, and Sam, the pictures and the stories spread word of the now unveiled threat to other politicians and businessmen with dirty hands and sticky fingers.

Most of the corrupt labored to dismiss the attack as a single purposed assault and railed against TNI for their lawlessness, but they were subdued by the groundswell. Only a few took serious note. That number grew slowly as the symbol Clayton had penned and Sam had painted began to appear on buildings and bumpers as graffiti and professionally reproduced stickers. Interest, impact, and effect would come. 'Luke 12:48' methodically became a rallying cry and replaced 'John 3:16' in the end zone crowds at venues across the nation.

When the luster of the assault burned brightest, radio dee jays held contests on what Clayton's acronym stood for until, as John LaRoy had predicted, the truth broke. TNI was 'The New Illuminati.' Fervor began anew and awareness fanned the flames of like-minded men and women until copycats sent threatening letters to their own local wayward officials. No one thought The New Illuminati was a joke any longer. Moves were being made across the country. Small hacks were perpetrated. Then the first bombs went off. The newsboys from Tampa were a thousand miles away in the still warm winter sun, but they had lit the fuse and the country would never be the same again.

20

The newsstand had been busy. Sam sat on the duct taped covered stool behind the worn linoleum covered counter and thought about the silent prediction he'd made to no one that the *San Francisco Chronicle* would sell out in record time. It did. Knowing what he knew – that he'd snapped all four appendages of the Mayor of the City by the Bay in an accounting for the politician's betrayal of his city and his wife – Sam could have ordered ten-fold his usual number of the *Chronicle* and made a few extra dollars, but years of special forces training stopped him. He wouldn't deviate from any routine and in doing so, offer up a chink in a seemingly impregnatable armor. As it was, Sam had flown to San Francisco, broken the mayor, and returned to Tampa without leaving a ripple in his wake.

The lessons of a lifetime carried him to the crying politico's shattered side on cash, falsified identification, and practiced deception. All three had come at various times and in various quantities from his father. A smile grew at the realization. His father, Samiste Ciampiano Sr., was a first generation American who immigrated from Ficuzza, Sicily permanently after several clandestine trips to the States at the behest of the ruling Trafficante syndicate in Tampa. A part-time bone breaker and full-time book maker, Sam Sr., aka the Hammer, ran the last of the city's newspaper stands. He had raised his son by himself after his teenaged wife fled, without his objection, from the violence that flourished around her baby's father. While his wife's running was accepted and almost understood, there was no question that his son, only a baby, would never be permitted to go with his mother. So Sam Jr., *Po' Martello*, the Little Hammer, grew up motherless, and inherited his father's thick arms, tenacity, and the newspaper stand. Before his death, Sam Sr. had shielded his son from the elder Ciampiano's business affairs, but Sam Jr. was too quick to not learn the ways of the street and lessons of loyalty and honor regardless of their shadowed origin.

There was a second Sam in his life – a fictitious uncle draped in red, white, and blue. Uncle Sam. This Sam built granite walls on the bedrock solid foundation of a street tough, but devoted and patriotic immigrant's son. Uncle Sam's Army honed *Po' Martello* into an elite machine and sent him off on raids around the world to fight wars few people were even aware of. Sam had left the military behind him sooner than he wished, but carried forward the unique training and physical skills of a special forces combat soldier.

The stillness of life in the old newsstand was never what Sam had wanted. Yet here he was. No longer a soldier. No longer his deadly Army of One. When the quiet of the newsstand had threatened to swallow him in the darkness of its confines as he closed the front flap each day, redemption had flashed almost simultaneously in a pretty face from yesterday and an opportunity from an old friend.

Karen had felt a pull toward the handsome face with the empty eyes. Risking much against unknown returns, Karen had injected herself into his life. The whirlwind began as a gentle trusting breeze, but it gathered itself and launched the lovers into something they enjoyed and needed. They balanced one another and filled gaps created and left empty years and years before. They may have maintained that pleasant balance a lifetime had not Clayton Rand surfed through a hundred channels to watch a twenty second news video of burning Cyprus trees.

Clayton, of course, had his own unique set of skills – on the other side of the moon from Sam's – but as powerful or more so when measured in reach and impact. He had used his intellect to hack and burn the commissioner's bank accounts and those of his co-conspirators easier than the Cyprus had been cleared. When Clayton was finished, he surreptitiously turned the evidence of the original crimes over to the District Attorney's Office.

That prosecutor, Jack Aaron, scratched his head through his tasseled gray hair as he sat at his disheveled and crowded desk and wondered out loud why a political animal/criminal would all but turn himself in. Jack's second, his chief investigator Marcus Pete, didn't wonder why the commissioner and others had exposed themselves at all. Marcus focused on how.

While they worked their local angles, Clayton's vision had already spread. The philandering, coffer dipping Mayor of San Francisco provided the perfect foil for TNI – The New Illuminati. But computer manipulation wouldn't suffice. Clayton needed – wanted – an escalation, a confrontation. Clayton needed someone with Sam's talents and Sam desperately longed for an outlet to save himself from an implosion. When their high school friendship renewed itself over the tattered newsstand counter, Sam was as good as in the mayor's home office snapping his knees like dried branches from a dead tree.

The trip west and Sam's subsequent painting of Clayton's Illuminati's triangle and eye on the wall of the mayor's estate served as a notice to other politicians and businessmen with like-minded low ideals and perverted moral compasses. That was what Clayton had intended. What was unintended but equally expected was the attention the assault brought from the FBI. Jack had been fanning the flames of his local Bureau office through his old friend, Calburn Denti, who saw the same picture as Jack, but until the San Francisco caper, TNI hadn't garnered much consideration. Now attention was coming in spades as The New Illuminati topped everyone's list.

Convinced by the events in San Francisco of the validity of The New Illuminati Cal had been laboring to convince her of, Director and Special Agent-in-Charge of the Southeast Region for the FBI Alyn Nuary, now scrambled to thrust herself into the case. She understood its media frenzy nature would guarantee her the accolades and notoriety she thirsted for if she could be nearby as others did the grunt work.

So Sam waited in the deep shadow of the newsstand while news of his attack on the mayor spread across communities and through fraternities of both pursuers and criminals. Within each faction, and within the public, the same wide range of opinions pined with various degrees of enthusiasm. Some decried the lawlessness and physicality. Others applauded it. Some felt the attack was a singular event. Others saw a harbinger of things to come – even longed for it.

Within the cocoon of the newsstand and his purposeful electronic isolation, Sam was nearly oblivious to the rumblings stirring up across the country. He had scarcely read the headline of his own making before slipping a copy of the *San Francisco Chronicle* under the counter. There had been more missions in his recent past than he could remember and he'd never looked at a news account of what he participated in. They were seldom close anyway and were mostly vague details tailored by the military to pacify or inflame the politicians and the public in equal measure. The military bartered news releases with members of Congress for appropriations while the politicians pounded their chests in exchange for votes and another term to feather their nests. The bulk of Sam's work never openly entered either the public or even the political arena. Anything that did, he ignored. The mayor and San Francisco would be no exception.

Sam's old high school classmate and untethered partner in the nearly mystical enterprise that had become The New Illuminati came out of the bright sun of the early afternoon and leaned on the counter enough to catch the shade of the overhanging coarse plywood flap. Clayton could see Sam clearly in the shadow, sitting on the worn rusty chrome stool reading a dog-eared book recommended long ago by Karen.

"Hey, Sam."

The book drifted down, as if he was being rudely interrupted though he'd already seen Clayton, as he saw everyone who approached the stand, long before they realized it. "Clay," was all Sam said in acknowledgement.

"How've you been?" Clayton asked as a primer.

"Alright."

"Been busy?"

"Some. You?"

"Same shit. Different day."

"I know the feeling."

"How's business?" Clayton struggled as he fought the urge to ask about the obvious.

Sam didn't answer. Instead he half slipped from the stool and reached beneath the sill. The only saved copy of the *Chronicle* came out in his hand and dropped on the counter in front of Clayton with a crack that resembled a slap in the face. Sam never said a word.

The appearance of the rag and the abrupt smack were by design. They combined into the slightest jolt. If Clayton had any second thoughts – second thoughts that would prompt the changing of his mind – Sam would like to learn of it sooner over later. From behind the counter, Sam knew there was nothing to tie him to Clayton as far as Clayton's Frankenstein was concerned. Even if the Illuminati should crumble, there was no connection Clayton could confess that would impale Sam. Anything the wealthy computer whiz might offer would only be conjecture at worst, hearsay at best, and it was thin in both columns.

Clayton scanned the headline in silence, "Mayor Attacked." He leaned closer to the paper and started reading feverishly. He looked up on occasion at Sam, who had returned to his book. Though Clayton had seen the story *ad nauseam* as recounted by the television news cycles earlier in the day, there was something exciting about reading it and doing so in front of the man responsible.

He read for another minute, but he was scarcely seeing the paper, so intense was his longing for an eruption of words. "What happened?" "How'd it go?" "How'd you do it?" But he held back like an anxious child in front of the veteran warrior. Instead, his mind raced on ahead without words or details or facts.

He imagined Sam's fists punching the mayor in the face as the corrupt politician cowered and flailed in a feeble attempt to defend himself. Sam's punches landed every time and the man cried and begged. Again and again the blows found their mark. Now, beneath the sounds of the punches themselves, Clayton could hear bones cracking. The nose was the first to give way. The mayor's hands gave up and fell away. Beneath a vicious flurry, the mayor's face turned into a blood splattered pulp and he lapsed into unconsciousness, near death.

"Hey, bud. You got anymore *S. F. Chrons*?" a voice interrupted.

"Out," Sam answered, with the appearance of not even having noticed the man working his way down the counter toward Clayton.

"Shit. Any more coming in?"

"No."

"I gotta read my news. Can't trust the cable to give you the straight dope. They get half an idea and talk about it for twenty minutes without saying a thing. They roll out two or three of their buddies – call them experts – and make a big show out of it. Most of them just hawking their latest book of bullshit. Like I'd plop down twenty-five bucks to read their opinion."

Then the man noticed the paper beneath Clayton's hand. "You buying that?"

"I-"

"He already did," Sam said.

"Wanna sell it? It's used," the man laughed. "Two bucks. Fastest money you ever made." He was already pulling two one-dollar bills from an old cracked brown tri-fold wallet.

"No thanks," Clayton answered. "I haven't finished it."

"You from California?"

"No."

"I am. I like to get my news from the source. Know what I mean? Here," he said as he pushed the *Philadelphia Inquirer* close to Clayton. "I'll buy you another paper. You don't mind, do you?"

"I like this one," Clayton said as he folded the *Chronicle* up too neatly.

"Ah, come on–"

"I'm not done," Clayton said with a rising force in his voice. Then he looked at Sam and repeated the words again. "I'm not done."

Sam nodded almost imperceptivity in acknowledgement.

Clayton turned away from the stand, annoyed with the Californian, but invigorated by just seeing Sam and knowing an alliance – albeit an unspoken one – was steadfastly in place. Clayton's yellow note pad held ideas and his mind had the knowledge. Sam had the muscle and his body the skill. The

New Illuminati had been transformed to something more than bytes, it had real teeth, fangs in fact.

"Bytes and teeth. That's funny," Clayton laughed out loud to himself as he tucked the *Chronicle* tighter under his arm while he jogged across the street.

Five hundred miles away in Atlanta, Alyn Nuary had forgone the call to Calburn and busied herself with a series of memos and documents in support of the seasoned veteran's report on the fledgling investigation in Tampa. The events in San Francisco had stoked the odds that Cal had been correct and rather than waste time with him now, Alyn elected to engage in damage control of her own miss-steps. At the heart of her ruse was Special Agent Denti's memorandum, outlining what he had thus far pieced together and his vision on the direction of the case. Alyn placed her signature and initials on each page – customary practice signifying agreement and pledging resources. Then she backdated the final signature. The package was photocopied then placed in a secure inter-departmental envelope bound for Washington and her boss, John LaRoy. Her conversation with Calburn had only been a few days ago. She felt she could easily reason away any perceived delay by pointing a manicured finger at the mailroom. Regardless, months from now, members of the Bureau outside the immediate chain would have no premise on which to base questions over dates. Time had a way of blending days, especially those closely packed. She'd appear to have been instrumental from the onset and well positioned to reap the benefits. Calburn would have to be dealt with – pacified – or better yet, sequestered. It would require more thought and an examination of available assignments balanced against what he knew and could contribute. In the final analysis, everything would be generated, approved, and orchestrated by her. Otherwise, a high profile opportunity would slip away and could land on another, less deserving, dinosaur of a grunt that would only squander the chance at rising to a new level.

Her package complete, she ordered in her administrative assistant. "Take this down to the mail room for immediate delivery to Washington. That 'Confidential' label on there is for a reason," she pointed obnoxiously. "I want it sent ASAP, but I do not want it stamped in any other way whatsoever. Is that clear?"

"Yes, ma'am. No stamping. It'll go internal."

"Is there another way?" Alyn said sarcastically.

"No, ma'am. Not for 'Confidential' material. We do date and time stamp—"

"Not that one," Alyn pointed. "Is that clearly understood? This is the second time I've told you."

"Yes, ma'am. Understood." The admin spun away holding the package that held the contents that supported Calburn's documented hypothesis. Then Alyn went to work plying her trade on the phone lines.

The admin walked briskly down the hall and bypassed the elevators for the stairway and made his way down three flights at a jog to the mailroom.

"Hey, Mac," he said offhandedly as he tossed the package across the plain gray steel desk. "Nuary wants this sent to Washington."

"I'll see if I can squeeze it in," he said from a grin. "She always wants her stuff on top of the heap."

"She said to send it with no date/time stamp."

"That'll happen," the ancient mailroom attendant said with no small hint of sarcasm. "Nothing's left this building without a date/time stamp in the thirty-five some odd years I've been here so I don't think it's happening now."

"She's the Regional Director."

"I don't give a shit if she's J. Edgar-fuckin'-Hoover in drag – which likely could have happened. I get my orders from a whole lot bigger fish than her skinny self-serving ass."

"She won't like it."

"She doesn't have to."

"What do I tell her?"

"That I don't give a shit what she wants."

"Then what?"

"Tell her to call the Man."

"She won't call him, but she'll be on your phone in five minutes."

"And I'll be on that same phone in ten telling my bosses what she wants me to do and then somebody with a big foot will plant it right in her sexy ass. Before it's over, they'll be pissing right in her liposuctioned, Botoxed, plastic surgery-diced up, puffy lipped face!"

Both men laughed hysterically.

The teller grabbed the package and looked up at the delivery boy. "Turn your back."

"What?"

"Turn around a minute. I always gotta teach you college boys how the Bureau works. Go ahead, turn around."

The admin complied. He heard a machine whirl behind him and what he assumed to be the big envelope being tossed into a mammoth gray receiving bin.

"So?" said the grizzled old mailroom attendant.

The admin turned around and scanned the desk and looked beyond in different areas.

"What you waiting on, boy?"

"Well, the package—"

"Taken care of. On its way to Washington. It'll be in the halls of the mighty by five AM."

"And the time stamp?"

"Did you see me stamp it?"

"No."

"Because you told me not to stamp it, correct?"

"Yes."

"I'm a government officer. I follow orders. Let's leave it at that. I got shit to do. Have a good day," the elderly clerk said as he looked away and waved his hand, dismissing the admin assistant as though he were nothing to him.

"Thanks, Mac."

"For what?" the old man said without turning around.

"For the lesson."

"Glad you caught it. You're learning, kid. Now get out of here. I got shit to do."

As the admin wandered back up the stairs, with far less a sense of urgency than a few minutes ago, his boss was in her office, as he had left her.

Nuary would normally be calling her boss, another dinosaur by her standards, but she had to wait out the dateless package's arrival in Washington addressed to his attention. She decided to do a series of lateral moves and contacted several agents and supervisors she knew, who she also knew would be interested in talking to her. She could tell by the way they eyed her when they thought she wasn't looking. Going lateral in the Bureau she could plant seeds outside of her siloed Region and Division and the fruit they would bear would come back as gospel and be credited to Alyn Nuary, "that wiz of a Director in Atlanta." She could care less that the phrase would be followed by, "You know, the looker with the great ass." That meant nothing. There was a pot waiting at the end of this rainbow Denti had conjured up and Nuary knew that it needed stirring in order to make it come out gold in her favor. She'd planted her thoughts in various fields with ideas, several steps short of original, and when the harvest came she would weave the vines to her liking. The case, the glory, and the rewards would be hers.

She brushed back her bottle blonde hair and with one hand, slipped the dangling hoop from her ear. These were apt to be lengthy conversations if it went as planned. White tipped manicured nails danced about her phone like so many girls at a recital. She punched in numbers as her other hand worked a directory on her computer. Over the course of the next four hours she had several conversations – and each nearly identical in content and duration to the last. There were the perfunctory greetings, introductions or renewals after months or years without contact. The context centered on the San Francisco incident and 'her' ongoing investigation. After a strict series of comments and questions, nearly scripted and drawn from Calburn's memos, Alyn ended each call with adamant reminders to contact her immediately if the receiver learned of any advancements in the case with Nuary's empty promise to do likewise. Each time she hung up, Alyn noted in a mental checklist – "seed planted."

The last call was to a Supervisor she had bedded a year or two ago who now oversaw a large portion of the Forensics work that came in from the east coast. The boring rhythmic drone of the last hour's ringing was all she heard until the predictable click announced that someone had answered, though they sounded annoyed at the interruption.

"Agent Meyer."

"Jason? It's Alyn Nuary. How are you?"

Instantly the voice changed and was warm and inviting, even jubilant.

"Hey, how are you, Alyn? Wow, I haven't seen you in a while. Are you in town?"

"I wish I was. We'd have dinner."

"I'd like that," Meyer said with a softness that indicated he had forgotten or forgiven her prior misdeeds and was willing to talk to her and perhaps more.

"Me too. It's a funny thing, Jason. I was thinking about you the other day – maybe a day or so ago – wondering what you were up too, how'd you been, what was going on in your life. I even made a note in my day minder to call you and then this case of mine started to come together and it gave me the excuse I needed."

"No excuse necessary, Alyn. You know that. Call anytime."

"Thank you, Jason. I knew there was a reason I was thinking about you. I must have been remembering what a gentleman you are."

"Gentle? Oh, I don't know about that. As I recall, you weren't into gentle."

"Why," Nuary tried feigned blushing over the phone. "You're being indiscrete."

"My apologies. I forgot how shy you are."

"Thank you."

"Right."

There was only a slight break in the conversation before Jason continued. "So tell me, when are you coming to the Capital?"

"Hard to tell. Someone has to do the field work and send the results to you to keep you busy."

"You're calling about a case, aren't you?"

"No," she lied. "You've been on my mind. I told you."

"I know. You mentioned that, and you mentioned a case. Plus, I was under the impression that you meant what you said the last time we were together. Something like, 'Go to hell,' as I recall."

"C'mon, Jason. That was years ago."

"Not that long."

"I don't remember that, but if I said it–"

"You said it–"

"Then I apologize."

There was another gap of silence as Jason weighed his options and priorities. He sat back at the end of a long table that doubled as a lab desk. Meyer was thirty pounds overweight – a product of the sedentary life encouraged by that same desk. There had been excellent work behind him, but it had been lost for a time when a rendezvous with Nuary prompted the circumventing of protocol and ended with a reprimand for him and a commendation for her.

"I'll tell you what, Alyn. When you come to town next, call me and I'll let you take me to dinner to make up for it. How's that?"

"Seems fair. I'd pay for dinner to enjoy your company. Small price really."

"I'm glad you see it that way. Now, are you ready?"

"For what?"

"To tell me the real reason you called. Is forensics delinquent getting you a report or something?"

"No. No report."

"Alyn. I know you better than that. And I'll go a step further – it's alright. Whatever the real reason is, you tell me, and you got it – whatever it is. The only caveat is that dinner. Oh, and benefits."

"Benefits? What do you mean?"

"C'mon, Alyn. Get with the times. Haven't you heard about being friends with benefits?"

"No."

"We're friends, right? More or less."

"Of course we're friends," she lied again.

"Then it's simple really. Kids these days talk about being friends with benefits, meaning they're friends, not boyfriends and girlfriends, but just knock about friends who have sex when the mood strikes them. That's the benefits part. Great idea. I wish they had it twenty years ago."

"Benefits," Alyn said as if it were almost a question, but not quite.

"Benefits. You in or out?"

There wasn't a lot of thought. 'Benefits' was just a term for something Alyn had doled out for years. This was a new twist – having it laid bare in front of her. Generally there was the tease and the pursuit – cooing and wooing – until consummation of the affair. The real twist for her was the 'friendship' part. That didn't sit well and she almost tipped her hand, but literally bit her lip, sucked on it playfully, then answered simply, "Okay."

Jason wasn't surprised and it showed. "We have a deal then. Now, the truth this time, what do you need? Or rather, what do you want?"

"That's awfully cold," she scolded.

"True, but fair. It's much better this way. We both know the rules this time. What is it you want?"

She was caught in her own web, but it was, in her mind, indeed fair enough. "There's a case," she began then paused, leaving time for the 'I told you so,' or 'I knew it,' comments she was certain were forthcoming. When Jason said nothing to fill the intentional gap, Alyn continued, picking up speed in her voice as she did. "It's something I've been kicking around for some time, trying to make the pieces fit. It's a helluva case, Jason, and I think it's just getting started. This guy is good. Best I've seen. Some sort of computer nerd with an angry streak. What I think is–"

"Alyn?" Meyer interrupted. "Whose case is this?"

"What?"

"Whose case are we talking about?"

"Mine. Why?"

"I don't think so."

"What did you say?" the true Alyn began creeping out from the façade she had held in place thus far.

"I said, 'I don't think so.' Listen to what you're saying, Alyn. You're using all the right words, just the right cadence. You almost sound like someone who's actually had some good cases. 'Best I've seen...' What a crock."

"You arrogant sonofabitch."

"That's more like it! That's the Alyn I know and love."

"Forget it. Sorry I called." But when she didn't hang up right away, Jason knew he had her.

"Hold on, Alyn. Who's the cop in this story? I know it's not you."

"You ask too many questions."

"Got any answers? Remember, it was you who called me."

"You're a sonofabitch. I swear you are."

"You might be right, but you'll never know how big a one I am unless you tell me why you're so interested in somebody else's case. Who knows, I might be totally willing to play along, for benefits, then again, maybe not. I'm guessing I will. You already know I don't always make the best decisions. I fell for you remember? I might do something equally as stupid again."

Alyn was stunned though loath to show it. "You never fell for me."

"Yes I did."

"Whatever happened?"

"You started banging that Federal prosecutor from Alexandria."

"I did not!"

"Think about it."

There was a fleeting few seconds of silence. "I did, didn't I?"

"You did."

"Sorry about that."

"Forget it. We'll be together again."

"Pretty gutsy prediction. What makes you think so?"

"Benefits."

Another second ticked away. "Yeah, benefits," Nuary muttered. "Gotcha."

"So," Meyer said as he moved the phone to the other ear. "What's the caper and whose is it?"

"It's mine."

"Bullshit."

"It's in my region."

"That's better."

"So that makes it mine."

"Whatever you say. Keep talking, my friend with benefits."

"Have you heard about the assault on the Mayor of San Francisco?"

"That's not Federal."

"How wrong you are, Jason. It may not look like it now, but it will be after Washington catches up on my reports."

"Call me intrigued. How so?"

"I believe it's a part of a complex wave of crimes – all perpetrated by the same group – maybe out of the same base of operations. They're doing a lot of computer hacking and financial manipulation, but I saw this advance to physical assault coming."

"You saw it," Jason said sarcastically.

"Within the scope of my team. We saw it. Happy?"

"I'm Okay. It's kind of fun to listen to you squirm a little. This is really going to be fun in bed. I can tell."

"You're pathetic."

"Sure. Whatever you say, Alyn, but why not cut the flattery and tell me what you want?"

"I need to see the forensic reports out of San Francisco."

"The mayor's case?"

"Yes."

"That's doable. Possible connections to ongoing assaults on National figures. Yea, that's doable. What else?"

"What makes you think there's something else?"

"Because you haven't hung up and your lips are moving. You might have gotten those reports by yourself, though it is an easier sell coming from my Division. What else, lover?"

"Any forensic requests that come in from Calburn Denti or John LaRoy, I need to know about. The inquiry, the results, everything."

For the first time, Jason was quiet as he considered his thoughts. Alyn poked him back to awareness. "What's the matter, big boy? Too much for you?"

It took a few more seconds. "No," he answered. "Denti is no trouble, but LaRoy, that's a horse of a different color." On his end, Jason moved the phone again, sat up, and hunched over his desk and the receiver. "Alyn, I can't do that." He baulked again as his eyes chanced a dart across the lab and wished the door closed. "And neither should you. Christ, I have to sign away my life, have a retina scan, and give my first-born child just to get in the office every morning. What do you think would happen if I started giving out executive level reports?"

"Nothing. You're following the instructions of a Regional Director."

"Show me the memo."

"Jason... Remember where your benefits are coming from."

"I am. I'm thinking about my retirement check right now and wondering if they would forward it to a certain post office box in Leavenworth, Kansas."

"Aren't you being the dramatic one?" Alyn said as if it were an observation more than a question. "Fine," she added. "You want a memo. I'll give you one."

"More than one. I want one on every request you make."

"There's one case – this Illuminati group. So you'll only get one and you'll take it. It'll be in reference to an ongoing field investigation regarding the Mayor of San Francisco and all associated investigations. But there're no copies and the original memo gets sent back to me when I ask for it."

Jason thought for just a moment. "Done."

"And when I ask for it back," Alyn continued. "Our professional 'benefits' relationship is over."

Meyer laughed now, more relaxed in the thought that a memo, even a vague one, would shield him. "Fine. No heart wrenching long goodbyes. But I want to ask one more thing."

"You don't get to ask shit."

He ignored her. "Why this one? What's going on?"

"I told you ten minutes ago. You ask too many questions. You don't listen, do you? I ask the questions, Jason. Not you. Get me those reports. I'll be in touch." And she hung up.

———————

21

A pleasant sunrise was easing up the other side of a large bank of windows behind Karen. She sat in the quiet of an early Virginia morning on a pale coral couch which, though not an oversized stuffed behemoth, engulfed her just the same. She wore the bottoms of a faded soft cotton draw-string set of pajamas. Her top was a baggy white t-shirt emblazoned with a Sunshine State tourism ad promoting Tampa as the jewel of the Gulf Coast – "Tampa Bay – Memories That Last a Lifetime," it read, over and around a colorful print of sun, sand, sea, and breeching dolphins.

She pulled her feet up under her and sipped a cup of black coffee from a plain white mug. Though it was a delightfully warm day – made more so by the wakening sunbeams painting themselves across the floor in front of her – Karen cradled the mug like a weary cowboy warming his hands on a tin cup. She was tired. Although the clock tried to convince her she had slept her customary eight hours, her body and mind didn't feel it and the elixir in her hands had not yet had the chance to work its magic.

The night had passed behind her like all the ones since she had returned home from her last visit to the deep south. Sam was always on her mind as she wrestled with unrequited love. In the constant mirror that had been that afternoon at Sam's house, she relived the gruff words and actions of a man she had come to know via the hand of Fate and had come to love through a play of her heart. Now, weeks later, the cuts still bled and the wounds seemed just as deep. Karen had waded through all the glossy grocery check-out stand's rows of analysis and stages of a broken heart. Each one promoted a variation of a minor illness with cures that, before you could get off the couch and reenter society with one's head high, daring someone find a chink in your armor, you had better read the article on page thirty-five. Some intrigued her enough to trick a sale and proved entertaining enough, but predominantly, she passed them by. She deemed that time, coupled with her own efforts, would heal her when the clock and calendar dictated as much. Until then, the nights were restless and the days spent in an awkward pantomime of what she was expected to accomplish.

As it was, neither the days nor the nights served their intended purpose and she consequently met each with dread. Mornings were listless whitewashes of time and afternoons dragged with the dulled senses of a million other souls locked in cubicle cages. The nights were empty pits of unbearably quiet and loneliness.

The loneliness continued but the quiet ended on an uneventful Tuesday morning – uneventful until she was invited to a briefing across the Potomac. The request came through military channels and wasn't directed to her, but Karen, despite her distraction in Florida, had continued to silently and unwittingly see her star rise within JAG. The hesitant new officer in pressed white who had interviewed Sam over a year before had been replaced by a woman whose mastery of the field and the profession had not been overlooked. When the generic summons came from the Federal Bureau of Investigation, Karen was a top three contender for consideration. By 11 AM she was number one and driving into Washington on her way to the aging fortress of FBI Headquarters on Pennsylvania Avenue. She had little intel apart from a quick brief that referenced an ongoing investigation by the Bureau and the subsequent request for JAG's presence. Two words in the brief – "military precision" – were the rationale behind the short trip. Someone in the FBI was about to ask a favor. She'd seen it a dozen times. They wanted quick and easy access to the National Personnel Military Records Center in St. Louis. Any Federal Agent could do it, but Karen, via JAG, could do it faster.

If the uniform helped with the Bureau's police force manning the checkpoints, it didn't show. Karen was diverted and held for an escort. The entire complex was restricted and monitored. Another FBI police officer appeared in a few minutes and signed for Karen as though he was accepting a package from FedEx. The two exchanged obligatory good mornings and walked through heavy doors and began winding away from the street deeper into the massive building. They eased along plain white hallways with old white vinyl floors beneath painted concrete ceilings. There was no attempt at disguising the fact that every move was watched, recorded, and if desired, listened to.

Another checkpoint proved the last for the police officer, but not Karen. She and a new escort were stopped at the entrance to another interior floor and again at the door to a conference room that would never have been mistaken for a corporate boardroom. The walls were painted concrete blocks – pale yellow with outset panels of corkboard. The tables were plain metal frames with white plastic tops. The ceiling had the same corkboard suspended between harsh fluorescent lights. This room was simple by design in order to manage complex conversations and do so in a way that prevented any voices from escaping. A silent detector scanned the room for recording or transmitting equipment. Undetectable electronic white noise bounced from the walls and deafened any electronic ears that may have attempted to pry their way inside. The building, the halls, and the room were the stage, covertly yet successfully set.

Karen was a bit player, or so she thought. The lead actors were milling around the room and settling in at a u-shaped configuration of the plastic topped tables. The barren tables were collecting paper coffee cups and manila folders. Yellow legal pads graced by their faint blue lines slipped from computer briefcases, but the laptops stayed tucked away. An Army Major, dressed in crisp fatigues, shirt sleeves rolled up neatly to just above his elbows, walked to Karen and stuck out his hand casually.

"Lieutenant Auburn," he said as he twisted slightly to see the name tag pinned neatly to her uniform. "Doug Caulden."

"My pleasure, sir."

He studied her for the briefest moment. "Lieutenant Karen Auburn. Got it. I never forget a name or a face."

"Good to know. I'm not that fortunate."

"Thank you for coming over," the major said moving on. "How was the traffic?"

"Not bad today. I must have caught a window."

"You've received the brief? The suits are going to give us a bit more detail."

"What are we looking at?"

"Not completely certain yet. Interesting speculation though. Cybercrime to start."

"That's a bit outside the area of expertise for JAG," Karen said meekly, feeling more out of place than before.

"Escalation might put it back in your court." The Major paused. "Karen, this... I apologize. I'd like you to feel comfortable calling me Doug in this crowd. We are the only ones wearing the uniform. Please. No 'Sir,' 'Major,' anything. Just Doug. I've worked with most of the Washington Bureau before and they get confused by rank." He smiled. "They think they should only talk to Generals. It's hard to get them to understand that Generals know the least of anybody."

Karen smiled back. Doug Caulden was in his forties – Army through and through – with a pleasant face, sense of humor, quick mind, and demeanor that hinted he knew more than he showed.

Doug leaned in and spoke softer. "They do better if we relax protocol a bit and work with them on these affairs. Truth be told, they need to relax more than we do. You'll see more jockeying here than at Pimlico. Those two at the front?" he said as he motioned with his eyes. "Night and day. The heavyset guy is John LaRoy – FBI puppet master for Capitol Hill. If it happens between Maine and Miami, it'll cross his desk. Only answers to the Director. Straight shooter. No nonsense and a helluva keen street sense. The lady? And I use the term loosely. Forgive me in advance. That's Alyn Nuary, Regional Head for the southeast. Reports to LaRoy. I'll let you make up your own mind on her, but suffice to say, she'd plant her fancy heels in anybody's butt to make the papers. She has in mind to be the first female Director of the Bureau, but her technique will only take her so far. She might have peaked, but doesn't know it yet. Don't let her behind you."

Karen looked at the head table. "I've met LaRoy before," she said. "But I doubt he remembers. It's been at least a year. I was in a terrorist briefing with him. He's sharp."

"That's an understatement. LaRoy is probably the best cop in the country. Plus he's well connected. Great combination if he's on your side."

"Is he on our side in this one?"

"Pretty sure."

"What's our contribution?" Karen asked. "I've been over here a few times. Generally they're looking at one of ours and want us to speed up some records or produce someone who's deployed."

"Not this time. LaRoy called me yesterday. This one might have legs."

"What do you mean?"

"I'm not JAG, Karen. He could get records from most anyone, no offense."

"None taken. But I'm not following."

Doug surreptitiously pointed to the Ranger patch on his shoulder. "Special forces. I wouldn't be here if John didn't think there wasn't something else to this."

"Folks?" LaRoy said loudly as if cued. "Take a seat."

As the collection of sleuths and soldiers settled onto plain chairs near their yellow pads, LaRoy stepped away from the front of the room and, bypassing several others, walked straight up to Karen. He put his thick hand on her shoulder as if welcoming an old friend.

"Lieutenant Auburn. Damn glad they sent you. This one's ticklish. We need JAG's top gun."

Karen was shocked and couldn't hide it. "Thank you, sir."

Unlike Doug, LaRoy said nothing to stem the formality, but his tone and a second pat on the shoulder served as an acknowledgment that was immediately disarming and very comforting.

"You bet. Welcome aboard." He moved back to the front as he talked to everyone. "Let me tell you what we're looking at here."

Before his delivery began, Karen had slipped into a chair next to Doug. She looked quickly around the tables and gauged the others. She didn't know the names or faces, apart from LaRoy and the quick reference to Nuary. As it turned out, neither did the others. Calburn Denti, up from the FBI office in Tampa, helped her out and himself.

"Excuse me, John?" Cal interrupted. "I am at a disadvantage I'm afraid. You know the Major and Lieutenant, but I don't believe I do."

Nuary, not to be outdone by her underling, jumped in. "Who are our guests, John?" she said with a wave of her hand toward the uniforms in the room before crossing her arms and leaning back beneath a condescending flash of a slim smile.

With no apology, LaRoy snapped out names and pointed around the room. "We've got two of the best. Major Doug Caulden, USSOCOM – that's Special Operations Command for you civilians. Lieutenant Karen Auburn – top shelf from JAG. The in-house crew is Cal Denti, up from Tampa, where this shit storm started. Alyn Nuary, Atlanta Regional Director. And Jason Meyer, forensics.

"Everybody knows who the hell I am so you also know I don't do tent cards, sticky name tags, or any other warm-fuzzy bullshit. If somebody in this room asks you a question and looks at you sort of funny, just tell them who the hell you are. And know this – nothing goes on with this caper that doesn't cross my desk. If that don't cut it with you, too goddamn bad. Any cowboy bullshit on this one and I'll kick you so hard I'll break my leg off right in your ass. I'm the only cowboy in the room. I'm John Wayne and you are my deputies," he said as he waved his big hand around the room.

LaRoy smiled at his own joke, but the room was split. Doug, Karen, and Cal Denti smiled and relaxed. The humor seemed lost on Meyer, and Nuary actually bristled and looked around the room for support, but found none.

The big man clapped his hands once hard and began to roughly rub his chin and mouth so much that it muddled his first words. "Here's what we know, what we think we know, and what we don't have a goddamn clue about." There was a brown legal folder in front of him. It wasn't tied, but LaRoy jerked the string. He pulled out a fistful of folders and bound reports. As he opened one and appeared to absently flip through the pages, he reeled off what he had effortlessly committed to memory when he had read the first dispatches from Tampa.

"There's some hanky-panky with bank accounts down in Cal's old stomping grounds. The local PD catches some councilman with his hand in the cookie jar and next thing you know, somebody moves all his money into a stock you wouldn't touch with a ten foot pole and he loses his ass. Maybe it starts there, maybe it doesn't, or more likely, that's the first thing we get wind of. Cal? I need you to back up – put it in reverse before we go forward. See if that was where it started. Maybe there's more. Maybe that commissioner wasn't the first go-round. We need to go right there – right to the goddamn source."

"I've got awfully good people on the ground," Cal said. "In the DA's office. I–"

"You haven't assigned any of our own people?" Nuary interrupted.

"Yes. I–"

"Who?"

"I assigned myself."

"Perfect," LaRoy cut it off. "If you say the DA's got good people, that works for me. You spear head it and let Nuary know if and when you need warm bodies to do the leg work. Give him whatever he needs, Nuary. Meyer, line up somebody to attach full-time to this thing. What else, Cal?"

"There's more financial manipulation–"

"That's you, Meyer," LaRoy blurted. "Sorry, Cal."

Cal didn't miss a stroke. "The next jump is to the congressman."

"Sick sonofabitch," LaRoy said, unable or unwilling to curb himself.

Cal smiled slightly, relaxed, and paused, knowing LaRoy was launching.

"And that sonofabitch was a United States congressman," LaRoy said as he began his rant. "Drops his pants in front of the entire world. He had a thing for little boys and that doesn't win you many votes. All his dirty pictures get sent to the media. Makes zero sense – zero sense – so obviously, somebody jerked the congressman's pecker and I mean jerked it hard. So hard, he keels over in his driveway dead as a doornail. Meyer? We've got the prick's hard drive, right?"

Jason nodded, but ignored his yellow pad.

"Now, when I was in school," LaRoy continued. "A text was what the teacher called my geography book. I think she hit me with it a time or two. I probably had it coming. Facebook. Damn dumbest thing I ever heard of." LaRoy tossed his hands in the air. "Hey, everybody! I had ham and cheese on whole wheat for lunch! Look at me. Oh, here's a picture of it. Tomorrow I'll send you a picture of it after I pinch it into my toilet."

LaRoy smiled. Major Caulden laughed out loud and dropped his head. Cal shook his from side to side, but couldn't dislodge his smile. Jason looked at the others to measure the room's reaction before revealing his own. It was an even split. Karen's eyes were wide, but Nuary's jaw dropped so far and so complete it jerked her head down.

"The only people who care are other morons who want to 'share' pictures of their cat. It's a waste of technology," LaRoy ranted as he ignored his rough joke and the room's reaction. "But I want somebody on that piece of plastic and crawling inside – like they're in that goddamn *Matrix* movie – and not come out until they have a smoking gun in their hand. There is no way this scumbag did this to himself and the timing exonerates the wife, so someone, maybe our Illuminati crew, tapped into his system. It'd take somebody awful damn good to do that and that very fact gives us our first of two breaks so far. The geek squad tells me they can count on two hands the people who can do what I just explained and not leave a trace. When I say not a trace, I mean nothing. No... What do you call it, Meyer?"

"Electronic finger–"

"Yep. Electronic fingerprints. None. Nothing. Sharp sonsabitches."

Jason recovered. "Geek squad?"

"Don't get your panties in a bunch. Information Technology. That better? Our Information Technology geeks."

Jason dropped his head, but smiled.

"Up to this point it's bullshit," LaRoy picked up again. "Computer hocus-pocus whatnot. But then it gets interesting. Cal, bring everybody up to speed."

Nuary leaned forward and opened a file. "I've got the assault report right here, John."

"Thanks, Alyn. But I asked Cal to call the Special Agent-in-Charge out in the Bay office last night to get the straight dope. What do they got, Cal?"

"Go ahead, Cal," Nuary said. Denti let it hang long enough to acknowledge how out of place she was.

"The short of it is we think these Samaritans are escalating."

Nuary interrupted. "Samaritans? Felonious assault – maybe attempted murder – let's choose our words wisely, Agent Denti."

Cal looked to LaRoy briefly, but was ready to shoulder the responsibility if need be.

"That's on me," LaRoy said. "I'm not taking a big pro stance on beating the shit out of mayors, but Samaritans was mine. I'll cut it out now that we have what they're calling themselves. Go ahead, Cal."

"Let me back up for the local members of the team who may not be aware of the history. The Mayor of San Francisco was caught having an affair. The girlfriend learned she wasn't the sole focus of entertainment and began the typical jilted lover laundry list of accusations. Except these were pretty heavy duty and they stuck. We're looking at major campaign finance misappropriation, big money construction bribery, kickbacks, bid rigging, influence peddling – he's the poster boy for malfeasance. But somebody, our Samaritans, that is, Illuminati, just to keep it simple," he said purposefully. "Throw down the gauntlet. Somehow a full page ad appears in the *San Francisco Chronicle* asking the mayor to do the right thing by the people."

"Or the 'right thing' according to our perps," Nuary added. "And let's stress a big 'maybe' when we look at this leap from Tampa to San Francisco. Go ahead, Cal," Nuary mimicked LaRoy.

Accidently, Karen found herself looking at Cal Denti as Nuary was talking. Cal was looking anywhere but at his boss and had been captured by Karen and her bright white uniform. At the word "perps," they mouthed the word in unison and each looked away before they might chuckle. They instantly felt they had found a kindred spirit.

Cal cleared his throat gently. "That's true. It's three thousand miles from my bay to San Francisco's bay, but the technical requirements to pull off that ad are similar to what John referenced with the pedophile congressman. With that as the lure, what really makes us sit up and pay attention is when the mayor is shipwrecked in his home office."

"Shipwrecked?" Karen asked before she could stop.

LaRoy laughed. "And you're in the Navy, Karen?"

"He got beat up very badly," Cal said.

"I liked shipwrecked better," LaRoy said as he turned again to Karen. "Somebody opened a major league style can of whoop ass on the mayor. What's the diagnosis, prognosis, whatever they call it?"

"He won't be walking for months and may never walk without pain. The use of his arms is almost zero at the moment. He'll live but he's got a long way to go."

"But not murder," LaRoy said strongly, dismissing Nuary's suggestion. "If the fellas that went in that house wanted him dead, he'd be dead."

"John?" Cal interrupted. "It's 'fella.' Singular. According to San Francisco the witnesses are saying one man. Three victims and all they can give us is white male. The bodyguard and the mayor never saw him at all – just a blur and they woke up gagged."

"A blur...," LaRoy said as he got serious and leaned across the table in Karen and Major Caulden's direction. "You two have been sitting here nice and polite trying to figure out your piece of the puzzle. I'm going to give it to you. Just like the geek, I mean IT Department says, there's only a few folks who can do what we've talked about, the list is longer, but not by a helluva lot, of a single guy who can slip by the mayor's detail and tear a man a new ass and disappear like a puff of smoke. I'm thinking he's one of yours, Doug. I want to know the whereabouts of everybody associated with Special Operations Command and no exceptions. That clear? Don't make me call the Joint Chiefs. If somebody tells me, "Oh, that's the skunk works" or, "Those boys are black ops," I'll call bullshit so fast stars will be spinning on collars. Follow me, Doug?"

The major was already nodding in agreement. "I'm thinking that this is that second break you mentioned."

"You'd think right. Anybody going to squawk about getting you current deployments, re-assignees, retirees, everybody?"

"They'll want it highly restricted."

"You, me, and Karen. Fair enough?"

"Fair enough."

"If you find some turkey squawking to their mommy about ringing the bell or a chicken caving in on hell week, I want to know about it."

Cal raised a finger instead of his hand. "Ringing the bell?"

LaRoy looked at Doug. "Tell him, Major."

"Special Forces selection. If you want to quit, all you have to do is ring a bell in the courtyard of the training camp. There's a world of regret for some of the men that ring that bell. It makes some of them say and do things they might not otherwise do."

Jason Meyer was put off by the uniforms and talk of Special Forces. "Just look for squawking turkeys and chickens that are good with computers. Redefines 'hunt and peck,' doesn't it?"

"Turkeys or anything else fowl," Major Caulden chimed, quick witted and diffusing.

"Christ," LaRoy moaned and the room with him, but it shed the tension.

"Sorry, John," Caulden said. "I couldn't help it."

LaRoy took it in stride, but didn't hide the seriousness. "Turkeys, buzzards, chickens, whatever. I don't give a shit if it's four and twenty blackbirds baked in a pie." LaRoy looked hard at the major. "Open it up and see if they start singing."

Nuary cocked her head to the side and would have wrinkled her brow if Botox hadn't rendered that impossible. "What?"

LaRoy leaned back, laughed out loud, and relaxed for the first time in several minutes. "Oh, you're not fooling me, Nuary. You're old enough to remember nursery rhymes, aren't you? 'Sing a song of six pence, a pocket full of rye.' That one."

There was an impromptu quick debate on who knew of or remembered the rhyming poem.

"I remember," Cal said as the room smiled without Nuary. "I just doubt 'nursery rhymes' is high up the popular trend in any search engine. Does forensics have any recent analysis on it, Jason?"

"I'm afraid not. It seems to have fallen from favor."

"Goddamn internet," LaRoy said. "Nobody reads to their kids." LaRoy pointed to Cal and Jason. "Anyway. Start beatin' the bushes until something runs out." LaRoy turned his attention to Doug and Karen. "And you two find me a dishonorable discharge for one of those blackbirds that got baked in a pie. Got it?"

"Understood," Doug said knowingly.

Blackbird.

It hit her.

Karen couldn't breathe.

———————

22

S am was leaning back on the tattered bar stool reading a paperback book that looked as used as the seat. The cover and finished text was bent behind so he held it easily in one thick hand. As always, no one came to the stand unnoticed.

"Hey, Clay," Sam said as he creased a page as a marker and tossed the book on the counter.

"What's up?" Clayton answered as he drew up on the stand.

"Selling a few papers. You?"

"Working."

"Yep."

"What else have you got going?"

"Nothing."

Clayton looked at the counter and touched it as if he was admiring antique furniture. "I don't want to pry–"

"Then don't," Sam smiled.

"Yea... I've got to ask – are you going to be able to keep the stand open? Things are a lot different than when we were hawking papers for your dad. It's all on-line, you know?"

"Yea, I know."

"Ever think of closing up shop?"

"I'll have to eventually. It has its moments. The tourists help, but it's quiet."

"Then what?"

"Retire," Sam grinned a little.

"Uncle Sam give you a pension already?" Clayton smiled back.

"No. No pension."

"You going to be able to make out?"

"I'll be alright."

"You sure, Sam?"

"The house is paid for. Dad left a few bucks. I don't need much. I saved everything I made when I was in."

Sam's eyes never left Clayton's face, but words lagged for them both. Clayton sighed and brushed at nothing on the counter as though wiping away crumbs. Perhaps they were memories.

"You'd whistle if you needed something, right?" Clayton asked him over the old counter as he picked up the paperback and leafed through it.

"Sure."

"Yea, sure."

"Yea, that's bullshit."

The ice got thinner beneath his feet, but Clayton was emboldened by the recent past. "The guys at the Columbia always liked you." He left the obvious hanging.

"You think they've been holding my dishwasher job open?"

"Or something."

"Dad wouldn't go for it. He was funny about who I ran with. I don't know how you got by him."

They nodded, smiled a little, and looked across the counter and the years. They were on a bridge that spanned the gap in the conversation. The figurative planks under them were made of common history – long past and present. It was solid. The old paperback in Clayton's hand temporarily filled any remaining cracks.

Clayton looked at the book's spine. The edges were worn away. The picture was thin and the yellowish backing was showing through. "*Sun Going Down*. Jack Todd," he read. "Any good?"

"Must be. Probably my third time through it," Sam smiled slightly to the side.

Clayton flipped back to the cover. "I'll check it out."

"Keep it. I think I know how it ends."

"Thanks, but I'm all e-book."

"I should've figured that."

"Your dad would be ashamed of me."

"A little. He liked you though. 'Good worker. Smart kid.'"

"You sound like him. You look like him too, except taller."

"He was tougher."

"He was that. I used to be so scared I'd oversleep and not make it here by five."

"He never used an alarm clock."

"And never late. For how long?"

"Somewhere over thirty years. Fifteen years longer than you could make a living selling papers."

Clayton thumbed the book and rifled the pages as though looking for something. He stopped and looked at Sam. "No slips? Didn't you inherit the other business?"

"No. Numbers haven't been popular for years. The government took it over when they were trying to catch the Trafficantes and saw how much money was on the table. They called my father a criminal, tried to shut him down, changed the name from bolita to lotto, and went into the business for themselves."

"Government," Clayton echoed Sam's sentiments.

"I think people played the same numbers all those years just to keep us in groceries. Dad would have never kept the stand open without them. No one even asks since he died."

"I don't know how he kept everything straight."

"Had a head for numbers. Like you." Sam huffed. "Shit. I remember you sitting under this counter with a tally sheet in one hand and a racing form in the other. Running odds and percentages. He'd let you do that and have me slinging papers up there on the corner like it was 1942. Yea, he liked you, Clay."

"But he loved you."

The grin returned to Sam's sharp jaw. "Yea, he did."

Clayton flipped through the book absently and let Sam enjoy the reflection in his own eyes.

"But he was always old," Sam laughed. "He was in his forties when I was born."

"I do sort of remember thinking he was your grandfather."

"No, he was my dad."

"No one was ever going to mistake him for anything else. He never missed a practice, let alone a game."

"If I wasn't grass-stained and dirty he'd make me walk home. Shit. If I was bloody, he'd let me drive."

Clayton laughed. "I believe that. I saw it happen."

"I know, but I was ten!"

They laughed together now and the hot Tampa street dissolved away and left two young boys laughing and remembering – their words dripping down on the old counter like melted ice cream.

Other memories crossed the counter as if they were quarters traded blindly for papers in days gone by. As remembrances do, the stories trickled to a stop and faded with the light in Sam's eyes and Clayton's smile.

Sam leaned back on the stool and rubbed his eyes with the heels of his palms then slid his hands behind his head and laced his fingers. "I guess now we're supposed to say, 'Those were the days,' or something."

Clayton flicked at a loose piece of contact paper that had given up trying to cover the linoleum covered counter. "No, we just smile, come back to the present, and go back to work."

"Sure."

"Do you mind if I bring up one more memory before we get back to work?"

Sam shrugged almost unnoticeably, but the cast of his eyes and lifting of his lip was ample signal.

"It's not as much fun as the others," Clayton said, half in warning for Sam, but in equal measure as though to test the width of the counter and the space between them. As much as he'd just had the dangerous man laughing at childhood games, Clayton had other recollections of seeing Sam hit the spring breakers – the college kids that filled the beach bars each Easter – in the mouth so hard they fell over each other and were stacked up like tossed cord wood. He'd seen Sam sweep a bar as if other men were a swarm of flies and his feet and hands sprayed Raid. He also knew what the papers he was leaning on had said had happened to the mayor of San Francisco.

"Is this where you ask me if I shot anybody in Iraq?" and Sam let his slight grin come back.

"No, further back. Sort of."

"Sort of? How's that work?"

"At your dad's funeral, and a hundred times before, I wanted to ask you if you ever heard from your mother."

Any smile slid behind the square jaw. "Heard from her? Clay, I've never heard from her. I don't even know where she is or if she's even alive. I never have."

Clayton looked into the guts of the paperback. "I'm sorry, Sam. I shouldn't have–"

"Don't stress it. Not knowing where she is stopped being an issue about the same time I drove my dad's car wearing that bloody practice jersey. Who she is was a big deal for a while, but I never had a clue. Still don't."

"Do you want to find her? I mean, you know what I do. I could probably turn her up if you gave me what you have."

"I have a name. One picture." Sam smiled. "It's one of those old Polaroid things. That's it."

"You want me to look for her?"

"Is this my pay?" Sam said as only half a joke.

Clayton was taken back. "No. Not ever. I was just thinking about it. If I could do something for you–"

"Like, returning a favor?"

"No. Just that... I mean–"

"Skip it," Sam said as he held the smile long enough to let Clayton off the hook. "We're straight. My mother was a kid herself when I hit the ground. Dad was thirty years older than her. Lucky he didn't get thrown in jail. She went to college somewhere and never came back as far as I ever knew. I stopped asking. He stopped telling. That was it."

The counter caught Clayton's elbow as he leaned and turned away a little. "If you ever change your mind, you'd tell me?"

"Sure."

Now it was Clayton's turn to smile, but as he did, he looked away and slipped an envelope in the book. "Just like you'd tell me if you needed a few dollars."

"Pretty much."

"But you'd never turn down work, right?"

"Not and still be my father's son."

Clayton returned the book to the peeling contact paper that vaguely covered the counter's back. "There's a couple of members of the Capitol Hill club that have been misbehaving. They're about to have some serious financial problems and hand the feds the smoking guns that I wish they'd put to their heads, but there's a senator who needs a visit."

"Sure."

"We only need a presence."

"A presence?"

"Like a tap on the shoulder in the dark kind of thing. She needs to know she's not untouchable."

"She won't be so easy if she ever needs a follow-up visit. A senator. That won't be easy the first time."

"I figured that. Anything I can do?"

Sam's wheels were turning – not spinning wildly, but grinding. He felt it in his head and the muscles of his chest flexed all but involuntarily. Clayton saw it.

"Is it doable?"

"Anything is doable. Comes down to intel on the HVT."

"Huh?"

"Don't worry about it." Sam picked up the book and put it in his back pocket. "How soon?"

"Pretty quick. There's a piece coming out in the–"

"Clay? I don't need to know."

"Right. That's right. I'm sorry."

"You asked what you could do. Can you access her schedule? They're touchy about people knowing where they are."

"It's funny how that changes when it comes to campaigns and money." Clayton pointed to Sam's pocket and the book. "It's in there." Clayton looked over each shoulder and in eyeing the passersby, brought out a fleeting furrow in Sam's brow. "There's a big twist," he said as Sam let the junior varsity attempt at a clandestine scan pass. "She's coming to you."

"That works for you?" Sam asked as he slid from the stool and walked the length of the stand and picked up an anonymous newspaper. "Maybe you don't want to shit in your own backyard."

"There's a fund raiser here in Tampa and she's giving a paid speech. I guess she's trying to boost the local candidates and stir up some rah-rah party loyalty."

"Okay."

"Cool. Alright. I'll... I guess I'll see you around."

"Yep," Sam said as he picked up another paperback from a small shelf it and other books shared with the old Mr. Coffee. Above the Ciampiano working library was the picture of the newsboys. Sam seemed to open the paperback to no particular place and started reading.

"That," Clayton said as he stepped away but pointed back to the new book. "That works for you?"

"What?"

"How you start anywhere in the story?"

"Yep. I know it pretty well. How it ends."

Clayton turned his head to see the title. Sam obliged, moved his hand, and held up a worn, but still bright yellow paperback. There was a drawing of a girl in a faded purple dress on the cover.

"Steinbeck. *Sweet Thursday*," Sam said.

"I don't know that one either."

"You know Steinbeck. Don't be a dick."

"I know Steinbeck, but not that book."

"It's the sequel to *Cannery Row*. You've heard of *Cannery Row*."

"I have the movie. Nolte and Winger. The dancing scene was a scream. I'll remind Raphael of it. He likes it more than I do. He'll want to swing over and watch it tonight. Any chance you want to come by?"

"None."

"Well, you remember–"

"No I don't."

"Raphael? Sure you do. He hawked papers for your–"

"I don't remember, Clay."

"Wait. He's in the picture," Clayton pointed. "We ran around–"

"Clay? Clay."

"What?"

"I don't remember him. Let it go."

It finally sank in. Clayton nodded and looked a little embarrassed. "Of course. Sorry. I get it."

"Take care, Clay."

"You bet. I'll see you, Sam."

"Sure thing and, Clay, read the book. It's better. Movie's good. The book is better."

Clayton leaned against the edge of the counter with both hands and eased away smiling, feeling forgiven. Now he pushed off as though he was shoving a sailboat out of its slip and he was embarking on an adventure.

"Aye-aye, Cap'n. See ya, Sam."

"Hey."

Clayton stopped and started to walk back to the counter as though he'd forgotten something important.

"High value target," Sam said.

"What?"

"HVT."

"Ahh... Gotcha. HVT, Jack Todd, Steinbeck, and the Thursday Girl," Clayton counted to four on his fingers.

"*Sweet Thursday.*"

"*Sweet Thursday. Sweet Thursday,*" Clayton repeated and drifted away up the sidewalk.

Sam read a paragraph and let Clayton disappear. He flipped the book closed and looked at the drawing of the good-looking girl on the cover. She had shoulder length brown hair, pleasant curves, and a pretty face in three-quarter profile. It was Karen. He ran his thick thumb the length of the girl. She'd been good to him – good for him.

"What have you been up to?" Sam asked the girl on the cover. He waited on an answer. When she continued to look away, he started to dream up one of his own, but brought himself up short.

"I'm going soft," he muttered to no one but the girl. Then he tossed Sweet Karen on the shelf with several other paperbacks and reached for the book in his back pocket and its envelope bookmark.

Less than a half mile away, the FBI, in the form of Cal Denti, had returned to Tampa from Washington. He was sitting three stories above Tampa in the disheveled office of District Attorney and professional friend Jack Aaron. Petey was sitting in – taking more notes than Jack, but otherwise asking and listening at the same pace.

"You've got their attention, Jack," Cal was saying as he sat comfortably amongst the rubble. "I was in Washington meeting with the Assistant Director for Criminal Investigation. He has a straight path to the Director, maybe the President as far as I know."

"Access to the top turd on a pile of shit isn't nothing special."

Marcus laughed. Cal smiled. "You can turn a phrase, Jack. The point is...," Cal stopped as he looked around the office. "How do you work in this? You can't possibly know what all these piles are."

"It's hard to believe," Marcus said. "But he does."

"Thank you, Petey. You're damn right I know what's in them. Now, do you want the phone number of my decorator or do you want to tell me what's going on?"

"What's going on is I was in a meeting run by John LaRoy – the Assistant Director. He's also over cybercrime. If it's going to get done – he's the guy."

"So...? What's he doing?"

"You're a pain in the ass, you know that, Jack?"

"He knows it. I tell him daily," Marcus smiled again.

"I'm just asking a question!" Jack blurted. "Jesus, you girls are sensitive today. What's he think? What's he got? Where're we headed? That's all. Jumping Christmas."

"Where we're headed is right back to Tampa. Maybe it started here, so we start here." Cal leaned forward and rested his elbows on his knees. "If the dead congressman and the mayor are connected as you suggest–"

"As I know."

"Then show me the connection. If this goes from local Tampa politics, to a Florida congressman, clear across the country, the calendar says it started in Tampa. Why? Who? How many people with ties to Tampa can transplant something like this three thousand miles? That takes money, coordination, and mostly, a very select talent at the keyboard."

"Why?" Marcus asked.

"Why what?"

"Why's he so talented? Could just be a hacker. They're all over the world."

"Run of the mill hackers are, yes. But why would a brainiac in Brussels care about a corrupt commissioner in Tampa? And this isn't the handiwork of a hacker."

"Says?" Jack's upturned hands asked.

"Our IT guys. This isn't a seventeen year old kid in a basement. He didn't learn this between games of *Grand Theft Auto*."

"Huh?" Jack looked at Petey for help.

"Mario Brothers? Pac Man, maybe?"

"Video games, Jack. Do you even have access to the internet?"

"He still uses an IBM Selectric," Petey laughed and pointed to the vintage typewriter sitting neglected in the corner of the office.

"What's wrong with you two wingnuts? Who said anything about a stolen car? Christ, stay on task here. And that old IBM is for when these fancy computers shut down. It's back-up. You'd know about back-up if either of you were a real cop."

Cal stood up and walked toward the door. "And you want to catch the guy who can slip in and out of computers across the country and not leave a trace? Help me, Marcus."

"He's just being an ass."

"No, he's for real," Cal feigned an anger he couldn't pull off. "You forget, I've known this guy for thirty years."

"You're right. It's real." Marcus was shaking his head, but still smiling. He looked at Jack and caught a wink from his boss and rolled his eyes.

"So, Cal," Jack said slowly, as though he was just catching on. "We've got a local genius who decides, for whatever reason, he is going to put a hurting on a loco-politico. Then he plies his wares against another elected criminal who likes to diddle little boys. Finally, he can't stand it and needs to see blood instead of just playing with his computer. He graduates to beating the shit out of still another political fat cat who's banging or stealing everything in sight. Sound right?"

Cal dropped back down in the chair. "You brought it to me, remember?"

"Yea, I did, but when I hear you say it, it doesn't even sound like there's been a crime."

"I didn't say it. You did."

Jack looked at Petey and feigned seriousness. "Any crimes here, Investigator Pete?"

"A few."

Cal pointed to the door. "You want me to go?"

"Oh, don't get your panties in a bunch, Denti. I'm just thinking out loud."

"You sound exactly like LaRoy."

"I like him then."

"I like him too and I want to get him what he's after. Can we get to work now?"

"We need to go back to the commissioner caper," Jack said.

"There you are. If that's truly where this started, that's where we'll find it."

"It?" Marcus asked.

Cal started to answer, but Jack cut him off. "It, Petey. It. The who. The why. The whole ball of wax."

There was tap on the door – the tips of three fingers gently brushing the wood. The three men went quiet.

"Was that a knock?" Cal asked the others.

"Oakes? Helfer Oakes?" Jack yelled. "Is that you?"

It was and the timid caller opened the door. In his hand was a long rolled poster.

"Get your ass in here, Oakes! Cal Denti, FBI, meet Helfer, our forensics team."

Cal stuck his hand out, but Helfer was holding the poster. As he fumbled and shuffled the paper tube, he busied himself fumbling his words.

"FBI. I, that is, we, the Forensic Unit, we haven't worked with the Bureau before. This is an honor. I hope–"

"Christ sakes, Oakes, don't tear up on me," Jack sputtered. "You're working with the man not taking his daughter to the prom."

"Don't mind him," Cal said as he finally found Helfer's hand. "You work with him so you probably already know he's a few bricks shy of a full load."

"Yes, sir. That is, no, sir. I–"

"Damn it, Cal, don't harass my forensic unit. Did you find it, Oakes?"

Helfer began to unroll the bulky paper out across Jack's already cluttered desk. Marcus and Cal began to position themselves to see.

"Get the door, Petey," Jack said, the humor having left him.

As Helfer, with Jack's eager help, unrolled the poster sized paper, Cal could see it was a map of the west coast of Florida. Jack moved dusty paperweights and stained coffee cups until he had the map pinned down at the corners. The large map had two nearly perfect circles, one shaded with green lines, the other red, and a large area of overlap as well as an obtuse rectangle in striped gray.

Jack looked the map over and ran his finger around the circles before he brought the others up to speed.

Cal finally asked. "This is what?"

"Coverage. Oakes has been running down the broadcast range of the biggest television stations in town plus big radio – the green, red, and blue – and the gray is what remains of the print stuff that trickles out."

Cal pulled at the conversation. "And?"

Jack rapped his knuckles on the delineators. "This is where our whiz kid lives."

Cal was quiet and looked down across the map.

Marcus couldn't contain himself. "Why's that, Jack? People could have picked the story up in Brazil."

"Yep. Could have, but unlikely. And what's more unlikely is that they'd give a shit. No, if it started with this thing – our commissioner – it was because whoever pulled that first caper is from here – has connections to this area – likes it here – and doesn't like thieving politicians."

"Jack, I don't know. We've had politicians turn before."

"I know – all of them – on the day they're elected. But this is different. Something triggered him," Jack said as he tapped the circles. "Not sure about that part yet, but he's here. He's here."

Eight eyes danced around the map and measured the circles and shapes as though through intense inspection, they would see a name, an address, or a face. The men watched the map as though it was about to move.

"You sure about this, Jack?" Cal asked gently.

"Pretty sure."

Cal tapped the map with his fingers. "This is a train of thought that pulled out of the station a while ago. You've been working on this a while, haven't you?"

"Shit, we can't sit around and wait for the feds to do anything."

"When I came over here to suggest we go back to the beginning, I didn't expect to find you there waiting for me. Good move."

"I'm still a cop."

"I know, but this," Cal said as he pointed to the center of the red circle. "This – admittedly a reach – is thinking. You're ahead of the Bureau."

"You say that like it's hard to do."

"Jackass."

Jack smiled and returned to the map. "Our boy's here alright."

"I'll humor you," Cal said. "Let's do a cross check on the tech geniuses inside Helfer's circles. There can't be many based on what I've heard."

Jack's shoulders dropped. "Who do you think we are, a bunch of hicks? The Keystone Cops? You think we haven't thought of that, Mr. FBI big-shot? I was born at night, but it wasn't last night."

"Why do I bother with you? Marcus," Cal turned his attention to Petey. "Did the DA here already ask you to run down a list of people in the Tampa area who fit the profile?"

"I'm on it, yes. It'll take a while, but we'll get it."

"It's not done?" Jack feigned anger.

"You mentioned it an hour ago over lunch!"

"Why are you standing here then?"

"You're excited about this game, aren't you?" Cal asked Jack.

"He can't sleep," Marcus added. "He's all wound up,"

"I can tell. He's in rare form."

"Maybe he's a tree hugger," Helfer blurted.

"Huh?"

"Jack? A tree hugger?" Marcus smiled.

"Not, Mr. Aaron. I'm referring to the uber-hacker in the circles," Helfer said as he pointed to his map. "He's the one that could be the tree hugger."

Cal didn't want to slip the chain of command across the agencies, but it only took a glance to prompt Jack.

"Start making sense, Oakes."

"Well," Helfer began as though he was testing the weight bearing threshold of an old floor. "You told me to plot the capacity and extent of the signals. I pulled the initial scopes based on basic power wattage, but there were too many variables. There's gain and line loss, noise ratios, irregularities in terrain–"

Jack put his hands over his ears. "Petey, make it stop."

"What are you driving at, Helfer? Are the maps correct? And where's the trees come in?"

"The trees could impact signal extension, but I've accounted for that under terrain. All those things impact end reception, but it's a moot point really."

"None of what you just said matters?" Jack asked.

"It does – for FM and standard air wave propagation of frequency bands."

"Petey, slap him in the back of the head and see if he starts making sense."

Marcus actually pulled his hand back. The hard working forensic unit lurched ahead to the point.

"I don't think radio is involved. You were asking what enticed this person. It was the videos and the signal extent was carried by cable. Of course they were available via standard air, but the cable strength and clarity would–"

"Holy shit," Jack said as he leaned back in his chair and breathed for the young scientist. "Oakes you just talked for ten minutes without breathing – some type of physical record – but in the end everything you said means nothing? What's wrong with you? Really? Have you gone off your medication? Are you sleeping well?"

"I thought it important to rule out–"

"Facts, Oakes. Just the facts. Sergeant Joe Friday cop work. Cut to the goddamn chase."

"I refined the cable reach on the dates they were broadcasting the story of the commissioner's scandal to have the most exact data possible."

"Good. Perfect, Helfer," Cal said as he pointed to the map. "And that's what you've charted?"

"Yes, but when I referenced the dates on their data tapes, I was seeing one shot over and over. The video they kept running was of the cypress trees getting pushed into burning piles by bulldozers. Lots of bulldozers. Big bulldozers. And a big fire. A really big fire."

Jack looked at Cal and on to Marcus. Helfer had found it. Cal knew it too. Any hesitation in his mind was melted by the roaring heat of the burning cypress. He looked at the map, put his hand on Helfer's shoulder and gave it a squeeze of respect.

"Good work, Helfer. That's the piece that was missing." Cal looked around the scientist to the investigator. "Marcus? See if you can add a 'Green' filter to your search criteria. Even if it doesn't change your numbers. I like it."

Jack slapped the map and stood up. "Like it? I goddamn love it! Nice piece of police work, Oakes. By God now you're Joe Friday. Damn nice." Jack looked at Cal and motioned to Marcus and Helfer. "There. What do you think of that? Helluva crack team. Tampa doesn't play paddy cake. FBI. You don't know shit. What do you feds got? Nothing. You know only what we tell you. If—"

"See you later," Cal said as he cut Jack off and went to the door. "Marcus, call me and I'll assign a few agents to help you work that scan. Helfer? When you want out of this insane asylum, call me. That was good work. You convinced me. He's local. Now, let's find him."

––––––––––––––

23

The junior high school field trips to the U. S. Capitol Building had nearly all been canceled. It was too expensive for school districts struggling to meet basic needs, balance wayward budgets, not raise taxes, and still field a football team. Security was Jack Benny tight. Transportation was impossible with traffic constrained to no vehicles larger than an open pickup truck for fear of diesel soaked fertilizer bombs masquerading as Ryder trucks. Parents had become hesitant to sign permission slips to send their children into what had taken on the appearance of war zones. Concrete barriers dotted the streets. Heavily armed patrols roamed. Monetary woes meshed with fear and the concrete barricades to relegate United States History and government to virtual tours.

The massive cast iron dome of the Capitol Building might still conjure up pictures of Winnie the Pooh's tiered beehive in the mind of an elementary school aged virtual visitor, but the production and activity inside would never have been mistaken for the industrious bees. Hundreds of millions of dollars in safety and security upgrades and modifications yielded a return on investment that wouldn't register via anyone's definition. Despite the additional layers of protection afforded the sitting Congress, many members continued to cite personal over national security concerns. Though now there were gas masks under their seats in the House Chamber and they were pushing through a measure that would permit them to be armed, elementary school teachers were still throwing themselves over their students when gunfire erupted outside their classrooms. Congress argued the validity of lies – one side of the aisle terming proposals as political posturing while the other screamed cover up – as their approval ratings hit historic lows in contrast to indictments and ethics investigations which soared to new highs. Still, nothing changed as the fox continued to guard the hen house and when trapped, was judged by other foxes who saw the plight of their colleague as their own potential future and were loath to set a precedent that would one day bite themselves in the ass. To a man or woman they bemoaned members of their body breaking their own

Congressional Rules, but to punish in accordance with severity and amend rules and regulations would jeopardize their own circuitous revenue streams so the status quo remained.

Political gridlock had long settled in as the norm. The notion of transparency vanished beneath campaign promises that disappeared as quickly as the litter following the walk to 1600 Pennsylvania Avenue and the swearing in of a new Congress.

The day might have been just another day in the campaign cycle that never truly ended. Donors were courted, wined, and dined with the contributions of other smaller fish in hopes of landing a briefcase full of cash. Tit for tat political favors and votes were traded like so much *Monopoly* money. The eyes of the legislators above the phony red power ties or red conservative women's business suits, some topped with gaudy hats that cried out for attention, but in truth guaranteed only the wearer's place as a clown in a circus act, ignored the contents of bills coming to the floor. Instead they focused on the contents of their campaign war chest, the juggling of contributions verses pathetic campaign finance law, and personal business interests listed in their spouses or children's names. It was an old story dating back to the first days President Grant was accosted in the lobby of his hotel as he waded through requests for favors on his way to work.

This morning there was a soft rumbling careening through the marble halls of Capitol Hill. Security and augmenting members of the FBI were busy documenting and collecting individual letters that had arrived at the office of every member of Congress. The letters were veiled threats – not unusual even when sent to all members of Congress – but they referenced the dead Florida Congressman and the Mayor of San Francisco and, more importantly for the security detail, the letters promised more "scrutiny and impact." Hundreds of members of Congress had no idea the letters had arrived. They purposely didn't review their mail. They remembered the Anthrax attempts from years prior. It was far better to let an hourly employee take that initial risk.

Even if the letter was a simple request or lauding the congressman for their perceived involvement in a local or national issue, the elected name seldom saw the letter, email, or learned anything of the request. They didn't have the time or the interest. They were consumed with the next campaign and their side bets in a personal economy that lined their pockets while the people they represented languished in their unknown roles as a smiled at means to an end. The constituents existed only for their numbers of votes. The people on main street received the obligatory oversized picture postcard of their representative's family at election time and were counted on to retain the incumbent one more cycle to "finish the job I've started" as though it was for the people they labored.

But the assistants talked. "Looks like everybody got one." "The FBI took ours." "Does the man know?" "Not yet." "I told that bitch of mine. Screw her. She wants us as unpaid interns and runs us in the ground, or bitches constantly to cover her stupidity, but cries in public how the minimum wage is unfair. We work for 'experience,' she claims. Then why not have the unemployed work for free to bolster their résumé? No votes in that." "Oh, and her travel? Don't get me started. One trip to Italy costs more than most people make in a year." "If the voters at home only knew the truth about what goes on here." "Are we about to go to war with Italy or something?" They laughed. "She goes every year – 'fact finding mission.' What a pathetic liar."

By day's end, most of the Hill knew about the letters. Very few members of Congress had asked to read the copies their disgruntled assistants had made before the originals were turned over to the Bureau. Those residents of the Hill that didn't know or cared less were more attentive the next day when a copy appeared in the *Washington Post*. The droning news cycles – Clayton's bane – talked of nothing else while the *Post* itself, calling the *San Francisco Chronicle* and the FBI for support, scrambled to salvage their back door relationships with conduits for leaks – members of Congress – when it suited their agendas, but who now were accusing the paper of collusion.

TO MEMBERS OF THE UNITED STATES CONGRESS

WE THE PEOPLE are tasked with the enormity of placing a few in positions of making decisions for many. The model is both necessary and flawed. The behavior many of you exhibit cannot be categorized as 'flaws.' They are violations of your standing body's ethics rules at least, felonies at worst. These actions are compounded by the weight of responsibility incumbent in your office. When you betray the needs of the grandchildren of those you serve, you have betrayed us all. As some have learned and all will come to know, there is a balance due. You are to be held to the light of accountability. We the People demand your immediate accordance with the laws the rank and file live under daily.

MEMBERS OF CONGRESS – Cancel your planned meetings with lobbyists. The money you desire, funneled through the legal veil of contributions, serves you alone. If the project or legislation was true to your constituency, facts alone would carry the floor. The appointments, promises, and cash would not be necessary. What warrants that stock in your family member's name and what guise of doing right for those you represent does it lend itself to? A simple test – minus the campaign contribution, would you still truthfully and vigorously support the measure before you?

MEMBERS OF CONGRESS – Shirk the normalcy of chicanery. Know to do right and do it. Seek other like-minded men and women and dispel the violators least you be violated.. Seek out and hold accountable those you have channeled into government office. Their mandate is to propel our Nation forward and care for all its citizens, yet they seek to operate and profit from dark corners. If your appointees seek refuge behind our Constitution to prevent their misdeeds being known, see it for what we know it to be and expose them to the light of justice. If you do not, we will, and their guilt will spread to your hands for your neglect and complicity.

MEMBERS OF CONGRESS – We are more deeply engrained than you are. Your time is fleeting across the landscape of our great Nation, whereas we have been here from the beginning. We know you. We are watching from within and without. We have had enough. Stop now. Do the will of the People. Do only this. Infractions will be costly, as *to those whom much is given, much is required.* We are coming. This is the time of

The New Illuminati

Luke 12:48

The warning – typeset a digit at a time around the molecules of the bricks that comprised the firewalls of the *Washington Post* – was having the intended impact through the halls of power and along thousands of Main Streets across the Nation.

In the chambers of both Houses, pairs of legislators leaned close to each other in their padded black leather chairs and exchanged speculation and actualities in veiled tones, from sweating foreheads, and with hands that looked clean but weren't.

"The Amberstone account is empty."

"What did you say?"

"Amberstone. Empty."

"Are you drunk?"

"No, but I will be as soon as I can."

"There's three million dollars in that account."

"There was three million dollars in that account."

"Are you sure?"

"I checked it three million times. I'm not stupid. You saw the article. Someone is playing us off against each other."

"Does Coyote know?"

"I'm headed up to see him now. I thought you'd like to join me."

The pair of thieves slipped from their chairs like eels to go up into the rotunda to find another bandit. They set off up the hallowed aisle that had been witness to acts of dedicated public servants who had labored unselfishly to birth a nation. Their crisp white shirts and power ties – dry cleaned on the government dime – trailed a stench that resembled road kill splatter after several days on hot asphalt. The smell permeated the distinguished walls of the Chamber over a hundred and fifty years of paint, paper, and plaster. The stench was fear and it was warranted.

In the north wing of the Congressional building, an admin assistant who had interviewed for a position advertised as 'Girl Friday' forty-five years prior and proceeded to shrug off countless title iterations through 'secretary' to 'administrative assistant,' was boldly entering her senator's office. She carried a steno pad – a constant from days long passed – still employed for shorthand notes. The relic of shorthand may as well have been a CIA top secret code as she had discovered many years ago that people could not read it. Occasionally she marveled, with disappointment, how the legions of girls in the "steno pool" had evaporated along with the art. Still, she employed the archaic technique, dated each entry and filed the spiral bound green paper books away. They were now a trove of dates, actions, votes, visitors, and skullduggery that had occurred throughout her extended employ. And like the author of the inflamed listing in the *Washington Post*, she too had long since had enough of the back door shenanigans of Capitol Hill. Perhaps she would assemble her legions of notepads and write a tell-all book. She sooner thought of turning them over to the FBI in hopes that someone there could read shorthand.

She dropped the *Washington Post*, folded carefully to Clayton's full page editorial, on the senator's desk.

"Shall I cancel the meeting with that man with the God awful black hat?"

"Who?" answered the aged politico from behind the tidy desk, surrounded by awards and pictures of him with past Presidents.

"You know quite well, sir."

"I am afraid I do not, Miss—"

"Oh, that goddamn lobbyist!"

The senator leaned back in his chair. "Nonsense. This business," he said as he brushed the newspaper as shooing a fly. "This is rubbish," he laughed. "The *Post* runs this, pleads ignorance, and the media can fill up a few days of news cycles as they wait for a plane crash or a sex trafficker. Maybe a good school shooting to boost ratings."

She had headed for the door, but the last words stopped her cold. Her voice wanted to explode, but forty plus years in the company of craftsman at manipulation vented the steam quietly. She turned slowly and made her way back to the desk.

"Mr. Senator, you of course, know what is below the main floor of the rotunda of our building?"

He all but ignored her. "Are you having a troubled day, Miss—"

"On the contrary. I am quite well, thank you."

"It pleases me to hear that," the senator said, eyes cast down on the article again. "I am in the midst of a fifth term. I am rather accustomed to the layout of the Capital, but I'll indulge you. Why do you ask?"

"It is a crypt, sir."

"Yes. If memory serves, it was intended for George Washington."

"Very good, Senator."

"Is there a point in your somewhat insolent line of questioning this morning?"

"There is. The crypt is empty. It has gone unused for all these years."

"Per President Washington's wishes I believe."

"Correct again, sir, but perhaps that may change."

The senator laughed. "Seems unlikely George will change his mind—"

"Correct. President Washington will never be placed in the crypt." She laughed with him and he relaxed until she released the words behind the laugh. "Which leaves room for many, many others. It's empty now," she said as she tapped the paper on the senator's desk. "But, God willing, not for long."

He was slow to respond. "That rings of sedition. Perhaps I should ask for you to be escorted from the grounds if you find your work so distasteful that, and please feel free to correct me, you are abdicating the murder of sitting members of Congress."

"I wouldn't dream of that. How horrible," she said as she picked up the paper though her boss wasn't finished with it.

"Then what you said—"

"Is accountability. You're an attorney, Senator," she said as she moved toward the door. "Execution of criminals is not murder under the law, is it?"

"No, it is not, however—"

"Accountability, Senator," she said as she left the inner office holding the newspaper high as though it was an artifact to be preserved and displayed. "Accountability."

The senator hollered to the outer office for someone to close his door. It happened and he was on the phone.

"Tell me whose stunt this was? Was it ours? ..... What do you mean no one knows? .....Forget that. Nothing is theirs or ours. Christ, we perpetuate each other's bullshit. I've been in this chair nearly forty years, I know how the game is played. I want who's running this. There has to be a stalking horse sent out. No one is going to give this the go ahead. Not something with this potential. Not on their own. .....Well, find out! Send somebody to the *Post* and talk directly to Green Lantern. Nothing comes off the Hill without crossing his desk. .....When? Jesus Christ, have you been—. Did you read the damn thing? Someone's gonna get their dick caught in a wringer over this and it won't be mine!"

Similar conversations were being jumbled together all through the Senate side as well as the House. The executive branch had launched a full-throttle, but covert game against an unseen enemy. When the *Post* had hit the sidewalks of Washington, impromptu strategy meetings were pulled together in the backs of taxis and limos, in bathrooms, and the Oval Office.

"We have to strike while the iron's hot."

"What does that even mean?"

"Can I get somebody in here making decisions for the entire country that is over thirty?"

"Cowboys. Branding cattle. Use the brand while it's hot. Be quick. Move fast. You ever watch a real western movie or just reality TV?"

"You old bastards. Cowboy movies. Get real."

"Who can we turn with this?"

"I know a junior senator who's got half his family working no-show jobs in his home State's AG's office. He was trying to impress me with a cash funnel on transportation bids – the idiot."

"We already own him. He can't keep his pants on or his mouth shut. Who else?"

"Hell, everybody! My vote is we give up everyone who has an investigation ongoing. Where there's smoke, there's fire."

"What's that – ninety, a hundred members?"

"That list is no good. We've got key players in positions that would make that list. We need to focus this on the ones we need out of the way. The timing is off, but if we can get some mileage out of this we could get control of the House."

"Cut it back to ones we don't already own or control. That way we can get these vigilantes – real or maybe someone with deep enough pockets to buy full pages of the *Post* – to do our work for us and get rid of members whose votes we can't be assured of."

"Decent plan. But is this Illuminati thing, as the FBI calls it, for real or is it all bullshit?"

"Illuminati? That's their name?"

"I got it from the Frisco Congressional District."

"Somebody see if you can get our friends at cable to stop showing that Bible verse every two minutes."

"Bible thumpers automatically look like loons. We'll be fine."

"If this group is real, they'll be caught soon enough. It's probably three guys in camouflage on the roof of a shack in Montana trying to get a Wi-Fi signal."

"Just let it pass."

"What's the Bureau saying?"

"They're being real tight. That tells us they think it's the real deal. I couldn't get much, but they've got investigations coast-to-coast."

"How do you want to leak the names we want leaked?"

"Use the *Post* again. That way we give the bad guys the list of members we want to turn the heat up on. People will think it came from this Illuminati outfit and we give them time to do their damnedest while the Bureau plays catch up."

"We can buy our Montana geeks enough time to do some real political damage across the aisle. I've got a couple in mind I want on that list even if they don't have investigations underway. Pricks don't want to play ball? Watch."

"Just political damage? We onboard with this? The tone of that write-up is pretty ugly and I heard the mayor out west is in a bad way."

"That's a jealous husband – local politics at best. These guys are hackers – geeks. They jerk off to gigabytes and hard drives."

The group laughed.

"Nice."

"We can leak anything and blame this New Illuminati group regardless."

"Lethal."

"Thank you."

"Has anyone looped in Rebel?"

"Hell no. No point. He doesn't want to know anything about anything."

There was more laughter.

"We'll tee it up. He'll wait four weeks and make a 'profound' announcement – something we write up for the teleprompter. As long as he can keep reading, he'll be fine."

"And send Revival to Africa–"

"She wants to go to Italy–"

"Spain, I think she said."

"Wherever. Just pack her off."

"Here's a thought. If this Illuminati group is the real deal, they may not like Rebel fundraising while Rome is burning, or Revival flying around the world."

"Maybe, but I don't know if they've got the balls for that. In the Congress they only have to worry about the FBI."

"Only?"

"I wouldn't want the Feds after me, but don't you think Secret Service is worse? I mean, those guys have no rules to play by. If somebody raises a hand, or the Secret Service even thinks they're going to, that dude is going down."

"Here's another thought. Everything I see and hear is that SS is pretty tired of Rebel and his entourage giving them a hard time over everything."

"Not a chance. Though the Castle is occupied by arrogant incompetence, that Detail is too professional not to do everything they can. I know most of them. They're good men and women being treated like shit, but it doesn't take away their pride. They'd jump in front of a bullet or tackle the Pope if he made a wrong move."

While the casual dark comic banter continued in offices along the fringe of the West Wing and the floors beneath it, on the streets of Washington and in the real world well beyond the beltway, America was responding to the trickling down of Clayton's illegitimate *Washington Post* editorial.

TELLURIDE, COLORADO: "About time."

"Hang 'em. Remember that old Charlie Daniel's song. 'A big tall tree and a short piece of rope.' That's how I see it."

"You can't hang everybody."

"They know who the bad apples are."

"People voted them in there. Vote them out."

"To be replaced by what? Another crook? I looked at a governor's race in the last election cycle and the people had to choose between a Democrat who stole fifteen million in a bank fraud deal and a Republican who stole fifty million in a Medicare scam. How do you pick a winner in that lot? Odds are better at a dog track."

"Just different kinds of dogs, I guess."

"That's right. And if they can't get the nomination in their party, they switch, or try being an Independent. Phony, thieving, lying, pieces of shit."

"You're painting with a pretty broad brush."

"Well, explain to me how anyone is supposed to elect someone who is an honest hard worker, who will be thinking of their State, when the choices have both been indicted or under criminal investigation?"

"Were they convicted?"

"They both took the 5th."

"That's legal."

"Legal sme-gal. If you didn't do anything wrong, just tell the truth—"

"I know – the whole truth and nothing but the truth."

"So help you God."

PETOSKEY, MICHIGAN: Thirteen hundred miles away, the finest man in the county was sliding into a worn booth in a clean but dated diner. The seat was deep green vinyl – any pattern worn away by years of Wranglers, Lees, and Carhartts attached to men who worked with their hands. The corner of the bench seat was gray with a few tattered layers of duct tape making no attempt to hide the patch, but effectively holding the battered stuffing in.

The waitress never came for his order and the pattern – worn as deep as the seats – flowed to the kitchen through the waitress somehow without a word said. The cook – forty years both simple chef to the diner and faithful husband to the waitress – saw the man pass the open order shelf between the counter and his griddle, over the double coffee pots, and below the stainless spinning wheel that the waitress clipped orders to and spun to her husband. The cook had the man's two eggs sizzling before he was settled in the booth.

Five stools from the register, two young men were sharing hot morning coffee and stories. They were also sharing a newspaper, folded open to Clayton's letter, but the paper wasn't the *Washington Post*. This was the *Morning Times*, a seventy-year-old publication with a readership the size of the few small towns it served. The paper had gotten physically smaller over the years, but had added color and was available online now, but generations still subscribed and picked up the daily if for no other reason than to read again what they had already seen at the last sold out high school wrestling match or just to see who had died. The *Times*, like the *New York Times* and every other newspaper in America, was running a front page spread on Clayton's handiwork though more than half were calling it a political ad against the incumbents.

"Tell me that ain't some shit there?" one said as he jammed the paper with a finger that carried a touch of grease under the nail.

Before his partner could answer, a quart size mayonnaise jar with a slot in the top that looked like it was hammered through with an old screwdriver twenty years prior, stopped at the end of a perfectly placed slide right next to his coffee cup. The original label of the jar had been torn away leaving behind traces in hard glue. Yellowed tape held a new label of sorts – a faded green order slip – that held equally faded ink letters that said simply, 'Curse Jar.'

He looked at the label and sought out the slider of the jar – the waitress at the register end of the counter.

"That ain't swearing."

She just pointed to the jar and went about her business.

"Shit ain't swearing," the offender said in an inaudible whisper as he reached into his faded jeans for a quarter.

"She'll bounce you. I've seen her do it."

On cue, the waitress passed behind the counter stools with the coffee pot bound for any half empty cup in the diner.

"This isn't the Brass Lantern Bar and Grill, boys. You want to use that language, go on out to the bag and gag at the strip mall."

The quarter dropped in quietly, the jar was moved a comfortable distance away, and the pair returned to the newspaper on the other side of the cursing allegation.

"Whoever ran this ad is getting my vote in November."

"I don't know that there is a 'whoever' behind this. From what I hear, it's a new group."

"Like a super-pac?"

"Maybe."

"Who are they behind?"

"I don't know that they're behind anybody. Looks like they're laying the law down to everybody to fly right or get grounded right quick."

"I like them even more."

The coffee pot leaned over their cups and gave them free warmers.

"You just don't know with politics. What looks good and right could have a whole other agenda no one sees until it's too late. By then everyone is talking about some other fire that's burning–"

"Or made out to be burning."

"Yep – or made out to be burning – and the thing that had everyone so riled up to start with has been given its Last Rites."

"Or buried so deep in some bullshit piece of legislation those dimwits—"

A used spoon reached out from a hand that somehow had its fingers entwined in the handles of six dirty coffee cups and tapped the Curse Jar. The speaker scarcely broke stride and dropped in another quarter.

"Those dimwits in Congress vote it through without even reading the fine print."

"And we pick up the tab."

"You called it."

"You bet."

They both stopped long enough to sip their coffee and stare at the newspaper as though a further explanation would somehow be available in the sixth or seventh reading. Nothing new was forthcoming, but it didn't matter.

The coffee pot stopped again. It was only for a splash, but the waitress and her elixir lingered over the newspaper. She pretended to try and read it upside down, but like most Americans, she'd already read it at least twice. And like the paid talking-head pundits, she'd run through a myriad of possibilities as to origin and potential fallout. But rather than share ideology via the network and cable shows with a tuned audience already presupposed to the political leaning offered, the waitress traded views, suppositions, and playful barbs with the chef in her life.

"What a tragedy we've come to this," she said as she pointed to the piece with the spout of the coffee pot. "It's the fall of Rome."

"Rome?"

"Decadence. Spectacle passing for entertainment. Political corruption. No accountability. Such a great country, but for such a short time. There's the real tragedy."

"Brightest candle burns out the quickest."

"There you have it," the swearing diner acknowledged what he felt was wit at its sharpest.

The waitress smiled a smile of beautiful relaxed disarming brilliance. "But we're not finished yet. Maybe we can pull the fat from the fire in the eleventh hour."

"You think?"

"Not me," the man with the quarters said. "Washington makes the rules they go by. It's the fox guarding the chickens. We're done for."

The waitress warmed the coffees again and used her stained decanter to point discreetly across the diner to the man sitting in the patched green vinyl booth.

"Not if we could get that guy in the White House."

The diners glanced without much discretion.

"He wants to be President, does he?"

"Not bad enough."

"What's that mean?"

"To put up with all the nonsense when he knows he'd never win."

"Not a winner, huh? People like to back winners."

"Oh, he's winner. At least he was. He was governor when you two were learning to read and write."

"No kidding?"

"No kidding. Balanced budget. Don't spend more than you take in – just like any family. Stretched a dollar. Cut frills. He found a nice balance between taxes and leaving people and business with their own money to invest, lose, save, grow, spend – whatever suits you. Made the government smaller, cheaper – efficient is what most people called it."

"But he couldn't win the White House?"

"Couldn't even win that second term as Governor. People were for him, but the 'Machine' wasn't. It came out later that he'd cut too many frills by their standards. Seems they didn't want to wash their own clothes – wanted the State to pay to dry clean everything. He wanted them in the Capital, working. They wanted ten weeks' vacation. He wanted them to contribute to their healthcare – like the rest of us – they wanted the State to pick up the tab.

"When it was said and done, he'd carved so much out of government, they turned on him. Less government is less people, less money. Less power. They don't want that. Most politicians are in office only to keep themselves there. From the day they win that first election, everything is geared toward winning the next one. Any real work is window dressing. So they ran him out. They convinced enough people that we needed more government to save us from ourselves. They had the money to buy more yard signs and more TV ads than he did. Ran a campaign to get out the *right* vote as they saw it, and not just every vote, and it fell in their lap.

"He lost. And when he tried one last time four years later, his own party said their new guy had created a bunch of jobs. And it was true. Sort of. He had created jobs – all the government jobs that man over there had cut.

"So the cronies got their power back. Taxes went up, interference in our lives went up, disability claims went up – free phones, free everything – 'You don't have to work. Let the government take care of you.' Government went back to doing what it does best – keeping itself going and growing."

"Dolly?" It was the chef at the serving counter. He had the man's breakfast ready.

She scooped it up, delivered it without a word, and left the light green check on the far corner of the worn Formica topped table.

Across the country, in diners big and small, old and new, waitresses and patrons traded coffee for conversation about Clayton's posting. Bars, like Dolly's Brass Lantern, took up political concourse. Going beyond the plaintively easy, "Damn government," standard diatribe, residents of bar stools – from dimly lit gin joints to trendy neon infused clubs began yakking up the power of one vote and the greater power of the Illuminati.

PHOENIX, ARIZONA: "I never vote."

"Why?"

"Doesn't change anything."

"No kidding. Not if you don't vote. Duh. Of course it can't change anything. It's like the lotto. You can't win it if you ain't in it."

"Good analogy. Politics and the lottery. We have the same odds at getting a decent politician as we have of winning the Power Ball Jackpot."

"It's not about the result, moron, it's about the process. You have this right. You should use it."

"Here it comes – 'People have died to give you the right to vote.' Am I right?"

"You're as dumb as a box of rocks, you know that?"

"It's a waste of time. Just like this conversation. But that *Washington Post* piece was interesting."

"Forget that. If just half of the people who feel like you changed their thought process and got involved – voted – we wouldn't be in the shape we're in."

"Waste of time. Politicians have always been thieves and liars and always will be."

"Absolutely true – as long as that attitude is the prevailing wind. But if we all stood up – voted our conscience instead of party lines or popularity contests – it could be different."

"Are you going to start singing Kum-ba-ya?"

"No. You're too dumb to remember the words."

KANSAS CITY, KANSAS: "Well, I gotta get to work and pay my taxes so the President can fly Air Force One to Florida to deliver pizzas or make sure he doesn't miss his tee time while the rest of us go to hell in a hand basket."

"He's got to scoot to a fund raiser while our diplomats are being butchered. It's a tough job, but somebody's got to do it."

"I'm waiting on the next selfie he takes at a funeral. Maybe he'll wait until they fly home some more dead soldiers."

SALINAS, CALIFORNIA: "Did you see that piece in–"

"Are you kidding? Everybody has."

"What do you think?"

"Where do I sign up?"

"Me too."

"I'm so tired of watching the news. They throw mud at each other and don't manage the country. We suffer while the President goes golfing. It's a four year gig – show up and work! We have problems everywhere."

"The guy deserves a day off."

"All the time? He's not stocking shelves in the Piggly Wiggly, you know? These decisions have an impact on generations of Americans. We're nearly twenty trillion in debt. Am I the only one that thinks that's a problem?"

"He did make a lot of promises."

"Transparency. No lobbyists. Sonofabitch. The President and that entire mob on Capitol Hill. Damn joke. Liars and thieves."

"Not all of them."

"No, not all, but the few good ones are undone by the rotten apples. We can't get decent ones on the committees that matter. Remember the Super-Committee? Best of the best? Save us from sequestration? Nothing happened except they tried to close the World War II Memorial, which doesn't take anybody to keep open! Congress can't do anything because they're all trying to get rich and re-elected. Case closed."

"I vote for Bill Gates. No one can buy him off."

"He won't run. None of the really bright guys run. They know the playing field and that they could get elected, but then those bastards already in would emasculate them and shove them off on an oversight committee for the growth of pine trees in the northwest because they're scared to death of a man with brains, sense, and conviction."

"Easy does it. You're getting kind of hot."

"We all should be hot. And we should make it so hot in Washington it flushes the roaches out."

NEW YORK, NEW YORK: "Did you read that thing in the *Post?*"

"I did."

"And?"

There was a long pause as a drawer in the mammoth glass topped desk slid open. When the woman bent to retrieve the newspaper, the man who had posed the question got a clearer look behind the mesh chair and out the floor to ceiling window. Outside was a thirty story drop for the eyes to Wall Street and the grid of the largest city in the United States.

The newspaper came out of the drawer and was set gently on her desk. The article was face up, but she opened the paper and flipped it over. Several pages later, she spun the newspaper on the slippery glass until it faced her caller. She pointed to a three-line piece in a precinct's police blotter.

He read it.

"So?"

"That man stole twenty-three dollars. He was sent to jail on Riker's Island."

"And?"

"I had a senator in this office last week who stole four million – just that I know of – and we sent him to Washington."

"I follow. Four million buys a lot of votes."

"Four million buys advertising. Advertising buys votes. Winning buys you the chance to steal more and win again with the proceeds. But, this article," she said as she flicked a manicured finger at the paper. "It's given me pause. We're not blameless in this mess. We bankroll the lobbyists to pay the senators to pass the legislation we want to boost profits and our bonuses."

"We're accountable to our shareholders remember. They expect profits."

"Like this? Preying on greed to fulfill our own greed? There must be a limit, an end. What if we all played by the rules they taught me in business school – supply and demand sets pricing. Produce a quality product–"

"Build a better mousetrap."

"Build a better mousetrap. That's right, but we don't make mousetraps. We don't make anything. We shuffle papers and juggle numbers until someone wins and someone loses. Then the winners tell us how wonderful we are and pay us commissions to leverage the regulations so we can do it again. Even better this time. We ratchet up the stakes until we break the camel's back per Lehmann Brothers. And you know how many people went to jail following all that manipulation that costs billions of dollars?" She wasn't expecting the obvious answer and didn't wait for it. Instead she motioned to the newspaper again. "Only the guy who took twenty dollars. Only him."

WASHINGTON, D.C.: "Stop worrying, will you? You sound like a school kid who thinks the bully is waiting in the parking lot for him."

"This doesn't bother you?"

"The FBI will track that blown out advertisement to somebody at the *Post* or somebody's Super Pac. Three days from now it's forgotten. Probably just the *Post* being the *Post* – looking for a ratings sweep."

"That's television."

"Same difference. It means nothing. I'm flying home in a couple hours."

"Aren't you having hearings tomorrow?"

"Somebody is. I've got things to do. We're headed down to Florida for tarpon. Beautiful fish. Great strip clubs too. You should come. All you do is meet the mayor of some Podunk town and talk about oranges for five minutes and the whole trip's paid for."

"Another day maybe. I'm sticking close to town for a few days. I'm hearing rumblings. People are missing money."

"Damn fools. They're always allocating money from one pile to another and forgetting who did what. It'll all come out in the wash."

"Not that money. Personal."

"Same thing. They give every call girl with big tits their credit card for a blow job then act shocked when their account gets tapped. I keep a separate card for 'business expense' with a low limit. Submit it for payment through the comptroller every month. Never a problem. I do the same with the House Bank. If they charged me a dollar every time I overdrew my Congressional account, I'd be bankrupt."

"Well, apparently, everyone isn't as clever as you. The upside is that the food banks around the country are pretty flush from what is trickling out. I hear almost every church with a website has gotten a donation. The FBI is looking at the Red Cross, Doctors Without Borders, and a bunch more, but no hints as to who's bestowing the cash. They know account numbers, but no one's taking credit for making the gifts. The FBI is starting to think there's a reason for no one talking."

"That's kind of funny, actually."

"Unless it's your money buying the water, medicine, and blue tarps for Haiti. You might stop laughing PDQ."

"The Bureau will run it down."

Before the shadow of the junior representative cleared the door, the would-be fisherman was checking some shill accounts buried in his brother's name. When he saw the zeros, his heart skipped a beat. Then his eyes saw red. He called his woe-be-gone brother who he would find clueless. The next day the majestic tarpon went unmolested as the Congressman cancelled his trip to "attend to pressing matters of National importance."

HELENA, MONTANA: "New Illuminati. That's a clever sounding name, ain't it?"

"Illuminating. Shed some light on the subject."

"More like watching the rats scramble in the barn when you turn the lights on."

"Instead of turning the lights on, I'd like to see the lights go out on some of those rats."

"Reads to me like that's the suggestion."

The early dialogues, debates, and conversations had taken place and continued, not knowing the process had already grown legs. It was moving through the digital world on marionette strings worked by Clayton and others with such ease it was fast becoming reckless merely by repetition.

For those that did not vote and those that did, a new stretch of highway where their discourse intersected was laid out in front of them. It seems they no longer had to wait out the election cycle.

TAMPA, FLORIDA: Sam put a copy of the *Post* under the counter and slid the full-page ad from the guts of the paper and read it. He smiled from within a cradle of calm. It was the way of one whose placating grin grows in equal measure from the page and the fore knowledge that grants an understanding and secret confidence. On the first pass, Sam thought of the millions of Americans who would read this in the next several days. From those millions, he knew only two who had the tacit grasp he did and could share his secret smile. By the third read however, a notion drew across his mind like a curtain. There may well be others – perhaps many others. Clayton's recruiting may not have ended at the counter of the newsstand. The computer genius's work had served as the primer. Other explosions had their own ignition source. Sam read it again.

It didn't matter. He had been a part of many teams in the past though this group would never stand up to interrogation. They would likely cave as quickly as the members of his very first team – that little league crew of nine – who could outplay any other eleven-year-old team in the state, but held the secret of who pried their way into the concession stand and stole candy bars for only as long as it took to ask the question.

The smile widened as he folded the page and tucked it under the counter. He leaned back on his stool and buried his chin in the palm of his hand as he flipped through an itinerary in his head and saw where it would intersect the senator Clayton had referenced. This published referendum would ratchet up the stakes. Sam continued to review his plan for tapping the senator on the shoulder – Clayton's definition of "a presence." The publication and the fallout would add to the difficulty, but it was still possible.

———————

24

The senator was squirming in her seat far worse than she had when she was answering questions under oath from the House Ethics Committee regarding her aborted and abysmal financial disclosure documents. She had control over that interrogation. After all, the committee members asking the questions had to tread lightly for the roles would be reversed soon enough for most. Far better to leave the stones that covered the merry-go-round of pre-IPO stock deals undisturbed. But now, in the back seat of a limo crossing Florida on the I-4 corridor, she was squeezing her knees together and grinding her ass into the seat.

"How long until we're there?"

The aide looked at her watch. "About ten minutes."

The senator grimaced, hunched over slightly as though pained and jammed her hand into her crotch.

"I'm going to wet my pants," she whispered. "Ask him to hurry," she said as she pointed with her makeup caked chin toward the front seat.

"We're a little behind schedule," the aide said to the driver. "Try to save us a few minutes, will you?"

"Yes, ma'am."

The car lurched only slightly, but nearly as quickly died under the weight of the surrounding traffic coming together as it dumped off the interstate into downtown Tampa. The senator peered out the nearly black tinted windows at the crushing traffic and the lights of the city beyond. She sighed. "My husband can't go and I can't stop. Isn't that awful? Getting old, I suppose."

"You look great, Senator," the aide lied.

"Looking great is the easy part. You get used to the needles after a while. Oh, they still smart like the devil – especially right here," she said as she leaned toward the practiced assistant and pointed right between her eyebrows. "Must be a bone there."

It took every ounce of restraint for the young professional to not say, "Yes, a bone. It's called your skull."

There was another contortion that even the Botox couldn't compete with until the senator reined in the urge and looked again out the windows during a temporary reprieve.

"Shouldn't we be picking up an escort? I need to get to a bathroom or I will go right on the floor. Can you imagine? At least I wore a dark suit. A little won't show, will it?"

"No. It'll be fine. Here," the subordinate said as she produced a tablet and tapped the screen until a list of names and photographs opened. "This is the mayor, members of city council, top donors–"

"Oh, perfect. Give me that. It will get my mind off it. Anything glaring going on here I need to address?"

"No, I anticipate a very calm night. The crowd will be very small."

"Oh?"

"Not because of you, Senator," the aide apologized. "The per-plate was very high – appealing to the most ardent donors."

"Then call it 'select,' not 'small.' I don't care for the ring of that."

"Yes, ma'am."

"That works out well though. I'm headed back to Orlando tonight, is that right?"

"Yes, Senator."

"Good. Good. My daughter is at Disney and I want to have breakfast with my grandchildren."

"It's all arranged, Senator. They are in the bank of suites being held for staff and security."

"Oh, well done. Could you get my grandson a badge or something? If he's my security detail," she smiled in her oblivion, "he should have a badge. He'd like that."

The aide wrote with her fingertip on the screen and saved herself a note as the car eased from traffic around a few corners – tight for the big car – and into the parking lot of the high-rise hotel.

"Thank you, Lord Jesus! Let me out of here before I have an accident. While I kiss the babies, you find me a ladies' room. Then come get me. Don't dawdle. I'll be fine once I'm up, but don't keep me waiting. And clear the bathroom out. I hate it when women want to chat over the stall. Idiots. They're just idiots."

The aide skated through the tiny throng and found her local contact. They were invisible in the long shadow cast by the senator as they scoped the banquet room, set up with elegant place settings arranged in a hierarchy of donation amounts that sat the largest contributors closest to the senator and the dais. Two security guards from the congressional office dressed in crisp dark blue suits followed and gave the room a perfunctory once over.

An advance crew had done the security setup and screening along with local police.

"And where is the nearest ladies room?" the aide whispered.

"Just around the corner."

"And the next nearest?"

"In the lobby."

The aide pushed open the outer bathroom door into a small privacy foyer. A second door led into the restroom proper where she walked up the row of stalls and back. It was clean and neat and most importantly, empty as she gave each door a push as she passed. The stall nearest the door was taped securely shut with an 'Out of Order' sign affixed to the door. She knelt, being careful not to touch the floor, and looked beneath the door. No feet. It was empty as well.

"Peeking under bathroom doors," she thought. "Mom and Dad would be so proud of my 'big job' working for the government." Now she spoke out loud to herself and the granite encased lavatory. "What a job – trying to find a place for the Wicked Witch of the West to squat."

She opened the inner door, stepped through the bathroom's vestibule, passed the first door, and spoke to one of the dark blue suits on the detail. "Tell anyone that comes by, this is temporarily closed. Send them to the lobby. There's another one there." Then she went off to find her boss with the tightly pressed thighs.

"My apologies, Senator, but you have a call from Washington," she said as she held up her cell to no dearth of groveling local politicians and donors. "It's the Majority Leader."

"Ah, duty calls. Please excuse me," the senator smiled brightly beneath eyes as wide as saucers. "I'll be right back."

In three hurried steps she had the phone to her ear, but was addressing her assistant. "Was it so hard to find a ladies room? I am in physical pain here. So inconsiderate."

The plain clothes guards followed her and met the other waiting at the bathroom. One eased the outer door open, being politely careful not to look inside.

"It's empty, Senator," the aide said as she peeled away and waited along the wall with the trailing security detail.

The senator didn't pause to let either door close completely, but Sam was watching. He had one hand on the latch and the other on the stall door behind the 'Out of Order' sign and tape. In the fraction of a second between the closing of the inner bathroom door and the senator's, Sam's stall snapped liked a rat trap. The only sound the senator heard was the tearing tape. She felt the push of her stall door and the heavy quick weight of a thick arm around her throat as Sam's forearm flexed only enough to compress her carotid artery. She passed out in seconds – unable to scream or resist the hint of a blue jacket covering the arm at her neck. There was no sound except the trickle of urine down her leg into her Italian made shoes and out across the floor.

A stopwatch began to click in Sam's head the moment he let his arm slip off the senator's neck. He snatched her by one ankle and dragged her through her own piss out of the stall and over to the gold accented basins. When she came to a minute later, thick plastic zip tie handcuffs were tight around her eyes, wrists, and ankles. Other ties laced her ankles up behind her to her wrists, completing the hog-tie through the drain pipes of the sinks. She wasn't going anywhere.

The last tie held a half empty toilet paper roll securely in her mouth and tight around her head. Her hands were turning purple, but Sam knew she wouldn't be bound long. It would only be long enough to hear the message. The clock in his head was ticking as Sam leaned in close to the senator's ear and heard her wheezing through her nose and saw her skinny chest heaving.

"Listen very closely. You have read the warning. Now you feel our teeth at your throat. You don't have the money, power, or people to stop us because we are those people. We are in the Congress. We are in your office. We are in the hallway outside. How do you think we got in here?

"It all stops," Sam growled as he jerked hard on the zip tie running through the senator's mouth. "Now. Do you understand?"

The senator nodded vigorously.

"No you don't. So I'll tell you what will happen. You'll cry out you were attacked for no reason – conveniently forgetting your mail fraud, insider trading, land swaps, theft, and perjury. Your selfish waste of taxpayer's dollars won't stop. You won't change and you won't influence others to change." Sam put his finger against the tie running across eyes that were streaming tears and pushed it into an eye until the senator lost sight of the blurred creamy binding and saw the rebelling flash of lightning inside the pressured eyeball.

"And then we will come for you again. But not gentle like tonight." He poked her eye harder and she moaned. "And we will put a bullet through this eye from six hundred meters and you'll be dead before your lying, thieving, rotten, soulless corpse hits the ground.

"Tell your friends it's over. Luke 12:48. 'From everyone who has been given much, much will be required; and to whom they have entrusted much, of him, or her, they will ask all the more.' We're not fanatics. We're not crazy. We're not criminals. You are the criminals. And you will be held accountable."

Sam stepped quickly into the bathroom stall and picked up the senator's purse from the puddle. He rummaged until he found a lipstick container. He dropped the purse in the toilet and took the lipstick to the mirror. He drew the pyramid and eye of the Illuminati over 'Luke 12:48,' just as he had done in San Francisco. There would be no mistake as to who had taken the senator to task. When he put the lipstick in his pocket he slipped his arm around the senator's neck again. She struggled, kicking her urine soaked shoes off in the process, and tried to cry out, but couldn't.

"You don't like this, do you?" Sam whispered. "You're afraid. You should be. Good night, bitch. Next time it will be forever. Think on it."

Sam effortlessly choked her out again.

He stood up straight and looked in the mirror over the vanity. He was not nervous, sweating, or even breathing heavy. He straightened his tie and tugged at his dark blue suit coat until it lay flat. It did little to hide his bulk, but that was okay. He wasn't planning on hiding to make the short trip across town.

The 'Out of Order' sign and the tape came off, was wadded and stuffed into a pocket. The layout of the ladies room was perfect. Sam opened the inner door and moved calmly and quietly against the wall where the outer door would shield him when it opened. Then he waited, predicting the timing of the opening door to the minute. If he had to fight his way out he knew he could, but he was certain he would walk out as unnoticed as he had walked in.

The door opened and Sam caught the inside handle and held it open, deathly still as though the aide had intended it to stay that way. The aide was going through the inner door without looking back. In a second, she was yelling for help.

Three Congressional officers rushed in while the fourth stopped a Tampa cop from doing the same. "Watch the hall," is all he said then bolted into the bathroom.

When he last cleared the inner door, Sam slid from his hiding stop, pulled a business card from his coat, and stepped outside. The dark blue suit was disarming and when he handed the officer the card, it took his eyes down away from Sam's face.

"Call an ambulance," Sam ordered then stepped around the corner while the card still captured the officer's eyes as he grabbed the radio microphone on his shoulder.

While the officer snapped the request into his shoulder microphone the card dangled from his fingers. It looked official – carried a government seal and a generic name. On the back, in small type it read, "Luke 12:48."

Sam was in a stairwell. He picked up a small duffel bag tucked behind a fire hose and began stripping the coat and tie as he headed down to the basement garage. When he emerged, he was wearing a baseball cap and sunglasses though the sun had already set.

Sam fell into the security of back streets he had known since he was a boy. Several blocks later he emerged in the bustling streets of Ybor City – his neighborhood within Tampa. In minutes he was bouncing up the steps of his house while sirens wailed in the distance.

————————

25

The big Boeing KC-135 was warming up four engines. The vibration sent a smooth shudder through the cavernous body of the plane. Almost lost in the quivering massive tanker, Cal Denti felt his phone vibrate in his jacket pocket and heard a faint familiar ring. When he pulled the phone out, he saw the initials 'J L' on the screen.

"You better get on a plane," sufficed for John LaRoy's salutation.

"You hear this?" Cal yelled as he held the phone out for a moment into the loud yawning interior of the KC-135. "I'm Space-A on the tarmac at MacDill. I'll be at Andrews in two hours."

Jack Aaron sat uncomfortably in the din beside Cal. He repeatedly tightened his seat belt.

"I'll have a car there," John LaRoy said as an answer to the sound of the plane's engines.

"What?"

"I'll have a car ready," LaRoy yelled.

"I can't hear you, John. Send a car over."

"I'll pick you up myself! Call me when you land."

"I'll call you when I land."

"Good. I'll see you in a couple hours."

"Okay! I'll see you in a couple hours!" Cal nearly screamed then powered down the phone and put it in his pocket. He tugged the harness that served as a seat belt and felt the flying fuel depot begin to roll. Jack looked around at the stories high mass of steel he was riding in.

"Are you sure this thing can get off the ground?" he yelled in Cal's ear.

"She'll get up. Relax."

Both men on the plane, and LaRoy in Washington, spent the next two hours replaying on a game board in their minds the few moves they knew of, speculated on the ones they didn't, and in the process, thought of ways to catch up to somebody who was so far ahead of them any trail that might have shown the way was ice cold before his footprint could disappear from unmarked ground. It seemed to Cal and LaRoy – eight hundred miles and thirty thousand feet apart – that the writer of the verbal assault on members of Congress was leaving as much of a trail as skating in soft socks across a polished marble floor. Cal was on the knees of his mind looking for disturbed dust. LaRoy was brow beating the electronic forensic unit for the same thing, but while they struggled, Jack had a name on a scrap of paper in his pocket.

Spread out five miles below the KC-135, the country was experiencing hints of an anxious shift that was currently being painted as crime. Two hundred years earlier they had dressed as Indians and ripped tea from the holds of ships. At the time they were dubbed criminals, yet among the classic literature on Raphael's elaborate shelves were history books that described them as patriots and freedom fighters. For the politicos of the time – King George among them – they cowered and sent their army and police against the purported hooligans while they whispered to themselves and each other that the devil had come for his due.

People had long grown numb to the seamy underside of the Beltway and Washington politics. They did not know who to believe, so they believed no one. Americans who traced their heritage back two hundred years were as powerless as those who just lowered their hands at their citizenship ceremony. All their hopes and dreams were being scattered like so much chaff in the winds of arrogance, incompetence, and greed. Clayton's published ultimatum, and stories from the Halls of Power that were beginning to leak out, provided direction and encouragement. By the time Cal touched down at Andrews Air Force base, the news cycles were jammed with back-to-back breaking stories from coast to coast and the momentum had only just begun.

The assault on the senator stole the headline, but it was soon outpaced by volume. It began with the massing of flash mobs outside local congressional offices and the homes of lobbyists and CEOs. Each had been implicated via investigations ranging from local authorities to state and federal agencies and the ethics committees of both houses of Congress. Clayton's fingers were cramping as he tapped into banks of tweeter lists and said enough in less than one hundred and forty characters to incite people across the country to descend on heretofore unknown addresses and the shrouded peddlers of power who resided there. By noon, thousands massed in the streets and manicured yards of a hundred men and women who were being figuratively pulled naked and crying into the harsh light of accountability.

Congressional appointees who had three months ago hid behind the Fifth Amendment in order to stall until their incriminating emails could be purged, now hid in their basements. They cried out for protection from the same government they had stonewalled as the citizenry they had lied to marched on their homes with metaphoric pitchforks and blazing torches.

Local police were quickly overwhelmed and responded by expressing their sympathy with the crowds as criminal indictments and ignored subpoenas were communally bantered across barricades between police and protesters. The authorities implored the citizenry to not cross the line from civil assembly to crime.

Then the first rock was thrown.

_____

26

The beer bottle was as cold as a stare from the back of a limo at a cardboard shielded denizen of an underpass. It had been frosted over ten minutes ago as Clayton held it in his hands. It relieved the ache. He had abused his fingers the night before and most of the morning in draining accounts, making donations, and educating the public. Sparks from his keyboard lit infernos that were raging from coast to coast. Washington was being razed by an internal, unquenchable, and invisible bonfire that relegated fires set by the British in 1814 to the ranks of a marshmallow toast.

Members of Congress and scandalous business operators had screaming matches that brought down cell networks and lobbyists. Each blamed the other for what would total billions of missing dollars and stock swaps that left each holding worthless paper. In the marble hallways and outer offices, assistants winked at each other as they passed and pulled childlike imaginary zippers across their mouths then rolled their eyes. Despite the restraints of the zippers, many were placing clandestine calls to contacts within the media, planting or cultivating 'breaking news' on a growing list of yet another 'friend of the people' who was crumbling under the weight of revelation. For the staff members, many understood they were cutting off the hand that fed them, but they had seen enough. For those that had profited themselves in a comparatively small measure, several placed calls, not to the media, but the FBI. Selfishly they were looking to leverage a way out and distance themselves from the men and women in red ties and business suits who sat framed by American flags behind their big desks in the innermost offices. Those calls were lighting up the proverbial switchboard across town at FBI headquarters.

Seven stories above Pennsylvania Avenue, John LaRoy had just been introduced to Jack Aaron.

"Cal puts a lot of stock in what you say and do, DA. If he ranks you that high, so do I. What can you tell us?"

Jack was uncharacteristically quiet. He couldn't be timid if been baited with treasure, but was now remarkably reflective. Marcus had talked and listened to a dozen scenarios before Cal picked Jack up for the impromptu trip to Andrews Air Force base and the meeting with the FBI. The answer was already in Jack's pocket and on his lips, but the question of, 'What if?' rested behind it on the tip of his tongue and found its way out as a scout moves on point ahead of a company of soldiers.

Jack looked at Cal and smiled slightly, but spoke to John. "He's a real sweetie, ain't he?" as the old Jack returned with words passing through a genuine smile of worn friendship that was about to be tested. "Now, just because you said something nice about me, don't get to feeling I'm going to be extending any liberties. You're still picking up the check for dinner."

Cal was quick. "I took care of your airline ticket."

"Shhhiit..." Jack leaned forward toward LaRoy. "The sonofabitch had me balanced on the tires – riding in the wheel well – from MacDill to Andrews."

"I've known him over twenty years," LaRoy said as he woefully shook his head, "and I've never known him to do anything nice for a person."

"Selfish bastard, really. Must be hell to have to try and manage him."

"It is. Left to his own devices, I wouldn't get anything accomplished in Florida. I appreciate you helping him out down there."

"Glad to do it," Jack said as he sat back. "I think a lot of you federal boys."

Cal rolled his eyes. "Please..."

LaRoy's eyes stayed on Jack. "Don't wait with your hand over your ass at dinner. He never picks up a check unless it's made out to him."

LaRoy and Jack laughed. Cal lowered his head and took it. The exchange was the coarse banter common among brothers, old friends, and men of like mind. Cal knew it and recognized it for what it was. Though at his expense, the few minutes of harsh ribbing and his relationship with each man instantly established a trust between the two top cops and reminded Cal of the similarities between the men and why he liked them both. Any commonality he could nourish would soon be pressed into service. He endured a few more jokes, as though he wasn't in the room, as the callous laughter would soon enough segue into the real dialogue and a discussion that would be riddled with uncomfortable silence.

"A bunch of us were having lunch the other day," Jack was saying. "I'm going to the head to take a leak and I hear some new intern with the feds tell the maître d' he's got a message for Agent Calburn Denti. I point across the dining room to a couple of tables shoved together and tell him Denti's over there. The kid asks me which one's Denti so I tell him, "The one with his back to the check!"'"

Jack erupted in a boisterous laugh at his own joke and took LaRoy with him. The pair were swept away by a fire hose of fifth grade zingers aimed at the defenseless FBI agent.

"I haven't had lunch with him in years," LaRoy said around a dying laugh. "When he comes to Washington, he always eats with the brass... because they can't trust him with the silver!"

Jack was tearing up and LaRoy's side was aching.

"One time...," Jack sputtered. "One time we were headed to lunch and this panhandler comes up to Cal's window at a light. The guy says, "How about a dollar for a sandwich?" And Cal says, "I dunno, let's see the sandwich!""

LaRoy roared and pounded his desk. Jack was leaning over in his chair laughing and rested his crying eyes on the heels of his palms.

Cal pulled a chair closer between LaRoy's desk and Jack. "Are you girls about through?" he asked sincerely as he leaned back and crossed his legs, brushing at nothing on his knee and pulling the razor-sharp crease neatly in line.

LaRoy took a deep breath and wiped his face with his hands. "Yeah, I'm tapped out. How about you, DA?"

"Yep, I'm good. That was funny."

"You two should look for open mic night at the Improv. You'd be a real hit."

"Don't take it too hard, Cal," LaRoy said. "And we can't quit our day jobs until we get out from under this shit storm. We opened fifteen new cases out of Congress in the last twenty-four hours and my guess is there's plenty more members on the Hill with their dicks or tits in a wringer, but they don't want us to know. Whoever's driving this steamroller has really hit a nerve."

"They're pretty good drivers too," Cal said as the transition from nightclub act to investigators was completed. "They seem equally adept at upper echelon hacking or scaring the b'jesus out of our senators."

"Some of our senators need the b'jesus scared out of them," Jack said as he stared across the desk at LaRoy, all their punch lines long forgotten.

Cal knew Jack's comment was the tipping point. From here on out, there would be no more laughter. LaRoy would drive.

"I appreciate you guys coming up here on short..., on no notice. With the senator getting snatched off her shitter in Tampa, your theory on origination of this vigilante has picked up a load of credibility."

Jack looked at Cal. "I was thinking they might be Good Samaritans, instead of vigilantes. What do you say?"

"That's one perspective, and not an uncommon one across the country."

Jack squinted a bit and looked at both men. "What's our perspective?"

"What's yours?" LaRoy asked with the seriousness of a judge at sentencing.

The first of many of those periods of silence Cal dreaded slipped into the room and took all the oxygen out. The three men shifted their eyes from one face to another, all the while looking inward for a private answer. Somewhere there had to be consensus and it was struggling against oaths taken years ago.

Jack turned it back on LaRoy. "What's yours?"

"You first, DA"

True to form, Jack grinned. "You show me yours, I'll show you mine."

"Guys," Cal said as though he was breaking up a high school fight that hadn't seen its first swing yet. "That's a question that doesn't need to be asked or answered. We're upholding the law – enforcing the law here. Clearly–"

"Let him answer," Jack pushed.

The silence descended again. Almost a full minute – an eternity in a waiting staring match – eclipsed only when Cal stepped into the awkward void. "We all want–"

"Wait," LaRoy snapped and welcomed the silence. "Maybe we all don't want the same thing." And the silence gripped every man by the throat.

27

K aren's hair was blowing across her face from the eighty-five mile per hour Georgia wind as she screeched south on I-95. The cross-referencing data John LaRoy had asked for had been gleaned and placed on her desk. She had scarcely opened it. There was no stopping back at her apartment or even long enough to gas up her car. She went from her office to the interstate and was running south as fast as she dared. Before Karen hit the highway, she had taken out her phone's battery. She didn't know where all this would end, but wouldn't leave anything someone like her could use. Sam's name was on the list inside the big envelope on the passenger's seat.

A thousand thoughts later, Karen saw the first 'Welcome to Florida' sign. Her eyes looked out the passenger window and watched the sign with its iconic oranges pass by in a blur. Beneath the window, on the seat, the big envelope captured her eyes for the umpteenth time as though staring at it would somehow change what was inside.

As Karen raced across the Georgia-Florida border, in Atlanta, Alyn Nuary's phone was ringing with news that would forever prohibit the genie of Sam's name on the list from ever being returned to the bottle.

"Nuary."

"It's Jason."

"Oh, my sweet little Jason. Didn't we have a nice dinner in Washington?"

"Swell—"

"And after? Did you enjoy your 'benefits package?'"

"I loved it, but the price is too high for me."

"What's the problem, dear?"

"Pretend you care."

"My, you're harsh. What's wrong, sweetie?"

"There's movement on that Tampa/San Fran case."

"I should say. It's all over every news outlet in the country. Seems to be a bounty on senators. There must be video."

"Not like you'd think. The early reports coming in say the feeds are all blank around the hotel – hallways, foyer, entrance, parking garage. Somebody scrubbed everything. We've located one grainy image from a place across the street. Can't tell anything except that a big guy walked out of the garage wearing a baseball hat and sunglasses just after they found the senator trussed up like a Christmas turkey. We can't even tell if he's black or white. Six two to six four. Maybe two twenty to two fifty. Big guy."

"No video from inside the hotel?"

"I told you, scrubbed. Nothing. All blank."

"Has to be an inside job. Somebody erased the tapes–"

"Tapes? And you bust LaRoy's balls for being in the dark ages? There's no tape. Everything is digital. They were hacked. These people are too good, Alyn, and you haven't heard the scary part."

"So scare me."

"You want this or are you gonna be a bitch?"

"Yes and yes. What is it?"

"LaRoy's scan of Special Operations personnel – active and inactive. It came in this morning."

"Anything to it?"

"A Tampa connection."

"That damn Denti... Who's seen it?"

"The log lists just three copies going out – all with encryption – one to LaRoy, one to that major with SOCOM – also in Tampa, that's scary part number two by the way – and another to the JAG officer."

"Special Operations is in Tampa?"

"Hub for SOCOM and then some. Command structure, administration, transportation, etc."

"Isn't that interesting," Nuary mused. "Maybe the Seals and Rangers are behind this. Wouldn't that be quite a twist?"

"The twist would be our heads snapping off our necks."

"The entire thing – the money transfers, the assaults – could all be black ops."

"Assaulting our own senators?"

"Maybe she blocked their appropriations."

"I'm done," Meyer said in a harsh whisper. "I'm not messing with these people. They just knocked the shit out of a sitting United States Senator. You think they can't get to people like you and me? I'm done."

"Send me the report."

"I don't know, Alyn. This is getting dicey. Too many internal players. Spec Ops? Are you kidding?"

Alyn put her finger in her mouth as to gag, rolled her eyes, and dropped her head. "Let me see the report and when I come to Washington for my promotion ceremony and distinguished service award, I'm all yours."

He flinched.

"But what if—"

"Send it."

Meyer hit send on his internal email account. The transfer bar flashed for a millisecond and the report was on its way.

"It's coming, but this is the last of it. I tell you, I'm out."

Nuary's email pinged and she saw the email drop in. She clicked it and unfolded the report with active links of names leading to service details and assignments.

"You don't know where you got it," Meyer said when he heard the ping through his receiver.

"Not to worry, darling. I've already forgotten," Nuary said and hung up the phone.

Alyn began clicking through the files, reading histories, training, rank, awards, theaters of conflict, and current assignments or locations. She sorted by location and found the men attached to SOCOM in Tampa. Most sported a lengthy dossier. One stood out for its brevity – Sgt. Sam Ciampiano. Alyn stared at his picture.

"Handsome. You resigned?" She scrolled through two sketchy pages. "Basic training like any grunt, then what? You disappear? Where'd you go? They have you driving a truck because you can't spell your name? What?"

She went back through the short description. "You're a pretty non-descript guy, Ciampiano. Somebody catch you banging the base commander's wife? Why are you on this list?"

One more scan through. "Last known location – Tampa. That it? Guilty by geography?" She looked at his physical records. Six feet, two inches. Two hundred forty pounds. "You're a big one. How do you look in a baseball hat and sunglasses?" Nuary was ready to click ahead until three letters caught her eye – J A G.

"Location verified by JAG," she read as she parked her elbow on the padded wrist support in front of her keyboard and leaned onto her palm. "Why does JAG want to know where you are, Sergeant?"

———————

28

"Are you a Democrat or Republican, John?" Jack was asking LaRoy.

"Neither," came the answer like a crack of a whip. "Independent, and fiercely so, as they like to say."

"Why?"

"Well, I'd be a Libertarian if I could pull it off, but then the administrations that come and go every time the White House changes its pants wouldn't think they could sway me to their side and I'd be working some bullshit tax evasion case in Palookaville instead of talking to you."

"So these politician types aren't your best friends?"

John LaRoy answered by leaning back, flexing a tense jaw and giving a jagged point toward Jack with his square chin. "We're a couple of old dogs, DA. My guess is we're cut from the same cloth. But I generally don't go down a road unless I know where the hell it's going. Just a suggestion, but why don't you just let 'er rip and let me know what's on your mind. What do you think, Cal?"

There was another gap that had moved beyond awkward to an ardent tenseness that carried a discomfort on its back.

"Jack?" Cal said. "If you have what I think you have, you have to provide it. These are serious charges."

"Or what?"

"We could subpoena you."

Jack laughed. "That's the best joke of the day. A subpoena in this town isn't worth the paper it's printed on. I see people every day snub their noses at the government over a subpoena."

"Congressional ones, yes," LaRoy said. "I've seen that too, and I'm not happy about it, but a subpoena from us, from the Bureau? That'll land you in the pokey."

"That a threat?"

"Not even remotely. It's a reminder."

"Thanks, but I know the law pretty good."

"That was never in doubt. I'm wondering – by the tone of this conversation," LaRoy said as he glanced at Cal. "Why you even came to Washington?"

"Let's stop," Cal said as abruptly as a deer jumps in front of a car and with the same result.

"Cal? Do you have what the DA has? You better tell me now or I'm going to get real pissed at you."

"I don't. We've been working it as Mr. X. Jack and his team pulled it all together."

"Let him keep fishing then," LaRoy said. "But I'll have that bait."

Jack let it pass and took a deep breath. "Call me curious."

"About whether I'll do my job? That doesn't sit well."

"I don't give a shit how it sits, John. Like you said, I think a lot of Cal here – though don't tell him that – and he says you're a good egg. So, I'm willing to haul my old ass up here and out on a limb. I'm just curious if anybody else is out there."

"Jack, let it go," Cal said, softer now and avoided the traffic this time.

"I just want to know if I'm the only sonofabitch who is wondering if I'm on the right side of this pile of horseshit," Jack said as he turned his palms face up. "Simple as that."

"Simple as that?" LaRoy heated up. "Simple as that, Jack? None of this is simple. In fact, it might be the most far flung case in the Bureau's history. This thing would give J. Edgar a hardon. But if you're looking for a conspirator to let these people walk–"

"He didn't say that, John."

"Damned if he didn't."

The pause came into the room again and sat on the edge of the desk between the men as a hawk sits on a branch and watches for the mouse to betray himself. When one moved, the game would be over or the game would be on – only the Fates could determine which it was to be.

Jack stood up and pulled Cal and LaRoy straight up in their chairs as far as they could go without standing themselves.

"I'll get someone to show you out," LaRoy said as he reached for his phone.

Cal threw his hand over LaRoy's and pinned down the phone as he shot up from his seat. "What are you doing, Jack? Goddamnit–"

"A cramp," Jack snapped. "I got a cramp." Jack massaged his thigh ever so slightly then in the same motion slipped his hand in his pocket. When it came out it flipped a folded three by five red lined index card on LaRoy's desk.

"Clayton Rand."

Cal's hand paroled LaRoy's from the phone. Cal retreated to his chair as LaRoy picked up the note and read the name he'd just heard. His eyes begged the palpable as they came up from the card.

"I don't have all that for you yet," Jack said as he motioned to Cal. "Tinkerbell and me will go back south after he squeezes whatever he can out of your forensic geniuses."

"So who's Clayton Rand then?"

"The only guy who can do what we've seen done who also could have seen the newsreel about my county commissioner who was being pretty liberal in his definition of development." Jack dropped back in his chair. "That's where this all started. I said so from jump street. Cal agrees with me."

"We've put a lot into this," Cal said. "This Rand is looking real good for it as far as capability, availability, probability—"

"Probability? As in 'probable cause' type probability?"

"Not yet. That's why I came up. I want to kick it around and see what forensics has developed."

"How about you, DA? That why you came up too? Kick it around?"

The break was short and Jack grinned. "Sure."

LaRoy leaned back in his chair. "Jesus-take-the-wheel. I've had some thin ones, but making a man guilty because everyone else is innocent is a piss poor case."

"That's why we're here."

"I'll slap the IT geeks around again. Right now they've got squat. The hotel that got dropped on the senator has fifty cameras for monitoring and surveillance. All blank before, during, and after the assault."

Jack sat back down. His imaginary cramp had slipped away. "Somebody erased that many tapes?"

"Just what I said, but no tapes, my friend. All digital. The hotel got hacked."

"Sounds like my boy, Rand. He's good. He's not going to leave anything to find."

LaRoy sighed. "Or any reason for a jury to find him guilty."

"Doesn't mean he isn't."

"Have you got a tail on him?"

Cal was back in. "Yes, we're tracking him – sort of unofficially. We could use a little help with the subpoenas. As you said, it's a little thin."

"Patriot Act will get it done."

"A strong hand to rattle the roost beneath a couple of judges would do the trick."

"I'll get one for you, but if he's everything you think he is, unlikely he'll trip up there."

"I know. He's too intelligent to do something that obvious. He's not going to give us anything on the electronic end."

"Never know. Let's get it in place."

The slight pause was eclipsed by grinding gears whirling in the heads of the three lawmen. LaRoy leaned forward over his desk. "Say, Jack? Newsreel? How old are you? I thought I was an antique."

Jack smiled while Cal answered. "He's not as seasoned as he lets on, John. It's just that he thinks old."

"He 'thinks old,' huh?"

"Yea, I think old," Jack fidgeted in his chair and grinned.

LaRoy laughed and conveniently forgot all the talk about tree limbs as he tapped the index card against the top of his desk.

"Tell me more about Clayton Rand."

29

"What's on tap for tonight?" Clayton said before he closed the door to Raphael's behind him.

"For which palette?" A bottle hissed like a perturbed snake under the release of its cap and Raphael handed his friend the cold one in exchange for an answer.

"Audio visual."

"B squared."

"Bogey and Bacall?"

Raphael smirked. "And who was that 9th grade teacher that said you had no future in math?"

"Ah, that would have been Mr. Rossillo. He was a wise man."

"He was."

"And you were his pet."

"I was everyone's pet."

"And still a kiss ass," Clayton jabbed.

"No argument, but it got me into Stanford."

"Whereas I had to settle for MIT, is that what you're trying to say?"

"It's a fair enough program, but as I recall you got in by the skin of your teeth after a rather unimaginative tenure at Rensselaer."

"Shit. You wish you could have gotten in Rensselaer."

"Over Stanford? Have you been drinking without me?"

"No, but I am now," Clayton said as he took a long pull.

"Cheers," Raphael said as he held out his bottle – a wisp of frosty breath exhaling from the bottle's throat.

"To tomorrow – whatever she may bring."

"Tomorrow."

The bottles' clink took on the report of a starter's pistol and the night was on.

"Which one?" Clayton asked over a throat soothed by the cold beer.

"Which what? Which tomorrow? I'm thinking the day after today."

"Which 'B-two' are we teeing up?"

"I'm leaning toward *To Have and Have Not*. Any preference?"

"That's tough to beat, though I'm a *Big Sleep* kind of guy."

They wandered in the company of their beers to the theater room and collapsed on the overstuffed recliners.

"And well I know, though that always has surprised me, I must say."

"I watch it for the General, not Bacall or even Bogey."

"The General?"

"Bacall's father. The old man—"

"I know the character, but why?"

"I'm not sure, maybe I just want to live to be that old. Or that rich."

"You're already that rich. Probably richer. And you don't spend the money you have now."

"Then it must be living to be that old. What's his line as Bogart is sweating his ass off? Something about living off heat – like a spider. Shit. We have to watch *The Big Sleep* now. I can't remember the line."

Raphael was leafing through his hard copy catalogue as Clayton looked inside his mind for the line from the film he couldn't quite get right.

"It must be the heat you like," Raphael said as he scanned his DVDs. "Things are heating up all over the country. I'm sure that pleases you."

"It does. And it should please you and everyone else in the country who still cares about it."

"Not so strangely, I believe you have merit. But I do hope you have found contentment in starting the game and can now step away."

"Not hardly."

Raphael stopped and physically leaned forward. "Clay, you've prompted a dialogue that is akin to striking a match to a powder keg. Get away from it before it blows."

"Away? I want to be in the middle of the explosion! I want to see these rotten bastards turning on a spit as the flames from that powder keg singe their skin until it blisters."

"Jesus, Clay, you're sick. But, alright. I get it and I applaud you. I really do. But some discretion is in order now. A United States Senator has been beaten in a bathroom not ten miles from here. And I just heard somebody kicked a congressman square in the balls in New York. You have to protect yourself."

"In New York? I hadn't heard that. Where?"

"Manhattan, and don't pretend you didn't know it was coming. I shudder to think how many minions you have flying around the country doing your bidding."

"Manhattan. Who got slapped?"

"That moron congressman who was sending pictures of his prick to his girlfriends. And he didn't get slapped. He got kicked – square in the nuts. There's a video of him lying on the sidewalk rolling off into the gutter holding his crotch. The authorities and your friends in the media think there must be a video of him getting punted, but it hasn't surfaced. The cops are saying the crowd pushed between the assailant and the police and the guy got away. For now."

"Good!"

"My guess is he's an MIT grad. Stanford is well above kicking people in the balls."

"To hell with Stanford. Damn, that is great news."

"That he got away? I would hope you made provisions to get the guy out of there after he puts the boots to a congressman."

"That too, but it's more important that people are taking an active hand – or in this instance, foot – in bringing accountability to bear."

"People? You mean your flunkies. Wait! I don't want to know."

"This conversation sounds reminiscent of another."

"Forget it. Let me find B and B."

Raphael massaged a small keyboard that had replaced the half-empty beer in his hand. The wide flat panel screen came to life with the iconic Warner Brothers shield and the beer took up residence again in Raphael's hand. As the preamble credits flashed by to the heavy beat of the melodramatic music, Raphael was swallowed by the deep comfort of his chair. Clayton was watching his friend instead of the screen.

"I really had nothing to do with that congressman in New York, Ralph. I just touched that first fragile snow drift at the top of the slope. The people are the avalanche. They've been waiting for someone–"

"Like a messiah?"

"Oh, God no! Someone like those nameless, faceless guys who dumped the tea in Boston Harbor."

"We have them already."

"Not like this."

"You mean violent?"

"Could be. Not always. Whatever it takes to wrench this country back from the brink. You're better at numbers than I am. You know we can't survive with a twenty trillion dollar deficit and a populace that thrives on free cell phones. Social security disability claims are up six hundred percent – that's a symptom of a diseased society – and politicians will feed that sickness as long as they get their share. They don't want a cure – they want to treat the illness. That's where the money is."

"So you are a doctor as well as a savior?"

"Cut it out. I'm a citizen who's doing what I can to help our country.

"You're a patriot."

"Damn right."

"Save the nation." Raphael held up his hands like a revival preacher.

"From people whose greed is cutting all our throats, yes," Clay said. "Are you in or out? I can't keep up."

"I don't hear you. I'm watching the movie."

"Here comes the General," Clayton said, easily distracted by the film.

"I know. I've seen it once or twice."

"Shhh. I can't remember the line."

The two watched Bogart sweating on screen playing the campy private eye as his character chats with the General in a sweltering greenhouse. When Clayton heard his sought for line he raised his bottle in salute.

Raphael raised his out of respect for the film. "Now you can sleep," he said.

"Sleep the big sleep."

"Be careful what you wish for."

"World peace? A cold beer? A soft bed?"

"How are you sleeping, by the way? How many blue pills are you tapping into your hand these nights?"

"None. Never better."

"Is that true?"

"I swear. I've never been sleeping better."

"A life of crime suits you then."

"I've found my calling."

Their sparring matched the snappy, jostling dialogue on screen between the matinee idols and real life husband and wife.

"From what I can gather, your new profession has a career life span equal to an NFL running back."

"Well then, I've got a good two more years to go."

"Would you consider an early exit – go out on top as it were?"

"I haven't reached the top yet."

"Those published letters seem to have had the desired effect and caused David to take action against Goliath. Wasn't that the plan?"

"Part of it."

"And part two involves kicking people in the nuts?"

"It's a start."

"You know, they're not going to let you keep spoiling their fun. They have to be looking – especially after what happened to the senator."

"Fuck that bitch."

Raphael sat up. "Clay. You have to stop. Someone's going to get hurt. I mean killed."

"Hopefully."

"That's not funny. You've made your point. You've got to stop."

"No, I do not have to stop, Ralph. And why would I?" Clayton himself sat up. "After two hundred years we've finally gotten these bastards at least thinking about doing the right thing."

"Out of fear."

"Who cares why? We can put so much pressure on them they start to play by the rules or find another game."

"Are you listening to yourself? That is so naive. You think a couple of assaults and some missing money is going to make people righteous? Holy shit, you have gone off the deep end in a bad way."

"That's only the beginning. We can strip them – take their money and you take their power. Take away the power and the only ones who'll want to be in the game will want in for the right reasons"

"You're not making sense, Clay. Just stop. Maybe you are that good at what you do. Maybe they don't have enough to catch you yet. Quit while you're ahead."

"I can't."

"Why?"

Bogart was sliding along the seat of a cab and making playful small talk with the female cabby. Raphael was watching Clayton while Clayton watched the television and didn't even see the action or hear the chatter.

"Have you read the Constitution lately?" Clayton asked.

"Not lately. Why?"

"How about the Declaration of Independence?"

"Same."

"You know the part, 'When in the course of human events...' and so on and so forth?"

"Sounds familiar," Raphael answered with measured hesitation as though being lured into a trap.

"A few lines below that there's a sentence that's stuck in my head. 'That when any form of government becomes destructive of these ends, it is the right of the people to alter or abolish it.' Do you know that part?"

"It doesn't mean what you're making it out to mean. It means alter – change – as in voting them out or making amendments, provisions, guarantees."

"Vote them out?"

"Yes."

"You're the one who's being naive. You can't get them out. It clearly says 'abolish.' Politicians are like ticks – they sink their teeth in the public tit and you can't get rid of them unless you kill them."

"So, that's how this ends, Clay? You kill everyone?"

"That's not the end. That's the beginning." Clayton took a drink and enjoyed the sharp banter of the film. "This is a classic film. Watch how Bogey moves. Listen to the timing in their voices. The plot is already there. The characters are fleshed out. You know how it will go. It's the same with us."

Somewhere outside an army was forming.

"You can't put this kind of magic back in the bottle," Clayton continued. "I could leave now, but it's already happened. You can stop right now — stop watching the movie — stop watching what happens across the country. It's alright." His voice edged to a near whisper. "It's alright. You can stop now. You know the ending."

"No, I don't know."

"Quiet," Clayton softly scolded. "Watch the film."

"Not yet. Tell me what's going to happen."

"Just hit rewind — about two hundred years," Clayton said as he scooted to the edge of his seat as though he was watching the movie for the first time. "You'll see it. The story of revolution is the oldest love story there is."

They were whispering now.

"Love story?"

"Love of country."

"Help me out here," Raphael pleaded in a whisper. "Help me see it. Explain it to me."

Clayton dismissed it all as his eyes brightened with the reflection of the glow from the television. "Shhh... This is the good part."

THE END
Part 1

Turn the page to read a teaser from **Return to Power – The New Illuminati, Part 2**, available now @ Amazon.

If you enjoyed **The New Illuminati**, share my work with family & friends. Also, please post a review @ Amazon & Goodreads!

Thanks so much,

David-Michael

S am Ciampiano had thought it was only a game. There was a big, paper covered, hard, one-dimensional board of squares with bright colored headers emblazoned with street names. Dollar signs dotted the board and play money was tucked here and there – purposely hidden or left to peek out and watch the game until pressed into service. The board folded neatly in half along a black cloth seam that was worn and frayed to gray by use. The cardboard box that held the board and the multi-colored money was the same – battered and bent at the edges, torn at the corners. Some of the game pieces had lost themselves over the years, but the game was still playable. The tokens were interchangeable and essentially meaningless as he remembered. His father had fancied a rather large military embossed brass button ahead of the tiny original pieces. Sam never let on he knew, but the big button was easier for the senior Ciampiano to move with his gnarled fingers – some of which had never been properly set when broken against the forehead of a man who had the temporary good fortune of having ducked just right. Sam himself had once played an entire game as a frail safety pin simply because he did not want to be the shoe. The memory struck him as comical now that he was living in the world's biggest shoe, just north of the heel.

Thoughts of the board, the pieces, and the playing of the game reminded Sam of his life in a way he figured few others who ever shot the dice considered. He was a reflection of the game board – a little battered and worn, frayed at the edges – and also felt as if a few pieces were missing. One piece was a substantial part of his heart he was coming to understand might never be found again.

While he wasn't stuck on Mediterranean Avenue without chick nor child and caught at the mercy of another player steeped in green and red plastic houses and hotels, he had crossed the literal Mediterranean, though he didn't recall collecting two hundred dollars as he passed Gibraltar. His Mediterranean Avenue had been the final maritime leg of a cramped and harried exit from Tampa and had, over the course of two months, discreetly deposited him in this coastal town within the Province of Bari. Sam didn't know where the next roll of the dice might land him, but for now he worked, rested, and willed himself to enjoy his freedom in a simple unassuming way. The past and the future churned behind his eyes, the scruff of a light beard, and beneath a short billed, dark blue fisherman's cap as he sat on the steps of a five-hundred-year-old stone fort in Monopoli, Italy.

He looked out across the cobalt water of the Adriatic Sea to the east. King Charles the 5th – Emperor of Rome and the King of Spain, Italy, and most of the known and New World – had the fort built in the 16th Century. It had been long abandoned as a parapet of defense for Monopoli and the centuries had seen the massive structure assume a myriad of services, including a historically brief return to its military origins during World War Two. A plain smooth concrete machine gun bunker stood nearby in stark contrast to the fort's ancient carved blocks of stone. The fort would no doubt remain long after the elements had washed the concrete and steel bunker into the depths of the sea.

For now, the fort and its heavy bolted doors were still and the only witnesses as Sam tied countless three-inch fishing hooks to their thick leaders for the next day. He would be out on the water well before first light catching the local cash crop. The fish would be traded for a few Euros to the cooks who would be waiting along the shore when he and a dozen others like him, in small brightly painted wooden boats of blue and orange and red, came in. Much like his time spent selling newspapers back in the States, this job required an early riser. And also like the newsstand, he'd often sell out early if the catch or the headlines were right and garnered enough attention. Regardless of his haul, Sam saved the best fish for the *Osteria Perricci*.

Perricci's Café was on a street barely eight feet wide. It was more sidewalk than street, but it had a street's name, *Via Orazio*. The restaurant made up twenty-five feet of the first floor of a row house that had no obvious end and filled the block three or four stories high in a haphazard fashion that resembled an unsquared deck of cards. Construction of the houses through the centuries slapped the face of any building code. It was that way through the whole of what locals called Old Town – the aged coastal neighborhood that surrounded the small single-handed fishing fleet, the fort of Charles the 5th, and the oldest of the churches. If and when any city inspector came around looking for building violations they were sent away with their boxes checked and their stomachs full. If they came by too often, they went away hungry, but with boxes still checked, usually by fingers still swollen inside splints meant to keep the pinky immobilized until it could heal from being crudely disjointed. The same applied to the health *ispettore* who presumably oversaw the cleanliness, fit, and output of the kitchen heart of the café which would cook Sam's catch. For an inspector sighted in on *Osteria Perricci*, a trip to *Via Orazio* was brief and he seldom passed within the shadow of the café's deep maroon double doors. As soon as any resident saw him, they were on him like gulls buzzing baitfish, screeching a threatening alarm as if his presence was a personal affront to their sensibility. Everyone in Old Town Monopoli ate at *Perricci's* from time to time, as they did a myriad of other local, innocuous, nearly invisible eateries, and to suggest the quality or cleanliness was less than *primo*, even by the *ispettore's* mere presence, was a poor reflection of the neighborhood and the decency of *Via Orazio's* residents. It simply would not be tolerated.

Sam heard and saw these attacks – and attacks is what they were – from the one foot wide iron railed balcony of his single room, two floors above the *Osteria Perricci* kitchen. Mr. and Mrs. Perricci, the owners and only waitress and sole cook, were pleased to offer the finest and freshest *pesci*, complements of Sam's morning constitutionals into the Adriatic, to their usual guests in exchange for Sam's room and board. Some months before, Sam had passed beneath the iron balcony escorted by the Perricci's oldest son, fifty-year-old Antonia Jr. On that first day, the men had hurried by Junior's daughter, Palma Isabella, as she swept unseen dust away from the front of the café. Palma, named for her grandmother, was in her early twenties and the picture of Italian beauty with dark hair hanging long and loose like a frame of raven walnut around dark but glistening bright eyes and a smile that shattered mirrors for their inadequacy at reflecting perfect angles of grace.

The man with Junior Perricci was handsome with a profile chiseled from granite. Isabella could see his muscles ripple even beneath an oversized shirt as he walked with the balance of a dancer. Over his broad shoulders was a large black canvas zippered bag. Her father's hands were empty and he motioned quickly to Sam as they walked by and into the restaurant.

"*Zio*," Junior said to his daughter. "Uncle."

Sam scarcely looked up at the beautiful, innocent dark eyes that looked for his. As Isabella brushed the mane away from her face and smiled politely, she thought it curious to see an American in her father's company.

Zio. That was enough for now. To Isabella, uncles came and went from the small room upstairs every year or so. None stayed long and each disappeared unnoticed. She treated them graciously, but would never ask anything further about them. The uncles never offered more than a courteous good day or thank you. If any, young or old, had thought anything of her as she became a woman, it was fleeting and unannounced.

To do otherwise would have been foolhardy at best for men on the run and deadly at worst for offending their protectors.

Junior kissed his mother and introduced Sam with a wave of his hand, but no name. "This is a friend of ours."

Palma smiled and nodded. As her husband stepped from the kitchen the wordless scene repeated itself, but this time Isabella was the door. Her grandfather nodded at his introduction and asked Sam in Italian if he spoke the language.

"*Un po'*, a little," Sam said respectfully as he saw his father in the old man's face and mannerisms.

Antonello Sr. nodded again and motioned Sam towards him. He offered to take his guest's bag but felt the heft and thought better of it. Instead he led the way to the stairs which led up from the kitchen. Junior and Sam followed. Isabella followed them all with her dark eyes before she drifted back to her broom in the street.

Upstairs in the small room the three men talked briefly. Junior translated what he could, but his English was no good and Sam's Italian was leaving many gaps. After three minutes of frustration, but before any misunderstandings, Junior stepped out on the tiny iron balcony and yelled to his daughter.

"Isabella! Come quickly! *Vieni! In fretta! In fretta!*" and he clapped his hands as though it would make her faster.

As it was she was at the door to the upstairs room before another attempt was made in either language.

"You are a guest of my family, Mr. Ciampiano," Junior began again with Isabella translating close behind. Her English was unpracticed, but sound.

Antonia Sr. perked up. "Ciampiano? He is Italian? Where is his family from?"

Isabella translated.

"*Mio padre.* South of Palermo. Ficuzza," Sam said in broken Italian.

"Sicilian? Always the Sicilians," Antonia said as he shook his head.

"His friends are our friends in Ficuzza," Junior said, waving off Isabella's translation. "Mother's town. We have an obligation."

"*Certo.* Of course. But American. Why American?"

"The favor comes to Ficuzza from America, Papa. Don T."

Isabella translated on her own something Sam had known from the moment he stepped unseen through the back door of The Columbia Restaurant in Ybor City.

Sam had slipped into the vast wine cellar beneath the restaurant unnoticed and waited. He knew the maître d', a long-time fixture at the restaurant and aged friend of his father, would soon be down to select wine for a diner as he did so often with equal parts care and regularity. It was only a few minutes before Sam heard the cellar door open and the humming of the maître d' as he descended the steps.

"Mr. Guzimon?" Sam called gently, not wanting to alarm the old man. "It's Sam Ciampiano."

"*Il Piccolo Martello!* The Little Hammer! Ah! Your father – such a man!" He stopped short. "Why are you down here? Do you need wine?"

"*Grazie, no.* I need to speak to Don T."

"Ah." The maître d', a small man made smaller and almost frail by age, hesitated only a beat. "Yes. Yes. Of course. *Un minuto.*"

Sam stopped the old man as he turned to go. "You haven't selected your wine."

"They can wait."

In a small back dining room of the sprawling restaurant, Mr. Guzimon spoke discreetly in a big man's ear. He in turn whispered to the head of a small table of men enjoying a light lunch appetizer of Spanish Bean soup. When the head of the table heard the message he set his spoon down gently and wiped his mouth with his cloth napkin.

"Excuse me a moment," the Don said as he laid his hand on the shoulder of the man seated at his right. "Come with me," he said in a low voice as he stood and left the rest of the men to their soup as they questioned each other with only their eyes.

Without a word, Sam exchanged warm hugs with the Don when the pair from the back room descended the stairs and met him in the cellar.

"*Martelletto*, what do you need?"

"I have to get out of the city – the country. Can you help me?"

The old men looked at one another for a moment before returning to Sam with tighter eyes. The one from the right hand began to ask. "What has happen–"

"No," his boss said firmly. "Go. Send me Guzimon."

When the man cleared the top of the stairs, the head of the table put his big hands on Sam's broad shoulders, squeezed, then patted Sam's hard face. "You are a good man, *Martelletto*. Your father was a good man. I know you come here with respect and in great need. Why is not so important."

"*Grazie*, Don T."

"This is a great country, Sammy. To leave it is a big thing."

"It is impor–"

"Shhh. Not a word – to me or anyone. I will learn soon enough. You know the ways of the street. Guzimon will take you to a safe place. Some time, later maybe, he will come and take you to the port." The Don looked at the palms of his own hands and held them out as if for inspection. "These hands will... Arrangements will be made. Passage. It will not be comfortable, but you will be safe. When you arrive, do exactly as my emissaries request."

"You know I will."

"I do know. I do. When I have learned enough and know it to be safe, I will send a word for you."

"It may never be safe, Don T."

"I understand. But you will be safe, *Martelletto.*"

"*Grazie.* I'm sorry to come like–"

"Nonsense. If you had gone anywhere else, I would be offended."

Sam wanted to say that he was so grateful and could never repay the kindness, understanding, effort, and risk, but he also knew that it didn't need saying. Don T beat him to it and released him of the burden.

"Your father paid this fare for you many times over. This is my payment in return and still I am indebted."

Mr. Guzimon was coming down the stairs.

"Take him through the old tunnel," the Don directed. "Bring him food. Pack a healthy bag with cheeses and breads that will keep. See to it he has wine. And books. Find me good books."

"Yes, my Don."

"It is a long trip, *Martelletto.*"

"Don T, I have to ask. There is a black bag hidden inside the couch at my father's house. I could use it."

"Your house may have many eyes on it."

"I'm sure of it. Mr. Abreu, my neighbor. He could get in."

"I know him," Mr. Guzimon said.

"See if he will do me this favor," Don T said.

Mr. Guzimon nodded.

"Goodbye for now, my Little Hammer," the Don whispered. "We will see each other again."

Sam hugged his benefactor and was rewarded with a kiss on both cheeks and a wad of cash, all Don T had in his pockets.

Sam looked at the money and eased it back. "If I can get the bag from my house, I will be okay."

"We will get the bag, but this is walking around money to keep your pocket warm." Without waiting for an argument that respect would not permit, Don T directed Guzimon. "Take him."

Guzimon touched Sam's arm. "This way, *Martelletto,*" and the pair disappeared in the maze of the wine cellar.

In the oldest portion of the basement, beyond the current aging wine, was a small storeroom that appeared as discarded as its contents. The light switch was an antique black Bakelite knob that connected fabric covered frayed wires that ran up the wall and passed in ceramic tubes through the ceiling joists. A single dirty bulb, held up by cobwebs as much as ancient wire, hung in the center of the room. The bulb glowed to life. Dust covered wooden wine crates, some still showing wisps of dry rotted straw packing, were strewn and stacked about. The odd indistinguishable kitchen apparatus, unused for decades and as lost as its original purpose, completed the cluttered room.

Sam followed Mr. Guzimon to the far wall and watched him open a tiny door that was nearly invisible before it was disturbed from beneath its coat of dust. The maître d' looked at the size of the door and the size of his charge. Sam was thinking the same thing.

"It gets bigger inside," Mr. Guzimon said as he tugged the door open.

Inside was another black knob light switch similar to the vintage one in the storeroom. It was turned with a loud click and several lights came to life and showed a musty narrow corridor built of brick with a low vaulted ceiling. The passageway was about five feet high, three feet wide, and looked to be at least eighty feet long.

"It will take you beneath the street." The maître d' clasped his hands as though to pray. "Ah. In the old days it was used to move coffee beans from the roaster to the café. They kept the roaster across the street for fear of burning down the café. They nearly did so, many, many times." The old man waved his hand at the tunnel as if blessing it. "Sometimes," he smiled. "Sometimes other things passed through the tunnel."

Sam smiled in return and put his hand on Mr. Guzimon's shoulder before ducking through the door.

"Thank you, Mr. Guzimon."

"There is a room at the far end. We will bring you up through whichever building is most clear. I will be back with something to eat and wine after I see to Mr. Abreu."

Sam hustled through the tunnel to the sound of Mr. Guzimon closing the small door behind him. At the opposite end, as he'd been told, was a small room with a dusty desk, but a bed that appeared fresh. He walked the small room then sat down. His eyes scanned for anything useful then settled into the palms of his hands to reflect on the last several hours and to wait on the protective, guiding hands of others. Don T and Mr. Guzimon were vital and his safety and escape rested on them alone. But number one on the short list of people he owed his life to was a petite brunette looking at him over the counter of his father's newsstand from beneath a wide brim floppy hat and shrouded in huge cheap sunglasses that nearly covered her face. It seemed an eternity ago already, but had only been hours.

"Sam," Karen had said, not at all like a question and without looking up from the newspapers she absently flirted with in her hands.

The voice brought him away from his book more than his name. He looked across the counter at the sunglass-cloaked face that was ignoring him.

"Karen?" he said with equal parts disbelief and surprise.

It was a question that wasn't seeking an answer. Sam knew the woman behind the lame disguise was his recently burnt out flame, Lieutenant Karen Auburn. That was a given. If there had been room for a follow-up question, it would have circled around why she was in Tampa at his newsstand and not at her JAG desk in Washington.

Karen didn't look up, but knew what to say to shock Sam's focus away from her sudden appearance to her true purpose. "You're being watched."